BOOKS BY
ROBIN MCKINLEY & PETER DICKINSON

The Blue Sword	Robin McKinley
Chalice	Robin McKinley
The Door in the Hedge	Robin McKinley
Dragonhaven	Robin McKinley
The Hero and the Crown	Robin McKinley
The Kin	Peter Dickinson
The Outlaws of Sherwood	Robin McKinley
Spindle's End	Robin McKinley
Sunshine	Robin McKinley
Water: *Tales of Elemental Spirits*	Robin McKinley and Peter Dickinson

ROBIN McKINLEY PETER DICKINSON

•••

fire
Tales
of Elemental Spirits

♦♦♦

FIREBIRD
AN IMPRINT OF PENGUIN GROUP (USA) INC.

For Jessica and Karen

FIREBIRD
Published by the Penguin Group
Penguin Group (USA) Inc., 345 Hudson Street, New York, New York 10014, U.S.A.
Penguin Group (Canada), 90 Eglinton Avenue East, Suite 700, Toronto, Ontario, Canada M4P 2Y3
(a division of Pearson Penguin Canada Inc.)
Penguin Books Ltd, 80 Strand, London WC2R 0RL, England
Penguin Ireland, 25 St Stephen's Green, Dublin 2, Ireland (a division of Penguin Books Ltd)
Penguin Group (Australia), 250 Camberwell Road, Camberwell, Victoria 3124, Australia
(a division of Pearson Australia Group Pty Ltd)
Penguin Books India Pvt Ltd, 11 Community Centre,
Panchsheel Park, New Delhi - 110 017, India
Penguin Group (NZ), 67 Apollo Drive, Rosedale, Auckland 0632, New Zealand
(a division of Pearson New Zealand Ltd.)
Penguin Books (South Africa) (Pty) Ltd, 24 Sturdee Avenue,
Rosebank, Johannesburg 2196, South Africa

Registered Offices: Penguin Books Ltd, 80 Strand, London WC2R 0RL, England

First published in the United States of America by G. P. Putnam's Sons,
a division of Penguin Young Readers Group, 2009
Published by Firebird, an imprint of Penguin Group (USA) Inc., 2011

1 3 5 7 9 10 8 6 4 2

THE LIBRARY OF CONGRESS HAS CATALOGED THE G. P. PUTNAM'S SONS EDITION AS FOLLOWS:
McKinley, Robin.
Fire: tales of elemental spirits / Robin McKinley and Peter Dickinson.
v.   cm.
Contents: Phoenix / Peter Dickinson—Hellhound / Robin McKinley—Fireworm /
Peter Dickinson—Salamander man / Peter Dickinson—First flight / Robin McKinley.
ISBN 978-0-399-25289-1 (hc)
I. Animals, Mythical—Juvenile fiction. 2. Short stories, American. 3. Short stories, English.
[1. Animals, Mythical—Fiction. 2. Fire—Fiction. 3. Short stories.] I. Dickinson, Peter. 1927–
II. Title.
PZ5.M2335Fir 2009
[Fic]—dc22   2009004730

ISBN 978-0-14-241945-8

Design by Richard Amari
Text set in Kuenstler Roman

Printed in the United States of America

CONTENTS

fire
Tales
of Elemental Spirits

PHOENIX

PETER DICKINSON

Summer 1990

Ellie came into the story very late on. It happened because she was oddly fascinated by the wood. Not that it was very different to look at from any of the several patches of woodland in the enormous grounds of the great country house, some of them really big—forests almost—others no more than a couple of dozen trees. This one was in between, lying in a wide dip in the rolling parkland, on one side of the picnic area, with the house itself in a similar dip on the other side.

Ellie, as usual, finished her lunch long before the others, and rose.

"Where are you off to?" said her mother.

"Can I go and have a look at that wood?"

"What about it?"

Her brothers glanced up from their Game Boys.

"It's a wood," said Jim. "That's enough for Ellie."

"Lots of mouldy old trees," said Bob.

"It looks interesting," said Ellie. "I want to know what it is. I think there's a notice board by the gate."

"Oh, all right," said her mother. "Stay in sight. Don't be too long. I'll wait for you here."

◆ ◆ ◆

The notice said

PRIVATE
Dave's Wood
Conservation Area
Nature trails 2–5 p.m., week-ends only. Tickets at East Gate.
School parties by arrangement. Call 731 4492

Ellie made a note of the number.

The gate was locked. There was a solid-looking fence, high as a man, running in either direction. She walked along it to the right, peering into the darkness under the trees. The wood was full of bird-song. Apart from that, she couldn't see anything to make it special for anyone else, but, yes, some of the trees did seem to be really old, and for her that was deeply fascinating. It made her skin crawl to think how long they had stood there while people had come and gone. As the fence curved away she looked back to the picnic area, where Dad and the boys were getting to their feet. Mum was looking towards her. Ellie waved. Mum waved back and settled to her book. That was all right. She'd be happy to sit there reading all afternoon. It was Dad and her brothers who wanted to do stuff. Ellie walked on.

She was watching a jay hunt for grubs along a dead branch when the yobs caught her. She worked out later that they must have seen her coming from some way off and lain in wait for her, and then she'd got it dead right for them, dead wrong for herself. She'd actually stopped at a place where a kink in the line of the fence hid her from the picnic area. The first she knew about them was the jay's wild alarm-cackle, and then a tap on her shoulder.

"Hi, babe," said a boy's voice, trying to sound like a man's.

Her heart bounced. She started to turn. A hand clamped across her mouth as she tried to scream. She bit it. The boy cursed, but merely shifted his grip so she couldn't bite then grabbed her right wrist and twisted the arm up behind her back.

"Grab her pack, then," he muttered. "What you waiting for?"

Another boy—so there were two of them—started pulling the shoulder-strap of her satchel down her left arm. She wrestled with them, sobbing, trying to kick out, trip one of them up somehow.

"Stop that, you lot! Lay off!" said a different kind of voice. A kid's too, but even and confident. It seemed to come from the other side of the fence, over on her left now after the struggle.

A moment of startled silence. A snarl of curses cut short by the flare of a photoflash, bright in the corner of her eye. Ellie sensed the sudden uncertainty in her captors' grip and wrenched her head free and yelled, gulped breath, and yelled again at the top of her voice.

The hands let go of her. By the time she'd turned to face them, the kids who'd attacked her were scuttling away, holding arms in front of their faces.

Shuddering and sick, she turned again. A boy was watching her from the other side of the fence. He looked younger than she was, somewhere about ten, and concerned for her but extraordinarily calm, as if what had just happened was something he dealt with every day.

"You all right, miss?" he said. "You got someone with you?"

"My . . . my . . ."

An absurd apprehension overcame her that her mother had heard the scream and was now running down the path towards the wood. Please not! It was all right now. If she found out . . . and Dad would be even worse. . . .

She darted away from the fence, far enough to see. No, she was still reading, and didn't even look up. Still trembling, Ellie came back to the fence, noticing now the expensive-looking camera slung round the boy's neck. He was a short but solid-looking kid with steady, dark brown eyes.

"Wow!" she said. "Lucky for me you were there! With that, too!"

Her voice came out as a gasping whisper.

"Reckon so," he said calmly. "Photographin' that jay you was watching. Wonderful thing, that camera. You goin' to be all right, miss? Keep an eye out for you, shall I, till you're back with your folk?"

"Oh . . . yes. Yes, I suppose so. I'll be all right. . . . I'm fine. . . . Er . . . how do I come on a nature trail? Is it just schools, or can anybody . . . ?"

"Best you call Welly. Tell 'er about you, shall I? Got the number? Give us a name, then?"

"Me? I'm Ellie. What's yours?"

"Dave. Welly and Ellie. She'll like that."

"Is this your wood?"

"Name runs in the family, manner of speaking. But you call Welly. Good-bye then, miss."

He nodded to her and turned away.

In a way the strangeness of the encounter was a help, for as she walked slowly back towards the picnic area, Ellie found herself puzzling about it, instead of living over and over again the horror of what had happened. What a funny kid! It wasn't just his calmness and assurance, the way he'd dealt with those louts, or the very odd way he'd put everything he said, or his accent—she wasn't good at accents, but she was pretty sure he was English, only talking the sort of English you might hear a couple of old guys, real country people, talking in a village shop. But underneath all those surface things something stranger yet, far stranger.

Her mother was still reading when she reached the picnic area, and closed her book with obvious reluctance, marking the place with a parking ticket. "Your hair's a bit of a mess, darling. Was it as interesting as you hoped?"

"They do nature trails. I'd love to go on one. Can we come again?"

"I expect so. The boys are mad on that stupid railway."

Ellie called the number that evening, as soon as she'd finished her homework. A woman's voice answered. It sounded a little shaky.

"Hello?"

"I'm supposed to ask for Welly."

"Speaking. And you must be Ellie. You want to come on a nature trail?"

"If that's all right."

"Well, so many people ask. . . . Is there anything you particularly want to look at?"

"Oh . . . I'm interested in the birds and animals, of course, but really it's the trees. You've got some lovely old ones, haven't you?"

"Indeed, yes. In that case . . . it'll have to be in the morning, so get here as early as you can. We do parties in the afternoons. Just call me the evening before."

"That's wonderful, if you're sure. Oh, wait, please. I wanted to say thank you to Dave. He was terrific! I'd have been in a real mess without him."

"Yes, he told me. I'm thankful he was around. I'm afraid you can't talk to him now—he's trying to photograph an owl. But I'll tell him. Oh, just one thing. Did you tell your parents what happened?"

"Er, no, I thought . . . but I suppose . . . I mean, those boys might—"

"That's all right. I called the security people and they picked them up at the gate. They'll deal with it. They may want Dave's photograph, but he says your face is completely hidden. With luck you won't be involved. But perhaps you'd better bring your mother at least as far as the gate this time, so that she can decide for herself if we're safe people to leave you with. The tour takes about three hours, tell her."

"All right. You'll say thank you to Dave for me, won't you?"

"Of course."

◆ ◆ ◆

Welly and Dave were waiting for her at the gate into the wood. Welly was in an electric wheel-chair, an old woman with white hair and wrinkled and blotchy skin. She had a really nice smile. Ellie couldn't guess how old she was—older, she thought, than either of her own grannies. Welly's hands trembled slightly all the time, but her eyes were bright with life. Dave seemed just the same as before, about ten, a bit short for that age, but stockily built without being fat, and with that strange, calm look as if nothing that happened was ever going to faze him. They all shook hands.

"This is extremely good of you," said Mum. "We bought a ticket at the gate. Two pounds. It didn't seem nearly enough to pay for your time. You said three hours, Ellie told me."

"Our time is our own, and we can do what we wish with it. I assure you, Mrs. Ford, it'll be a pleasure. We are both passionate about our wood, and Ellie seems really interested. I hope she can stay the whole three hours."

"Yes, of course, if that's really all right. I've made up a picnic for her."

"We wouldn't have let her starve, you know."

Mum laughed uncertainly. Ellie guessed that she didn't know what to make of Welly, any more than Ellie did of Dave. But it was only twenty minutes to the library, so she'd get over two hours' book-choosing and book chat. And everyone was happy.

◆ ◆ ◆

"Dave will take you round," said Welly. "We've got two parties this afternoon, and I get tired stupidly soon these days."

It wasn't a trail at all. They left the marked path almost at once and checked the whole wood out, almost tree by tree. The birds and animals seemed not to notice them, even when they climbed an immense old oak to which Dave had attached steps and handholds so that he could keep an eye on a bat colony that roosted in the hollow of its trunk, as well as the nest of a green woodpecker in a rotted limb. Astonishingly, the bird stayed on its nest, untroubled by the flash, with a chick's head poking up beside its wing, while Ellie took several photographs.

"Used to me," Dave explained.

Unlike normal guides, he talked very little, just showed her things and let her decide for herself, though he answered her questions willingly enough, for instance when she asked how long the bat colony had been there.

"Let's see now," he said slowly. "Great storm, eighteen ninety-seven, that's what took 'er top out. Give 'er time to rot 'ollow, forty, fifty year, maybe. An' the bats were there, definite, come nineteen seventy, and maybe twenty year earlier.

"Dessay it'll be in the diaries," he added after a pause, as if by way of explanation that he hadn't been working it out from memory.

◆ ◆ ◆

"I trust you've had a good time," said Welly, when they returned to the cottage in the clearing near the middle of the wood, where they'd left her over two hours before.

"Oh, it was wonderful!" said Ellie. "I wish it had gone on for ever! And you've got two parties this afternoon. That's six hours."

"Parties don't get three hours," said Dave.

Welly paused from ladling stew into three bowls and looked at him.

"She'd do," he said. "Given she's willin'."

Welly returned to her ladling. She seemed not to notice the way her hands trembled. Dave carried the bowls to the table.

"Best you sit there," he told Ellie. "Just let old Vick take a sniff—she won't 'urt. Likes to know who's what, an' she don't see much no longer. All right, girl!"

Ellie sat. An old spaniel heaved herself up from beside the stove, limped across and sniffed at the hand Ellie offered.

"Vick the Fourth, she is," said Dave as the dog went back to her snooze. "'Nother name as runs in the family."

That sounded like a private joke. Ellie didn't get it.

"Take your jersey off if you want to, my dear," said Welly. "I'm afraid I need it warmer than most people can stand. Now, you can have your picnic if you prefer, but this is very good. Dave makes a lovely stew. The rabbits are out of the wood."

Rabbit stew! More and more Ellie felt she was in some kind of dream. Mum could do without cooking any more than she had to, so mostly at home they ate microwaved stuff out of packets. Mum would have been horrified by the mere idea of rabbit, too. But here she was with her mouth already watering at the smell, in this wonderful old cottage room with its log fire burning on the huge open hearth and its Aga and its long-lived-in feel, and this strange, strange couple.

Welly spun her chair deftly back to the table. Dave took a large bib out of a drawer and tied it round her neck, then sat opposite Ellie and hacked three chunks of bread from what looked like a home-made loaf.

"Now," said Welly, "you're right. Not everyone that calls and asks to visit us gets this kind of treatment. The fact is that we have been looking for someone like you, to help us. This wood is rather special. You'll have seen at the gate that it's a conservation area, but there are plenty of those these days. What makes it special is that it has been one now for almost a hundred years, and, uniquely, diaries have been kept of everything that happens in the wood, including an annual tree census and a five-year census of all the wild creatures that live here. It is now time for both. I can no longer do my share, and Dave can't do it all, so we need a helper. We could no doubt find one by advertising, but that would mean an adult and there are various things against that. They'd probably have ideas of their own, rather than being content to do it our way—"

"Never work level along of a kid," said Dave, "'lowing I might maybe know best. An' the birds an' animals, they're used to me—saw that, didn't you? You won't bother 'em, neither, not like a grown man's going to."

"That's certainly the case," said Welly. "It makes the task so much easier if the creatures don't keep hiding from you. But at the same time, any helper has to know what she's looking at, as you appear to do—"

"Knew a beech from an 'ornbeam," said Dave.

"So, my dear, are you prepared to help, if it can be arranged?" said Welly.

"Oh, yes please!" said Ellie.

That was how she came into the story, and so late on. From their very first meeting, she had felt that there was some kind of a mystery about Dave, and a story to go with it, and as time went by, she became more and more curious, but she was afraid to ask in case they were offended and she wouldn't be able to come again. On her fourth visit, her resolve cracked.

By now it was the school holidays and she had come for the middle of a week, three whole days with the two nights in between. This also meant that Dave didn't have to be careful not to show himself on weekdays. Officially, he lived with his father in London during the week and went to school there, then came up and stayed with his grandmother at week-ends and in the holidays, while his father went mountain-climbing. Since there were no school parties to be guided round, on weekdays he and Ellie had the wood to themselves. They spent the whole of the first day working through a single section of it, doing the trees systematically, filling in the forms that Welly had prepared for them and adding the animals and birds as they came across them. Ellie would do one tree and Dave a neighbouring one, so that Ellie could call to him if she needed help. In the evening Welly entered the results on her PC.

Ellie slept in a small room at the top of the stairs. She guessed that it was Dave's, though it was far too tidy to feel like a boy's room—like her brothers' at any rate—and that he had moved in with Welly on the other side of the landing so that she could have it.

Next day they went on with the census and were busy and happy until late in the afternoon, when they were measuring the girth of an oak tree. This was the immense old fellow in whose hollow branch Ellie had photographed the woodpecker's nest. It had in fact lost more than that single limb, and they had both spent almost an hour up in its crown recording the progress of its decay. Now their joined tapes met round the base. Ellie held their ends together on one side, and Dave drew them taut on the other and read off the inches. He couldn't be bothered with centimetres, he told her.

"I don't know," said Ellie as she straightened. "Somehow it

doesn't seem to matter that it's lost its top. It's still the emperor of the wood. But that must've been a storm and a half, Dave."

"That it was," said Dave. "That it—"

If he hadn't caught himself but just carried smoothly on, Ellie mightn't have noticed the repetition, or grasped what it must mean. As it was, she froze for a moment, then turned slowly and stared at him. He waited, unreadable as ever.

"You were there, weren't you?" she said. "It was almost a hundred years ago, and you were there. How old are you really, Dave?"

"One 'undred and ninety this New Year past," he replied, untroubled. "Gettin' on a bit, you might say."

Midwinter 1899/1900

On the last night of the old century, or the first of the new one, Dave Moffard was woken by a single tremendous crash of thunder. Outside the wind roared through the trees of the wood and whined between his two chimney-pots like a man whistling through a gap in his front teeth. If there was rain, the noise of the wind drowned it. A little later he caught the whiff of smoke borne on the same fierce wind.

Wonder what's caught it, he thought. Timber of some kind— leaf-litter burnt with a sourer smell. There were a few dead trees in the wood, but nothing he'd have guessed would catch that easy. Though you never know with lightning.

Must be past midnight, he thought. *'Ello there, Nineteen-hundred. Never reckoned I'd live to see you in. 'Appy birthday, Dave Moffard.*

He fell asleep and slept on until less than an hour before the late midwinter dawn. For a man his age, Dave didn't sleep too bad.

As on all other mornings, he first lit his lamp and riddled the ashes out of the stove, opened the dampers, fed in a few small logs and a couple of larger ones and put the kettle on for a pot of tea and his shaving water. For breakfast he had porridge cooked overnight in the oven, and then a morsel of ham with the tea, chewing slow and careful because his teeth didn't fit that well. He shaved—harder to do these days, with his left eye so clouded and his right beginning to go the same way—then fed the stove again, put the tea-pot on it to stew a bit more, half-closed the dampers and looked out of the door. Dawn just breaking on a cold, clear day, but dry. No rain seemed to have fallen, then, after all that bluster. The wind had dropped too, to not much more than a breeze. It was still threaded with smoke.

"Let's go an' 'ave a look then, shall we?" he said, talking not in fact to himself but to Fitz, an old setter three years dead and not replaced because it wouldn't have been fair on a young dog, with Dave likely to snuff it first. They never really get over it.

He fastened his boots, heaved himself into his greatcoat, shoved on a hat and a double pair of gloves, wool first and then thick leather, picked up his stick and went out. Time was he'd have taken a gun, but his eyes weren't up to it now, nothing like. He'd slowed down disappointingly quickly in the last few months—there'd been days when he'd barely put his nose out of doors—but he was feeling noticeably better this morning.

He moved upwind at a steady shuffle, leaning on his stick to ease his right leg. Well before he reached it, he guessed the source of the smoke. The Cabinet House. Must've caught it good and proper. Yes, there it was, no more than a shell of walls, roof fallen in, nothing left of timbers and partitions except ash and embers on the ground and an odd reek of something sweet and sticky drifting on the breeze. Hundred and twenty years, getting on, it had stood here.

Dave knew that because the date was carved into the lintel stone. *Enter and wonder—1781.*

It was the fifth earl who'd built it, to house his collection. Pretty well all the earls had been mad on something or other, and the fifth had been mad on collecting. Used to go travelling round Europe and beyond with a couple of dozen servants to look after him, buying up anything that caught his fancy, provided it was odd enough. Built the Cabinet House, all little fancy turrets and spires and what have you, to hold his collection in special glass cases. Then he'd got a fever—Egypt or somewhere—and died, and the sixth earl had come along, not interested in collecting but mad on shooting, and planted up Dave's wood for pheasant-cover, all among grand old oak trees— been there hundreds of years, some of them. Had to have a game-keeper, of course, so he'd built a house for the fellow—Dave's house now, because he'd been gamekeeper here following on from his father and his grandfather. So all his long life, there the Cabinet House had stood while the wood grew round it, full of its knick-knacks—dragons' teeth, locks of mermaids' hair, funny-shaped nuts, bottles from pharaohs' tombs, that sort of rubbish. Dave was sad to see it go. *Might've lasted me out,* he thought.

Forty years back, the eighth earl—book mad, he'd been—had fetched some of his scholar friends along to look the lot through, and they'd gone off with anything worth while for their muse-ums. There hadn't been anything left to be sad about, really, except memories.

Dave stood in the doorway gazing vaguely over the pile of ash with the remnants of heat beating up into his face. *Warmin' my old carcass through,* he thought. *Doin' something useful at last.*

Sudden as a blink, almost, the sun rose, slotting its rays through a gap where a fallen tree had brought down several of its neighbours. There was a movement in the ashes a little way over to Dave's right. He peered at it with his good eye and decided it was more than just an eddy of wind stirring the surface. Something underneath. He scuffed the fringe of ashes aside, took a half pace forward, gripped his stick by the ferrule and reached out, trying to rake the thing towards him with the crook.

Poor beast, he thought. *What a way to go. Put you out of your sufferin', shall I?*

He took a quick stride forward, this time onto hot embers, thrust the crook into the heart of the heap, hooked it round something more solid than ash and dragged it free. It cheeped plaintively as it came, disentangled itself from the crook, and stood, shaking the ashes from its feathers. It was a baby bird, about the size of an adult rook, its eyes newly opened, its body covered with astonishing luminous yellow down that seemed to ripple with the heat of the fire, and the tiny fledge feathers along its wings a darker, almost orange gold. The beginning of a scarlet crest sprouted from the bald scalp. Dave had never seen anything like it before. It was an absurd creature, but wonderfully appealing. It seemed unharmed, though the crook of his stick had blackened perceptibly during its brief raking in the embers.

Nor did it seem to be bothered by the heat even now. It stayed where it was, gazing imperiously round the ruin, seeming wholly untroubled by the human presence, and finally gazed directly up at Dave with its head cocked a little to one side. *Well, what now?* It asked him, plain as speaking.

Dave was too interested to be amazed. Even in a very ordinary bit of English woodland like this there were enough amazing creatures to last a fellow a lifetime—one more didn't make that much difference.

"Up to you," he told it. "But if 'eat's what you're used to, you're goin' to catch your death stayin' out 'ere. Couple more days and this lot's goin' to be chilling off good an' proper. If you want to come 'ome with me, that's all right. You can sit on the stove if you've a mind. In the stove, for all I care. But you're goin' to be too 'ot for me to carry by the look of you, and I'm not havin' you burnin' my gloves, and I'll need my stick. Let me see now. You go back an' keep yourself warm while I see what I can fix."

The bird cocked its head to the other side and settled down in the ashes, shuffling itself down into their warmth. Dave poked around outside the wall and found a half-burnt beam that must have come from immediately under the eaves, to judge by the section of cast-iron guttering still attached to it. The timber had smouldered away enough for him to be able to lever one of the iron gutter supports free with his stick. He dragged it across the clearing to a molehill where he kicked and scuffed it in the loose earth until it was cool enough for him to pick up without scorching his gloves. He carried it back to the doorway and with some difficulty knelt and, propping himself on his stick, leaned as far out as he could, with the back-bar of the gutter-support just touching the ashes. Lifeless though they looked, the residual heat rose, roasting, into his face.

"Well, get on with it," he gasped. "Can't stay like this more'n a second or two."

The bird didn't hesitate but shrugged itself clear of the ashes, waddled over and climbed on to the support. With even more of an effort than when he'd knelt, Dave got to his feet. He stood for a moment, swaying in darkness, with his heart battering at his ribcage, but when his vision cleared he saw that the bird was still clinging grimly to the gutter-support. He also saw that the life in it was like the fire in a live coal, and that if he didn't get it back to his stove very soon, it would die.

By the time he reached his door, he was reeling and gasping

again, and a pulse of pain had begun to flood across his chest with every thump of his heart. He nudged the latch up, barged into the room and across to the fireplace, dropped his stick, grabbed the mantelshelf for support and lowered the bird onto the stove. It flopped off the support and huddled itself down onto the hot metal, its hooked beak tapping feebly at the lid.

Dave dropped to his knees, almost toppling clean over, but caught and steadied himself. He groped in the hearth, found the lever bar and, still kneeling, hooked it into its slot and dragged the lid clear. The bird scrabbled itself over the edge and dropped out of sight.

Dave closed the lid and with a long gasp allowed himself to collapse forward onto his gloved hands. He stayed there, panting, with his head hanging down between his arms, until his heartbeat eased and the pain in his chest receded. He found he'd been muttering to himself between the heavy, indrawn breaths.

"Near goners, the both of us. . . . Both of us perishin' near goners. . . . What the devil for . . . did I want to go doin' a fool thing like that?"

At length he crawled across the floor and pushed the door shut. He crawled back to the stove, dragged off his gloves, found his stick and used it and the arm of his chair to haul himself to his feet. With shaking hands, he poured out a mug of tea. It was now stewed until it would have tanned hide, which was how he liked it. He added sweetened condensed milk to cancel the bitterness and, still in his coat and boots, settled into his chair. He sipped slowly, thinking about the bird.

One of the knick-knacks in the Cabinet 'Ouse, he decided. *Old earl picked up an egg or two in his travels, didn't he? Maybe this one needed a bit more 'eat than most to get it goin', same way sycamore seed needs a bit of frost. Funny all those scholars comin', and still missin' it—kickin' thesselves in their graves, I shouldn't wonder. Any road, I'll be keepin' this to myself for now. Not tellin' nobody about it, that I'm not.*

From time to time, he heard the bird fidgeting around inside the stove, but without any sounds of distress, so he left it alone. Normally when he fed the fire, provided it was drawing well, he just pitched a couple of logs in without looking and put the lid back on, but obviously he'd have to stop doing that now, so he fetched the tongs, chose a couple of logs, lifted the lid and peered inside. The bird had rearranged the burning wood to its liking and was now huddled down into a regular nest, just like a wild bird out in the wood.

"Watch your 'ead, sonny," he called, and lowered a log in with the tongs. The bird looked up as it came and nudged it into position. The same with the second log. *Quite the little Lordship*, thought Dave as he closed the lid. *But I could do with a creature about the house again. Been missin' that since old Fitz died. Better be gettin' a few more logs in. Wonder what it likes to eat.*

So, on the first day of the first year of the new century, which was also the hundred and first year of his own life, Dave Moffard embarked on a fresh relationship with a fellow creature.

For the first couple of weeks, he didn't see much of the bird. It was very little trouble. Regularly, morning and evening, it would cheep loudly, and he'd lift the lid of the stove, reach in with the tongs and lift it gently out onto the top. It would strut to the edge, twist smartly round, raise its rapidly lengthening tail plumes and excrete forcibly over the rim, jet-black tarry pellets that stuck wherever they landed and hardened like rock as they cooled. After the first couple of times, he stood ready with a spare bit of board to catch them.

It then stayed in the open for several minutes, gazing round at the room with an air both fascinated and baffled, as though Dave's cottage were the last place on earth where it had expected to find itself. This gave him a chance to study it properly.

It was fledging fast. As the true feathers showed through the down, it became clear that they weren't all going to be of the same glowing orange-gold as the primaries, but might be anything from a deep smoky amber to intense pale yellow—any of the colours, indeed, that you might see among the embers on an open hearth with a good fire going. It was also growing. Soon, he realised, it would be the size of a bantam, and he was going to have trouble getting it in and out of the stove. This despite the fact that it didn't seem to eat anything. He'd tried offering it scraps the first few times it had appeared—bread crumbs, shreds of mutton, a beetle, a little of the buckwheat he used to keep for the pheasants and so on—but it hadn't been interested. Then on the third morning it emerged with a live ember in its beak. Once it had relieved itself it laid the ember on the stovetop and used its beak to hammer it into fragments, which it then picked up and swallowed as neatly as a pigeon picking seed off fresh-sown tilth. When it had finished them, it stood and gazed at Dave with a bright, unblinking stare.

"All right, sonny. Got you," he said, and the bird turned away, satisfied.

His gamekeeping had given Dave a wide experience of the intelligence of birds, from the idiocy of the pheasants he reared to the wiliness of some of their would-be predators, but even by the standards of magpies and jays he found this impressive.

He didn't get a chance to report the loss of the Cabinet House until Tom Hempage dropped by four days after the fire with Dave's weekly basket of provisions from the Estate Farm kitchen. The bird stayed out of sight and didn't make a sound while Tom was in the room. He was under-gamekeeper so this was a busy season for him. Not that the tenth earl was specially interested in shooting—politics was his form of madness—but his New Year house party was a major event in the political calendar, and it was important to have sport to offer his guests. Dave's wood was awkward for a lot of guns to shoot, so they'd been banging away elsewhere. Tom said he'd report the fire, but he doubted anybody would be by until the last of the gentry had left.

It was another fifteen days before anyone else came, and by then the bird was fully fledged and its mode of existence had undergone a marked change. It was as if the true feathers acted like some kind of overcoat, insulating it from the cold. Perhaps, too, it now had less heat to lose. Though warmer to the touch than any animal Dave knew of, it was no longer literally scorching. At any rate it had abandoned the inside of the stove and taken to perching on top of it during the day, and roosting on a ledge up the chimney, with the flue-pipe running close by for warmth. It could fly short distances from the very first, without any of the normal clumsiness of young birds learning the knack, but as if it already knew how and was limited only by its plumage not yet being fully developed. By now it was a splendid creature, a blazing and commanding presence, like a living embodiment of the sun. In his head Dave had already been calling it Sonny. *Spell it either way*, he thought. *No disrespect*. He began to be afraid that once it was fully grown it would decide that his cottage was nothing like grand enough for it and fly off to find its true destiny. Though he had known it less than three weeks, he would have minded that fully as much as he'd minded the death of old Fitz.

His visitor, when he came, was Mr. Askey, the estate manager.

They went out together to inspect the ruins of the Cabinet House.

"Still getting about then?" said Mr. Askey. "You seemed a bit shaky last couple of times I came."

"'Ad a bad go all through the back-end. Wasn't sure I'd be lastin' that long, to be honest with you. But I been feelin' a deal better lately."

"Looking it too. But then you've never looked your age, anything like. . . . We took it, by the way, that you wouldn't want a lot of palaver about you reaching your hundred."

"No, sir. Tell you the truth, sir, I've not been easy about that. Mebbe I've been wrong all these years about 'memberin' Trafalgar, eighteen-oh-five. Could've been Waterloo, mebbe. Eighteen-fifteen, weren't it?"

For the life of him Dave didn't understand why he'd answered as he had. The time for making a fuss about his birthday was over, and anyway Mr. Askey wasn't the sort to make a fuss without Dave's say-so. They knew each other well, ever since Mr. Askey had been brought in by the ninth earl (mad on improvements) as his new manager, planning, among other things, to build a series of model cottages for all the estate workers. Mr. Askey had first visited Dave twenty years back to discuss moving him into one of these, had at once recognised his obvious dislike of the idea and had come up with a scheme that pleased everyone. Dave would stay where he was on a pension, but still taking care of his wood for the benefit of the occasional gentleman who wanted a bit of rough shooting rather than the big organised drives; the earl would have his model cottages with a new, dynamic head gamekeeper to see to the rest of the shooting. It had been Mr. Askey who'd organised various perks, such as the weekly provisions, as part and parcel of the pension. He was that kind of thoughtful. And from time to time he liked to drop by and talk about old times on the estate, usually because he needed to know how something had come to be the way it was, but often enough just because he was interested.

He was a good man, and a friend, and Dave didn't like telling him less than the truth. Maybe that showed in his voice, judging by the sharp, considering glance Mr. Askey gave him before he grunted and walked on.

After that, though Mr. Askey continued to visit Dave, an unspoken constraint seemed to lie between them, not diminishing as the days and weeks, and then months, went by. Meanwhile Sonny throve. By the time the bluebells filled Dave's wood, he was a magnificent bird, about the size of a peacock, though a far more graceful flier. On any clear morning, as soon as it was light, he would strut out of the door, flip himself up onto the hitching rail beside the porch, luxuriantly stretch his wings and then launch himself out and up to the topmost branches of the great old oak on the far side of the clearing. Once there, he turned east and waited for the sunrise, and as soon as the first rays flamed off his plumage he stretched his wings wide, as if to gather all the sunlight he could reach into himself, raised his head and sang.

The notes were about the same pitch as those of a pigeon or a dove, but this was no mere two-note call, repeated and repeated, but a true song, as elaborate and melodious as that of a thrush. Dave used to stop whatever he was doing simply to stand at his door and listen.

By this time Sonny was too large to get into the stove, so Dave tried offering him a shovelful of embers on the hearthstone. On dull days Sonny might nibble at them a bit, but at the first break in the clouds he would be out and away up into the tree-tops. After a while Dave came to the conclusion that he lived mainly on sunlight, but then, one murky day after several similar ones, with the smell of more rain coming already strong in the wind, he did his annual spring clean-up of the clearing, raking the fallen twigs and branches into a heap on his bonfire site and setting them alight. Sonny, who normally seemed to expect to have everything done for him, for once lent a hand, strutting around and gathering twigs into his beak and adding them to the pile. Then, once the fire was lit and the flames burst through, he hopped into the midst of them and nestled himself down, twisting this way and that like a blackbird having a dust-bath. The smoke, Dave noticed, had a curious spicy smell. Sonny spent all morning on the bonfire, and came out glossy with heat, not the smallest feather singed.

"Fire an' light," Dave told him. "Fire an' light. Them's what you need, eh? I don't know what we're goin' to do for you come wintertime, now you can't fit into the stove no more."

By high summer Sonny was no longer confining himself to Dave's wood. The first sure sign of this came when he floated down into the clearing one June dusk with a dead adder in his grasp, which he laid at Dave's feet, just as a cat might bring a dead mouse home to show to its owner. He then carried the snake to the bonfire site, poked it in among the bits and pieces waiting to be burnt and piled more stuff on top of it. He flipped to the top of the pile, spread his wings, stretched his neck skyward and crowed, a sound nothing like his daybreak song, but one clear, long cry of triumph. Unkindled, the whole pile burst into flame. Sonny stayed in the middle of the blaze until the pile was embers.

"Full of surprises, aren't you?" Dave told him. "Kemp Moor, that must've come from, that snake. Nine miles off if it's an inch, and you won't find adders anyplace else round here. On'y you best watch out 'ow you go gadding about. Anyone spots you, they're goin' to want to get 'old of you and stick you in a zoo."

He wasn't in fact seriously worried about the possibility. For all his incandescent splendour, Sonny could be strangely difficult to see in full sunlight, even with a darker background, and became completely invisible against a clear sky. Just as any normal smokeless flame does, he seemed to be subsumed into the general glare. And even in murkier weather he was very good at concealing himself. Neither Tom Hempage nor Mr. Askey nor anyone else said anything about an exotic bird that had suddenly appeared on the estate.

From then on Sonny repeated this behaviour at least every other week. Only adders, apparently, would do, though there were plenty of grass-snakes actually on the estate. And he may have been looking for them further afield, as he twice spent a whole night away, not reappearing till the following evening. If there was nothing waiting to burn on the bonfire heap, he would build a pile for himself, so after the first two or three times Dave took to dragging bits of fallen timber home from his walks round the wood.

This pattern persisted all summer, until the leaves began to turn, the swifts had already gone and the swallows were gathering. The only slow change had been that as the days shortened, Sonny seemed to become even greedier for the sunlight. In any bright spell he spent his time at the top of the oak, sometimes slipping in and out of the cottage five or six times a day as the clouds came and went.

At the same time the pyres he built for himself became steadily larger. In dull weather he spent most of his time flitting round the wood finding dead branches and wrestling them free from their tree.

More than once he came and fetched Dave to bring home something too heavy for him to drag, though it was remarkable what he could manage for himself. Then he let Dave break it up for him, but insisted on building the pyre himself, finishing with an elegant pyramid, neat as a wren's nest, with a tunnel in the side into which he would insert the adder when he brought it home. Dave was fascinated by the whole procedure, though he had no idea what it meant.

By now Sonny was spending two or three nights away at a time searching for the adders. Dave became used to these absences and wasn't worried. All the same he immediately recognised the day when Sonny finally left as being different, and by the time the morning hymn was over, Dave, listening from the porch, knew it for what it was. Though the hymn to the sunrise had varied from day to day, it had always been full of joy, joy like a leaping flame. This morning it was longer, slower, and suffused with the melancholy of fading embers. It was farewell. Farewell to the summer. Farewell to Dave. Like the swifts and the swallows, Sonny was heading south.

As soon as the hymn was over, Sonny came swooping down and straight in through the door of the cottage. Dave turned and followed, and found him perched on the arm of his chair. Slowly Dave sat, and they contemplated each other for a while.

"Well, good-bye, old fellow," said Dave. "Been a real pleasure 'avin' you around. And an honour, if you don't mind me sayin' so. Done me a power of good, you 'ave. I don't know what I'll do without you, but never you mind. I'll find something. Not that I blame you. You've got to go where the sun goes. That's where you belong. I wouldn't want to keep you 'ere, supposin' I could. It wouldn't be right. Don't you go frettin' about me. I'll be all right."

His voice had grown croaky by the time he finished, but he wasn't ashamed. Sonny would understand.

Sonny stared at him for a little while, nodding his head up and down. Then he twisted his neck round, reached and neatly tweaked a feather out of his tail plumage and laid it on Dave's lap.

"Something to remember you by, eh?" said Dave, utterly delighted. "That's nice of you, very nice indeed. I'd been hoping to find one of those come moult time, supposin' you do that. Not that I'm going to forget you. Not a chance. . . . Well, you'll want to be off, I suppose, and I'm not going to keep you. You've a long way to go."

Sonny hopped onto his shoulder as he rose, and let him carry him out. He hopped onto Dave's offered wrist, gathered himself and leapt, wide winged. He swung out and up round the clearing, a blaze of brightness against the summer-weary foliage, and continued the rising spiral like a soaring hawk until the sunlight struck him and he vanished.

◆ ◆ ◆

In one sense Dave missed Sonny dreadfully, more than he'd ever missed any of his dogs, even old Fitz. But at the same time he felt extremely fortunate to have been given such a season of wonder in his old age. Very few people, he was sure, could have had such luck. It hadn't been anything he had been entitled to, let alone allowed to hang on to when the time came for him to lose it.

Furthermore, he had told Sonny the truth. The bird had done him a power of good. He felt in better heart than he had for years, and it needed no effort of will to do as he'd promised and find things to occupy his time. Two bits of good luck came his way. Tom Hempage, not normally one for chat, told him as if by way of gossip that the old bitch at the farm had whelped late, both in her life and in the year. As she was the best dog the farmer had ever had, he wasn't willing to lose any of what was sure to be her last litter, but she hadn't enough milk for all of them and they were looking for people to wean the pups and look after them until they were old enough to train. From the awkwardness of his manner Dave guessed he had been told to ask without seeming to, and this was the best he could do. Without thought, he said he'd be glad to take one on.

He got the last of the litter, a bitch, small even for a runt, proving his guess correct. The farmer would only have kept her for sentimental reasons. He wanted a home for her where she would be more of a house pet than anything that would one day make a working gundog.

"We'll show 'em, eh?" Dave told the brindled scrap, and she looked up at the tone of his voice, the flop ears attempting to prick. A good sign, he thought. No reason she shouldn't train. Though he didn't expect to keep her beyond the spring if she turned out any good, he named her Vick, after a bitch he'd had seventy years back, when the Queen had still been just Princess Victoria. And she did what he'd wanted, keeping him busy enough, stopping him brooding about Sonny. For that reason, and against all his principles—his previous dogs had all been kennelled outside—he went along with the house-pet idea enough to have her indoors and let her curl up on his lap in the evenings. Only, last thing at night, after he'd shut Vick into her box and put the lamp out and lit his candle, he'd take Sonny's feather from the pot where he kept it on the mantle shelf and run it gently through his fingers, and for those few moments the blazing presence would be vividly with him in the room.

And then, a few weeks later, George Hand, the head gamekeeper, dropped by for a bit more than the usual chat about old times. Apparently his lordship was planning some really big shooting parties that winter, and George would be needing to drive the woods as much as they would stand, so there weren't going to be much by way of breeding birds left by season's end, and he'd be needing to stock up all he could, come spring. Did Dave feel up to lending a hand?

"Glad to 'elp," said Dave. "Just 'ave to see 'ow I come through the winter, mind you, though I'm a mort better than I was this time last year. But I'll start takin' a look round, see what needs doin'. Do it myself if I can, ask you to send a lad up if I can't."

So from then on, Dave quartered the wood more systematically than he'd been doing on his daily excursions, checking out the movements of jays and magpies and such. To help persuade them that a man carrying a gun meant no harm he took his with him. Vick, as soon as she was big enough, went eagerly along, learning to walk to heel, to sit until called, and so on. One bright January morning, extending this process, he told her "still," and made her stand motionless while he took notional aim at a magpie. To his astonishment he found that if the gun had been loaded he could perfectly well have shot the bird.

Until that moment, though he had been vaguely aware that his eyes were getting no worse, he had no idea they had grown so much better. Testing them one at a time he found that the right eye was now almost unclouded, and the left, which a year ago had been seeing little more than a blur of light, was now making out definite shapes and distances through the mist. He was completely delighted, of course, though he didn't take the apparent miracle for granted, merely hoping it would last. But for some reason he was wary of telling anyone about his good luck. There was something uncanny about it.

◆ ◆ ◆

It turned out a harsh winter, with deep snow and hard frosts followed by a messy thaw, but he bore it better than he'd have believed possible. One still, clear March evening he was checking over the cages, ready for the first pheasant chicks, due next week, when he heard a soft and complex call from overhead. His heart leaped, and he looked up in time to see Sonny detach himself from the general blaze of sunset and settle onto a cage frame. He gazed around for a minute with his usual hauteur, then hopped down and stalked over to inspect Vick. She sat to greet him, as she would for a human visitor, her tail wagging vigorously.

"Nice enough little dog," Dave told him teasingly. "No substitute, mind you."

Sonny turned his head to stare at him, acting disdain, but obviously amused.

◆ ◆ ◆

The pattern of the years was set. Sonny spent his summers with Dave in the wood, migrated with the swallows and returned before them. Each time he came he found Dave looking a little younger. Curiously it was Tom Hempage, not Dave himself, though he occasionally fantasised about the possibility, who first decided that this was no mere appearance, but was indeed the case. Being a quiet and private man, Tom would not have spoken of it to anyone—none of his business—but Mr. Askey had asked him to keep an eye on Dave, so he mentioned it to him. Mr. Askey waited for a couple more visits to decide for himself, and then, one rainy summer afternoon, brought it up directly.

"You're actually getting younger, aren't you, Dave? It's happening."

Dave sat for a long while, staring at him in silence. All round the clearing rain dripped from the sodden trees, a sound like the endlessly passing minutes that compile the centuries.

"I've wondered," he muttered at last. "But it don't make sense. Really it don't. Do it, Mr. Askey?"

"You're a hundred and five, Dave. I looked you up in the parish register. There's no mistaking. I did that—five years ago it must have been—when you first told me you weren't sure about it after all. I was puzzled at the time, but I reckoned you had your reasons, so I didn't say anything. Do you mind telling me now?"

"I . . . I don't know. . . . I really don't know. Maybe it was something . . . something Sonny—"

He froze and looked away, desperate with agitation.

"Sonny?" said Mr. Askey gently.

There was a rustle from the chimney and Sonny slipped deftly down into view to stand on the stove. It was an entry quite as imposing as that of any Grand Duchess descending a great sweep of stairs to greet her noble guests.

"My goodness me!" whispered Mr. Askey, and rose, like Vick apparently recognising Sonny as belonging to an order of creation at least on equal terms with humankind. Sonny eyed him back, just as appraisingly, until he settled back on his chair.

"Can you tell me anything more?" he asked, watching Sonny make himself comfortable on the stove.

With a feeling of immense relief, Dave told him what had happened from the beginning.

"Well, well, well," said Mr. Askey, when he'd finished. "I think you've managed to make friends with a phoenix, Dave. The Phoenix, I should say, as I believe there's only one at a time. Not that I remember much about him. I'll ask Mr. Frobisher. I won't tell him why, of course. The fewer people know about this, the better. We don't want the world and his wife coming to gawp. But I'll have to tell his lordship. I can't go behind his back. Don't worry. He'll see it our way, I'm pretty sure."

He spoke with confidence. The earls, for all their varied madnesses, had carried some persistent character traits. They looked after their own. Though they didn't intrude into their people's lives, none of their servants, tenants or dependants, except for the hopelessly self-destructive, had ever died in want; and they thought that what happened on their estates was no business whatever of the outside world.

◆ ◆ ◆

A week later they were sitting on the bench by Dave's porch, with Sonny on the hitching rail beside them. The weather had cleared, and the sun at that time of year rose high enough above the tree-tops to reach almost all the clearing. Sonny wasn't doing his disappearing trick, and in that strong light, seen against the darkness under the trees, he seemed literally to blaze. It was hard to believe that that intense shimmer of brightness wasn't true flame.

The effect was perhaps enhanced by his obvious amusement at what was being said. Now Mr. Askey closed his notebook, checked the time on his fob-watch, glanced towards the entrance to the clearing and leaned back

"So there's not a lot they agree about, you see," he said. "Only one at a time—that's clear—and lives for anything up to three thousand years each go. Comes from Egypt, and something to do with the sun god. When his time's up, he builds himself a pyre and sets light to it and is consumed, and the next Phoenix comes out of the ashes. Right? And then there's a few bits and pieces fit in—his enemy being the Serpent—that goes with those adders your friend brings home—and maybe the fellow who talks about the miraculous egg he makes each time to hold the ashes of the old Phoenix— all myrrh and covered with jewels—I've been through the Cabinet House inventory—that's in the Library still—and there's a phoenix egg in there, all right—fifth earl picked it up in Heliopolis—nothing about jewels, of course. . . ."

Mr. Askey was reaching for his fob again when a man walked into the clearing and came towards them with the peculiar prancing strut that was immediately remarked upon by anyone who spoke of meeting him for the first time. Both Dave and Mr. Askey rose.

The tenth earl was now in late middle age. A small man, filled with a peculiar, eager, electric energy that should have turned him into the complete figure of fun his enemies made him out to be, but somehow had the opposite effect. A high complexion; green eyes, slightly pop; short-clipped moustache; leather gaiters and a long tweed jacket, belted and reaching almost to the knees; a fur deer-stalker: all a deliberate self-caricature, an arrogant challenge to jeerers. Completely effective.

"Afternoon, Askey, afternoon, Moffard—keeping remarkably fit, they tell me."

"Thasso, thank you, m'lord."

"Excellent, excellent. Talk about that later. Now, then . . ."

The earl turned towards Sonny. They eyed each other as equals. It was easy to imagine that in his time Sonny had faced pharaohs with the same gaze. Without any self-consciousness, the earl held out his hand for Sonny to shake, but instead Sonny stepped onto his wrist, spread his wings wide and with a long, smooth movement closed them either side of the earl's head and at the same time arched his neck forward until they touched foreheads. After a moment or two he straightened, refolded his wings and returned to the hitching rail. The earl took a pace back, spread his right hand over his heart, bowed his head, then turned to the bench.

"Well, well, well," he said. "When it comes to sheer majesty, they could learn a thing or two from him at Windsor Castle, eh, Askey? You're right, of course. Have to keep mum about this. Talk about that later. Moffard first. Told that last census fellow you weren't sure, eh? Could've been Waterloo you remembered, not Trafalgar?"

"Best I could think on, m'lord."

"Do for now. Do for now. But you'll need to start taking the long view, Moffard. Won't wash twenty years on, will it, leave alone fifty? Think you're going the whole way? Right back to the cradle?"

"Maybe so, m'lord. I'd not put it past him. No way he can tell me."

"I'll not be there to see it, more's the pity. Better start planning for it though. World's changing, Moffard. Government's getting its nose into all our lives. Happening more and more. No way we can be sure of keeping you hid, not for a hundred years. Two choices that I can see. One—keep moving on. Live one place for a while, soon as it looks like you're going to be spotted, move on. Wouldn't fancy that, eh?"

"That I wouldn't, m'lord. Lived here all my life, I have. Allus thought I'd be dying here."

"Feel the same myself. Right. That case, four or five years on you're going to have to start play-acting you're getting older. And then you'll fall ill, take to your bed, and your nephew'll show up to look after you. . . . Oh, come on, man. If you don't have one now, you'd better start having one—sheep farming out in New Zealand, maybe, spitting image of you, everyone tells you. And now, when you're poorly, he takes you on. Anybody comes to the house, he's the one they see. You're in your bed upstairs. Maybe Dr. Pastern could pay you the odd visit—think we can let him in on this, Askey . . . ? Yes, Moffard?"

"Beggin' your pardon, m'lord, but Sonny'll see to that. First thing you said when you set eyes on 'im, weren't it? 'We've got to keep mum about this.' Same with Mr. Askey 'ere. Same with me, when 'e weren't nobbut a chick. Almost the first thought come into my 'ead—I wasn't lettin' on. Thassow 'e is. None sees 'im as he don't want, and them as sees 'im don't talk. That's right, Sonny, aren't it?"

All three turned towards the hitching rail. Sonny gazed back at them with a look of arrogant confidence that in a less impressive creature would have been smug. The earl chortled, unastonished but delighted by a successful turn in the intrigue.

"Capital!" he said. "Pastern can sign the death certificate when the old lad officially pops it. You're going to be chief mourner at your own funeral, Moffard—there's not many get a chance like that. Now, Askey, we'll want a trust or something—look into the terms of the entail—deeding a ninety-nine-year lease on this wood to Moffard and his heirs and assigns. Think that's on, eh?"

The talk slid into a morass of the legal intricacies attendant on any ancient entail. Dave listened with growing anxiety, sufficiently marked for the earl eventually to notice.

"Yes, Moffard. Something troubling you?"

"Beggin' your pardon, m'lord, but this aren't anything I'm due. 'Undred years now you done right by me, you and your family, more'n right. No call for you to take on another 'undred years."

"Nonsense, Moffard. We'd do it any case. Besides, there's your friend here. We've had half the monarchs of England knocking on our door over the years, sold whole estates to pay for the honour of lodging them. I tell you there's not many of them did us more honour by their presence than your friend here. Shan't see him through myself, but nor'll I die happy not being certain the two of you are going to make it. You follow? Good man. Now, Askey . . ."

Dave gave up trying to understand the legalities, his mind too numb for thought, but his hand unconsciously fingering at a dull ache that had started towards the back of his lower jaw. Not toothache—he had none left to ache—but—

Lord above! Got one comin' back!

It was this discovery, as much as anything that the earl had said, that forced him at last to think about the reality of what lay ahead for him, to try to peer through mists and shadows down the diminishing perspective of the years to the mysterious vanishing point of his own unbirth. For some time after Mr. Askey and the earl had left, he continued to sit there, until he was roused by a sharp rap on his right knee—Sonny's peck, demanding his attention.

As soon as he saw he had it, Sonny turned and strutted off round the corner of the cottage. Dave found him by the open shed where he kept his larger tools. Here Sonny pecked at the spade he wanted Dave to bring, then rose and, flying from branch to branch, led the way to the clearing where the broken walls of the Cabinet House enclosed the low mound of its remains.

Sonny settled onto the top of this, scratched at the surface and stood back. Obediently Dave started to dig. Below the first meagre layer of grasses the mound was still almost pure ash. He heaped the first spadeful to one side, and Sonny immediately started to scrattle through it like a chicken scrattling through loose soil for insects and seeds. Finding nothing, he stood back again. They repeated the process with a second spadeful, and a third, from which Sonny picked out something about half as large as a hazelnut and set it aside. From then on most spadefuls contained one or two of the things, varying in size from an acorn to a grain of wheat. There was a distinct pit in the top of the mound by the time Sonny decided he'd gathered enough.

The harvest was more than Dave could have carried in his cupped hands, so he unknotted his neckerchief and gathered the things into it. Sonny supervised the operation closely, picking up some of the smallest that Dave had missed. Dave knotted the kerchief into a bag and carried it back to the cottage, where he spread a larger cloth on the table and spilt the contents of the kerchief out onto it. The rattling and rubbing of transport had loosened much of the ash that had coated the things, and now Dave could see, or at least guess, what he'd dug up. The things were hard and shiny-smooth, some rounded, some faceted, but all glowing or glinting with the colours of fire.

Sonny stood beside the heap looking enquiringly at him.

"These for his lordship, then?" Dave asked him. "Wonder what they're worth. Pay for our keep for a good while on, eh?"

With a feeling of intense relief at no longer being wholly beholden for his own safeguarding through the difficult years ahead, he watched Sonny soar up to the canopy of the trees to bask in sunlight until it was time for him to sing his evening hymn.

March 1915

In the same week that the news came from France that the heir to the earldom (mad on soldiering) had been killed by a random shell on his dug-out in a quiet section of the front near Arras, Mr. Askey died of the cancer that had long been killing him. On the estate the trauma of the major event wholly obscured the minor. Mr. Askey might have endured his slow and agonising passing almost unattended if Dave (now officially Ralph) Moffard hadn't sat and slept by his bed through four days and three nights, mostly just holding his hand, sometimes talking a little, dribbling water between the tense, grimacing lips and injecting the prescribed doses of morphine with tenderness and precision.

For most of the time the drug only partly masked the pain. There was a brief spell of full relief after each injection, and then a slow return of the torture, like a jagged reef emerging from as the tide recedes, until the final stage in which the groans became sobbing cries and Dave could do nothing but hold his friend's hand and suffer with his suffering while the seconds limped ever more slowly past until the cycle could be repeated.

Late on the afternoon of the fourth day, when both already foresaw another endless night of trudging across that Sahara of unmerited punishment, Dave heard a sharp rap on the window. He crossed the room to look through the slit between the curtains and saw Sonny perched on the sill. Astonished—it was at least a week sooner than he'd ever returned before, and the winter had not been kind—he raised the sash to let him in.

"He's bad, Sonny, bad," he gasped. "Anything you can do for him? Oh, Sonny!"

The moan from the bed shuddered into a howl as the cycle entered its last phase. Sonny flipped deftly to the foot-rail and perched there, gazing dispassionately down the length of the bed at the living mask of Tragedy on the pillows. Dave came and stood beside him, gripping the rail. Without warning Sonny arched his neck and struck at Dave's wrist, a precisely weighted peck that left a single bead of blood shining on the skin. He repeated the blow against his own breast, and withdrew with another bead, this time a fiery orange, at the tip of his beak. When he placed the second bead upon the first they mingled, and at the same time mounded up and seemed to solidify into a single jewel that glowed like an ember in the darkened room.

Sonny contemplated it for a moment, then picked it up, stalked the length of the bed and placed it neatly between Mr. Askey's lips.

There was a pause, and the mask became human, became the face of their friend, drawn and lined with illness, but known, admired and loved.

Mr. Askey opened his eyes and looked at them and smiled.

"Oh, that's good," he whispered. "That's good. That's good. Thank you for everything, Dave. Thank you, Sonny. Glad you made it home in time. Give my respects to his lordship. Tell him it's all been worth while, all worth while."

He closed his eyes and died.

◆ ◆ ◆

The earl bore the loss of his heir characteristically. His only known show of emotion on the subject came when some titled tub-thumper publicly congratulated him on setting an example to the nation by giving his son's life for the cause. He glared at her briefly, then snapped, "Don't be a fool, woman. I didn't give it. He did," and turned his back on her.

Fourteen years later, he was to endure another bereavement when his grandson (mad on motor-cars) killed himself at Brooklands while road-testing a straight-eight speedster of his own design, leaving a great-grandson to inherit the earldom at the age of five when the old man eventually died in 1932.

◆ ◆ ◆

Summer 1934

The madness that caused the eleventh earl eventually to be known—notorious, even—as the Green Earl was not immediately apparent. The seeds from which it was to grow were probably sown soon after his great-grandfather's death by a Miss Wells, recently engaged as governess to his two elder sisters.

Miss Wells was a tall, plain young woman in her early thirties, with a wide mouth, wide-set eyes and a pale but not unhealthy complexion. She had a look of pleasant calm, with reserves of determination below the surface. She was a governess because she had been denied a formal education beyond the age of twelve, when her mother had fallen ill from an hereditary disease and her father had withdrawn her from school to help with the household chores. From then on she had educated herself in her spare time, choosing subjects that interested her, at first generally botanical, but concentrating more and more on native British trees, since there were subjects for her to study locally in the Forest of Dean, where her parents lived. By the time of her mother's death and her father's almost instant remarriage, she was a considerable expert on some of the larger species and had had technical papers published in professional journals; none of this was much practical use to a woman turned out of her home with no more than a token allowance and with no academic qualifications whatever. One of her brothers-in-law, a motoring crony of the young earl's father, had recommended her for the post of governess, and the post had seemed right for her the moment she set eyes on the woodlands that mottled the estate. It was not surprising therefore that at almost the first opportunity she visited Dave's Wood. Since it was the afternoon on which the girls had their riding lessons and the nursery maid had her afternoon off, she was in charge of the earl, so she took him with her. Besides, there was a Mr. Moffard, whose permission she would apparently need. If he proved difficult, she could tell him she wanted to give the earl a botany lesson.

There was no such difficulty. Mr. Moffard seemed a courteous old man, though somewhat withdrawn. Just before leaving, Miss Wells asked him if he had any idea of the age of the magnificent oak tree that stood on the other side of the clearing opposite his front door.

Mr. Moffard seemed to open up a little.

"Not to say for sure, ma'am," he answered. "Seventeen 'undred eighty-two she was there, full-grown—that's in the diaries—an' there's oaks in there 'alf grown as aren't down as full-grown for another 'undred, 'undred an' twenty years. So give 'er a couple of 'undred on before the diaries, I reckon she was a young'un when the Armada come by."

"Not a Domesday oak, then?"

"Ah, no, ma'am. Fewer of those than folk make out, and what there is more dead than alive. An' Domesday this'ld 'a' been forest far as you could see. Thissair wood's maybe a bit o' that left over, but there aren't a tree in it anythin' near that old, not in the diaries, neither."

"Do you mean you've got diaries about the wood going back to—seventeen eighty, wasn't it?"

"Eighty-two, ma'am. Fifth earl begun it. Liked collectin' stuff, 'e did, anything old, almost, and gettin' it written down in a book. Sees thissair wood, full of old trees. 'Get 'em all writ down,' 'e tells my great-granddad. Thassow it begun, on'y no one never told us to stop. You interested in trees, ma'am?"

Miss Wells looked at him almost shuddering with excitement.

"More than anything in the world, Mr. Moffard," she said. "May I look at your diaries?"

"Really old ones, they're over in the Library at the House, ma'am. Eighteen forty-two thissair lot go back to. . . . Careful, m'lord! She'll bite, 'cos she don't know not to. Get 'er out for you, shall I?"

Miss Wells had managed to keep half an eye on her charge as he nosed cautiously round the room. The obvious danger came from the log fire burning in the enormous open hearth. It was piled surprisingly high, even for a dull, chilly April afternoon, but so far the earl had been more interested in the mass of other attractions in the room, all stowed as neatly as if in the cabin of a careful sailor. His latest find had been a small crate, adapted into an animal cage. She watched briefly while Mr. Moffard opened it and fished out a fox cub for the earl to look at and touch, and then turned to the diaries. There was almost a shelf of them, in different shapes and sizes; each covered two or three years. She opened the earliest and was immediately enthralled. Every major tree in the wood seemed to have its own entry, with a number, a code for its location, and then a record of its progress through the year: measurement of girth, first bud, leafing, flowering, general health, creatures using it to nest and roost, loss of branches and other damage (a close-range blast from a shot-gun to an ash in one instance) and so on. She pulled out a diary forty years on to see what had happened to the ash, and found that it was now dead all down one side. Another twenty and it was gone, apart from an entry recording the fungi on its stump.

By this time she could hardly think for excitement. She knew of no other record in the country remotely resembling this in completeness of detail. She glanced up to check if Mr. Moffard was yet free and saw that he was putting the cub back in its cage. As he came towards her an oddness struck her. Her heart sank.

"These are quite extraordinary, Mr. Moffard," she told him. "But . . . but . . . I mean, it's been over ninety years, and they're all in the same handwriting."

"Ah, no, ma'am. Just the two of us, me an' me uncle. Spittin' image of 'im, I am, folk tell me, an' it's the same with the writing. Remarkable long life 'e lived, too. Born 'tween the last day of seventeen ninety-nine, 'e used to tell folk, an' the first of eighteen 'undred an' and nowt, and din't—"

"That's extraordinary, Mr. Moffard! So was I! A hundred years later, of course, but between the last—"

There was a stillness in the room, a sudden surge of tension, enough to startle Miss Wells into silence and a quick check round the room. She gasped, suppressed the automatic shout of warning and rushed towards the fireplace. The earl was standing actually inside the chimney breast, having worked his way in between the glowing mass of embers and the side wall of the chimney, and was now leaning forward over the fire to crane up into the dark cavern of the chimney above. She reached in, grasped his arm and dragged him out.

"Oh, but please—" he began.

At that moment her fears seemed to be justified. A glowing mass slid down the chimney and landed in the heart of the fire. Flames blazed up around it, too bright to look at. They settled. The mass shook itself and became a distinct shape, which rose and stepped forward onto the hearth. Miss Wells found herself staring at a bird about the size of a farmyard cock, with apparently normal avian plumage, except that it was a brighter, fierier orange-yellow than she would have imagined possible.

The earl turned to her, earnest-faced.

"Welly, you mustn't tell anyone," he commanded. "It's a secret."

"No, no, of course not," she muttered, still staring.

"That's the Phoenix, that is," said Mr. Moffard calmly. "Seems 'e's wanting for to meet you."

Summer 1990

"We been makin' a game between us, Welly and me, when you'd get it," said Dave. "She said as it wouldn't be that long now."

"But how . . . how . . . ?"

"Livin' backwards. This ninety year that's what I been doin'. 'Undred afore that was forwards, same as anyone else, so put 'em together and I'm an 'undred an' ninety. 'Ard to take in, I dessay, but don't you fret on it now. You'll get it soon as you've met Sonny. Nothin' to be feared of—'e's been around since you first come, on'y you won't 'ave seed 'im. 'E'll be down when 'e's through with 'is 'ymn."

Ellie continued to stare while Dave returned to his notes as if nothing of more than passing importance had happened. At last he looked up and grinned at her, a normal boy's grin of pure, harmless mischief.

"Bit much to take in, I dessay," he said. "Come along, then. Wouldn't want you to miss this."

They walked together back towards the cottage, past grown trees, some of which, Ellie was creepily aware, must first have shouldered their way out of the soil long after the boy beside her had been born. The idea made her shiver, not with fear, but from its sheer strangeness.

Back at the cottage she settled beside Welly to help her enter up the day's notes on the PC while Dave cooked—strong tea with lots of sugar, and fried potato baps with bacon scraps and onion in the mix, greasy but crunchy crisp on the outside, and utterly contrary to all Mum's dietary rules. Delectable. She was finishing her second helping when Dave picked up his mug, handed it to her and rose.

"'Bout time now," he said.

Welly backed her chair from the table and wheeled herself to the door, down the ramp and round beside the bench, where Dave and Ellie settled. All three waited in silence.

The front of the cottage was in shadow now, with the setting sun just lighting the topmost branches of the trees along the eastern edge of the clearing. Above that the sky was a soft, pale blue. The evening was full of the good-night calls of birds. They hushed, and the whole wood waited.

The song began so softly that Ellie wasn't sure at how long it had been going on when she first heard it, a series of gentle, bubbling notes, close together but distinct, so like a human melody that Ellie felt she could almost have put words to it. It became louder, wilder. Ellie closed her eyes and in her imagination saw the song as a swirling fountain of individual droplets above the trees, each note glittering into rainbow colours in the sideways light, the fountain rising and spreading into a circling canopy of light, which then un-shaped itself and fell in a gentle shower onto the waiting leaves below.

Again she couldn't tell for certain when the song ended, but as she opened her eyes the birds of the wood resumed their calling.

"Layin' it on some tonight," said Dave. "That's for you, Ellie. 'Ere 'e comes."

Ellie followed his glance in time to see a large bird launch itself from the top of the oak opposite, glistening with the reflected colours of the western sky—or so she imagined. But when the bird glided down into shadow, the sunset hues stayed with it until it landed, glowing, on the hitching rail beside the door.

Ellie rose—it seemed rude to stay sitting—and stared, her heart pounding. The bird gazed back considering, judging, her.

"This is Sonny," said Welly's voice behind her. "He's the Phoe-nix. You've probably read about him. But I've always found it easiest to think of him not as a magical creature out of a story-book, but as a god. He comes from Egypt, where they didn't have just one god, they had lots. But he's the only one left. Go closer. He won't hurt you."

"No. No. Of course not," murmured Ellie, allowing her feet to drift her towards the hitching rail. The bird drew itself up and spread its wings wide as she approached, until it seemed to tower over her.

Yes, she thought. *It's a god. Of course.*

She bowed her head and the wings swept forward until they lay gently against either side of it, a warm, soft, feathery touch. She felt the bird's brow against her own, the fringes of its scarlet crest min-gling into her hair-line.

They stayed only briefly like that and straightened. Ellie stepped back, feeling not exactly changed, not altered or tampered with, but renewed, fully herself and confident in that selfhood. The gift of the Phoenix. Something she would have until she died.

"That's 'is blessin'," said Dave. "Worth 'avin', eh? It'll be gettin' cold for 'im now, an' 'e'll be wanting to sit on 'is fire, so we'll be goin' in an' we'll tell you about it all."

◆ ◆ ◆

It was well past midnight when Ellie crawled into bed, exhausted beyond belief with the excitement of the day but still for a long while unable to sleep for the muddle of thoughts and memories jostling through her mind. . . .

◆ ◆ ◆

. . . Sonny, the one and only ever-living Phoenix, blazing on his great mound of embers on the hearth below but filling the whole room with his presence. . . .

◆ ◆ ◆

. . . Welly and Dave curled up in each other's arms in their room on the other side of the landing, husband and wife for forty years now, he getting younger all the time, and she getting older, and still in love. . . .

◆ ◆ ◆

. . . And then, almost word for word in her mind still, what they had told her:

". . . We'd been together, as people say now, almost since the day we met. I don't think it was anything Sonny did to us—we just fell for each other, didn't we, love?"

"That we did. Couldn't think what were 'appenin' to me. Thought I were getting' the 'fluenza, maybe."

"But we couldn't get married because of Dave needing to change who he was every twenty years or so. That was tricky enough as it was without my having to account for a series of missing husbands. But then, in the winter of nineteen forty-nine—No, I'd better go back a bit. From the very first I wanted to know as much as I could about Sonny—"

"Like that, Welly is. If it aren't in a book, it aren't real."

"I started in the library here, reading everything I could find about ancient Egypt, and I advertised for a tutor—we could afford that, because of the very generous arrangements his lordship had made for Dave here—"

"Sonny payin' 'is debts, that come from. Showed me a pile of jewels in 'is bonfire 'eap to give to 'is lordship, an' then 'e said I got to 'ang on to 'alf of 'em—"

"As well as a ninety-nine-year lease on the cottage and the wood. It was still extremely generous, but it meant I could hire a tutor, and I found a wonderful old man, a retired professor of Egyptology who lived in a large old house in Hampstead piled from floor to ceiling with books. I boarded with him all through the war when I was doing war work in one of the ministries. I couldn't tell him why I wanted to know about the Phoenix, of course, but he got interested and dug out everything he could find, and he taught me to read hieroglyphics, and best of all he got me a place on a dig one of his ex-pupils was running in Heliopolis, and Dave came too—"

"Wanted to see where Sonny spent 'is winter, a' course."

"The earl vouched for him so we could get him a passport because he didn't have a birth certificate. We used to walk in the desert in the evenings, and Sonny would meet us. He seemed to have much more power there—"

"Only natural, 'im bein' closer to the sun."

"We were excavating a temple of Osiris, and he'd come to me in my dreams and show me how it used to look in his day, so they were very glad to have me on the dig because I seemed to be such a lucky guesser—they used to joke about my having second sight. And then on the last night of the year—we'd told them it was our fiftieth birthday, but of course it was really Dave's hundred and fiftieth, only his fiftieth from when he began to go backwards—"

"Sonny's, too."

"In this cycle, anyway, though . . . Yes, Ellie?"

"They didn't have our centuries did they? Back in ancient Egypt, I mean."

"Takes what 'e can get. We got centuries now, so that's what 'e uses."

"He has to have some kind of a cycle that the humans he lives among find important. In Egypt it was a hundred and twenty years, but it's centuries now. Anyway, my friends on the dig held a party for us, and when it was over Dave and I walked out into the desert and Sonny met us and took us to his temple. It was buried deep in a dune, but Sonny called and a patch of sand slid away and there was a hole we could crawl through—pitch dark, but as soon as we were in, Sonny blazed into light and there it was. Oh, Ellie, it was perfectly wonderful, quite small, but untouched—never been found by anyone, or looted or excavated. Every wall covered with paintings or hieroglyphics, all looking as if they'd been done yesterday. . . ."

"An' that's where 'e married us."

"Yes . . . that was where he married us. . . . I'm sorry . . . I've never been able to talk to anyone else about it before . . . that's why I'm crying. It was so beautiful. It sounds lonely, but it wasn't, because he brought them all back, everyone who'd ever helped him before, the way we're doing, not to see or hear or feel, but *there*, crowding into his temple to welcome and bless us, his fortunate, fortunate friends. . . .

"Of course, when I got back to England I longed to tell my old professor about it, but I couldn't. So Sonny sent him a dream instead—"

"Payin' 'is debts again."

"Yes. There's a sacred text carved onto a stele at Luxor. It's so battered that no one could read it, and scholars had been arguing for years about what it meant. When we got back from Egypt, I found a letter waiting for me from my old professor, telling me that on New Year's Eve—the night we got married, remember—he'd dreamed he saw the stele as it was when it was new. It seemed to be lit by flame, and he could read it right through. And he was so excited that he woke up and found that he still remembered it, so he switched on his bedside light and wrote it down. He got up next morning thinking it would be complete nonsense, but he looked at it and saw that it must be right. The Society of Egyptologists gave him their Gold Medal for the paper he wrote on it, and he told me that now he could die happy. He was over ninety."

"That's lovely!"

"That's Sonny, that is. You better get on, Welly, or we'll all be fallin' asleep."

"You're going to tell me why you really want me. Aren't you?"

A pause, and a sigh from Welly.

"We can't make 'er. An' Sonny won't. Tell 'er that."

"I suppose it's a place to start. You see, my dear, after that first time, I used to join a dig and go back to Egypt every winter. Dave would come for a little while and I'd take a break to be with him, and wherever my dig was we'd go to Heliopolis and visit Sonny and his temple. So I got to read all the hieroglyphs and the scrolls, one of which was about the temple ritual. The important thing was that there were always two special priests—sometimes one of them was a priestess—and one of them was getting older and the other one was getting younger. And on ritual days, especially the midwinter solstice, the other priests would make a fire on the altar and the Phoenix would appear and bathe in his flames to renew his strength. Then, right at the end of the cycle when one priest was a very old man and the other was a babe in arms, they'd build a special pyre on the altar and on that last midnight they'd lay the baby—the priest who'd been growing younger—on the pyre, and the Phoenix would appear and nestle down onto the baby as if it were brooding a chick. Then, on the stroke of midnight, the baby would be unborn, and the Phoenix would take its spirit into himself and the pyre would burst into flame. In that same instant, somewhere in Egypt, a new baby would be born, and the old priest would start to live backwards.

"The priests would watch all night, and in the dawn light they would see a pile of ashes where the pyre had been, and on top of it a great jewelled egg. Then, as the sun rose, its first rays would shine through the eastern portal of the temple and strike the egg, and the shell would open like a flower and the baby Phoenix would be there, ready to begin the cycle again. All that was then needed was for the child who had been born at the sacred moment to find his or her way to the temple and be recognised."

"Weren't like that when poor Sonny were born, not a bit. 'Ad to make it all up for 'isself. Touch an' go from the start. Still is."

"Exactly. We don't know what went wrong with the cycle. The pyre must have been built and lit and the egg formed, but something prevented it ever being hatched. It may even have been Sonny's way of enduring the Christian centuries when it would have been difficult for the cult to survive. But the fifth earl picked up the egg up somewhere, still described as a phoenix egg—that's another mystery—and brought it to the Cabinet House, and Dave was born close by at midnight on the turn of the century, and the cycle could begin again. We don't know whether Sonny arranged for that himself, or whether it was just the bit of luck he'd been waiting for.

"But I don't think he can have known about me, or he'd have arranged it differently. I've got this hereditary disease. My mother died when she was forty-eight, and one of my sisters when she was fifty-three. None of us who've had it has ever lived beyond sixty, that we know of. So Sonny's kept me going thirty years beyond my time. He can do that. There's no record in the scrolls of any of the growing-older priests having died before the cycle was up, and it was a hundred and twenty years then, remember. That's a tremendous age at any time. A lot of Egyptian mummies have been carbon dated, and their average age at death was thirty-one."

"Taken it out of 'im, it 'as, an' then some, doin' it for Welly. An' the summers, they aren't nowhere near 'ot enough for 'im, not comparing to Egypt, and flyin' out an' 'ome spring an' fall, that's takin' it out of 'im too. 'E gets old, same as anyone else, each time round, on'y 'e's found this way o' stayin' immortal. But like I say, it's goin' to be touch an' go for 'im this time, an' touch an' go for Welly, an' that means touch' an' go for me. Don't care to think what'll happen if I get to be unborn 'thout Sonny bein' around to sort things out."

"In a few years' time, Ellie, I'm going to be almost completely helpless, and Dave's going to be five, going on four, and Sonny's going to be trying to survive our English winters on sun-lamps and log fires. In Egypt there were always other priests who helped our predecessors survive those difficult years. Now we are alone."

"And you want me to help."

"We are asking you to join the Priesthood of the Temple of the Phoenix until the cycle of the death and rebirth of our god is fulfilled."

"All right. Can you wait till I've finished school? I don't think my dad will want me go to university, not if he has to pay for it."

"I think we can do better than that. I've already talked to his lordship. When you've finished school, he'll take you on as assistant forester on the estate, with special responsibility for the wood. I'll introduce you to some of my forestry friends—I still keep up with them by e-mail. You'll have the diaries, and once we've gone, there'll be no need for you to keep the wood secret. You'll have an absolutely unique resource to bargain with. Any university that runs a forestry course will be thrilled to have you."

"I don't need any of that. Really I don't. I . . . I'd do it whatever it cost me."

"Mebbe you would, too, but Sonny aren't goin' to let you. 'E'll look after you, 'cos of 'e pays 'is debts. Not a lot o' gods you can say that of."

At long last Ellie drowsed off into sleep. Her last conscious thought was *I wish I'd been at their wedding. It must have been wonderful. Perhaps Sonny will send me a dream.*

He did.

Midnight, 31 December 1999

A cold night, almost clear. The moon already set. A swath of brilliant stars overhead, and another to the east above a horizon of low hills, visible through a gap in the trees. A large hand torch illuminates part of the clearing, in its beam a pyramidal pile of logs with a flattened top. A light ladder rests against the pile, and an elaborately patterned cloth is draped over its top.

The person holding the hand torch turns. Now the beam illuminates an object something between a hospital stretcher-trolley and a high-tech wheel-chair. Propped on it, swathed in shawls and piled with rugs, lies a very old woman with a bundle on her lap. The torch is settled on the foot of the bed, so that it once more illuminates the pile. Its bearer moves up beside the bundle, opens it and holds its contents to the old woman's face, as if for her to kiss, and moves into the light of the torch. Now it can be seen that she is a young woman, heavily wrapped against the cold, but the baby she is carrying is stark naked, though apparently almost newborn. Carefully she climbs the ladder, kisses the baby, places it in the centre of the cloth and folds the four corners over it. The underside of the cloth is brilliant with jewels that flash with all the colours of fire in the torch-light. She descends and returns to the trolley, bringing the ladder with her.

Now she folds back some of the bedclothes from a mound near the foot of the bed. The mound stirs, stands, and reveals itself as a large bird. It shakes itself, spreads its wings, and flies heavily to the top of the pile, where it nestles down onto the cloth that wraps the baby, like a hen brooding its chicks. In the torch-light its plumage seems to glow dull orange, and when the torch is switched off continues to do so.

Steadily the glow increases until it illuminates the whole clearing. Both women are weeping, but the older one is smiling too. The younger one reaches in under the blankets to hold her hand.

Just as the glow becomes too bright to look at, the whole pile bursts into flame. The young woman lets out a long sigh of relief.

"Made it," she says quietly. "All three of you made it. I was afraid he wouldn't be strong enough."

"Yes," whispers the old woman. "He was strong enough. And in a few years I will be too. Strong enough to go and live with him in Egypt where he belongs.

"Somewhere tonight, Ellie, a child has been born. I think it will be a boy this time. I don't know where, but it doesn't matter. Perhaps we'll meet him in Egypt, or perhaps you'll find him here and bring him to us. For you will come and visit us. Often."

The pile burns fiercely. The flames that roar up from its summit completely hide what has happened to bird and child. A strange reek fills the clearing, like incense with several elements left out, both sweet and peppery, mingling with the ordinary odours of burning. Myrrh.

The two watchers wait in silence. They wait almost without stirring through the small hours of the night while fire slowly settles into itself and star after star rises steadily above the eastern hills. At one point the young woman bends to connect a fresh set of batteries to the cables that are keeping the bed warm. Apart from that, neither stirs or speaks. Once again, after a centuries-long hiatus, the priests of the Phoenix watch the night through in stillness and in silence.

By the time the stars are beginning to disappear into the paling sky above the eastern hills, the fire has become a smooth mound of embers with, cupped into its summit, a rounded object bigger than a man's head, glittering with fiery jewels set into a glowing orange background, darker than the embers of the fire. The egg of the Phoenix.

The older woman begins to speak. The younger bends to listen to her whisper.

"Ellie, my dear, this is something that hundreds of thousands of people of many different faiths, for century after century, have passionately believed in, longed for and prayed for. And now we two are going to see it with our living eyes. We will see our god reborn."

Ellie smiles at her and turns to watch for the moment of sunrise through the gap she cut last week with her chain-saw.

Only we'll never be able to tell anyone, she thinks.

HELLHOUND

ROBIN McKINLEY

Miri had been the sort of child who believed that every pony with a star on its forehead had been born a unicorn and had agreed to give up its horn to become a pony and bring happiness into some child's life.

"After Tamari, I don't see how you kept that one up," her mother said. Tamari was an exquisitely beautiful half-Welsh pony, dark dappled brown, with four white socks and a perfect four-pointed white star on his forehead. He also had the temperament of a back-alley mugger. "Do you remember the time Tamari cornered that poor little sap Trudy behind the manure pile and you had to rescue her?"

"Or the time Jojo jumped out of the paddock *next* to Tamari because a single fence between them wasn't enough?" added her father helpfully.

"Lovely form too. Nobody knew Jojo had it in her. We started entering her in hunter classes after that," her mother said.

Miri smiled faintly. "Some unicorns mind more than others, after the change."

Her brother Mal guffawed. "Don't forget Peggy."

Peggy had been one of their mother's reclamation projects. "Jane, I really think—" Miri's father had begun, as they watched the poor bony thing totter down the ramp of the horse trailer. They were used to her coming home from the horse-rescue with a new four-legged adventure, but this one looked beyond what food and love could rehabilitate. "She came up and put her nose under my arm," Jane said defensively. "What was I going to do?" Peggy had become a stalwart of the lesson program and the weekend trail rides, and while most of her welts and weals healed without trace, there was a peculiarly matched pair of marks behind her shoulders that Miri said were wing scars, and named her Pegasus.

It was an old family routine, trotted out for old friends and relatives rarely seen; after the friends or relatives had exclaimed over how grown-up the children had become since they'd last seen them, her father told the unicorn story and her mother brought up Tamari, and if the visitors were still enjoying themselves, Mal said, "Don't forget Peggy."

There were lots of animal stories in their family. Her father's fish tanks were scattered all over the downstairs (and terrariums full of invisible chameleons and tree frogs upstairs); her brother had an African grey parrot who said things like, "Are you *sure* you locked the stables?" and "Have you cleaned the tack yet?" with deadly accuracy; and her mother usually had two or three (or four or five) cats underfoot in the house (the tanks and terrariums all had cat-proof lids; the African grey had a permanent "make my day" look in her eye) as well as several generations of mousers patrolling the barns.

And then there were the horses. Jane ran a riding stable. She gave lessons on her own horses and boarded other people's. Tamari had been a boarder. When Jane had finally told his very nice owner that he had to go, the owner had sighed and said, "He's been here almost a year. That's almost twice as long as he's ever been anywhere else. I was beginning to hope . . . oh, well." Tamari was a show pony; his manners were always as perfect as his looks at shows, and he had the trophies and ribbons to prove it. It was only when he was home again that he turned into something out of a bad creature feature.

Miri wanted a dog. When she'd been very young and they had first moved to the then-derelict farm, there had been a man who came several weekends in a row with what seemed to Miri, at six, to be at least forty terriers—ferocious ratters, who had dealt implacably with the resident population. Twelve years later the man was still coming occasionally (her mother refused to put down poison, and there are always rats around a barn), although he had less hair than he'd had and more waistline, and the number of terriers had dwindled to three. Miri had been fascinated from the first by the gallant, indomitable little dogs, even though she couldn't bear to watch them at their grisly business for long. And the boarders often had dogs; her mother occasionally permitted barn privileges for these on a case by case basis—and on the understanding that any dog caught misbehaving was instantly banned.

Miri's favorite was a border collie named Fay. Fay's owner Nora had once told Fay to lie down at some little distance from where she was hosing her horse off, so she wouldn't hose Fay too. But the hose and tap were at the edge of the driveway, and Fay was lying in the middle of it. Miri and her mother were coming back from a show with two tired, eager-to-be-home horses in the trailer when her mother had to stop because Fay was lying in the way. Her mother tried a gentle toot on the horn. Fay raised her head long enough to direct a withering glare in their direction, and then laid her head back on her paws.

Her mother laughed. "Well, that put us in our place. Go tell Nora to call her dratted dog, will you please? She's got that radio turned up so loud she can't hear us."

But Miri liked Oscar too, and Sammy, and Bramble. Miri liked dogs.

"I want a dog," Miri often said.

"No," her mother equally often replied. "There are enough animals around the place already."

"Enough of *your* animals," Miri said.

"What is Balthazar, then?" said her mother. "Chopped liver?"

Balthazar was Miri's horse. He could do anything, including nod, count, and lie down on request, but his chief virtue in her mother's eyes was that he and Miri led the weekend trail rides and, with Miri on his back, nothing ever bothered him: rabbits, raccoons, frisky ownerless dogs appearing as if by magic, plastic bags left by careless picnickers fluttering threateningly from the undergrowth, horses and riders who behaved rationally and competently in the outdoor arena having sudden inexplicable meltdowns without a fence around them: all the standard trail hazards. Unflappability had a price above rubies at a stable that needed weekend trail rides to make ends meet, and for this he was forgiven anything, including how much he ate. He had been—and for that matter still was—the best birthday present Miri had ever had.

She still wanted a dog.

"A stable needs a dog," she said. "The next time somebody tries to break into the tack room, it would bark."

Her mother winced. Her insurance premiums had gone up after the last claim. "No," she said firmly. "It would *not* bark. It would be asleep on your bed, and your bedroom's on the wrong side of the house."

"What do you have against dogs?" said Miri. "You *like* animals. We even have guinea pigs because when the Stantons emigrated to Australia they didn't have anyone to give them to so they gave them to us. We have *tortoises* because that stupid man at Dad's office thought they could live in the fish tanks, and Dad's as bad as you are and couldn't say no." Her dad cleaned the tortoise cages. Miri only mucked out warm-blooded animals.

Her mother sighed. "Dogs are too much like horses—I mean the kind of care they need. They're not all like Fay. *Fay* wouldn't be like Fay, except Nora has put a huge amount of work into her. Cats will almost look after themselves, if there's enough space for them to keep themselves amused in."

Miri didn't say anything. Space to keep themselves amused in, in Miri's experience of cats, was under some human's feet, and what about the cat food? If all the money for cat food went to dog food, they could have *two* dogs. Two *large* dogs. But it wasn't that she didn't want not to have cats. She felt there was a principle of fair play involved.

"Dogs you have to do things for. You have to train them, and you have to know where they are all the time. You have to *be* there for a dog."

"We *are* here. We're *always* here. We're going to be here *forever.*"

Jane gave her a harassed look. It was true they hadn't been away on a vacation in four years, since their last barn-sitter had left without warning after two days. Their stall-cleaner had arrived the next morning and found the barns closed and dark, and the horses still waiting for breakfast. (Also the cats, the fish, the tree frogs and the tortoises. Four years ago had been before either the guinea pigs or the parrot, Dorothy. Miri rather thought that her brother would never be able to go on vacation again, and wondered what any possible future wife would think about a parrot going on the honeymoon with them. He'd lost at least one girlfriend already on account of Dorothy: a happy, contented African grey is both jealous and demanding, and Dorothy recognized a challenger and behaved accordingly.)

"Honey . . . are you still sure you want to work here full-time after you graduate from high school? Including living at home and all? Because you know I can't afford to pay you enough to let you move out." Miri knew. Her dad did the books, and was always trying to make both her and Jane pay more attention. She also knew because when she was still too young to be much use, they'd had live-in barn help. Her family had quite a few live-in barn help stories too.

"Mom, it's a dead issue. We've got all these *plans* for what we're going to do once I'm here full-time, remember?"

Her mother laughed. "I remember only too well. With you working twenty-four hours a day we're going to have the money to build an indoor arena in three years. I feel I must have brainwashed you or something. Kids are supposed to want to grow up and leave."

"And I want to grow up and stay. You didn't brainwash me, you just gave me *all* your DNA." It was a family joke that Miri was her mother's clone: they were both small, dark, tough, compact, horse-obsessed, and couldn't add a column of figures to save their lives.

"Well, here's my best offer, then. The day after you graduate from high school, you can get yourself a dog."

It took her almost a week after graduation to make time to go to the dog pound. The primary school got out a week before the high school did, and the barn was immediately deluged with little kids wanting extra lessons. Miri was good with kids, especially the ones torn between adoring horses and being scared to death of them. Some of these then transferred their adoration to Miri, and would only take lessons from her. Every time she looked at her schedule for a space to shoehorn another lesson in, she thought of the indoor arena, and found time.

She knew her mother was hoping she'd forgotten about the dog . . . but that Jane also knew her well enough to know that she would not forget.

So one day—finally—at lunch she said, "Carol's mom cancelled, poor Carol's sick, and I moved Harriet to last thing. If you can spare me, I'm going to the pound this afternoon."

Jane gallantly refrained from sighing, and said immediately, "Of course we can spare you. Remember to buy dog food on the way home."

Miri suppressed a grin. Her mother also knew her well enough to know that if there was no farm dog by dinnertime, it could only be that a roc had stooped from nowhere, picked up the car with Miri in it, and was bearing them away to an unknown island in the Pacific.

She drove very carefully on the way to the pound. She had had her license from the moment she was old enough to be legal, and had been efficiently backing horse trailers around corners at the farm some time before that; it wasn't the driving. It was that today was a special day. Today she'd have—she'd finally have—a dog. It wasn't even only the dog: this would be the first time she'd done something clearly, absolutely, definitively *hers*. She loved the farm and the riding stable, and had every intention of staying there for the rest of her life. (She even had the site picked out to build her own house on, if she managed to acquire a husband who had a job that earned genuine money so they could afford to. But the site was only on the other side of the driveway plus a few trees from the old farmhouse. There was six A.M. breakfast for horses to think about, and you wanted to be within earshot for sounds of trouble.) And budgeting for the indoor arena was her idea (maybe she had one or two of her father's genes after all), but it was still something she was doing with her mother. A dog would in a way be the first step toward making the riding stable genuinely individually hers too.

Ronnie was behind the counter at reception. "So, how does it feel to be a grown-up and have to start paying your own bills?" he said jovially. Ronnie coached the local Little League team Mal had been on, and had six dogs of his own, all from the pound. He tended to specialize in the hard-to-place ones, so he had three-legged dogs, blind dogs, old dogs and hyperactive incontinent dogs. He also had a very patient wife.

"It feels okay. I'm only working forty-two hours a day for seventy-five cents an hour—that's pretty good, isn't it?"

Ronnie whistled. "Your mother's getting soft."

"Yes, that's what I thought. So I decided I'd better get a dog fast before she tightens up."

"Good plan." He lifted the end of the counter and came out. "I'll take you round. Do you have any idea what you're looking for?"

"Not really. Something that can put up with a lot of cats and people and won't chase horses."

The pound was nearly full, so there were a lot of dogs to look at. And most of them were barking. Miri began to think there were more advantages to cats than she'd realized. Her head started to hurt, and it was hard to *look* at each dog, especially the barking ones. But shouldn't she want a dog that barked? In case it happened to be on the right side of the house the next time someone tried to break into the tack room.

They turned down a row of large runs. "I also don't want anything that it takes two days' salary to feed for *one* day," said Miri, as something that looked like a cross between a St. Bernard and a Shire horse shambled up to the front of its run to look them over.

"They're not all like Marigold," said Ronnie. "Some of 'em are just tall."

Miri stopped at a run a little over halfway down the row. This dog was not only not barking, which was unusual enough, but it was curled up in a far corner with its back to them.

"This one's a funny one," Ronnie said. "You won't want him, though. Nobody does. I'd've taken him home by now, but my wife says six is enough. He's a complete gentleman; he wouldn't chase your cats or your horses. But you won't want him. He'd scare your little kids."

Miri's curiosity was now fully aroused. All she could see was a long reddish-chestnut back: part setter, maybe.

"I'm going to take him home soon anyway, though," said Ronnie. "I hate seeing him like this. Some dogs almost don't mind being pound dogs, but he's a sensitive soul, and he's been here too long. He's pining, poor thing. No one even stops to talk to him, let alone take him home." He unlocked the wire-mesh door and went in; Miri followed. "Hey there, my friend," said Ronnie. "You've got a visitor. Come say hello."

The dog raised his head and looked back over his shoulder at them. He had a long narrow head with lopped-over ears, and a slightly bristly red coat—although more streaky merle than setter. He also had enormous, slanted, almond-shaped eyes, with slightly drooping lower lids. But the interior of those lids was a brilliant *scarlet* red, flame red, and the rim all round was red; and the eyes themselves were a curious reddish brown, almost the color of his coat. The whites of his eyes, visible at the angle he was looking at them from, were also scarlet red.

"Oh," said Miri.

"The vet can't find anything wrong with him. He seems to see perfectly well, the eyes don't seem to be sore or tender and there's no swelling, no wounds; the lab reports all come back negative. He just looks . . . odd. Somebody saw him by the road and called him in; but when Diane went out with the van she almost didn't bring him back, because of the way he looks."

The dog was looking at them sadly. Miri wasn't sure how she knew this; it was hard to read an ordinary dog expression in those eyes. But she was sure she knew what she was seeing. It wasn't just what Ronnie had said about him.

"So, dog, how's it going?" she said, and held out her hand tentatively.

The dog looked at her for a moment longer and then slowly uncoiled and stood up. Oops, thought Miri, well, he's certainly one of the tall ones. He waited, watching them, before he turned around so he was facing them, and paused again, still looking at them. The way he moved reminded her of the way you move around a nervous horse: slowly, gently, with lots of pauses, and watching carefully both for any reaction and any opportunity to try to make friends. This was suddenly so clear to her that she grinned, and held her hand out more positively. The dog cautiously walked the length of the run to them, stared into her face a moment longer, and then dropped his vivid eyes and lowered his head to put his nose in her hand.

"It's only that he's a hellhound," Miri said. "That's why he has those eyes. I'll take him."

Ronnie, grinning so hard his face was in danger of splitting, left her in the run with her new dog and went in search of a collar and leash. She glanced down. The hellhound looked up immediately. The scarlet of his eyes seemed to swirl and flicker, like real flames.

When Ronnie returned, he was apologetic. "This is the only one I could find in his size," he said, holding out a loop of bright red. Miri laughed.

"No, I think red's exactly right. Anything else would only make it worse."

He was a rather beautiful dog—except for the eyes—and she was already getting used to them by the time she'd buckled the collar round his neck. He ignored all the frenzy from the other dogs as they made their way back through the rows of kennels to reception. There was a surprising amount of paperwork to adopting a dog—and it cost more than she was expecting too. Drat, she thought, there goes the indoor arena for an extra—oh, six minutes or so. While Ronnie went into the office for the adoption forms she stood by the counter and looked at her hellhound some more. Her hellhound looked back. The faintest suggestion of a wag rippled through his hindquarters and tail.

"I wonder if you know anything?" she said. "I mean any of the ordinary dog things. I wouldn't want to guess what you really know." She'd done a lot of dog-minding and dog-sitting for people who came to the barn so she didn't feel at a total loss, although there was a strange fluttery feeling in the base of her throat. As Ronnie came back again, holding a wad of papers, she stooped down and tapped the floor. "Lie down," she said. And then she heard herself add: "Please?"

The hellhound had obligingly lowered his head to watch her. He looked at her tapping finger and put his nose on it. Then he looked at her face again—and she had the extremely disconcerting sensation that he was changing his mind as he looked at her, thinking something on the order of, no, I can't keep it up. Keep what up? she thought. That you're a dog? Or that you're *not* a dog?

He lay down. He lay down like the statue of a jackal on an Egyptian tomb, or like a stone lion in front of a library. She almost felt that she ought to stay crouched in front of him.

She stood up.

"Wow," said Ronnie. "I don't think I'd be teaching that one to fetch my slippers, though."

"No," she agreed. "But any self-respecting tack-room thief ought to take one look at him and run away."

She'd named him Flame by the time they got home. She found herself pressing the gas pedal more gently as she turned into the sandy, gravelly drive to the barn, as if by doing so the truck's wheels would make less noise, and she—and Flame—would be able to slip in unnoticed.

Of course this is not what happened. The old truck, perhaps as a result of over ten years of pulling horse trailers, had developed a unique wheeze, not unlike a horse with broken wind. ("If you had a horse that made a sound like that, you'd retire it," said Miri's father. "Ned," said Jane with dignity, "it's a *truck*.") So even though there were always cars and trucks (and frequently old croaky cars and trucks) pulling in and out of the stable-yard, Jane, Mal and Ned—and two of the current regiment of barn cats—were all standing at the edge of the drive by the time she'd parked and turned the engine off. Mal's summer job—he still had two years of high school left—was second shift. Just my luck, though, she thought, to have picked a day when Dad is working at home. Oh, well. Maybe better get it over with. . . .

She climbed out of the driver's side and paused. Flame was sitting up in the passenger seat, so her family could see that there was, indeed, a dog.

"Well, come on," said Jane. "I have a class to teach in two minutes. Let's see him. Her."

"Him," said Miri. She opened the passenger door slowly, and clipped Flame's leash on. Then she led him round the back of the truck to where her family was waiting. The two cats ran away. Flame paid them no attention.

"Good god," said her father.

"Oh, poor thing, but what's wrong with him? It's not contagious, is it?" said Jane.

"Yuck," said Mal. "I thought you wanted a *dog*."

"He's a hellhound," said Miri. "That's all. There's nothing wrong with him and it's not contagious. Ronnie gave me the letter from the vet that says so." In fact the letter didn't say anything of the kind: it hedged. That the writer was puzzled and confused was apparent; but the letter did say that the vet hadn't been able to find anything wrong with Flame.

There was a little silence.

"I hope you bought a large bag of dog food," Jane said finally.

"Yes," said Miri, but her heart sank. Her family *liked* animals; Flame wasn't that awful, was he? Didn't anyone even want to say hello to him? Give him a pat? She hooked the leash over her wrist and dropped her own hand on his head; the hair on the top of his head was very silky, as if it had been specially organized there to be good for stroking.

"Sorry," said Jane, who could read her daughter very easily. "He's just—I wasn't expecting a hellhound." She stepped forward and then dropped down on one knee. The huge scarlet eyes looked at her gravely. She reached out and stroked her hand down his bristly throat and chest. "And a dog brush with the dog food. No mud and no burrs past the mudroom, okay?"

"Okay," said Miri, smiling with relief. At least Jane wasn't going to try to banish him from the house.

A long pink tongue unrolled from Flame's mouth, and he just touched the back of Jane's hand with it. It was barely a lick; it was more like an acknowledgement.

"I think he's trying to charm me," said Jane.

"Is he succeeding?" said Miri.

Jane and Flame stared at each other a little more.

"Yes," said Jane. "I rather think he is. You've got a lesson yourself in half an hour, you know, and I'm not at all sure how Lynn is going to react to your hellhound." Lynn was one of Miri's timid ones. A good lesson with Lynn was getting her off the longe line for a turn or two around the arena by herself. "What are you going to do with him while you're teaching? I don't want him loose till we know he'll behave and—er—"

"You don't want mass panic if the kindergarteners all catch sight of him at once," said Miri calmly. She was feeling much better now that her mother was (more or less) won over. One or two of the kindergarteners at a time were fine, but in aggregate they were unfortunately prone to shrieking. They *enjoyed* shrieking. Flame might bring on quite a bad attack of this.

The kindergarteners were, in fact, the nine- to eleven-year-old group, but Mal had started calling them that three or four years ago when he wasn't much older than they were, and despite Jane's having forbidden him to do so. Possibly because most of them had had a crush on him, they'd decided en masse that they liked the name, and the Kindergarten Quadrille was now an established part of the barn's annual horse show, and places in it were much sought after. (Miri had said sourly, about a year ago, that having a crush on Mal was still a requirement for entry. Mal had knocked her down and sat on her—they were in the hayloft at the time—and Jane had said that if they wanted to behave like eight-year-olds, then bedtime was eight o'clock and Saturday night curfew nine.) The class Jane was about to teach was kindergarteners, and so was Lynn.

"I'll introduce him to Lynn," she went on, trying to sound more confident than she felt. "She'll like being first. And if fraidy-cat Lynn is okay with him the other kids won't want to be anything else." She looked at Mal.

He too could read her easily. "It'll cost you," he said.

"Okay," said Miri.

"*What?*" said Jane. "What's going to cost? What are you two up to, under my nose?"

"Mal's going to help the kindergarteners adjust to my hellhound."

"*I* haven't adjusted to your hellhound yet."

"*I* haven't adjusted to *Dorothy*. And I bet Flame's table manners are better than Dorothy's!"

"*Flame?*" said Mal. "You didn't tell me his name was *Flame*. The price has just gone up."

"Children, children," said Ned.

"There's Lynn's mom's car," said Jane. "You'd better figure out what you're doing fast."

There were a few rather hairy moments in the first few weeks of Flame's tenancy, but Jane said, "We haven't lost any customers, and that's all that matters. The rest will sort itself out." Lynn had, in fact, given a little gulp and sob—almost a shriek—but Mal had sauntered in with Miri and Flame, and Lynn (who was nine) wasn't going to look like a *real* kindergartener in front of Miri's gorgeous brother. Miri, not knowing what else to do, tied Flame to a tree outside the small arena they used for private lessons, where he had the shade and the shadows disguised him. Lynn glanced his way nervously a couple of times, but Flame didn't do anything but lie quietly, and she soon forgot him.

By the time Lynn was leading her horse back into the stable Mal was working his wiles on Jane's class. They couldn't believe their luck that Mal was actually *hanging around* to talk to them. Miri thought, watching them, he could tell them to go jump off a cliff, and they'd all say, where? What cliff? But there weren't any cliffs nearby and all he said was, "Hey, Miri's got a new dog. He's really cool. He's got these scary red eyes. He's a hellhound. His name is Flame. Want to meet him?"

They all giggled at *hellhound* but with Mal there watching there was no shrieking. And one or two of them were even brave enough to pat him.

She collected the new name tag that said FLAME with the stable phone number on it the next day, and began letting him cautiously off the leash when she was cleaning tack or mucking out or anything she didn't have to concentrate on. By the following week he was accompanying her when she took horses in and out to the paddocks. He never showed the least inclination to chase anything—despite several of the cats' best efforts—and the horses didn't react to his red eyes. Balthazar liked him: he'd reach his nose down over the half door of his stall to say hello. She still tied him up when she was giving lessons, but Ned rigged up a running line between two trees outside the two outdoor arenas so he had room to move around, although all he ever seemed to do was shift to whichever end was nearer where Miri was and lie down.

The price of Mal's cooperation had been that she pick him up after all the parties he went to, for the rest of the summer—and he was invited to a lot of parties. Fortunately he didn't go to very many of them—Dorothy wouldn't let him. But he still managed one or two a week. Since his job got out at eleven, this meant that she was picking him up at four or five o'clock in the morning—occasionally she was lucky, and they went on till after six, when the buses started running again. She'd pointed out that even extortion has its limits, and by six o'clock she was out feeding horses, with a cup of strong coffee steaming on the windowsill in the feedroom. He'd promised that if it was after six, he'd catch the bus to the end of Highland Road, and walk the rest of the way home.

But usually the phone rang at four or five. This had been its own problem, because the farm was in a dead zone, where cell phones didn't work. So on party nights Miri had to remember to unplug the three other phones in the house, leaving only the one in her room— and then to plug them back in again on her way out of the house. Five wasn't so bad; she was usually thinking about getting up then anyway. Four was rough. She was still asleep, dawn was barely a smudge on the horizon, and by the time she got home again it would be too late to go back to bed.

Flame always came with her. He was, of course, sleeping on her bed, and when she got up, he got up. It obviously never occurred to him that he might be left behind, and she was glad to have him with her. The parties were not always in places she particularly wanted to be at four or five in the morning. Usually Mal was waiting on the street for her—sometimes with someone else who needed to be dropped off home—but once or twice she'd had to wait.

On one of these occasions three guys who were obviously the worse for their night's entertainment had seen her and come reeling over to . . . she wasn't sure if they meant to scare her, or if it was just that they were too drunk to notice the effect they were having. She'd turned the dome light on so she could read while she waited, which was probably why they'd noticed her. She tried to ignore them, but they were banging on the driver's window and laughing. One of them went to the front of the truck, grabbed the bumper, and started rocking it. The other two thought this was hilarious.

Flame was curled up on the passenger seat. He'd let this go on for about twenty seconds, but when the rocking started he slowly uncurled. He didn't have enough room to stand up on the seat, but he put one forepaw on the gearshift and the other one delicately between Miri's legs, and leaned toward the window. He put his nose very close to the glass, pulled his lips back and *growled*.

"Jesus H. Christ, what the hell is *that*?" yelled the noisiest of the three, who was the window-banger, and backed off a step. The bumper-rocker stood up. Flame turned his head so he was staring out over the steering wheel. Miri *felt* rather than heard Flame's growl deepen.

And the man screamed. He threw his hands up in front of his face, and backed away, stumbling over the curb, falling onto the hood of the next car. His two friends grabbed him, and the three of them ran.

Mal, at that moment, appeared at the top of the steps of the one house on the street that still had lights on in all its windows. Miri unlocked the door for him to get in. "Is everything all right?" he said.

"Everything's fine," she replied. She was still stroking Flame with hands that trembled very slightly. Flame slithered over the back of the front seat and lay down in the narrow strip between the seat and the back of the cab, where mysterious bits of tack tended to accumulate. Miri had cleared it out and put a blanket down for him.

"Your hellhound's eyes are redder than usual," said Mal.

"It's just the dome light," she said.

"It wasn't a very good party," said Mal. "I'd rather have been home with Dorothy. You won't have to come here again."

"Good," she said.

The one thing that still worried Miri about Flame was that she didn't have time to walk him enough. He had the long legs and deep chest of a running dog but mostly all he ever had the chance to do was wander around the stable-yard, and when she was teaching she still tied him up.

Mostly the addition of a hellhound to the Greyhaven Stables

went remarkably smoothly. The cats were adjusting; or all but Camilla, one of the house cats, who had decamped to live with a family about a mile down the road. Jane was a little testy for a day or two, but once she had been assured (several times) that the Johnsons were happy to have Camilla, she got over it. The guinea pigs, let out of their cage, hid under the sofa, but the guinea pigs had always hidden under the sofa when they were let out of their cage. Dorothy, once she had ascertained that Mal was not very interested in Flame, put up with him, and deigned to learn his name.

One or two more boarders' dogs had been banned because they couldn't get along with Flame, but most were wary but polite. Flame tended to ignore other dogs, although he made an exception of Fay, who adored him, and would rather lie under his tree with him than go out on the trail with Nora and her Pinto horse, Carey (short for Caramel Cashew Swirl), much to Nora's disgust. "Well, she's spayed," Nora said. "There's not a lot of trouble she can get into." Flame would occasionally rest his chin on Fay's back.

"She's like one of the kindergarteners with Mal around," Miri said to Jane. Although the kindergarteners were having a bad summer; Mal had a steady girlfriend. Mal often had girlfriends, but they rarely survived meeting Dorothy, and after he'd lost his first sweetheart to his parrot he'd started bringing new girlfriends home quickly to get it over with. After Kim, he never seemed to mind when they disappeared, but then, for Mal, there were always more girls out there.

Leslie was different. In the first place after high school she wanted to train to work in a zoo, and had been working summers and weekends at the little local sheep-pigs-and-llamas kids' petting zoo for two years. She was fascinated and thrilled by Dorothy, and while as rivals for Mal's affection they had to be mortal enemies, Leslie got round this by ignoring Mal in Dorothy's presence, and Dorothy couldn't resist playing to an apparently worshipping audience. Leslie was even fascinated and thrilled by the tropical fish and the invisible tree frogs and chameleons, which was a first, and put Ned firmly on her side. And she'd been the only person ever to meet Flame without an initial cringe. "Oh, wow," she'd said, and immediately stooped to make friends.

She was also extremely pretty.

Jane started calling her the Paragon. "Cynic," said Miri.

"There has to be *something* wrong with her," said Jane.

There was. She had two left feet. "I'm *all* left feet," she said. "I'm not just chosen *last* for volleyball or whatever, whichever team has to have me bursts into tears." And Mal was determined to teach her to ride.

Mal wasn't horse-obsessed like his mother and sister, but he (like Ned) helped out when they were shorthanded—which was, as with most stables, rather often—and was rarely cranky about it. He was also quite a good rider himself, to his sister's considerable annoyance, because he had a natural gift for it and she had to work hard for every tiny scrap she learned.

"Don't worry about it," said Jane. "It was just like that with my brother and me."

"The brother who made his first million when he was twenty-four and has a ranch in Wyoming?"

"He's never in Wyoming. He's too busy earning his next million. You wouldn't want to be like that, would you?"

"I'd get out to Wyoming more often," said Miri.

But Mal, being a natural rider, didn't have a clue how to teach someone who wasn't. Jane and Miri assumed that teaching Leslie to ride would fizzle out: Mal couldn't teach and Leslie couldn't learn. But it didn't. Mal kept asking if any of the beginner horses were free and if so when, and Leslie kept showing up looking determined, and trying to give Jane or Miri money, which they kept refusing.

The afternoon that Leslie appeared in a new pair of riding breeches and riding helmet (she'd been using one of the stable's helmets), Miri said, "Okay, look. This is silly. *I'll* give you lessons. Mal couldn't teach a tadpole to swim."

"It's not him," Leslie said. "Two left feet, remember? It's me."

"Then why do you want to learn to ride?" Miri said with genuine curiosity.

Leslie turned away and stroked the cheek of Rainbow, who had her head over her stall door, hoping for stroking. "Because . . . oh, because I'm used to being good with animals. I'm resigned to being horrible at sports. I've always avoided riding lessons because I was afraid this would happen—because I knew this would happen—but I'd *love* to be able to ride, you know? I don't have to be good—like you or Mal—just—oh, I'd like to be able to go trail-riding with Mal. And canter where there's a good place to canter. And jump over the big log."

"Okay," said Miri. "It's always good to know what you're aiming at. I'll teach you to ride till you can canter out on the trail" (to herself adding, on a carefully selected bombproof horse) "although I don't promise any jumping. We'll see how it goes. Okay?"

Leslie, to her surprise, hesitated momentarily. "How much does— do you charge?"

"Save your money for a car," said Miri. "So I don't have to pick Mal up after any more parties."

◆ ◆ ◆

Leslie was hard work. Miri pulled every trick she knew about teaching riding out of her hat and Leslie still needed two bounces for every stride when she tried to post to the trot. She could drop her legs straight down the horse's sides when her feet were out of the stirrups but as soon as she put them back in the stirrups she stiffened up and began to crouch. "Let's play a game," said Miri. "Let's pretend that you *don't* know that you have two left feet. Let's pretend you're just an ordinary person who wants to learn how to ride."

"It's hopeless, isn't it?" said Leslie.

"It is *not* hopeless, damn it," said Miri. "Stop trying to *make* it hopeless, you know?"

"Sorry," said Leslie, and sighed.

Once Miri was (relatively) sure Leslie wouldn't fall off at the walk, she took her out on the trail, thinking that a change of scenery would be good for both of them. Leslie was on the (bombproof) Peggy, and Miri on Balthazar. Balthazar was disappointed by all the walking, but he was accustomed to such disappointment. And Flame came with them.

At first they did the baby loop which only took about fifteen minutes and you were never really out of sight of the barn. But Miri's sharp eye took in that, out on the trail, Leslie occasionally forgot that she was all left feet and couldn't possibly learn to ride, and relaxed. Once, when she'd forgotten for more than a minute, Peggy put her head down and blew.

"There," said Miri.

"What?" said Leslie. "Did I do something wrong? Isn't she supposed to do that?"

"No, you did something *right*. You stopped *perching* on her like a bird on a wire and she relaxed and started to enjoy herself."

"Oh, am I *hurting* her?" said Leslie in deep distress.

"Okay, I take it back," said Miri. "You *are* hopeless."

There was a brief tortured pause, and then Leslie laughed. "Oh. I get it."

"Good," said Miri.

But after that Leslie did begin—just a little—to learn to ride. Miri stopped trying to teach her anything in the arena, and they went straight out onto the trails, leaving the baby loop behind and diving deep into the preserve. And Flame always came with them. Once, when Leslie began one of her (regular) apologies for how much time she was taking away from all the other more important things Miri should be doing (which would then lead into another attempt to pay for lessons), Miri interrupted and said, "You're doing me a favor. I've been worrying about giving poor Flame enough exercise."

Flame, hearing his name, came lolloping up to them, tongue flying, his eyes so crinkled up from grinning that he looked almost ordinary.

"I wonder what his background is," said Leslie, and Miri could see her immediately as the zookeeper to be: focussing on the strange animal she has been presented with. "There's a lot of sighthound in there somewhere—deerhound maybe."

"Very likely," Miri said neutrally. He looked as much like a deerhound as he looked like any dog. Since she was the only one who brushed him, she was the only one who knew that he had not merely the common system of a longer coarser outer coat and finer softer undercoat, but a third coat beneath the second, dense and almost prickly, almost as if it might be suitable for repelling hellfire. He also had two extra pairs of ribs, disguised by the length of his back. If it had been only one extra pair she probably wouldn't have noticed; but she'd thought, stroking him, that his ribcage seemed to go on a surprisingly long time, and so she counted, and checked the result with a helpful website on dog anatomy. She might have asked the vet about this, except that she had recently observed, while checking for ticks, that his testicles had regrown. He had, of course, been castrated at the pound. She didn't want to get Ronnie in trouble for having released an unneutered dog, and if Flame stayed healthy, the vet might not notice the testicles. She wondered if the pound's vet had noticed the ribs and the third coat, or if he'd just been totally distracted by the eyes.

There were other anomalies. The last inch or so of his tongue had a narrow smooth white streak down the center, like scar tissue, as if his tongue had once been forked. He ate charcoal out of the fireplace. (He would have eaten charcoal briquettes too, only Miri felt sure that the chemical stuff that made them burn faster and hotter wouldn't be good for anything to eat, even a hellhound.) She'd known Labradors that ate *anything* including charcoal, but Flame did not also eat bricks, shoes, houseplants and small pieces of furniture—just charcoal. And while he liked to lie in front of the fire like a normal dog, he liked to lie facing it, staring into it like a philosopher—or a hellhound. The flicker of the flames on his wide-open red eyes looked like the reflection of a forest fire.

But he had perfect manners around the stable, the horses, and the clientele. There were one or two nervous parents who didn't like him, but Miri simply learned who they were and made sure he was tied up under his tree when they were due to arrive. And he was now proving to have perfect manners on trail rides.

It was still only Leslie, Miri and Flame. Miri had suggested they invite Mal some time—even that Leslie was ready to go out with Mal by herself—but Leslie said, "Oh, not yet. Please. If you can stand it a little while longer. I can almost relax now, when it's just you, but I know I'll stiffen up again as soon as anyone comes with us—especially Mal. But I've been thinking, what I'd like to do is tell Mal I'm taking him on a picnic for his birthday—and then tell him at the last minute it's going to be on horseback. Is that a good idea, do you think?"

"It's an excellent idea," said Miri.

"Oh, I *hope* so," Leslie said in her earnest way. "I mean I'm *trotting* now and everything. You are *so* patient. I guess you have to be, to be a riding teacher, but it's still pretty amazing. And I really don't understand why you've put so much time into me. It's not just Flame."

"Don't you worry about that," said Miri, who found taking Leslie for a trail ride twice a week a nice change from her nervous kinder-garteners, "I'm going to get it out of Mal later."

During this conversation Miri hadn't been paying attention to how far they'd come. It was true that Leslie could trot, and Miri was considering whether it was time to risk a canter. It would be really great—not to mention having Mal in his sister's hip pocket for the rest of his life—if his girlfriend could canter by the time his birthday picnic happened.

And then Peggy, bombproof Peggy, shied.

She didn't shy very far, and she shied into Balthazar, who put his ears back and held his ground. Leslie, who was only clumsy and not a fool, merely said "*ugh*" and dragged herself back upright again; a good instinctive convulsive grab for Peggy's mane had kept her in the saddle. Both horses were standing, tense and alert, looking in the same direction. Miri now noticed that Flame was standing right in front of them, looking in the same direction too, with his tail and his hackles raised.

"Damn," said Miri. "I didn't notice where we'd got to. I wouldn't have brought you here, although it's not usually as bad as this."

"*What* isn't?" said Leslie.

"Our haunted graveyard," said Miri. "Don't tell me you haven't heard that story?"

"Oh," said Leslie. "I guess. But I thought it was like Pegasus and unicorns."

"When I got old enough to answer back, I used to tell my parents that if they're going to bring a six-year-old whose favorite bedtime stories are all fairy tales to a haunted farm then they deserved what they got. There's still a rumor for anyone who remembers that my parents got the place cheap because of the graveyard, although the fact that the house only had electricity downstairs and the only indoor plumbing was the pump in the kitchen might have had something to do with it too."

"Wow," said Leslie.

"Yeah. We moved in the beginning of the summer so we had all summer to get a toilet and a shower put in. Mom and Dad decided I was old enough to have my baths in the pond but Mal had to have his in a plastic tub in the kitchen." She smiled reminiscently. "I don't think he's ever forgiven me. Anyway. I don't know what the graveyard's problem is and a lot of the time it's perfectly fine, you can go in there and look around and nothing happens. There's only six tombstones—all the same family—they all died within a few weeks of each other, in 1871. Probably flu or something, Dad says. It must have been awful for whoever was left, whoever buried them. When I started school here the kids all said that nobody had lived in the house since. It took me a few years to figure out that they didn't have electricity out here in 1871."

"You mean," Leslie said, "that it still spooks you."

"Yeah," said Miri, whose own hackles were trying to rise. There was a big tree to one side of the little path into the graveyard that led off the trail they were standing on. Every time she blinked there were, briefly, goblins sitting in its branches, chittering at her. "Who wouldn't prefer unicorns? The only reason I know it's usually okay is because Mal comes here a lot. He likes it. He likes it partly because his big sister is afraid of it—the big sister who got to have her baths in the pond when he had to have his in a big plastic tub in the kitchen, when she was six and he was four. But I think he really does like it too. He says the sky is bluer there or something. And he says if it's having a bad day he goes away again. I never bring the trail rides this way—in case of bad days. Like today."

"I thought we were still out in the middle of the reserve," said Leslie.

"That's one of the things I don't like about it, the graveyard," said Miri. "It's like you'll be out in the middle of the reserve and then suddenly you're coming this way. Usually I notice that time and geography have folded themselves up again and turn off before we get here, but I didn't today."

"Does it happen to other people?"

"Oh, yeah. That's why the kids at school were so happy to tell me I lived on a haunted farm. And I know that a lot of people told Mom she'd never get a riding stable going here because of it."

"I've lived here all my life and I'd never heard about it," said Leslie.

Miri told herself to get a grip, of course there were no goblins. It was a bright day, and maybe she'd been staring into flickering leaf-and-sunlight patterns too long and too hard and her eyes were tired. "Dad says even ghosts wear out eventually, like socks, and Mom says that the riding stable probably just sort of outnumbers it—them—now. You know, like when the development went up around the old Danforth house. When the first couple of houses went up the old Danforth place totally dominated. Now you can hardly see it. We're the development." She swallowed hard, and forced herself to look away. But she looked back again almost immediately. Flame was still standing, staring at the path, and at the tree. As if he saw goblins in its branches. "But if you go to the tourist center at the reserve and look at the map, there's a red box around the boundary with our farm and down at the bottom it says that there's something wrong with the earth's magnetic field here and it's easy to get lost so pay extra attention to the trail markers and don't use your compass."

"Maybe that's it."

"I don't think magnetic weirdness makes horses shy *sometimes*," said Miri.

"Look at Flame," Leslie said wonderingly.

Miri was looking at Flame, and thinking about the way the guy who'd been bouncing her fender had thrown up his hands and screamed. She didn't think Flame was reacting to the earth's magnetic field either. And it wasn't only Flame; both horses were staring straight at the little path that led only to the old cemetery. Some horses like to wind themselves up, so they can dance and act foolish; Peggy and Balthazar weren't like that. If they were tense and worried, they were tense and worried for a reason.

"Let's get out of here," she said. "There's a good stretch for trotting up ahead. Have I taught you half-seat yet?"

Miri cheated, teaching Leslie to canter. She taught her half-seat at the trot, and one day, when she was nicely balanced, her head up and looking straight ahead, her hands lightly but firmly against Peggy's neck, Miri said, "Peggy, *canTER*," and Peggy, veteran of many hours in the arena on a longe line, cantered. Balthazar, veteran of many beginner trail rides, kept pace exactly, in case some kind of rescue was required. But Leslie gave a little, quickly repressed squeak, and then settled down, keeping both her legs and hands steady. "And *waaaaalk*," said Miri at the end of the wide bit of path, and both horses dropped calmly back to a walk. Leslie turned a shining face to Miri, and Miri leaned over and patted her leg.

"That was *terrific*," she said. "Perfect. Now we're going to go back into the arena so you can learn to sit the canter, and *you are not going to stiffen up on me,* and then you're going to have the best birthday picnic ride that anyone has ever had, okay?"

◆ ◆ ◆

The day of the picnic dawned grey and drizzly and Leslie was on the phone to the farm at seven, twittering about the weather.

Miri had been expecting this, and had the portable in her pocket so she could answer at the first ring, before anyone had the opportunity to get testy about it. Everyone was usually awake by seven, but her father and brother would be pre-articulate, and cranky. Miri made suitable soothing noises to Leslie, including saying (truthfully) that it was burning off, and that the weather report had promised a fine day. She didn't add that the weather report had also said thunderstorms moving in overnight—it was a lunchtime picnic, after all—nor did she add that she didn't like the way Flame was behaving.

To any riding stable without an indoor arena, the weather was of paramount, and frequently bitter, importance, and she and her mother grasped any straw of prediction. Miri had discovered that Flame predicted the weather rather well by the way he met it when they first went outdoors in the morning, for Miri to feed the horses. If he went out blithely, head and tail high, then there was a fine day coming; to whatever extent he was slinky and furtive, to that extent it would be a miserable day. She told herself that his present manner, which seemed to be that there was something coming to get him which was immediately behind him whichever way he stood, leaped or swapped ends, was probably his response to the approaching storms; these would be the first thunderstorms they'd had since she brought him home from the pound. She just hoped it didn't mean the storms would get here early; she wanted Mal's picnic ride to go well almost as badly as Leslie did.

She let her eleven o'clock lesson warm up a few minutes longer than usual so she could say "happy birthday" and "have fun" as Mal and Leslie set off; also to run a falsely casual eye over Peggy and make sure that in her agony of perfection Leslie hadn't done something like forget to tighten Peggy's girth. When Mal graciously allowed a small giggling group of his admirers to wish him happy birthday Miri took the opportunity to take hold of Leslie's heel and give it a vicious yank. "*Relax*," she said. "Remember *relax*? You're already crouching and you're not out of the stable-yard yet."

Leslie gave a shaky laugh, and the heel in Miri's hand dropped about two inches. "Keep thinking about Peggy," said Miri. "You want her to have a good time too, right? Just nudge her forward gently—keep your hands and legs *steady*. Try—oh—try to make her take the bit down to her ankles—till you're holding the reins by the buckle. Do that every time you notice you've been crouching. Well, maybe not *every* time. That'll keep you busy."

Mal, in his detestably easy way, swung up into Twilight's saddle. He wasn't wearing his helmet, and out of the corner of her eye Miri just saw their mother bursting out of the barn where she was overseeing the Kindergarten Quadrille team tacking up, when Mal leaned over, put his hand on the back of Leslie's neck, and kissed her. For quite a long time. Jane was now standing beside Miri, who felt she could almost hear Jane's mouth closing with a snap. She could see several of the Quadrille members watching this performance in varying postures of longing and despair—and Leslie was quite pink by the time he stopped. Mal being Mal, he would know perfectly well that his mother had just almost bitten his head off for not putting his helmet on *before* he mounted. But he didn't look their way as he unslung the helmet over his arm and carefully strapped it in place; and he gave a careless wave as they rode out of the yard. Leslie waved too, but she looked back, her expression a combination of joy and consternation.

"They're too young to be that serious," said Jane.

Miri silently agreed that that hadn't been any old birthday kiss. "You and Dad were just that age," she said. "And I was born two years later, and you told Gran you were waiting tables while she looked after me when you were training three-year-olds and Dad was in college, and we're all still alive to tell the story."

Jane grimaced. "Don't remind me. I don't suppose you'd buy 'that's different'?"

"No," said Miri. "A baby wouldn't be nearly as much trouble as Dorothy."

By four o'clock both Jane and Miri were beginning to glance a little too often down the old road that led to the nature reserve. There was no reason the birthday party needed to be back yet; five o'clock was probably the time to start expecting them, and it could be later still; it wouldn't be dark till after seven. But the clouds were beginning to stack up, genuine thunderheads, grey and ominous. Five o'clock came and went, and the last lessons of the day. A couple of boarders were still out on the trail, but Miri (it being Jane's turn to get dinner: steak, for Mal's birthday) would come out, check around, and lock up later.

Flame had spent the day looking for goblins, and for the first time ever, when Miri tied him between his trees while she gave lessons, paced back and forth. It wasn't only Flame; Oscar had refused to get out of Cindy's car, and had stayed in the back seat and howled. Cindy left early.

They were heading back to the house, emphatically not saying anything to each other about wondering where Mal and Leslie were, when the two missing boarders came trotting down the old road. Jane and Miri stopped dead. Riders *walked* their horses back down that road, finishing the cooling-off process before the horses were put away; and both these horses had sweat darkening their shoulders and white showing around their eyes.

Miri could hear how hard Jane was working to keep her voice level: "You two don't look too happy. Or you four."

Miri made a grab at Applepie's bridle as he jigged past sideways, his nose curled into his own shoulder; it wasn't a good idea to let a horse trot into the barn. Applepie, recognising the hand of authority, stopped, but Miri could feel the tension in him just from his mouth clamped on the bit. Sheila dropped the reins with a sigh. "Thank you. I don't know what's got into him; I've never seen him like this. I know there's some weather coming but . . ." Applepie was middle-aged, round and—most of the time—placid, rather like Sheila; Sheila rode for exercise, not excitement.

It was beginning to rain.

Charis dismounted from Moose, who had never pranced in his life, but was trying to do so now. "This must be the mother and father of all storms, is all I can say," said Charis.

Miri thought, somebody tell me it's just the barometric pressure that is making my hair stand on end. But she looked at Flame, and he was looking back down the road the way Sheila and Charis had come—the way Mal and Leslie should have come, and hadn't—and he was so still he looked like the statue of a dog. The statue was entitled *Awaiting the Arrival of the Enemy*.

As Sheila and Charis led their horses away Jane said, "There's nothing we can do."

"No," said Miri.

"And standing around in the rain is dumb," said Jane.

"Yes," said Miri, but neither of them moved.

There was a little silence, and then Jane said, "I suppose we might as well go indoors and start getting supper ready."

Any other evening it was Jane's turn to cook Miri would have corrected her: "And *you* can start getting supper ready." Tonight she only said, "Yes."

They went indoors and were instantly mobbed by restless, fretful house cats. There being only four human ankles to twine around, Jessica, always the bravest, chose to avoid the crowd, and twined around Flame's. Mal's birthday cake sat on the kitchen table, under a meat save to protect it from the cats, but HAPPY BIRTHDAY MALACHI was still clearly visible through the mesh. There was a little pile of presents next to the cake. Miri listlessly started peeling potatoes, for something to do, something that would stop her looking at the cake and the presents.

Dorothy rocked back and forth on her perch in the living room, screaming, "Mal! Mal! Mal! Mal!" Ordinarily Miri could ignore Dorothy in one of her tantrums; tonight Miri wanted to scream along with her. Flame crept under the kitchen table and stayed there. Jessica and Charlotte joined him. It was a big old table with a lot of gnarly bent legs, and the cats disappeared in the shadows, but Miri could see Flame's eyes glowing if she looked carefully. She thought, he almost looks like a very large dust bunny. No, a dust hellhound. She hoped, if she ran a broom under the table, he wouldn't disintegrate. She finished the potatoes, pulled a chair out of the way and joined Flame and the two cats under the table. She put her arms around him and hugged him hard; he was warm and solid.

"You haven't hidden under the table since you were seven," said Jane in that too-level voice she'd used to Sheila and Charis.

I used to hide under the table because I was afraid that the ghosts in the old graveyard would come back here and get me, she thought, but she didn't say it aloud. "If you want to join us," she said, "bring a cushion. Two cushions."

Jane's hands had stopped rinsing lettuce. She was staring out the kitchen window. Even from under the table Miri saw the flash and when the thunder immediately followed the whole house rattled. She was pressed so closely to Flame that she felt the vibration when he made a noise; but it wasn't a whine, it was more of a groan.

"That looked like it was right over the old graveyard," said Jane in a voice even flatter and more remote than the one she'd been using.

Miri climbed out from under the table and joined her mother at the sink. She turned the still-running tap off. "You can't know that," she said.

"No," agreed Jane. She turned the tap back on, and went back to swishing lettuce. "But it might have been. It was certainly some-where over that way."

Miri stared out the window for a while. There was another flash of lightning, but farther away; the thunder, when it came, was only a distant growl. The sky was still dark grey, but the wind had got up, and the clouds were rolling and twisting around each other like enormous snakes. It was still raining; when a gust of wind threw a handful of rain at the kitchen window, Miri started, as if it had been deliberately thrown at her. "We still can't do anything," she said.

"No," said Jane. She was loading the clean lettuce into the salad spinner.

"We don't even know which way they went," said Miri.

"No," said Jane.

"And they could have taken shelter somewhere," said Miri.

"Yes," said Jane. She was about to give the salad spinner's han-dle the first pull when there was a blur among the trees at the end of the old road that led to the preserve. "Oh, no," said Miri, and Jane looked up, fractionally later, and gasped. Miri had her hand on the doorknob before her brain had confirmed that the blur was a galloping horse; but it was Jane, behind her, who'd seen who it was: "Peggy," she said.

Flame was there too, getting between their legs as they crowded out of the door. You don't run at a panicky horse; Miri made a grab for Flame's collar and discovered that he was already walking half a step behind her. "Oh, god," said Jane. Peggy was riderless, and alone.

She came to a bouncing, unhappy stop in the corner between the barn and the first arena, switching her forequarters back and forth as if looking for the way through. She turned around and saw them, let out a frantic whinny, and trotted toward them. Jane reached out quietly and took her bridle with a hand that trembled.

"Her reins have been knotted and her stirrups run up," said Miri. "They've *sent* her to us. Twilight—must have hurt herself. But they're okay. They must be okay."

"If they were okay," said Jane grimly, "Leslie—or Mal—would have ridden Peggy back. Whoever ran the stirrups up didn't dare leave the other one."

Miri was already jogging toward the barn. She could see Balthazar's head over his stall door: he always looked out when he heard her voice. Jane followed, leading Peggy. "You still don't know where to go," said Jane. It would be Miri and Balthazar that went looking; Balthazar was the most reliable horse they had, and he was at his steadiest with Miri.

"No," said Miri. "But Flame does. Look at him." She'd let go his collar as soon as Jane had pulled Peggy's reins over her head. He was standing at the nearer end of the old road, staring into the trees. His head and tail were high; as they looked at him he turned his head and looked at Miri, clearly saying, *Hurry up.* "Yes," said Miri, and ran for the tack room.

She led Balthazar to the mounting block and tested everything once more, forcing herself to pay attention; she was so preoccupied she wasn't certain that she could be trusted to buckle a bridle, to tighten a girth, things she did several times a day, every day, and had done for years. She checked the first-aid kit and the thermos of hot coffee twice: but even these were familiar adjuncts from the ordinary weekend trail rides. She settled her helmet on her head and swung into the saddle. Both wind and rain were lessening, but they were still going to get wet. Peggy was tied up in the breezeway. Jane had made the coffee in the tiny barn kitchen and then pulled Peggy's saddle off and was running her hands down her legs and looking at her feet, checking for any injury. Or possibly for any sign that whoever had sent her home was bleeding. She straightened up as Miri mounted.

"Good luck," was all she said.

Miri nodded. The moment Balthazar moved away from the block Flame took off. Miri asked Balthazar to trot. She already knew where they were going: they were going to the old graveyard.

The wind seemed to drive the rain into her eyes; she kept shaking her head and holding the reins with one hand so she could wipe her eyes with the other. But Balthazar seemed to know that he was supposed to be following Flame, and Flame clearly knew where he was going. Occasionally Balthazar had to slow to a walk to pick his way, and Flame would stop and wait for them, but Flame, who was never impatient, paced or danced in place; and once he lost himself so far as to bark, a single, sharp, commanding sound. Balthazar raised his head as if to say, "You might as well calm down; I know what I'm doing." Miri had to hope he did, because she couldn't see well enough to guide him. It was not only the wind and rain; it was also getting dark. And she was lost. And should it be taking this long to get to the old graveyard?

She thought, why am I so certain Flame is going to find Mal and

Leslie? That if I follow him I'll find them too? He glanced back just at that moment, his red eyes flaring weirdly in the twilight. He was an unearthly figure, and he seemed bigger, somehow, out here in the malign-feeling, restless, still-volatile end of the storm; he seemed nearly as big as Balthazar. Don't be silly, Miri said to herself, but her thoughts wouldn't shut up: he's the sort of thing that ought to live at that graveyard, they gibbered on, with the ghosts, and the—the lamias, or the vampires, or whatever. Even if he is going to find Mal and Leslie he could just be leading me to the same fate. Why did I know him at once for a hellhound? She watched the long bristly-feathery red tail ahead of her for a moment, thinking about her first sight of him, at the pound, when he'd turned around and she'd seen his eyes for the first time, and seen the hopelessness in them. I might as well mistrust Balthazar, she thought. I'm just not going to.

And at that moment she saw the old bent tree that stood or leaned over the path into the graveyard. And at the foot of it she saw a bulky shadow that she was sure wasn't usually there . . . and then it moved, and she saw Leslie's face looking up at her. Leslie was sitting on the ground holding one of Mal's hands with both of hers . . . and Mal was lying in a strange, twisted position. . . .

Miri nearly fell, getting off Balthazar. "It's okay," Mal said in a hollow hoarse voice nothing like his normal one. "I'm not dead or anything. It's just . . . I can't feel much below my neck."

Leslie said, "It had been such a lovely afternoon. Blue and clear and warm."

No it hasn't, thought Miri, startled. It's been grey and thundery-feeling all day, in spite of the weather report. But she didn't say anything. She was too busy staring at Mal. Don't move him, she thought. Spine injury. Don't move him. Mom'll have called the ambulance by now—I'll leave in a minute and tell them where to come. But she couldn't help herself dropping to her knees beside him and picking up his hand. It was like picking up a stone or a grain bag or a baking dish to put in the oven, except that it was warm. There was no tension, no response—no life. Leslie was clinging to his other hand; her other hand alternated between wiping her face—it could have just been the rain, but Miri could see her crying—and stroking Mal's hair. "Such a lovely afternoon. Mal brought me here, we had our picnic here. The storm came out of nowhere. It was—it wasn't *right*, that storm."

"Leslie," said Mal, in his stranger's voice.

"It wasn't right," Leslie said, and Miri realized she was near hysterics, near breaking down completely. "The lightning struck as if it was *aiming* for us. Twilight bolted—and that tree *reached* down and knocked Mal off. . . ."

"Leslie," Mal said again.

It wasn't the tree, thought Miri . . . and then she thought, how do I know that?

Flame was standing beside them, at the end of the path, staring toward the graveyard as he had stared into the forest while he waited for Miri to tack Balthazar up and follow him. As he had stared up the path a few short weeks ago, when Miri and Leslie had come this way.

"I ran Peggy's stirrups up and—and knotted her reins," said Leslie.

"She did that all by herself," said Mal. "I didn't tell her to. I was so proud of her."

And Miri saw that he was crying too.

"And led her onto the path and pointed her toward home and told her to go and she went," said Leslie. "As if she knew. I didn't dare leave Mal. I—In case of concussion, you know. You mustn't leave someone alone if they might be concussed, in case they fall asleep or—or go into shock. . . ." Her voice cracked on the last word.

Miri was horribly aware of the inert hand she was holding. The fingers lay limply in hers; she had to hold on with an effort to prevent the hand from sliding away from hers and flopping back to the ground. She saw the two riding helmets and the remains of the picnic piled up behind where Leslie and Mal were. In the middle of the crisis that little heap of human gear—Mal's useless helmet, which had not prevented what had happened—suddenly seemed the saddest thing she had ever seen.

She laid the hand down gently and stood up. She had brought blankets and the useless first-aid kit and a thermos of instant coffee with half a bag of sugar in it. She was embarrassed by the first-aid kit, by her adult-ed emergency training, by her ability to splint a broken bone on a healthy unbroken volunteer at the adult-ed center, while an EMT with a clipboard watched her. She'd never had to do more than put a Band-Aid on a graze, and once she'd created a sling for a sprained wrist. She unrolled the blankets and retied the first-aid kit to the back of Balthazar's saddle. She uncapped the thermos and made Leslie and Mal each drink some of the hot too-sweet coffee; Leslie drank a few sips mechanically, and then held the plastic mug awkwardly for Mal. *She does it better than I would have,* Miri thought. *They didn't teach us that in the first-aid course.* She laid one blanket over Mal as he lay, and tucked the other one around the sitting Leslie. Neither of them seemed to notice.

It had stopped raining, and the wind had died, but the feeling of tension and fear didn't ease. Almost as if they were in the eye of a hurricane.

"I'd better go tell the ambulance crew where to come," she said. She paused. She had to say something, but the words didn't exist. "Will you be okay?"

Leslie looked up, an expression on her face not unlike the one that had been on Flame's, that day at the pound. She didn't bother to try to smile, but she understood what Miri was saying. "Yes," she said. "We'll be fine." And Miri clearly heard in her voice that she wouldn't break down or have hysterics while Mal needed her.

But when Miri turned away, to go back to Balthazar, to mount up and ride back as quickly as she still could—dusk would be black dark soon, and if they were following a flashlight she'd have to dismount and both of them walk—there was Flame, standing in her way. She tried to brush past him, but he wouldn't let her. "Flame," she said, "we have to go back—well, I have to go back. If you want to stay here and—and guard them, that'd be good. But I have to go." And she reached over him to pick up Balthazar's reins.

And he bit her.

It was, briefly, as if the world had ended. The world, in some ways, had already ended; although she was still able not to think about what had happened to Mal, to her little brother, to one of the three people she loved best in the world, the awareness of it was horribly near. Still without really facing what had happened, she told herself that doctors were miracle workers these days, that hospitals had machines that could do *everything*, that Leslie, wonderful Leslie, had kept her head and wisely refrained from trying to move him, so that anything any doctor or any machine could do for him could still be done. But the encroaching darkness of this evening still felt like her own life closing in, as if, after this, there would be no dawn.

And then her dog bit her.

She looked down from what felt like a very long way away, as if she were floating up among the treetops somewhere . . . as if she might float away entirely. He had bitten her swiftly and decisively—but, she now realized, gently. He still had hold of her arm; she could

feel his teeth, but they weren't hurting her. She thought, I'm a bal-
loon and he's holding my string. Slowly she floated back down from
the treetops, till she could feel her feet on the ground, her breath
going in and out. Her dog's teeth in her arm. She let Balthazar's
reins drop back on his neck and said to Flame, "What is it?"

He let go her arm and turned away, trotting straight back to the
path to the graveyard. Slowly she unfastened Balthazar's tethering
rope, and looped it around a tree—a smaller, innocent tree, a little
distance from the path, and from Leslie and Mal. Then reluctantly
she followed Flame.

"What is it?" said Leslie.

"I don't know," said Miri. "But he brought me here. He brought
me a lot faster than I'd've been able to find the way myself, in
this weather. I'd like to see what he wants. It won't take long. I
promise."

As soon as she set foot on the little track into the graveyard she
knew something was terribly wrong. It was like . . . she couldn't
think of anything that it was like: that was part of the wrongness.
She felt dizzy and sick, and as if she was no longer sure which way
was up and which down; it was an effort to pick up each foot and
think where to put it down. Especially because her feet kept wanting
to go backwards; the one in front kept trying to pick itself up and
move it behind the one in back. She concentrated on Flame's tail.
She had been following Flame's tail for a very long time; leagues;
centuries; all the way from the barn to here, somewhere on the
journey unknowingly crossing a boundary to this other country
where this awful thing had happened to her brother. . . .

The path itself was short. When they reached the end of it
and the sky opened out before them she was astonished to discover
that there were streaks of sunset lighting up the retreating storm
clouds in gold and pink and pale orange, and the sky above them

was a glorious deep blue. There was a huge pale amber moon just above the trees. She was dumbfounded that such beauty could still exist, in this foreign country where her brother lay twisted and help-less where he had fallen.

The trees around the edges of the graveyard were black, and the crooked, leaning tombstones were black. All the rest was washed in the rose-grey of the sunset. Flame himself was a deep vivid russet, like a maple tree in October.

No; one other thing was black. There was a tall, hunched, half-human shape in the middle of the clear space; in the middle of the little cluster of tombstones. She didn't come here often, but she was sure that no such tall thing had ever stood where this one was now.

She stopped. Flame turned around instantly and came back to her; went round behind her and leaned against the backs of her legs. I don't want to go forward, she thought. I don't want to go any nearer that thing—whatever it is.

And then it opened its eyes, or turned its head, or threw back its hood. All of the rest of it was still black, lightlessly black, black as if light were an unconvincing myth, but it had red eyes. Large, slanted, almond-shaped, scarlet-red eyes.

Miri put her hands over her mouth to stop herself from screaming.

Flame backed away a pace or two and then *slammed* into her, and she staggered forward, away from the encircling trees, out into the graveyard. She dropped her hands and whimpered like a scolded puppy, but raised her face to the sky and tried to imagine the touch of the moonlight like a real touch: like the nose of your horse or your dog in your hand, against your face or your arm, hoping for something nice to eat, or at least a pat; saying "hello," saying "I'm here," saying "how are you?" saying "can I help?" The moon was a silvery gold. The shadows on its face were grey, and there was no red anywhere.

She felt Flame's nose on her arm, and then the sweep of his tongue, over the place where he had bitten her, minutes or months before. She did not look down. She did not want to see his red eyes. She stared at the nearest tombstone, so she need not look at the thing's eyes either.

You're too late. The boy has fallen; it's over. He loves it here; he always has. Soon he will be here forever.

No! she cried.

Yes. He will die, because he will not want to live. And his mother will remember how he loved it here, and so he will come here, although his sweetheart will struggle against this.

No, she thought. No, no, no. She raised her hands again, and put them on either side of her face and squeezed, as if this were a known tactic in an emergency, like artificial respiration for someone who has stopped breathing, like not moving someone with a spine injury. *No.* . . . And Jane would never let anyone she loved be buried here in this place, this awful place. . . .

buried

Why? she cried again. *Why?*

The thing quivered as if it were laughing, and so she knew it was the thing who spoke—if *speaking* was how to describe what it did. She heard it; that was enough—more than enough.

A third voice: *Do not ask why. There is no why. Because he can. That is enough. Because he is wicked. Because this is a place of power, and his kind are drawn to power.*

Ah, Gelsoraban. You appear at the most unexpected moments. I should have thought you had grown weary of mortals by now.

I should have thought you had grown weary of wickedness.

Again it laughed. *Never.*

Well, then.

But you were born—created—cast and carved as were we. You of all of us have gone away from us.

Not only I. Jry and Krobekahl and Strohmoront too.

It seemed to her that the thing went still in a way it had not been still before, and that there was no laughter in it anywhere. *That is not enough.*

To stand against the rest of you? To create light where you have brought darkness? No, it is not. But it is a beginning. We have begun.

And then the thing did laugh again. *Begun! You're a* dog. *What is Jry? A squirrel? A frog? Perhaps Krobekahl is a tea-pot or a chair. And I have the boy. And through him this place—this place of power, as you have called it.*

You do not *have him!* Miri said. *He is my brother! He is human—he is daylight and breathing!*

Not for long, said the thing. *Not for much longer.*

Give him back! she said. *Give him back!*

You can claim him, if you dare, said the thing, and it was obvious that it was sure she did not dare. *I would not want Gelsoraban to think there is no—what is it?—mercy in me.*

How? she said fiercely.

Why, said the thing, *you need only ask—nicely—each of the nice people who lie here already. Who have lain here for so long with no one but themselves to talk to. They are quite looking forward to someone new. I have promised them, you see. You will have to convince them to give him up. I do not think they will wish to do so. I think they will need a great deal of persuading. Too much, perhaps, for someone as young as you. Someone as fragile as you. For daylight and breathing are very fragile—especially after dark.*

She looked up. Sunset was fading quickly; the first stars were out above the remains of the clouds. Again she looked at the moon, and this time she willed herself to feel the moon's light like the touch of a friend. And then she looked down, into the blazing red eyes of the creature she'd brought home from the pound; the creature that looked enough like a dog—though it obviously wasn't a dog—that it had been taken to the pound. She remembered Ronnie saying: when Diane went out with the van she almost didn't bring him back, because of the way he looks. *Gelsoraban.* And the horrible black thing that had broken her brother knew him. Who—what—was Gelsoraban?

Flame gave a tiny, doglike whine. It was exactly the whine of a dog who is suddenly sure its beloved owner doesn't love it any more. It was like the look in his eyes at the pound; the look in Leslie's eyes when she'd said, "We'll be fine."

And at that moment the black thing laughed. That was its second mistake; it must have thought that would finish breaking Miri's nerve. But instead it drove her back on the things she knew. She knew that their mother would never let Mal be buried here. And she knew that if there was any chance for her brother, however remote, however dreadful, she would take it. And she knew that it didn't matter what Flame was or who he had been—or what color his eyes were. What mattered was that she trusted him.

It didn't seem right to stroke the head of something capable of defying the black thing—to stroke it like a dog. But this was Flame—Flame, whom she'd rescued from the pound, the top of whose head was particularly silky, as if to invite stroking. She drew her hand down his sleek head—and took a deep shuddering breath—and felt a little braver.

She didn't want to ask the black thing what she had to do to talk to the ghosts, and so she walked forward—*toward* the black thing as it stood in the center of the graveyard. Her stomach was threatening to turn inside out and her knees were threatening to drop her to the ground, but she crossed the few steps to the first tombstone and hesitantly put her hand on it. . . .

She was dead and trapped and cold and terrified and smothered by darkness and paralyzed and dead *and she couldn't move and couldn't breathe and she had never been so cold and this was darker than anything could be she was blind and* dead *and helpless and she could not see or hear or feel except fear and cold and this is what it was to be* dead. . . .

No. She could hear. She could hear the black thing laughing.

She could see too. She could see Flame's flaming eyes, even in this darkness, and she knew them for his eyes, not the thing's. She thought, how lucky I am you are not a dog. I would not be able to see a dog's eyes in this darkness. And I think I might be frightened to death if I couldn't see you—couldn't see your eyes.

She said—she tried to say—"Pardon me, is anyone there? I've come to ask—to ask you—if I could have my brother back, please? We would miss him so much and—and I know accidents happen, but it wasn't an accident, it was the black thing."

Loneliness. Loneliness, and dark and cold and death and . . . and going on and on. On and on and on and on and on. No change. Never. Just dark and cold and death . . . and loneliness. Especially loneliness.

Flame's eyes blazed at her and she thought, wait a minute. Why are these—people—stuck here? Being dead and cold and lonely? Most graveyards aren't haunted. She thought of the cemetery where her grandfather was buried. It was huge and beautiful and full of trees, and there were picnic tables and families came there on nice days and the kids played while the grown-ups changed the flowers and—sometimes—whispered the news to the person they were visiting. She'd always imagined her grandfather somewhere sitting on a long porch with a dog at his feet. The porch sometimes looked out over a wildflower field and sometimes it looked out over a lake, but the dog at his feet was always the dog he'd told her stories about, that he'd had when he was a boy. She couldn't imagine him as a boy, so he was the grandfather she had known, but she was sure she knew exactly what the dog looked like, and how he would lie at her grandfather's feet.

It was as if she saw him now. The porch, and the cottage behind it, stood in the wildflower meadow. She raised her hand and waved. The dog saw her first; he lifted his head and thumped his tail. Then her grandfather noticed her. *What are you doing here, girl?* he said.

I—it's about Mal, she said. *I—I have to get him back.*

Her grandfather ran his hand over his head, just the way his son still did. *You got a special permission, do you, girl?*

I—I guess so. She thought: I have a hellhound. With eyes as red as your wild poppies.

You be careful. Don't you come any farther this way.

There are some—people here, who—shouldn't be here, I think. I think they're lost.

You want to send 'em this way? You do that. I'll help 'em. You just don't come any farther.

Grandad—

Yes, girl?

I miss you.

I miss you too. But I sit here, watching you. Watching you grow up. Watching Jane and Ned grow you up. It's nice here. Peaceful. It's nice to have old Sunny with me too, and he leaned over and put his hand on the dog's back. *And I'll see you here some day, and that'll be wonderful. But that day's a long way off for you. I think you better go back now.*

Mal—

You send those people along of me, and go back to Mal. It's a long time for Mal too.

Her heart had jumped up from its leaden misery at her grandfather's last sentence, before she realized that it didn't necessarily mean what she wanted it to mean. *Oh, but*—she began, and then Flame was in front of her, bumping her backwards as he had bumped her forwards, into the old graveyard. And she heard her grandfather laugh.

Gelsoraban, he said. *You sure show up in the strangest places.*

And then she was back in the black, cold, dead place, surrounded by loneliness. She made a huge effort and said, "My grandfather will help you. He says so. You don't have to stay here. You don't have to be so lonely you let horrible black things k-kill people to give you some company. Come on. It's this way. Look." And she made an even greater effort, and she was no longer cold and dead and paralyzed, and she looked over her shoulder, and she could still see the meadow, and her grandfather, and Sunny. It didn't look too far. It didn't look like too far to walk, even if you were old and weak and had known for too long that you were hopeless and there was no way out.

And then the darkness and the cold began to break up, like storm clouds after a storm. There was something like a gentle breeze that blew past her; something like the rustle of people walking past you in the dark. It was a clean-smelling breeze, not rotten or moldy; it smelled of freshly turned earth, of the fields in spring right after the farmer has dragged his harrow over them.

There was something else too. Something she could not put a name to: *this is a place of power.* For a moment she felt borne up by something large and strong and—and—she had no idea, but she thought that if she could have seen it, it would have been beautiful. Beautiful and free. Free.

As the darkness cleared she found she was standing in the old graveyard, with Flame standing leaning against her, and her hands wrapped around his ears as if he were a sturdy tree limb and she had just fallen over a cliff. When she let go, her fingers felt stiff. It was a clear, calm night, with a million stars overhead, in spite of the bright moonlight.

There was no black thing standing among the tombstones, and the old graveyard felt strangely . . . empty.

And then there was a scream—Leslie's scream. Miri turned and bolted back down the path, in spite of the dark under the trees.

Mal was sitting up, and had put his arms around her and was saying, "There, there, I'm sorry I frightened you—I frightened the hell out of *myself,* believe me—but I guess I was just stunned some-how—I'm okay now—I'm okay—" And Leslie was clinging to him and crying and crying and crying.

Miri firmly put both Mal and Leslie on Balthazar, and walked beside them as they started home. Mal and Leslie had both tried to argue, but not very hard, and before they'd gone far Miri had her hand on Mal's leg to help keep him in the saddle, or rather to pinch him when he fell asleep. Every time she dug her fingers into his thigh and he twitched awake with an "uggh, take it easy, that hurt" she remembered the limp, insensible hand she had held when she'd first found them. Leslie sat behind him, and sometimes Miri had to let go of Mal long enough to pinch her.

Flame had shot on ahead of them as soon as they'd got them-selves sorted out and were started back in the right direction, and sooner than she'd expected she saw flashlight beams and heard voices, and then Flame reappeared, dancing like a puppy. "Here!" she shouted. "We're here!"

Jane reached them first. She threw her arms around Miri because, Miri thought, she had to throw her arms around someone, and Miri was the only person available on the ground. But Miri was glad to hug her back. Balthazar had stopped when Miri did, but when Leslie made to slide down so that Mal could dismount more easily, Jane put her hand on Leslie's leg and said, "No. You just stay up there. I'm sure you're exhausted. Flame—"

But she didn't have a chance to finish, because Ned was there and began saying all the same things, and by that time the first of several strangers had arrived, wearing what Miri guessed was a police uniform although it was hard to tell in the dark, and Mal and Leslie had to insist to each of them as they appeared (especially a very bossy woman who appeared to be the head of an ambulance crew) that they were fine and were happy to ride the rest of the way back and did not need a stretcher or anything else.

While this was going on Miri was discovering just how exhausted she was. She moved a little away from the gathering crowd around Balthazar and his two riders, bumped into something that felt like a tree stump, and sat down on it. It was very uncomfortable but for a moment at least it was better than standing up. She felt that even sitting up was almost too much, and slumped over, propping her elbows on her thighs. And then there was a flicker of red in the corner of her eye, and Flame put his nose in her ear. She sat up again.

She reached out to cup his long face between her hands. "Thank you," she said. "Thank you, thank you, thank you. Gelsoraban, or whatever your real name is. I don't know what you did but—thank you. I can't begin to . . . I'd feed you steak every day for the rest of your life only I can't afford it. Or foie gras or—or—" And she discovered she was crying.

A very, very long tongue extruded itself and licked her face. "Yes, you're right," she said. "Silly of me to get all collapsed and shocky when everything's okay. Everything's *fine*. Thanks to you. No. No, I'm *not* going to cry any more, I'm really not. I think you've got some extra *tongue*, like all those ribs. . . ." But her hands were shaking, so she took them back, and chafed them together. "I'm sorry I'm behaving like such a dork. . . ."

There was the oddest sensation in her head. It was a little like finding a parcel on your doorstep that someone had left for you, that you weren't expecting, that you'd overlooked. There was nothing so clear as words, but she realized that she'd been given an awareness that what had happened in the graveyard was as much her responsibility—her achievement, her victory—as it was Flame's. "I don't know," she said, because she was a human and words were what she used. "I don't know. I don't care. It doesn't matter. Mal's okay. That's all that matters."

Another awareness: that the old graveyard was now clear and clean. That the things that had been happening for over a century because it was neither clear nor clean would now stop happening.

"You mean cell phones will work here? The next time somebody casts a shoe and we have to walk home I can ring ahead and say we'll be late? That'll be *brilliant*. And totally lost and hopeless walkers from the preserve won't turn up at the stables and want to know where they are. Well, not as many anyway."

Jane's voice, and a cone of flashlight beam: "Hiding under the table and talking to your dog again, are you?" Miri told herself that Jane wouldn't be able to see anything that was the wrong kind of revealing by flashlight, but Jane came straight up to her and crouched down to give her another hug. "Honey, are you all right? I have the feeling more happened than Leslie or Mal is telling us." She paused to give Miri a chance to answer, but when Miri said nothing she went on, "We were just getting organized to start looking ourselves.

We've got cops, firefighters, and an ambulance, and a few guys from the preserve, and Leslie's mom is probably here by now too. I hated ringing her but . . . And then Flame came prancing into the yard and barked to make us all look at him—you know he never barks—and he gambolled around like a lunatic for a minute or so and then ran straight up to me and threw himself down and waved all his legs in the air, still barking and wagging his tail like he was trying to wag it off. And I said, without even knowing I was going to say it, They're all right. He's telling us they're all right."

There was another little silence, but this time it was a silence they both wanted to listen to.

"Flame knew where to go, of course, but I knew you'd been heading for the old graveyard, so we didn't have to argue much about coming this way first. Everybody else is kind of on hold. The cops were saying there's not a lot we can do now it's dark and the preserve guys were saying they know the ground really well and they'd be happy to do some looking anyway, it's not high summer any more, exposure, you know, if you're out all night and you're hurt. . . ." That wasn't a silence they wanted to listen to and Jane hurried on: "Look, darling, there are some stretcher-bearers just longing for something to do, and Mal and Leslie are refusing to get off Balt." Miri smiled a little at this. "Would you like a lift back?"

"No. Good grief. I'm just a little—shaken. It was—scary, you know?"

Jane said grimly, "Yes. I know. And it did happen at the graveyard? Mal says the lightning struck almost like it was aiming for him, and he fell off."

He didn't fall off. He was pulled off. "Yes."

Jane sighed. "You're as communicative as they are. Never mind. I don't care, so long as you're all back safe. Twilight's come home, by the way. She's got a very strange—what looks like a burn, on her flank, but it can't be a burn. If the lightning had actually struck her they'd both be dead, or at least really messed up. She's a little spooked but I hope she'll be okay. We'll turn her out for a week and see how she goes. Come on, child. If you won't accept a friendly passing stretcher you can at least lean on me." She pulled Miri's arm over her shoulder and stood up.

When they got back to the barn the ambulance driver, who'd been listening to the hospital dispatchers, told them there'd been a bad accident on the way out of the city, and the highway was blocked solid. So when he'd heard the message coming in on the barn machine he'd picked up the phone: Leslie's mother had been two miles from the nearest exit for the last hour and a half. (There were already two messages on the barn answering machine, and when they got indoors they discovered three more on the house machine.) Jane said, "Oh, poor woman," and to Leslie, "You aren't going anywhere tonight, you can sleep here." Jane rang back, told her to go home as soon as she could, said they'd ring again as soon as everyone else had gone, and put Leslie on the phone.

It was nearly eleven by the time the last of the searchers and rescuers had left. Miri was so exhausted she could hardly walk the hundred yards from the barn to the house. She hadn't decided what she was going to say about what had happened, and she hadn't had a chance to talk to Mal and Leslie about what they wanted to say, or not say. Fortunately the cop who tried to talk to her thought she was just tired and shaken—which was only too true as well—and patted her shoulder and told her to come in to the station when she'd had some sleep and fill a form out, please. It wouldn't be that easy with Jane.

When they got into the house, Leslie rang her mother again, and

Jane rescued the salad that had been sitting in the sink for the last five hours. They'd decided to save the steak and the cake till tomorrow; Ned started slicing bread. Miri looked dubiously at the peeled potatoes, and put them in the refrigerator. Mal was saying hello to Dorothy, who was carrying on, Miri thought, as if she knew the truth. The cats had decided that whatever it was, it was over, and supper was *late*.

Miri dropped her eyes to Flame. Flame was looking at her, but then he often looked at her. She sat down in the nearest chair—she'd leaned harder on Jane on the walk back to the barn than she wanted to admit—and Flame put his head in her lap. He was too tall to do this easily, so Miri slid off the chair and sat on the floor beside him and leaned against him. He put his nose in her hair and whuffled gently. Under the cover of Dorothy's shrieks and Leslie's conversation with her mother she said to him, "I don't suppose we're going to be able to talk to each other after this?"

There was no answer. She didn't really expect one. But she was having a hard time with what had happened a few hours ago. And she couldn't explain away the impossible part because she remembered Mal's lifeless hand in hers too clearly. She whispered, so that only Flame could hear her, "If the only way I get to talk to you is because . . . because something incredibly awful has happened, then I'd rather you were just a . . . dog." He whuffled a little more. His breath always smelled clean and sweet—a kind of running-water smell, like the stream through the nature preserve. It must be all that charcoal he ate. "How does a . . . a . . . become a dog? I bet Jry and Kro—Kro-something aren't squirrels or tea-pots. Maybe they're hellhounds, like you. I wish . . ." But she couldn't say what she wished, even to Flame.

Jane said, "Okay, everyone. This isn't going to be the best meal you've ever eaten, but we all need to eat—you three especially. Leslie, you sit there. Miriam, you may not sit under the table with your dog, even that dog."

It was hard to think about food at midnight. Flame got Miri's first sandwich but she managed to eat the second. It did begin to make her feel better, but that only made her thoughts even harder to duck or switch off. Jane disappeared briefly and returned carrying a bottle of wine and a corkscrew. "This feels like a special occasion," she said. "I mean a special occasion that doesn't have anything to do with Mal's birthday. I've had horses come home riderless before—memorably when you, Miri, took that four-legged maniac Padraic out against my express orders, and he lost you—"

Just as we were passing the turn off to the old graveyard, thought Miri, but she didn't say it aloud.

"But I've never had this sense of having someone snatched back from—from—from—" but she couldn't say it aloud. "And the way you all look isn't helping. You wouldn't be in shock like this—and I'm not sure Miri isn't the worst—if all that had happened is that lightning struck a little too close and Twilight took exception and dumped Mal. For one thing, if that's all that happened, the two of you would have come back on Peggy, instead of sending her home with her stirrups run up as a message that you needed rescuing."

There was a little silence. Finally Mal said, "So, tomorrow, whatever we say now, we get to blame the wine, is that it?"

"That's the idea," said Jane. "And the hour, of course. No one says sensible things at midnight. So talk. What the hell really happened?"

There was another little silence. Miri could hear the grandfather clock in the hall ticking. Dorothy was standing on one leg with her head under her wing. The only sound besides the clock was Ned eating his third sandwich. Mal reached out and picked up one of his presents. He'd decided to save opening them till the steak dinner, but he looked at the one he held carefully, as if he was going to guess what was in it. But Miri thought he was looking at his hand and arm more than he was looking at the gift. It was a small flat box and the wrapping paper was blue and white and the ribbon around it was red. Miri knew what was in it because she'd wrapped it: a gift certificate for a new pair of running shoes. His old pair were blue and white and red. All he had to do was go round to the sports shop and choose the new ones. He'd met Leslie when she had been one of the volunteer gofers for away matches for the cross-country team last year.

Mal put the little box down and picked up his wine glass briskly, took a giant swallow and set it down again with an air of resolution. "Okay. I didn't just come off Twilight. I broke my neck."

Silence again. Horrible silence. Ned stopped chewing. The clock went *tick tick*.

"I heard it. Tiny little crunch. And then I was on the ground and couldn't feel a thing below my neck. All I felt . . . It was . . . no. I don't want to talk about it."

Miri looked up just as the tears began to slide down Leslie's face again. Mal reached his hand out—the hand that Miri had briefly held—and covered hers with his. "I don't want to talk about it for *me*, not just for Leslie. Leslie was brilliant. Peggy was pretty stirred up by the lightning and Twilight taking off, but Leslie got her quieted down—and the storm left almost as fast as Twilight did—"

"As if it had done what it was meant to do," said Leslie in a strange flat voice—a voice very like Jane's when she'd said, That looked like it was right over the old graveyard. Leslie picked up her wine glass in the hand Mal wasn't holding and took a mouthful.

"Yes," said Mal. "It was a bit like that. But this is the wine talking, right? So Leslie tied Peggy up and—and found out I wasn't getting up because I couldn't, and she said that she mustn't move mc, and that she'd send Peggy home and you'd be sure to come looking for us and you'd even know where to come because Miri had told her that I liked the old graveyard, and you'd've seen the lightning strike.

"And it was pretty much forever, lying under that tree, till Miri and Balthazar and Flame showed up. . . ."

"Don't," said Leslie. Mal squeezed her hand. "Yeah. So Miri showed up and she . . . she saw it was pretty bad. And then . . . well, Flame went kind of nuts. That was pretty weird. Miri decided to see what he was carrying on about and followed him into the old graveyard."

Jane glanced at Miri and back at Mal.

"I thought she was kind of . . . you know, postponing the inevitable. About me. And . . . well . . . I don't know. There was this feeling for a little while like . . . I don't know, like the world was coming to an end, except I was already . . . I was pretty out of it. It's just I was even more out of it there for a while. . . ."

Leslie said, "It was like the sky had come down and was mashing us into the ground. It was like . . . it was like being in a waffle iron and they're closing the lid. I thought . . . I thought what had happened to Mal was making me crazy, that I was cracking up. And then suddenly it went away."

"Okay, it was like that for you too? That's pretty much what it felt like to me. Except when they opened the waffle iron and let us out I could move again. It was like everything that had happened since the lighting struck had been the waffle iron. Had been a bad dream. Except it wasn't. I *remember.* I remember just . . . kind of not *being* there, except for this awful . . . Also I *feel* like I've been in a waffle iron. I've fallen off horses before and I've never been beat up the way I feel beat up now. You're going to need a winch to get me out of bed tomorrow morning, I think."

Miri was looking at Mal when he turned to look at her. Leslie was looking at her too, and Jane. She couldn't see where Ned was looking but she could guess he was looking at her. She looked down at Flame to give her courage, and gently pulled his ears, one silky ear per hand. "It was Flame really. I didn't know. He—it really is—was—haunted, you know. The graveyard." *This is a place of power.* She taught riding at her mother's riding stable—no, she taught riding *with* her mother at *their* riding stable—places of power were nothing to do with her. Flame looked up at her, and the end of his tail twitched. She took a deep breath.

"Flame knew the—the thing that was haunting it. He's a hellhound, you know?" She wanted to laugh, but she was afraid she wouldn't be able to stop. "I guess he defected. But I guess he knows his old colleagues. This one knew him. It said I could have Mal back if I convinced the—the ghosts to let him go. The—the thing seemed to think that the way—the way Mal was, he—he wouldn't live long." *He will not want to live.* "And then . . ." But she realized she couldn't tell them about her grandfather, about Ned's father, not when they all still missed him so much, especially Ned. It would be like Mal talking about what happened to him after Leslie said *don't.* She might try to tell Jane about it later, some time when they were alone. "I—I guess I kind of told them that they didn't have to stay there. That they weren't trapped. They didn't seem to know—that was the thing, not letting them know. I think Flame must have stopped the thing from stopping them while I—told them. So they left. And when we came back out of the graveyard again Mal was sitting up."

There was another, longer silence. "Do you suppose Flame would like some wine?" said Jane. She passed Miri an empty plate and Miri poured a few drops of wine into it and set it on the floor. Flame came out from under the table and solemnly lapped it up. Then he raised his head and looked around the table as if checking that this was what he was supposed to do. Or as if he was including them all in . . . it was like ratifying a contract, thought Miri. Sealing a pact.

"I think the graveyard really . . . isn't haunted any more," said Miri. "Maybe cell phones will work here now."

"Well that would be convenient," said Jane. "Except that then we'll have to forbid people to use them while they're riding and insist they turn them off before they get on their horses. Leslie, you're dropping. Let me show you where you'll sleep. Miri, can you loan her a nightgown?"

Miri fetched an old, half-worn-out flannel nightgown because it was, in her opinion, the most comfortable and comforting, and then began to collect the dirty dishes and ran water in the sink. "For pity's sake, Miri," said her father, "go to bed. I'll do this."

Miri shook her head. "I'm not quite ready to go to bed," she said. "I don't want to have to dream about anything yet." Ned put his arm around her and they stood silently for a moment. Then he sighed. "It's one thirty A.M. and I believed every word you said. To-morrow morning I have to give a presentation to the trustees of a big charity so they'll hire us, and what happened here just now will all be nonsense. But at one thirty A.M. . . . thank you." He kissed the top of her head. "If you really want to struggle with the dishes, I'm going to bed."

Miri nodded at the billow of detergent suds. "You go. The horses won't care if I'm awake, so long as they get their breakfast. Your trustees probably would mind."

She didn't notice that Jane had returned till she began lifting dishes out of the draining rack and drying them and putting them away. They'd finished and Miri was mopping the counter when Jane said at last, "It's all true, isn't it? It's all true."

Miri said, "Yes."

Flame was sprawled in the middle of the kitchen floor, where they had to keep stepping over him, but neither of them had wanted to tell him to move.

"It's two in the morning, and I can say anything I like," Jane began, and paused.

"That's what Dad said."

"Do you suppose he was—Flame was—somehow—sent?"

Miri thought about his sad red eyes when she'd first seen him at the pound—about the depth of that sadness. Had she been drawn to that sadness because she was supposed to be? "No," she said, after a moment. "I think he—after he—after he defected, I think he's been having, um, culture shock. I think that's probably why he's . . . a dog."

"I don't like the way this conversation is going," said Jane. "Next you're going to tell me there's a lot of stuff like the graveyard—what that graveyard used to be—around."

Miri said, "I think there probably is. But there's a lot of stuff like us and Leslie and our barn too, isn't there? Like those two guys from the preserve who were going to look for Mal and Leslie even after dark because they know the area so well. Or even you telling Leslie's mom to go home, that Leslie can spend the night here. And we have Flame."

At the sound of Miri's voice saying his name, Flame opened his eyes and thumped his tail.

"Then maybe," Jane said drily, "you were right about Peggy and Tamari too."

Miri knelt beside Flame and began stroking his long extra-ribby side. "Maybe I am."

Flame moaned with pleasure, just like an ordinary dog.

Jane said, "Tamari's owner rang yesterday. She's got a new show pony. She says it's an angel. In fact that's its name—Angel. She says

Greyhaven is the best barn she was ever at and she wants to come back."

"But there's a catch," Miri said.

"She's still got Tamari."

Miri sat back on her heels and laughed. Laughing felt good. "Tell her we'll have him—at double rates. Because only you and I will be able to do anything around him, even fill his water bucket. Tell her that the extra money will go into the indoor arena fund—we'd be even better than the best barn she's been at if we had an indoor arena."

"My decisive new business partner," said Jane. "That's kind of the way my mind was going too. You're two years older and here all the time. We can cope."

Flame had raised his head and was looking at Miri meaningfully. She started petting him again. "And you know," she added, "I bet they'll write a big newspaper story about what happened tonight— isn't Leslie's mom dating a journalist?—and they'll get everything wrong because we won't tell them any of what we've been talking about, but we'll tell them about Flame finding Mal and Leslie and then coming back to the barn to tell you he'd found them and to lead you back. And I bet all these people come out to get a look at this weird hero dog with the red eyes. And I bet some of them decide we look like a nice place and they and their kids should take some riding lessons. And when we can put the indoor arena up in two years instead of three, we can call it the Flame Arena."

Now Jane laughed. It was a nice sound: easy. Happy. "Okay. It's a deal. Are you ready to go to bed yet?"

"Yes," said Miri. "I have to feed the horses in four hours. And I'm going to dream about the Flame Arena."

FIREWORM

PETER DICKINSON

This was the story Nedli told:

*Long ago there was only the Great White Owl, the spirit owl,
so there was always ice and snow and darkness. There was
never any thaw, never any long, warm days. No people lived
in the mountains. Then the Sun sent his children, the Amber
Bear and the Blind Bear, to drive the Great White Owl away
beyond the mountains, so that people could live here. She was
not the Blind Bear then, but as they fought the owl he pecked
out her eyes.*

*Never was such fighting. The earth shook, and the moun-
tains smoked and flamed and poured out burning rocks, but
in the end the two bears drove the owl away, and the sun
came, and the long, warm days.*

*The sun brought people, and animals for the men to hunt,
and roots and nuts for the women to gather. But the people did
not have fire, so they ate their food raw.*

*Now the two great bears grew fat and lazy in the good
times, and they found a cave far up Bear Mountain and went
to sleep, and the Great White Owl came back, bringing the
snow and ice and darkness.*

The forest animals did not know to go south, so they froze and died. But the people huddled into a cave. They broke branches from the forest and made a wall to keep out the wind and snow. But still they were cold, cold, and they had nothing to eat, and soon they would die. So they cried to the bears to save them.

Their crying woke the Blind Bear, and she said to her brother, "I cannot sleep for the crying of the people. Make yourself into a snow bear and go to the people and give them your old pelt, your amber pelt, to keep them warm."

The Amber Bear did as she said, and as he journeyed the Sun came up for a little while and saw a great white bear crossing the glacier, carrying an amber pelt across his back. The Sun's light struck sparks from the pelt and they fell on the glacier and melted a hole in it, and that is why in summertime there is a lake in the middle of the glacier. Only a few little sparks stuck in the hairs of the pelt.

When the Amber Bear reached the cave, he found the entrance blocked with branches. He pushed his way through, and as he did so those few sparks fell out and set the logs on fire. He left his old pelt on the floor and went back to the Blind Bear.

The people woke and found a great amber pelt on the floor of the cave and a fire at the entrance. They rushed down to the forest to fetch more branches to feed their fire, and there they found the frozen body of a deer. It was hard as ice, so they put it by the fire to thaw, but they piled so many branches onto their fire that when they came to eat the deer they found they had roasted all one side. So they learned that meat is best if it is cooked.

Now they had both warmth and food, and could live

through the White Owl season, until the two bears woke feeling mean and hungry, and fought the owl again and drove it away and brought the sun back.

That was the first of Nedli's stories. If you asked her whether it was true, she would tell you, "It is true in the spirit world. My stories are a way of seeing, and a way of saying."

◆ ◆ ◆

Tandin knew he was dreaming. The cave he was in wasn't the Home Cave, but some kind of a dream cave. It was pitch dark, but he knew that the Blind Bear was there, though he couldn't see her or smell her or touch her. Dream terror welled up, shuddering through him, forcing him out of his dream.

Just as he was waking, the Blind Bear whispered in his mind.

One word.

Fireworm.

And now he was swimming up out of sleep, sleep deeper than he had ever known. Only the Blind Bear's whisper drove him into wakefulness, ordered his eyes to open, forced him up onto his elbow, to stare around the Home Cave. And all seemed well. The fire glowed in the entrance. It glowed through the cave, lighting the overarching rock, glinting off the hairs of the great bear pelt that hung on the back wall, casting shadows among the huddled bodies of the sleepers around him.

There was a strange, sweet reek in the cave, dragging him back into sleep. His body sagged.

Fireworm.

What did it mean?

"Listen to your dreams," Nedli would say. "Mostly they are silly, but some are messages from the spirit world. You will know when it is one of those, but they come as riddles, and you must guess their meaning."

This was one of those, Tandin was drowsily sure. Fireworm? Another of Nedli's stories said that the Great White Owl hated fire, because it came from the sun, and sent the fireworm to take it away. For three winters people tried to fight the fireworm, but in the end they gave up and moved away. That was long ago, among different mountains. Probably it was only a story, a way of seeing, or a way of saying, but the dream had been so strong. . . .

He settled back down, but still the nightmare kept him from sleep. He tried to drive it away by imagining that he was lying with Mennel in his arms, where she slept among the women on the far side of the cave. Bast, her father, had forbidden her to speak to him, but he knew from the way she looked at him—

Fireworm!

The Blind Bear's whisper broke through the flimsy dream. Again he eased himself up onto his elbow and stared at the fire. It had burnt down to a heap of embers, with a few ends of branches smouldering round the edges. Why hadn't whoever was on watch been keeping it fed? Above the glowing heap he could see a section of the night sky, hard-starred, with the glittering flank of Bear Mountain cutting it off to one side. In front of that whiteness Barok sat with his back against the wall of the entrance, wrapped in his furs and fast asleep with his head on his knees. That was strange. Barok was a good man. Often he led the hunt. He wouldn't sleep on watch.

The heap of embers seemed to settle a little. The movement continued. Tandin sat right up, then rose swaying to his feet, wrapping his fur round his shoulders. His mother was dead and no one knew his father, so he slept in a place without honour, well away from the fire. He staggered between the sleepers towards it. Twice he stumbled on limbs, but no one woke. Now he could see a hollow forming in the top of the mound, embers slithering down its sides, like the sand in the little traps some ants make in summer. Any prey that steps into them loosens the sand and slithers helplessly down to where the ant waits at the bottom. . . .

Faster and faster. Tandin came wide awake.

"Fireworm!" he croaked. And louder, "Fireworm!" again.

No one stirred. He nudged a sleeper with his foot, prodded him hard. Dead? No, in Nedli's story the fireworm put everyone to sleep with his breath. . . .

Yes! That sweet odour . . .

Tandin stumbled to the entrance and into the harsh, clean mountain air. It scoured the sweet stench out of his lungs. His mind cleared, and he remembered how the men in the story had fought the fireworm. He laid his fur on the path, ran back to the cave entrance, grabbed Barok's axe from the rock beside him and started to hack chunks of compacted snow from the piled drift beside the path, heaping them on the fur. He folded the back legs over the pile, forming a bag which he could drag by the legs to the fire.

By now the hollow reached down to the floor of the cave, where it became a fiery pit going on down, with the embers still slithering into it. The pile was already more than half gone. With a huge effort, Tandin swung the bag up over the remaining embers, let go of the back legs and shot the snow pile down into the pit.

From down below came a hooting scream like the sound of a blizzard howling through a rock cleft. The sleepers began to stir.

"Fireworm!" Tandin yelled, and staggered back gasping to the snow-drift. Before he had half filled his fur, the hunters were stumbling out. As their minds cleared, they remembered Nedli's story. They elbowed Tandin out of the way and finished filling his fur. Two of them dragged it off to the fire while the rest hacked out more snow.

Inside the cave the women used some of the branches stacked ready for burning to rake as many of the embers as they could into a pile well away from the fire, and then fed them with broken branches. As the hunters flung bag after bag of snow into the pit, the howl from below rose to a deafening scream, which then faded away as it sank further and further down into the rock. Long after it had dwindled into silence, the hunters toiled steadily on, while the women swept and swept to clear away the black but still scorching embers that littered the floor.

At last they gave up and settled round their new fire, coughing and spluttering because it was no longer in a place where natural drafts carried the smoke out of the cave. No one slept again. Nedli retold the story of the fight against the fireworm, and they then sat mulling it over in sad and anxious voices, knowing that the monster was no tale-teller's invention to while away an evening, but was a creature of the real world, their ancient enemy. And it had found them again.

Towards dawn the hunters were discussing how to keep themselves awake on nights when the fireworm came. Someone said, "Its breath is very strong. All of us slept, even Barok, who was on watch."

"In the old days they made a snow-hole outside and went out two at a time to keep watch, coming back often to check the fire," said another voice. Others joined in.

"And still some could not be woken when it was their turn."

"The howling woke me."

"And me."

"It couldn't send out its breath when it howled."

"But Nedli says the fireworm comes in silence. What made it howl? Someone must have thrown snow on it. Who was awake?"

"Vulka was already at the drift when I came there."

They turned to Vulka, who shook his head, puzzled.

"No," he said. "The howling woke me too. But someone . . . his fur was half filled with snow . . ."

Frowning, he gazed round the shadowed faces. Tandin did nothing to catch his attention, but when their glances met and locked, he rose. A man without honour is no better than a woman. He dared not stay seated when speaking to hunters.

"Yes," he said. "The Blind Bear woke me. I dreamed I was in her cave. . . ."

He told them about his dream and what he had done on waking. They stared at him and turned to Nędli. She didn't only tell stories. She was their Old Woman, who remembered things that had happened before any of them were born, as well as all the lore of long ago, things that generations of Old Women had passed down. She sat among the women, and spoke for them, but spoke as an equal with the hunters. She looked round the circle and then rose.

"Let the hunters come with me," she said, and led them to the back of the cave.

"Who knows the name of Tandin's father?" she said. "Was it any of you . . . ? No . . . ? Lay your hands on the pelt of the Amber Bear and swear to me it was not."

All did as she told them.

"Perhaps the fellow's dead," said Sordan. "Or perhaps he was from another cave."

"Perhaps," said Nedli. "But the Blind Bear has called Tandin to her and spoken to him in his dream. I think he is a spirit-walker and it was Amber Bear that took human shape and fathered him, as long ago he fathered Tarr and Undarok."

"Those are only stories," said Vulka.

"Last night you thought the fireworm was only a story," said Barok.

"In that case let Tandin walk the ghost path," said Bast. "Let him ask his father to help us."

The other hunters ignored him, well aware why he should say that. There were ghost walkers in one or two of the other caves, but most who had tried to take that journey had either died or returned too crazed to live long.

The Blind Bear whispered in Tandin's mind.

Son of a bear, come.

He left his place by the wall, joined the circle of hunters and laid his hand on the pelt.

"Yes," he said. "Let me walk the ghost path. Set me on the way."

"You're too young," said Barok. "Grown hunters have died. Remember what Nedli has said. 'The ghost path is splintered ice beneath the feet, thorn bush tearing the flesh, bitterweed on the tongue, ice in the heart. It runs on the very edge of life, with a sheer drop down into the dark land of the Great White Owl.'"

"There is always a price to pay for anyone who walks the ghost path," said Daskan. "An arm, or an eye."

"Or his mind," said Bast, with relish. "Or his life."

"The Blind Bear calls me," said Tandin.

That settled it.

Nedli knew the ritual. She set everyone to preparing a feast but told Tandin to take extra furs and go and wait outside. As he went out into the pale and icy dawn, the Blind Bear whispered in his mind again.

Bears sleep at this season. Son of my brother, be a bear.

Something in him understood her meaning. He chose a place on the northern side of a boulder, so that the brief noon brightness shouldn't wake him, and scooped a hollow in the snow. Deliberately, bit by bit, he slowed his heart and his breathing. His eyes were open, but he was neither awake nor asleep. When Mennel passed him with two other women, going to fetch roots from the pits where they were cached, she turned aside and stared down at him in wonder. Tandin perceived her as if from very far off, and knew who she was, but did not stir.

The others feasted and boasted and sang, and as the sun began to sink, they came out and carried Tandin inside. By then his flesh felt as cold as raw meat would have been on a summer morning, but he was still slowly breathing.

On Nedli's instructions they had taken the amber pelt down from the wall and spread it on the floor. Now the women stripped Tandin of his furs and laid him on it and wrapped it twice round him and bound it in place with thongs. Six of the hunters hoisted him onto their shoulders and carried him down to the burial tree, with the rest of the people groaning and wailing the death chant as they followed.

The burial tree stood a little way into the forest at the top of a mound too rocky for anything else to have taken root. All round rose the cairns of long-dead hunters. The tree was very old, and dead all down one side. Most of the trees in the forest were pines of one kind or another, but this was an ash tree and leafless at this season. Two of the hunters climbed into the tree carrying thongs, which they passed over two branches growing side by side, a little way apart, one dead and one still living. The men on the ground tied one end of each thong round the roll of pelt with Tandin at its centre and hauled him up into the tree. It was almost dark by the time they turned away, still singing the death music, and left him there, hanging between life and death.

Though he could see nothing from inside the pelt, Tandin had been aware of all this and knew what was happening to him. Now he could feel the night gathering itself round him and the utter cold in which nothing could live beginning to seep through the layers of fur and hide and into his still-sentient flesh. Slowly it moved deeper, but before it reached his centre, a strange warmth began to pervade him, a glow without heat, a peace. The feeling made him drowsy, and he slept.

He was woken by a savage thump on his chest, a battering of wings and a tearing sound. The bundle he was wrapped in rocked violently to and fro. The pelt that covered his face was ripped clear, and he gazed up into a strange dark shape, outlined against moonlit sky. At the edge of his vision, on either side, two curving silvery lines pulsed to and fro, glinting where the moonlight caught plumage on the leading edges of the beating wings.

Now, knowing what he faced, he could make out two dark and shining rounds, faintly gold, in the dark shape above him. The eyes of the Great White Owl gazing down at its prey. And below them the gleaming curve of the black beak, poised ready to strike.

This is the price I must pay, he thought, *to be blind, like the Blind Bear. If this is what she chooses, I am ready.*

Something buffeted into the tree-trunk. The leafless branches clattered together. Twigs rattled down. A roar of challenge rose from below.

The White Owl screamed, leaped into the air and hurtled down, savage talons reaching for the challenger. Something thudded against the tree. The violence of the impact snapped the dead branch from which Tandin was suspended. His whole bundle swung down, still held by the thongs at the lower end, and continued to swing heavily to and fro while the battle shook the forest. From time to time he caught glimpses of the fight, the owl plunging once more into the attack, or the monstrous bear it fought reared on its hind legs, fangs gleaming in the moonlight, forelegs held wide, with immense hooked claws extended. At one point he saw its mask clearly. Where the eyes should have been there were two scarred pits. Yet it turned its head to follow the owl's flight and tensed to meet the next attack. He didn't see an actual clash, or how the fight ended.

But the owl was gone and the fight was over. Then, as the swinging motion diminished, he saw the bear chewing at the thong that still held him, where it was lashed and weighted with boulders at its further end. It parted, and he was lowered to the ground. His face was licked by a great rough tongue. A strange, fluid moment followed, in which his bones seemed to melt into flesh and both together into a juice which almost instantly solidified into flesh and bone. Dazedly he rose to his feet.

His four feet.

And the pelt he had been wrapped in was no longer fastened around him. It was part of him, his own hide.

His nostrils were filled with a wonderful, complex reek. He swung his head towards the other bear. Her features were dim and blurred, but her scent was as vivid as any human face, and as individual as a name: Blind Bear. She was in heat.

She nosed along the ground and picked up in her jaws a bit of broken branch with a length of thong attached to it, then turned away with a grunt and walked off down the mound and into the trees. Tandin followed her, snuffling her scent.

The ground sloped more and more steeply upward. They climbed between snow-draped trees until they reached open ground, a plunging snowfield on the flank of an immense spur of Bear Mountain, which soared majestically up on their left, though in the dim vision of a bear it was no more than a huge white blur. The Blind Bear climbed steadily on, twisting to and fro to avoid the deeper drifts. When she reached the ridge at the top of the spur she turned left. Tandin padded eagerly after her.

Still climbing, they followed a desperately narrow track along the spine of the ridge, often no more than a finger-width from sheer falls on one side or the other. On their left, below them, lay the glacier, and nothing but the darkness and killing cold and whistling blizzard of an arctic night. To their right it was somehow broad day, with the lulling odours of summer drifting on the breeze. So they climbed between life and death to the cave of the Blind Bear.

The entrance was a dark slot in an ice-sheeted cliff. Here the Blind Bear paused, rose to her hind legs and batted a large icicle from the archway. She sniffed at it briefly, marked it with her scent and padded on. Tandin sniffed at the icicle as he passed it. Its scent was entrancing. He didn't want to leave it, but neither did he want to lose the Blind Bear, so he picked it up in his mouth and hurried after her along a twisting tunnel. Other tunnels led off to the side, but the scent trail was clear and he found her waiting for him in an immense cavern, deep inside the mountain.

The darkness here was absolute, but her odours told him all he needed to know.

He put the icicle down and came up alongside her, rubbing his body against hers, then faced her. Both bears rose to their hind legs, clutched each other round the chest and with deep, rumbling purrs rubbed their neck-glands against each other. They fell to their feet and stood nose to tail, flank rubbing flank and noses snuffling at the other one's anal scent-glands. When both were fully prepared, he mounted her, and they coupled in the utter dark of her cave.

Tandin woke in his human body. He was lying on the bear pelt, naked, but the air was no colder than it might have been in high summer. He was still in the Blind Bear's cave, and she was there, and again he knew it before she spoke in his mind.

Your seed is in me. You will never mate with any human female. This is the price you must pay to walk the ghost path.

"I pay it," he answered, and like a witness to his oath, the rock returned the echo of his voice.

Now you must fight the fireworm. Twice you must fight it. The first time alone, in the spirit world, and again with your friends in the world where people live and die. Your weapons are by your side. Use them in both worlds. Now come with me.

Tandin groped by his thigh and found a piece of rough timber with a bit of thong knotted around it. It could only be the broken branch of the burial tree that the Blind Bear had carried all the way to her cave. He didn't recognise the other object. It was hard and smooth, about as long as his arm and as wide at one end, but tapering to a point at the other and, when he picked it up, heavier than any timber he knew. He rose. The Blind Bear grunted and turned away. He drew the bear pelt round him and followed the soft pad of her feet. He could still smell her, but no longer locate her by smell. Her scent was now only the heavy reek of some large beast.

She stopped as soon as he could see the pale slot of the cave entrance, its icicles glinting in the moonlight. He realised what his second weapon must be. Why had it not melted at all in the warmth of the cave? It was as dry as the dead branch and no colder to the touch. Strange, but no stranger than what had happened before.

"My honour and my thanks," he said as he came up beside her.

She grunted and he walked on until he stood at the mouth of the cave, looking out along the impossible path by which they had come. He didn't hear her come up behind him, or know she was there until her nudge against his spine sent him hurtling along the narrow path. He took an instinctive stride to regain his balance, and another, and another, and found he was racing along the twisting path, each stride a bound the length of a fallen tree, but light and easy and sure. So sure that there was never any moment when he felt a risk of missing his footing. It was as if the path were constantly reforming itself to meet his foot.

He understood what was happening to him from one of Nedli's stories. This was the spirit-walk. The hero Jerast, who had paid the price of an ever-running sore to walk the ghost path so that he could fight the Wolf-father, could do this. He sped effortlessly along the ridge, down the steep snowfield and into the trees. The forest barely slowed him. He twisted and jinked, but there was always a way. And the climb to the Home Cave was as easy as if he had been weightless.

He paused at the entrance and considered the weapons in his hand. For the moment he could see no use for the bit of branch, but the unmelting icicle seemed a ready-made stabbing stake. He was reminded of one of the hunters' main weapons; poles or shorter and stouter lengths of wood, sharpened at one end and the point then hardened in the fire. Some had thongs attached to them so that they could be pulled from the stricken prey with less danger of the hunter being trampled or gored in the process. So Tandin loosened the thong from the log, tied one end round the butt of the icicle and coiled the rest around his waist, tying it so that the icicle hung at his hip.

He laid the bear pelt down on the patch of rock that they had cleared of snow the night before and looked up at the moon to check how much of the night was gone. It was almost full, and still climbing the eastern sky. It struck him that this could be the last time he would see it.

In Nedli's story the people who had fought the fireworm long ago had found it was useless to block its entrance hole with rocks, because it chewed its way through them almost at once. It was better to keep filling the hole with snow night and day, so Sordan and

Dotal were sitting by the entrance, ready to do this next time. Their eyes were wide open, but Tandin was still in the spirit world and they seemed not to see him as he passed between them, not even when he thrust the end of his log into the embers of the fire and set it blazing. Instead of soon smouldering out, as a log would do in the world where people live and die, it continued to burn brightly, lighting the whole cave.

The new fire was close to the right wall, and the men and women were sleeping in two groups along the left-hand side, where a draft seemed to keep most of the smoke clear of the floor. The hole by which the fireworm had come was a black pit in the solid rock. The last load of snow had all but melted away. The hole went straight down. Its walls were almost smooth, without handhold or foothold. Confident in the near weightlessness of the spirit-walker, Tandin stepped calmly into it and floated down, with the flame from the log streaming above him, until he reached the bottom. This turned out to be a natural fissure in the rock, through which the fireworm must have made its way until it was directly below the Home Cave. It was no more than a boulder-strewn crevasse, almost impassably difficult going in the world where people live and die, but the spirit-walk carried Tandin along it with the speed of dream.

Several times he came to tunnels which the fireworm had bored through the rock to make its way from one fissure to another, and there he slid the icicle in against his back, beneath the windings of thong, and dropped to all fours, but still sped along, not crawling on hands and knees like a human but somehow shortening his legs and lengthening his arms so that he could run like a fox or a deer.

As he twisted his way through the massive foundations that underlay the familiar mountain landscape, he found himself becoming steadily more aware of their nature and structure, almost palpable to him in the spirit world in which he was moving, the unimaginable pressures and resistances that held them in place, the huge, uncaring, alien essences that informed them. Ahead and to his right, dominating them all, rose Bear Mountain. He could feel a core of heat deep below it and rising up through its centre, narrowing as it rose towards the summit.

The air in the tunnel grew steadily warmer. He sensed the forest-covered valley below the Home Cave as a slight easing in the pressure. The fissures and tunnels turned to follow it for a while, then turned again, and he could feel the renewed weight of the mountain spur up which he and the Blind Bear had climbed earlier that night. The ghost path along the ridge was like a streak of lightning in his awareness as he crossed beneath it, a vivid, jagged line, a landmark. And then something new, massive again, but different. Another sort of spirit, a great force locked into stillness. The spirit of ice, waiting through the endlessly returning seasons for the world to change, and the sun to return and release it into water. The glacier.

Now the fissure turned again, and then widened suddenly and became a large chamber filled with a strange, smoky glow. The air was warmer than a summer noon and smelt of earth and embers. Immediately he was aware of the presence of the fireworm. It had been asleep, but his coming had it startled into wakefulness. Not Tandin himself, but the flame he carried. He retreated round the bend in the tunnel and wedged his log between two boulders. It seemed to have burnt down its length hardly at all. Leaving its betraying flare behind, he stole forward.

He reached the cavern and looked down into a wide hollow. He could see places that seemed to have been shaped by the same method that had shaped the tunnels through which he'd come, but here they had carved out the cavern floor to form a great nest-like hollow in the solid rock. The glow came from a stranger creature than Tandin had ever imagined, lying on a darkly glowing mound of rocks at the bottom. At first it seemed to be nothing more than a huge, pale globule with fiery ripples pulsing over its surface, regular as a heartbeat. The only things he had seen anything like it were the fat, whitish edible grubs that could sometimes be found under the bark of rotting tree-trunks, but this was enormously larger. It would have filled the far end of the Home Cave.

There was a domed mound at its nearer end, on which, as he watched, a small round hole opened and emitted a wailing hoot. Further back, on either side of the mound, two cupped flaps had risen, which he recognised as ears. So the hole must be a mouth, and the two black spots a little above it must be eyes. The mound began to rotate to the right, paused and returned to the left, and returned again, hooting each time it paused, then waiting, and then resuming.

Until now the sleeping life in the creature had been veiled by the far stronger presence of the fireworm. On waking, its ache, its need, had instantly asserted themselves. And now, behind that, he could faintly sense the swarm of half-formed lives inside it. He couldn't for the moment see the fireworm, but felt it to be somewhere in the darkness between himself and the hooting creature. Then it came lurching into view.

It was at first sight less strange. Not as huge as he had expected, but still several times larger than any creature the hunters met in the forest, with a body like a tree-trunk, but smooth and oily, and a dismal, whitish colour, the pallor of a plant that has tried to grow beneath a stone. The head was away from him so he could see no features; the creature was blunt at the rear, tailless, with short legs thicker than a man's body, ending in wide and muscular feet with immense hooked claws.

When it reached the other creature, it uttered a soft hoot, as if to say "I am here." It seemed to have no neck and a head almost as blunt as the rear, with a huge dark eye and a small ear visible, but no sign of any nostrils, mouth or jawbone. They were mates, Tandin now saw, a male and female fireworm, however strangely different. And she was swollen to this shape by the growing brood of half-formed fireworms inside her.

He watched, sweating in the heat, while the fireworm reared onto its haunches. A flap opened across its belly. It scooped down into the pouch with its forepaws, and brought them out with the paws cupped around a heap of dark fragments. Somehow it lowered its head and blew on them from the mouth Tandin still couldn't see. He caught the faint glimmer of embers coming to life and watched while the fireworm shuffled itself sideways round the female, delicately tipping them in between its bulging underside and the glowing rocks on which it lay. With what sounded like soft moans of relief, the female subsided into a globule while the fireworm busied itself around it rearranging the heated rocks to cradle it yet more closely.

Satisfied, the male rose again onto its haunches and started to swing its head questioningly round the cavern. Now Tandin could see the mouth clearly, though he wouldn't have recognised it as such, a wrinkled and pitted area in the middle of a flat, round surface. Before the fireworm's search reached him he withdrew into the fissure.

There was no hunters' lore to tell him how to fight such a creature. He must get in at least one good strike, but where? Did it have a heart, even, to pierce, and blood to shed? Was there some kind of bait he could use, so that he could attack it from the flank? Yes, he had fire, the flaming log. If he could . . .

The rudimentary plan was still forming and he was unwinding the thong from his waist when he heard a movement from the cavern, a shuffling footfall, and another, and another. The fireworm was moving towards him. It had somehow sensed where he was, and now it was coming.

He snatched up the log and retreated to a point where the fissure widened. There he wedged it between rocks again, and, just as the fireworm came round the bend, scuttled behind a large boulder lying against the right-hand wall. Through a slit between the boulder and the wall, he watched it approach. As it came the puckered mass at its front end unfolded, stretched, and became a single circular lip surrounding a mouth as wide as the whole head and lined on all the surfaces that he could see with row behind row of blunt but savage-looking teeth. The front row protruded forward, while the whole head rotated steadily from side to side, as if already grinding its way through solid rock, each row of teeth replacing the one before it as that wore down.

The monster wasn't built to move fast, but it came steadily, picking its way over the tumbled surface. In places its low-slung body slithered on the rocks. As it moved out of sight behind the boulder, Tandin turned and tensed, gripping the icicle at the balance point, with the other end of the thong looped round his left hand.

The head came into view. The monster's whole attention was on the flaming log. Though one eye faced in his direction it seemed not to notice him—but the instant he moved the head swung towards him and that terrible mouth was less than a pace away. A waft of its sickly-sweet breath flooded over him. He could sense its numbing power, but here in the spirit world it could not touch him. With all his strength he flung the icicle into the grisly pit of a mouth, and immediately leaped aside.

He had already chosen a landing place, and another a stride further on, but he needed to take his eye off the fireworm to reach them. When he turned to face it, he found that its head had followed him round and the monster was already lurching towards him. It seemed not to have noticed the icicle down its gullet or the thong trailing out of its mouth. Desperately Tandin jerked on the thong as he retreated another pace. In the same moment a violent spasm shook the fireworm. Its body arched up, with its front legs heaving clear of the floor, and it emitted an enormous coughing roar, spewing the icicle out of its mouth while Tandin's tug on the thong brought his weapon flying towards him, passing over his shoulder and landing just beyond the blazing log. He pounced on it and swung towards the monster, without thought reversing the icicle in his grip, ready for a fresh throw. The flame from the log wavered for a moment as the weapon passed through it.

Tandin didn't notice. All his attention was on the fireworm. Another spasm shook it, far less violent than the first, and another even less. It turned towards Tandin and came slowly forward.

There was no time. *Get round to the side somehow*, he thought. *Strike low and into the soft patch behind the leg, to where the heart might be. Use the—*

The icicle twitched in his hand. He glanced down and saw it was streaming with water from its thicker end, so strongly that it was starting to wriggle and squirm. In a moment the stream had become a jet and he could barely control it, let alone throw it. In desperation he reversed it again and swung the jet on the fireworm, straight into the gaping mouth.

Instantly the creature recoiled and turned away, vomiting steaming water, and retreated down the fissure. Tandin pursued it, wrestling to keep the torrent of water aimed at it. He reached the cavern almost at the end of his strength, but with an enormous effort he managed to jam the icicle down between rocks again, with the force of the jet wedging it into the crack and holding it firm, and the water streaming down towards the central hollow.

By the time he had fetched the blazing log out of the fissure, the torrent had become a stream, tumbling down over the rocks, and still the flow-rate rose. It was as though all the winter snows of Bear Mountain were thawing together and forcing their way out through this one opening. He could even smell the familiar odour of snow-melt given off by the green and foaming cataracts of suddenly un-locked rivers in spring.

He turned to see what had happened to the fireworm. It had reached the other creature and was circling round her, rubbing its body against hers while they mourned together. Faintly through the roar of the torrent he could hear their hooting cries.

The water was now in the bottom of the hollow and was begin-ning to swirl round their nest. Clouds of steam rose from the burn-ing rocks. Tandin caught only glimpses of the fireworm and his mate. He seemed to be making no attempt to leave her, but as the flood rose and the rocks of the nest cooled and blackened she seemed to shrink, and before long was visibly the same kind of creature as her mate but with a much smaller head and short, feeble legs. Now she started to scrabble her way down to the water's edge and with a despairing lurch plunged in and tried to wade for safety of the slope beyond. The fireworm followed. But they had left it too late. The water was already too deep for her and she sank. For a little while the fireworm struggled to heave the submerged mass on, but then with a last agonising hoot gave up and collapsed and sank beside her.

Tandin watched for a while, but neither of them reappeared. His sense of exhausted triumph was threaded through with something different, something like regret, like loss. In their very strangeness, in the fireworm's tenderness towards his mate, in their love for each other, they had been wonderful. He was suddenly aware of his own utter isolation. The Blind Bear had told him he must fight the fire-worm alone, and so far he had simply accepted it, but now it struck him like the chill of winter whistling into the warmth of the cavern. Never before had he been on his own for so long. He had been born into a crowded cave, played and fought and learnt to do simple tasks with other children, dragged home logs with them as they grew older and stronger, helped the women gather food, run as a flanker on the hunt—never before anything like this. It was as if his only friends in the spirit world had been his enemies, the fireworms, and they were gone. And from now on it was going to be like this, always. Even when he was with the others back in the cave, inwardly it would be like this.

Sighing, he picked up the log. The flame still burnt, but far more feebly, and was weakening all the time. The spirit strength that had been his through the long night seemed to do the same, until he felt no more substantial than a puff of smoke. Like smoke he floated along the fissure, up the hole that the fireworm had made, and into the Home Cave. His kin still slept by the wall. The fire still burnt. He threw the log onto the embers and it burst into flame all along its length. He drifted between Sordan and Dotal, still watching by the entrance. Again, neither saw him pass. The bear pelt was where he had left it. He lay down and wrapped it round himself and gazed up at the sky. The moon was in the same place among the stars as it had been when he had entered the Home Cave. He drew a loose fold of the pelt over his head and went to sleep.

The hunters woke and ate before dawn, and at first light started down to the forest. Tandin slept on in the spirit world, so they didn't see him lying by the entrance. Instead, they found his body as they had left it, slung between two branches of the burial tree. They lowered him to the ground and realised that he was still breathing with faint, slow breaths, and that despite the freezing night his flesh was still as warm as meat might be on a summer morning. So they carried him up to the cave and set him down in the cleared space by the entrance and went into the cave to tell Nedli what they had done. She said that they must let him be and he would wake in his own time.

At dusk Tandin drifted up out of the spirit world and found himself in his own body, in the world where people live and die. He sat up, settled himself cross-legged and pulled the bear pelt over his shoulders. He saw the people going to and fro, preparing for the night and for a possible attack by the fireworm, but in his eyes they were like shadows or like dreams. They glanced or stared at him for a moment but left him alone. Someone brought out food for him from their evening meal and set it down by his side, but he didn't touch it. In his mind he was reliving everything that had happened, sorting through it, searching for its meaning.

It must have a meaning. It was a story that he had lived through, like one of Nedli's stories, a riddle. Nothing that had happened to him in the spirit world had changed anything. Before it could do that, everything had to be done again in the world where people live and die. He must fight the fireworm twice, the Blind Bear had told him. And using the same weapons. But the icicle was still in the spirit world, buried under the rocks in the fireworm's cavern, and the log was ashes on the fire in the Home Cave.

That was the riddle. The trick of a good riddle, Nedli said, is that things are and are not what they seem. The log had looked as if he might have used it as a sort of club, but what use would that have been against a creature like the fireworm? It hadn't become useful until he had thrust it into the fire, and then it had been the light that had guided him through the fissures and tunnels, and the bait that had lured the fireworm to him, and the heat that had released the stream of water from the icicle. And the icicle itself. It had looked as if he could have used it as a throwing-stake, but could he really have driven it through that thick and slithery hide to the monster's heart? And when he had struck his blow, flinging it down the fireworm's gullet, the fireworm had coughed it back out. But as soon as he had passed it through the flame of the log it had changed and become truly a weapon that he could use, first to drive off the fireworm and then drown both him and his mate.

So his true weapons had been not a bit of dead branch and a chunk of ice but the powers locked inside them, waiting to be freed. Fire and water, water and fire.

Everything else, he was confident, was as he had seen it. Nedli said that things in the spirit world were like reflections in still water. The clouds in a pool on a summer's day show what the clouds in the sky are like. You can shatter them with a thrown stone, but the clouds in the sky move on untroubled.

So the fireworm and his mate were still as he had seen them in the spirit world, and their nest was where he had found it, just below the glacier.

The glacier. Ice. Water waiting to be released. By fire. The lake that had been formed by a spark falling from the pelt of the Amber Bear. It opened every summer and froze over when the snows came, but was always there, deep in the heart of the glacier, a mass of water, more than enough to feed a torrent like that which had flooded into the fireworm's cave.

It was after midnight when Tandin came out of his trance. By then the food that had been left for him was frozen hard, so he took it into the cavern. Merip and Bond, watching by the entrance, rose staring to meet him. He greeted them quietly and went on, thawed the food by the fire and ate it. Then he wrapped himself in the bear pelt and lay down a little apart from the others and slept for a night and a day and a night.

◆ ◆ ◆

He woke a different man. Still Tandin, but changed. He had dreamed during that long sleep in the bear pelt that the spirits of all those who had worn it before him had each come to him in turn. They had spoken no word, but laid their fingers on his eyes and blown in his nostrils and their breath had carried into his mind all the secrets that each of them had known. Then they had left him with their blessings. He had started on his adventure as a young man without honour, a sleeper by the wall. He returned as confident in his own authority as if he'd been a long-time leader of the hunt.

When he woke and sat up, the others were already eating their morning meal. They fell silent, watching him. He was a spirit-walker, a figure of awe. He rose, drew the pelt over his shoulders, folding the forelegs together to hold it in place, and raised both hands in greeting. They returned the gesture, still in silence. He scooped a palmful of mashed root from the roasting-stone, beckoned to Nedli and went outside.

Though the sun had risen it had no strength, and the bitter night frost still hung in the air. It was too cold for an old woman, so when Nedli joined him he made her sit beside him, wrapped the bear pelt round both their bodies and kept her warm with his own warmth while he told her what he had done and seen.

"Tell the others," he said.

"Tonight," she answered.

"Good."

He sat for a while after she'd left him, simply becoming accustomed to his new self, then went down alone into the forest, where, still in the world where people live and die, he turned himself into a bear and began to become accustomed to that self also. He snuffled around, bear fashion. By smell he found a large, edible soil fungus, and a nest of honey bees in the leaf-litter at the bottom of a riven tree. He left them where they were for the moment but as the sun went down dug the fungus up and ripped the tree apart to get at the bees' nest. Then he stopped being a bear and with his clever human fingers hollowed the fungus out, putting the flesh inside into his pouch, so that he could scoop the honeycomb into the rind and carry it back for the evening meal.

So that evening they feasted, and when they'd done Nedli told them Tandin's Story. She had reshaped and reworded it, with many repetitions, and told it in the high, wavering story-teller's chant, making it into a story that would sit beside the stories of long-ago heroes that they all knew by heart, and would live in people's memories for generations after they were all dead. When she'd finished, Tandin explained what he thought the story meant and how it showed them the way to kill the fireworm. The hunters discussed it, of course, everyone having their say, or they wouldn't have been hunters, but no one disagreed, except about which of them should go.

"Let Tandin choose," suggested Merip, but Tandin shook his head.

"No," he said. "I am not the leader of the hunt. Let me be your tracker in the spirit world."

Clearly relieved, they picked Barok, and he chose six others, Vulka, Bast, Sordan, Dotal, Merip and Bond, to go with him. Next day they made ready, collecting food and extra furs, and binding them into bundles, and cutting shaped pieces of fir branch that they could bind to their feet and so walk on soft snow.

The morning after, Tandin was standing a little aside watching the rest of the party gather at the mouth of the cave with their families milling around them to wish them safely home when Mennel pushed her way out of the group and stood in front of him, her soft round features haggard, her firm young body sagging and listless, her brown eyes red with weeping. She, like all the others, knew the price he had paid, because Nedli had made that part of her story. He took her by the hands. She stared up into his face. Beneath the weeping, beyond the grief, he saw a bitter determination in her eyes. A bloodless whisper emerged from between his unmoving lips.

"Sister of my father, I have paid your price. This is Mennel. She is the pain of my wound. Give her to a good man."

He seemed to listen to an answer, but she heard nothing. She shook her head, refusing that future also, and turned away.

At this season, in the world where people live and die, it was a full two days' journey to the foot of the glacier, so at nightfall the hunters dug themselves a snow-hole in which to lie covered in furs and keep each other warm.

They did the same next night on the side of the valley in which the glacier lay, but this time Tandin didn't join them. Instead he turned himself into a bear, found a hollow under a fallen tree where he could safely leave his bear body for a while, and entered the spirit world. Once there, he started nosing along the snow-covered moraine, the tumble of rocks below the ice wall at the foot of the glacier, until he found the place he was looking for.

He knew it before he reached it. Just as, when he'd been spirit-walking through the fissures and tunnels that led to the fireworm's lair, the path along the ridge that he'd followed with the Blind Bear had become suddenly vivid overhead, so now he was instantly aware of the lair itself, vivid beneath his feet.

Having made sure of that, he climbed the moraine and nosed at the ice wall, probing for the spirits beyond it, different from those of the imprisoning ice—the spirit of the lake-water itself, and the spirit of fire, rising from deep below the mountain. Yes, of course.

That was the same heat that warmed the cavern and kept the lake from freezing when winter froze the world, and created a weakness in the ice wall that each spring, year after year, gave way and let the top half of the lake come roaring out, tumbling the rocks of the moraine aside and carving a deep gully down the mountain, while the covering ice collapsed and the remains of the lake were left open to the sky.

He was padding back towards the snow-hole where the others lay when a clamour of snarls broke out from the wooded slope on his left. Wolves, bringing down their prey. He turned aside and climbed between the snow-draped trees and found a small pack snarling and wrenching at the body of a young caribou.

Wolves will normally face and fight a single bear, however large, rather than leave their kill. But when Tandin growled at them the secret word that the hero Jerast had tricked out of the Wolf-father, the whole pack slunk away into the dark.

The caribou was struggling to rise. Tandin broke its neck with a blow and dragged the carcass back to the snow-hole. He buried it in a drift, meat for the next few days, then turned himself into the human Tandin and joined the sleepers under the furs.

They breakfasted before dawn and climbed down into the valley to look at the task ahead. Tandin showed the hunters where the fireworm's cavern lay.

"Good," said Barok, pointing at the cliff of ice towering above them, and the glittering ice-fall that had been the last outflow from the lake. "That's where the water's going to break through, so that's where we've got to melt the ice."

"We can't melt the whole fall," said Bond.

"The melt-water runs in the gully," said Bast, always on the look-out for anything he could object to. "It will put out the fire if we build it there."

"So we build two fires," said Dotal, "one to either side of the gully, right against the cliff. There's a lot of weight in that ice-fall. If we can weaken the cliff either side of it, it will pull the whole slab of cliff out."

"Another thing," said Vulka. "The timing's going to be tricky. We don't want the cliff breaking before the bastard's dug his hole up to our fires. Water's bound to put them out then, and he'll give up."

"Question is, how fast can the brute dig?" said Bond.

"And how long to melt the cliff?" said Sordan.

"Last thing, he was having a nap, Tandin said," said Merip.

They looked at Tandin.

"I don't know how fast he can dig," he said. "When he wakes and starts, perhaps. I'll see tonight, if I can."

"Right," said Barok. "We'll start by building a decoy fire. There." He pointed to a place a little way down the slope where the further wall of the gully had collapsed, half blocking it with a low pile of rock. "Best if he comes out there," he added. "Then, when the water fills the gully, it will flow down his hole. And tonight Tandin can see if the fire has woken him. All right? And we'll build two rock platforms close against the ice-cliff either side of the gully for our main fires. That way, when the melt-water starts to flow down the cliff it'll run out under the rocks. Then we'll all set about fetching fallen timber out of the woods."

"It'll all be wet," said Bast.

No one paid any attention. They were used to Bast. They shared the tasks out, and by the time the main party had heaved and trundled rocks from the moraine to build the platforms for the two larger fires, Vulka and Sordan had found enough small dry timber for Vulka to work his firebow and get the decoy fire started. Then they split into two groups and scoured the woods on the flanking slopes for burnable timber among the tangles of fallen branches and dragged it down to the gully. Tandin rested, minding the fire, and no one nagged or mocked him for not joining the work.

At nightfall the hunters retired exhausted to the snow-hole. Tandin joined them, but when it was his turn to keep watch, he fed the fire and then settled cross-legged with the bear pelt around him, entered the spirit world and probed with his spirit down through the snow and the permafrost into the rock beneath, and on down through that for the fireworm.

Yes. It was there, he sensed, but still sleeping. There was something uneasy about its sleep, though, like a troubled dream. How had it experienced their earlier encounter? he wondered. It can't have been totally unaware. Though, on the surface, events in the spirit world have no effect on their counterparts in the world where people live and die, at a deeper level they are the same event. Defeat and death in the spirit world aren't necessarily followed by defeat and death in this world. They may be felt only as a nightmare troubling the sleeper. But still, surely, there has to be some weakening, some loss.

Troubled himself, he didn't know why, Tandin withdrew from the spirit world, fed the fire and then watched the slow rising of the stars until it was time to go and wake Vulka.

Next day was much the same. All day they toiled at timber gathering, tying thongs to the butts of fallen trees and forming teams to drag them down to the glacier. At first Tandin joined the work and they seemed to welcome him, but still he didn't belong. They were a team of men, doing what men do—in the hunt, in guarding the cave from wild beasts, in confronting aggressors—understanding how these things were done by a team to achieve ends they couldn't have achieved as individuals. If Tandin had been merely a new recruit, they would have treated him roughly, putting him down, letting him make mistakes and then jeering at him for them and so on, until he had earned his place. Instead, they treated him with respect, warning him of risks, giving him the lighter end of a load, standing out of his way. It was not the same, and he sensed their hidden relief when he withdrew to rest after the midday meal.

By dusk they had enough piled up at the foot of the moraine for half a moon of ordinary fires, and had begun stacking it ready to light on the platforms either side of the gully. Meanwhile they let one side of their decoy fire burn down enough to provide a good bed of embers, and at nightfall roasted chunks of caribou meat over it and feasted, boasting and teasing, tossing the gnawed bones back into the fire.

That night, as before, they kept watch by turns, and as before, when Tandin's watch came round, he fed the fire and settled down and entered the spirit world. But this time there was no need to probe for the fireworms. Both of them were instantly clear to his inward senses, the female this time more strongly—her intense and desperate sudden need, her pleading. And his reluctance, his despair, his dread. He had nothing in his pouch to give her. The humans in the cave had driven him off with the terrible cold weapons of the outer world, and now, night after night, blocked his entry with the same things. They were ready to fight him again should he make a new tunnel. . . .

The cavern seemed to fill with the odour of charring flesh.

A change, a sudden attention, a focussing. A hope.

The fireworm had become aware of the new fire, almost directly over its head.

Now it began to move. Sideways at first—it couldn't reach the roof of the cavern to begin its tunnel—into the fissure, perhaps. . . . Ah, now, much more slowly it had begun to climb. It was drilling a fresh tunnel, upwards. Tandin could sense the steady, continuous effort, the pure power.

◆ ◆ ◆

Merip, whose turn it was to watch next, woke of his own accord and went to see what had become of Tandin. He found him sitting trance-held by the fire, so he kept his own watch and woke Bond in his turn. The others joined Bond before dawn for a breakfast of cold roast caribou and mashed root. Then they continued all morning with the task of gathering timber and were having their midday meal when Tandin returned to the world where people live and die.

When he woke, he told the hunters what he had seen.

"So how soon will the bastard finish his hole?" said Vulka. "He's been going for a night, roughly. How far has he got?"

"About a third of the way—a bit less, maybe," said Tandin.

"Give him a day and a night and a bit more—he'll be through tomorrow noon, then. We'd better get the big fires lit, Barok," said Bond.

"It doesn't matter if we don't get it melted till after he's through," said Barok. "The hole will be there."

"Provided he doesn't go blocking it up again," said Bast.

"I've been thinking," said Sordan, slowly, as if to indicate the speed of his thought processes. "They didn't wake up first night after we'd lit the fire, though it had been going long enough, surely— it was good and hot by then. But last night, all of a sudden, there was the female, wide awake and all eager. And Tandin said he smelt burnt meat down there. Right? Remember Denini and the birds' eggs?"

All the others laughed, even Merip, though the laughter was at him. He was a small, cheerful man, nothing like a typical hunter, never on his dignity but affable and easy-going. The women said that the other hunters had only allowed him to join them because he was a brilliant tracker. Denini was his woman, and he doted on her. When she'd been pregnant with her first child, she had craved birds' eggs, and Merip had had to spend good hunting days climbing trees to poke the nests down. The other hunters had mocked him for his solicitude, but he'd only laughed and said that it was for the sake of his unborn son, so that he could grow to be a hunter, fleet as a bird. And then the child had been a girl, and he'd doted on her too.

All this was good for a fresh round of teasing. Only Sordan, rapt in the seriousness of his thought, didn't join in.

"No, listen," he said, as soon as he got the chance. "What was the difference between last night's fire and the one before? Answer, we'd roasted caribou and chucked the bones on it. Now suppose somehow the female had gone and smelt that, down there—suppose Tandin had taken it down with him—"

"No need for any of that supposing," said Vulka. "What Tandin does is a sort of dreaming, far as I can make out. So you're dreaming, and a gust of wind blows a bit of smoke towards you, and you smell it in your sleep and make it part of your dream. Right, Tandin?"

"I don't think so," said Tandin slowly. "I started my watch well past midnight, and there wasn't any meat smell then, not with this wind. And I suppose there is something a bit like Denini about the female—"

"She's not fat, not even when she's whelping," said Merip indignantly. "And she doesn't hoot either."

That, and the whole absurd idea, was good for a fresh bout of laughter and teasing, which finished with Barok saying, "Well, I reckon we'll get the big fires lit before we pack in tonight, and if all we've got to do to bring the brute up here is sling our scraps into the fire, it's no great hardship."

He set the example with the rib-bone he'd been gnawing, and they all went back to work.

That afternoon they lit bundles of small stuff at their fire and poked them into the tunnels they had left for that purpose in the main wood-piles. More small dry stuff already laid in the tunnels quickly caught, and almost at once the flames were racing up through the logs with a jerky, scampering movement like squirrels running up a tree. Even in their weariness and anxiety the men laughed in triumph as both piles roared into flame.

Almost at once the fires were too hot to stand beside, and soon it was impossible to approach them for more than a few instants. The men had to choose their moment, strip off their furs, dart in with a branch or log, fling it onto the furnace and dart away. The flare lit the wooded slopes on either side of the valley. Now, from any distance, they could see how the separate updraughts either side of the ice-fall were carving two steadily widening and deepening slots into the cliff. A stream of melt-water came gushing down them, under the boulders of the platforms, down into the gully, where they became a single stream, slicing into the snow in the bottom of the gully, freezing into fresh ice-falls as they tumbled from boulder to boulder.

The three combined fires would have given light enough to work all night, but after a while the hunters became anxious that the ice wall would give way too early, so they broke off for their supper and then four of them left to rest in their snow-hole, while the others continued to feed the fires. Tandin took no part in their work now, but sat alone and apart, deliberately upwind of where they had eaten. Deep in the spirit world, immune to the appalling cold, he watched the fireworm's progress. Again the smell of charred meat seemed to reek through the cavern, and again each time the fire-worm returned there to rest the female soon drove it back with fresh entreaties. As it neared the surface Tandin began to be able to sense the exact point at which it might emerge. Sure enough, it seemed to be aiming not for the two great blazes by the ice wall, but for the far smaller decoy fire, where the hunters had roasted their meat.

Soon after sunrise, when the hunters hauled their first load of fresh timber out from the woods on the western slope, they found three men standing on the edge of the gully, staring up at the deep cuts that the fires had carved into the cliff either side the of ice-fall. They turned when Barok hailed them and came striding across the rocks, frowning, hands on axe-helves.

"The one on the left is Findri," muttered Dotal. "I gave him my elder daughter. They come from Upmountain Cave. Let me speak to him."

The others watched as he walked confidently forward to greet his son-in-law, calling his name. The scowls softened only slowly as he gestured and explained. The strangers turned to stare at Tandin, sitting wrapped in the bear pelt, as motionless as the rocks around him. Dotal came smiling back.

"Tricky," he said. "The glacier's their protecting spirit. But they've had the fireworm too—drove it off the same way we did—knew the stories, of course—they'd be glad to be shot of it. I told 'em what Tandin did. It's a good four generations since they'd a spirit-walker in their cave. They're going to give us a hand."

With the extra workers the log-stacks were quickly replenished and the fires roared up anew. The stream in the gulley was now a torrent. Twice more Tandin returned to the world where people live and die and told the workers that the fireworm was very near and looked like breaking through well before dark, but the third time it was different. Only a man's height from the surface and directly below the decoy fire, the fireworm had stopped digging and gone back to the cavern. Despite all the female's unceasing pleadings and scoldings, it was now deep asleep. But he had sensed no sudden alarm or caution before the withdrawal, only a feeling more like weary satisfaction.

"It's waiting till nightfall," he said.

The men had stopped work to eat and were sitting on the lower boulders of the moraine, gnawing the last bits and pieces of caribou and tossing the stripped bones down into the nearer of the two fires. Now they began to argue about when the ice wall would give way. As the fires had carved into the cliff either side of the ice-fall, the two competing teams had driven them steadily deeper by swinging fresh logs clean over the blazing piles to feed the further sides. The funnelling effect increased the updraughts, and large logs began to crumble into embers almost as soon as they had burst alight. In the short time the men had been eating, both fires had reduced themselves to great, glowing mounds and the noise from them dwindled to a fluttering murmur. In a pause in the talk the ice wall groaned.

The sound wasn't huge, just a slow, deep creak. They froze, and looked up at the ice-fall, towering almost immediately over them.

"Let's be getting out of here," said Barok.

The sound had hauled Tandin from his dream. He woke and heard the men calling to him as they scrambled down the moraine, and followed them along the track they'd cleared through the snow by their steady hauling of timber down from the hillside. Where the ground began to slope upward, they halted and turned.

It was now half-way through the short afternoon. The air, freezing even at midday, was already chilling fast, and seemed bitingly cold to bodies that a little while ago had been almost sweating in the glow from the fires. Again Tandin moved a few paces apart and returned to the spirit world, while the others huddled down in the lee of a low crag and waited to see what would happen.

Twice more the ice wall groaned, loud enough for the men to hear where they sat. But the fires were visibly shrinking. They seemed to glow as strongly as ever, but that was only in contrast to the fading light. Much as the cold of the coming night crept into their bodies, so tension, boredom and impatience suffused their minds. Continually they glanced to where Tandin sat oblivious and withdrawn. He gave them no sign at all until, with the last light fading and the stars plain to see, they heard a voice. Not Tandin's voice, but a voice speaking directly to them out of the spirit world, forcing itself between his unmoving lips, as eerie as the groan of the glacier:

"The fireworm wakes. He comes."

The hunters tensed, staring at the heaped embers of the decoy fire. Its outline blurred and wavered as the rising heat sucked in night-frosted air from the sides, heated it in an instant and drove it upward. Twice more the glacier groaned. None of them perceived the actual moment of change, the point at which the fireworm broke through and the embers began to slither down into the shaft it had drilled. The first they knew of it was a shuddering indrawn sigh from Tandin, and his own voice saying, "He's come. He's here."

Now they could see the ember-pile collapsing, sifting away inward and down. When it was two-thirds gone, with a pit at the centre and the sides of the surrounding pile no longer steep enough for the embers to tumble down, it stopped.

They waited, expecting no more. But now a shape began to emerge above the dully glowing heap, rising further and further—the huge, blunt snout of the fireworm, then its massive head and shoulders, black against the still fierce glow of the two main fires. The hunters leaped to their feet, gripping axes and spears, poised to charge down on their enemy. The hunt was on, and Barok took control. They looked at him for the order.

"Wait," he said. "He will hide in his hole. Let him come farther."

Somehow wedging itself with its hind legs against the walls of its shaft, the fireworm reached out and began systematically scooping the remaining embers towards itself, rotating its body in the pit as it did so, in order to clear the whole ring.

"When his back is towards us," said Barok.

They waited.

"Why do we not sleep?" muttered someone. "All slept in the stories."

"Too far?" suggested someone else. "Or his breath is blown away, out here."

"Move forward," said Barok. "No, wait, he has heard us."

The fireworm, its back now almost towards them, had paused in its steady rhythm of work, and visibly tensed, like an animal suddenly alert. Its great head angled up, but as if to sniff rather than listen. Puzzled, they watched it heave its whole body out of the shaft and start to crawl towards the nearer of the two main fires, moving with great difficulty over the rock-strewn slope because it was dragging beneath it, immensely distended and glowing with the stolen embers, the pouch that Tandin had seen in the cavern. And still it wanted more.

Seen like that, despite its size, it looked utterly vulnerable and clumsy.

"Now," whispered Barok.

The hunters stole confidently forward.

The fireworm reached the nearer fire, but instead of scooping up embers wholesale, as it had done before, it began to pick and nose through the fringes, choosing only here and there. The hunters were about half-way towards it when the glacier groaned again.

They paused. This was a different noise, with a sharp, cracking onset and then rising and increasing.

"Back!" shouted several voices, and they had already turned and were racing and scrambling over the rocks when the ice-cliff gave way and all other sounds were swallowed in its thunder.

Only Tandin, watching from the slope where they had waited, saw it happen. There was no visible warning. The sheer ice split open like a seedpod either side of the ice-fall. The section of the cliff that held it tilted out and crashed down between the fires, and the dark green wall of prisoned water launched itself into white and bellowing freedom. The central gully vanished in an instant. The fires were drowned. A few instants more and the fleeing hunters, though already on rising ground, were struggling in the fringes of the flood. Tandin saw one man swept away, and another almost, but grabbed from a rock by Bast and hauled to safety as he passed below. The survivors scrambled up the slope, glancing now and then over their shoulders at what they'd just escaped. When all were well above the flood-line they turned to look. Too exhausted by their efforts, too stunned by the colossal re-sults, they were in no mood to exult or triumph, but could only stand and stare sombrely at the careering water.

Of the fireworm they could see no sign.

They found its body next morning, as they followed the still roaring torrent down the mountainside, looking for their lost comrade, a hunter from the other cave named Illok. They had no luck with him, but they came across the fireworm lying sprawled among the rocks where the first great outrush had hurled it. Its pouch had relaxed in death, losing almost all the embers it had so striven for, and lay in flabby folds beside its belly.

Though they had seen the monster the night before, that had

been at a distance and in the uncertain glow of the ember-piles. Now they could stand round it and realise its true size.

At first they merely prodded the body with their feet and poked at it with their spears. Then Sordan slapped Barok on the shoulder, Dotal loosed the hunter's yodelling cry that signals a successful end to the hunt, and in a moment they were all glorying in their achievement, whooping and prancing and baying to the skies, the sound of their voices floating up over the snowfields towards the summit of the mountain.

Once again Tandin stood to one side. His feelings were very different from theirs, and at the same time utterly different from his exhausted but triumphant return after his contest with the fireworm in the spirit world. There was no hero in this part of the story. This had been something else, a team of men bringing off a difficult and dangerous task. Nedli might tell the tale, so that people in after time could know of a way to kill a fireworm, but she wouldn't do it in the manner in which she told her stories of heroes, because it is in the spirit world that they do their great deeds, not here.

Sordan was trying to hack off one of the fireworm's feet, to take back to the cave as a sacred object to hang on the wall, but his sharpest flint made not a scratch in the monster's hide.

That was as it should be, Tandin thought dreamily. He felt a strange fellowship with the fireworm, far deeper than he felt with the rejoicing hunters. It too didn't belong in the world where people live and die. No weapon of this world should harm it, even in death. It had taken a spirit force, the huge, cold spirit force of the lake, to destroy it. That was what the Blind Bear had been telling him when she'd given him his weapons in her cave.

His dream-state deepened. There was life of a kind still there in the great carcass, he realised. Just as a light still gleams in the eyes of a deer after the blood has stopped pulsing from the death wound and the breathing died away, so there was something, some last element of the fireworm's fiery being, still seeping out of its cooling hulk. But not out into this world above the rocks, into its bitter cold and wet. Back down into the world of fire beneath the mountains.

Like a lone wolf on a scent, Tandin followed the difficult trail, down and yet further down, until he entered the world of fire, and became one of its creatures. There were other creatures there, of many kinds, just as there are in this world above, and just as people were the masters here, so were fireworms in the world below. They had thoughts, like people, and loves, and longings.

They lived in the heart of the fires below, and fed upon substances in the fiery rocks, but they could not give birth there. Just as toads must leave the air to mate and lay their eggs, so a pregnant fireworm must go up among the chill rocks above to give birth, and her mate must carry up burning rocks to keep her and her unborn brood alive.

That was hard, but not dangerous, unlike her other need. To feed those unborn young she must have substances that couldn't be found among the rocks, but only out in the dreadful world above, in places where a fire has consumed the flesh of some animal and its ashes are scattered among the embers. This might happen, perhaps, where forest creatures have been trapped in a blaze, but far more reliably where humans make their lairs and roast their meat.

Perhaps that was only a guess, but the love was certain. The love of the fireworms for each other, and her need, and his courage in trying to satisfy it. He had watched over her, cosseted her, fostered her and made long and dangerous forays into the world above to fetch the precious substances—all so that the marvellous race of the fireworms should not be lost. And he had failed.

Tandin came dazedly back into the world of air with this thought in his mind, that what had happened was not a triumph, but a tragedy. And there was a hero in this part of the story after all, the one now lying defeated on the icy rocks of Bear Mountain with the hunters rejoicing round him. Some of the best of Nedli's stories, the ones that sang on in the mind long after she'd told them, were like that, tales of a hero who had triumphantly performed mighty deeds, and in the end perished in fulfilling the final one. Did the fireworms in the furnaces below the mountains tell each other such tales? And who would go back to the world of fire below to tell them what had happened?

But the story should still be told, if not there, then here. When a hero is forgotten, he dies a second death. Yes, once they were back at the cave the people there would want to know everything that had happened, and then one day, not yet, Tandin would take Nedli aside and tell her his thoughts, so that she could make a new story, as strange as any that she already told, The Fireworm's Story, to live in people's minds for generations not yet born.

Spring came. The hillsides streamed and the ice-locked rivers loosed themselves and roared and foamed with snow-melt waters. The days drew level with the nights and the Amber Bear returned from his wanderings, dragging the sun with him, and the Blind Bear woke and together they fought the Great White Owl and amid ferocious gales drove him northward.

This year there were no uncoupled young men in the Home Cave to go journeying to the other caves along the range in search of a woman for themselves. But the White Owl had taken Golan's woman, Sinasin, with a sickness he caused, first making her very sad and then, one night in the darkest part of the year, causing her to slip away while the watchers were changing places and lie down in the snow on her fur with nothing to cover her. Golan had found her there, frozen and dead, in the morning. So now he went to look for a new woman, confident that as a seasoned hunter he could have his choice. As well as the usual gifts he took something even more welcome, a new story, Tandin's story, which he told from cave to cave along the mountain range.

Now all summer others beside the woman-seekers came visiting the Home Cave on various excuses, but in fact to gaze at the hero, and Tandin found himself more and more marked out and set apart. So it had been all his life, one way or another. First he had been pushed aside as a fatherless child and a man without honour. Now he was the son of the Amber Bear. A hero. A spirit-walker who had paid as great a price as any of the old heroes. No one despised him for this, as they would have despised any other womanless man. It was a matter for awe.

But the aloneness was hard to bear, so more and more he retreated into the spirit world to roam the ghost paths and converse with the spirits of trees and of waterfalls. There was great kindness in trees, and great wisdom in waterfalls, a deep understanding of the flux and change of the world. The visitors to the cave would find him sitting all by himself on the bear pelt, his eyes like stones, his breathing slow and deep, his flesh chill to the touch, and know that he was spirit-walking far from that place, and stare at the hero.

One afternoon late in summer Tandin was on such a journey when he felt himself suddenly called—he didn't know how, or by whom. But the call was urgent, a desperate need, so he sped back along the ghost-paths and re-entered the world where people live and die. He found himself sitting in his usual place, on the bear pelt, and looking at a small group in front of the cave, two visitors listening to Nedli, and at the same time gazing at him with the usual wondering stare, and, a little apart from them, Bast, Mennel and another stranger, a man about Bast's age.

Bast was talking to the stranger, but Mennel was gazing at Tandin with a totally different look from that of the wonder-seekers, a despair and need so piercing that it had somehow broken through into the spirit world and called him here. And something else. For her—perhaps for her alone in all the world—Tandin was still who he had always been. But there was no hope in her look. She too knew the price he had paid.

He gazed at her dreamily, and for a moment he became a woman, thought a woman's thoughts, felt her feelings as she stood being bartered away by her father to be some stranger man's, his possession, his toy, his child-bearer.

All fell silent as he rose and drew the pelt over his shoulders. They watched to see what he would do. As he walked across he seemed to them to be floating an invisible distance above the ground. Bast and the stranger fell back a pace. Tandin took Mennel by the shoulders. She closed her eyes, and he licked them and sealed them shut and drew her to his side, pulling the bear pelt round her to enfold them both.

"Be a bear," he muttered in her ear.

She rubbed herself against him, flank to flank, purring deep in her throat. The stranger bowed his head in acceptance while Bast visibly calculated the prestige that might accrue to him from this new alliance.

Keeping pace without effort, Tandin and Mennel started down the path, still with the bear pelt around them. As they drew further away the shape they made seemed to become less and less like that of two humans wrapped in an animal's skin and more like the hindquarters of two shorter, bulkier beasts walking close together. By the time they disappeared into the forest, that was indeed what they might have been.

SALAMANDER MAN

PETER DICKINSON

Long before the man reached Aunt Ellila's stall, Tib recognised him as a magician. Though many people practised cottage magic, the high magic practised by professional magicians was illegal throughout the country. But the town of Haballun chose to be different, in this and many other ways.

Slavery, for instance. This was also illegal, yet Tib himself was a slave, bought by Aunt Ellila direct from the school, with an enforceable guarantee from the Guild that if he escaped and was free for more than a month, the purchaser would be compensated by a payment twenty times his purchase price. To make the guarantee effective, the Guild had hired a magician to design a system whereby each slave was branded on his left shoulder-blade and the brand then tattooed with an individual mark, linked to a scrying stone in the Guild head office. If Tib went missing, a clerk would dig out his sale-parchment and lay the stone on the copy of his mark, and an image would appear in the crystal showing exactly where he was hiding. Once recaptured, he would be punished for as long as he had been free in a manner that caused intense pain but did no physical damage, and then returned to his owner. As part of his schooling Tib had been made to watch would-be escapers undergoing this torment. Since he had been brought to the school almost newborn, he had sometimes wondered what freedom might be like, but if he'd ever felt tempted to try it he had only to reach over his left shoulder and feel the ridges and hollows of the brand to abandon the idea.

Aunt Ellila wasn't in fact a bad owner compared to some that Tib had heard of. "Aunt" was a purely formal title, dating back to the early days of the system, when owners needed to pretend to be blood relatives of their slaves in order to have an apparent right to keep them as servants. If Tib had had an actual aunt or uncle he would have called them "Gada This" or "Gado That."

Tib was Aunt Ellila's only slave. He cleaned the house and ran errands, but his main job was to help stack the heavy hand-cart and then haul it down to the market in the morning, with Aunt Ellila walking beside it and carrying the basket of her more fragile stock on her head. He then unstacked the cart, set it up as a stall, rigged the awnings and the screened area behind it, assembled the shelves and showcases, and finally unpacked the crates and brought the goods to Aunt Ellila to arrange as she wanted them. During the long, hot day he ran errands, parcelled up items sold, and so on, and minded the stall in the slack period at midday while Aunt Ellila went off to Defri's bar to dice and drink bhang soda with her cronies.

At other times he sat in the shade of the awning, apparently asleep but in fact on the look-out for sneak-thieves, the market police, and other trouble-makers. He was extremely good at this. It was what Aunt Ellila had bought him for and trained him to do from the first day she'd had him. A few months back a couple of other stall-holders had come round getting up a petition for more police patrols. What was the point? Aunt Ellila had asked them. It would only mean more police for the thieves to bribe, and so more theft to finance the bribes. Much better buy a kid like Tib, who could spot a gang at work a dozen stalls off, so that she could pass the word to her neighbours and they'd be ready for the bastards.

Magicians were a different kind of trouble. They were a lot harder to spot, for a start. It wouldn't be anything to do with the man himself, of course. This one, as usual, looked as ordinary as magic could make him—middle-aged, a bit tubby, brownish stubble, green headcloth, standard linen long coat, baggy pants, sandals and the vague air of a citizen with three or four everyday errands to do.

It was the way the crowd moved round him that was the tell-tale. The space between the stalls was thronged. No magician likes to be touched, unless he has chosen to be. There is always some slight leakage of power, so he sees that it doesn't happen. The throng between the stalls was a glutinous current, with slow eddies and churnings, stoppages and swifter impulses. But this man moved through it at his own pace, pausing briefly in front of each stall. When he did so, no one jostled into him. When he wanted to move on, a gap appeared in front of him, though whoever had been blocking his path only an instant before might be looking the other way. Tib spotted him for a magician as clearly as if he'd had a sphinxlet perched on his shoulder.

Tib yawned and stretched. His right arm, as if by accident, touched a wind-charm into tinkles. Rapidly he stilled the chime by closing his palms together over the cylinders. By the time he let go Aunt Ellila was re-arranging her stock, moving some items aside and bringing others into view, which she hadn't wanted any casual stall-browsers deciding to buy on a whim.

Her trade was in good-quality knick-knacks, jewellery and ornaments, bought either at house-sales or from other stalls. It was surprising how many people possessed, without knowing it, useless-looking objects of the kind that in fact had magical purposes, some startlingly powerful in the right hands. Aunt Ellila did not herself practise magic—not one of the twenty-seven magicians in Haballun was a woman—but was the fifth in her family to trade from this pitch, each generation teaching the next how to recognise such things. She had no children, but a twelve-year-old niece would be coming shortly to train as her apprentice, and eventually perhaps to inherit the business. Most of the twenty-seven magicians would look by from time to time to see if she'd picked up anything new, but Tib had no way of knowing if this was one of the regulars, as they all had spells on their doorways that changed their appearance whenever they went out.

The man paused, as expected, in front of Aunt Ellila's stall, but this time stepped closer. With a glance at Aunt Ellila for permission to touch, he picked up one by one the objects she had brought into view. Most he put straight back. Some he inspected longer. A few he weighed in his palm, closing his eyes, and put aside. Tib paid little attention. All this was standard magician stuff, and the market gangs weren't beyond having one of their number play the part to distract attention while they went about their work. But he was instantly aware when the dynamics of the sale shifted.

He glanced across. Aunt Ellila had a charming smile, and was using it to the full, but her eyes were narrowed. That meant, Tib had learnt, that she suspected a customer knew something about an object that gave it a greater value than she'd been going to ask. So he was surprised to see that the magician had picked out the broken camel toy. This was, or had been, a mechanical novelty with, as far as Tib knew, no magical properties at all. It consisted of a statuette of a camel standing under a banana-palm, gazing up at the unreachable fruit. A silk cord ran into the base, which, when pulled, was supposed to cause the camel to rear up and try to reach the bananas. It might have been worth a quick smile if it had worked. Tib had spent several evenings trying to get it to do so, without luck, and now Aunt Ellila only kept it on display as something to catch the eye, and in the faint hope that some fool of a customer might think he'd have more success.

The magician put it on the counter and pulled the cord. Nothing happened, but he picked it up all the same and held it between his hands. Watching him from behind, Tib could see no change in his appearance, but for a blink of time he ceased to be ordinary and became a presence, his true self. The next instant he had veiled that self in ordinariness. He put the camel back on the stall and pulled the cord again. The camel reared up and stretched with absurd, hopeless longing for the bananas.

Aunt Ellila clapped her hands. The magician replaced the camel on the shelf where he'd found it and assembled the objects he'd chosen. Aunt Ellila fetched two stools, and they settled down to bargain. Tib watched the passing crowd.

After a little while Aunt Ellila called to him.

"Just go and fetch us a couple of mugs of bhang, Tib. Mint for me, and . . . ? Mint for the gentleman too. And a pot of honey-jellies, but go to Selig's for those—they're better than Defri's. Take the money out of the till. Good boy."

Tib showed her the coins he'd taken and set off, going to Selig's first, at the other end of the market, rather than carry the bhang there and back through the throng. Selig's honey-jellies came from the same cook as Defri's, which meant Aunt Ellila wanted him out of the way, so he took his time. But Aunt Ellila enjoyed a good haggle, so he was surprised to find on his return that the bargaining was over. She and the magician were sitting where he'd left them but rose as he approached. Aunt Ellila was holding herself stiffly and not smiling at all. The magician sipped briefly at his bhang and put the mug down.

"Excellent," he said. "I will fetch the registrar's clerk."

He slipped into the crowd. Tib put the honey-jellies on the stall and handed Aunt Ellila the change. She threw it into the till un-counted, snapped the drawer shut and held out both hands in the imploring gesture of a street beggar.

"Oh, Tib," she croaked. "I'm sorry. I'm truly sorry. I . . . I've just sold you."

Tib's jaw fell open. He stared.

"I hope you got a good price," he managed to say.

"Beyond belief," she said, shaking her head. "Impossible. But . . . Tib, I told him I still didn't want it. Nothing would be enough. I . . . I've been hoping, when Zorya comes . . . you and she. . . . If she married you, then we could free you, and then you could run the stall together, and look after me when I'm too . . . too—"

She hid her head in her shawled sleeve and wept. Utterly stunned and bewildered, Tib put his arm round her shoulders and held her to him. Zorya was the niece who was coming to be her apprentice, but Aunt Ellila had never given him the slightest hint of the rest of her plans. He felt much as he had during the delirium of fever three years back, too dazed to think, too numb to feel.

The sobs eased. Aunt Ellila straightened, shook her hair out and used her shawl to dry her tears.

"He said it had to be you and no one else," she said angrily. "Something about a sign—that stupid camel—gods, I wish I'd chucked it out! So when he saw I wasn't just talking your price up, that I wasn't going to take *any* price, he . . . he . . . look!"

She reached into her neckline and hauled out the chain that hung there. Like everyone in the city who could afford it, she wore a collection of amulets against enchantments. They wouldn't have been much use against a professional magician, but it was still worth paying for protection against cottage-cursers, and the surpris-ing number of people who lived wholly unaware of their abilities and used them by accident. Tib had never seen Aunt Ellila's amulets, but thanks to the nature of her business, they would have been more effective than most. Now all that was left of the nine little symbols, tokens and figures that had dangled from the chain was a few splinters of bone, melted blobs and shreds of fabric.

"That was to show me what he could do if I refused," she said. "He was perfectly fair and open about it. He's even given me a replacement which he says will be a lot more use—I'm not going to wear it till I've had Dr. Cacada take a look at it, of course. And he's sticking to the ridiculous price he offered, but . . . oh, Tib, I didn't see what else I could do!"

"No . . ." said Tib slowly. "You've done your best. You've done your best for me all along, really. I've been extremely lucky. I owe you a lot, and I'm not going to forget it."

She looked at him, shaking her head, again on the verge of tears.

"You're a good boy," she said. "I'd like to give you something to remember me by. I was keeping it for when . . . when you. . . . Come."

She led the way into the curtained lair behind the stall where she dozed off her lunchtime bhang. It seemed to contain nothing besides the roll of mattress and the head-pillow that Tib had ferried to and fro every day since he'd been strong enough to push the cart, but she knelt, unhooked a few fastenings at the side of the roll and pulled out several small linen and leather bags. She put one aside, hid the rest back in the mattress and rose with the chosen bag in her hand.

"I suppose I've really known all along it was meant for you," she said. "Long before. . . . Anyway, the day I came to look for a slave, there was a beggar outside the school selling trashy little trinkets. Of course I looked his stuff over, the way I do. There was nothing on his tray worth even a glance, except this. I knew at once it had powers, though I'd no idea what they were. Still haven't. I bought it for a song and put it in my purse, but then . . . I hadn't actually been meaning to buy a slave that day—just wanted to see what was on offer, then go home and think about it, but the moment I saw you. . . . Anyway, oh, months later, when I was sitting over my bhang one evening, and you'd cleared supper and curled up in your cot and gone to sleep, I was thinking about what a lucky choice I'd made when I found you and fiddling around inside my bag for one of my little combs I'd put in it, but it had slipped down behind the lining, and so had this. I'd completely forgotten about it. I suppose that was why I'd never put it on sale, because it would be a bit like selling a piece of you, and now . . . and now . . . I'm going to lose you anyway, so you may as well take it. . . . Aren't you even going to look at it?"

Still in his daze of shock and grief, Tib found she'd already put the bag in his hands. He fumbled the cord loose and groped inside. His fingers touched something soft and flexible—a ribbon, he thought, but when he drew it out he found a golden band, not gold thread, but too soft and flexible to be wire. Running it through his fingers, he came to a stiffer part and found himself being stared at by two small purple eyes—jewels of some kind—and now he could see the shape of the head woven into the mesh. The thing was a small golden lizard. A pair of stubby clawed legs dangled beside the body, with another pair beyond. By then the body had begun to narrow towards the tail, but before he came to the tip there was the head again, lying, he now saw, on the hinder end of the body, with the tail itself coiling neatly round the neck.

"I think it's an arm-band," said Aunt Ellila, and then, as he slipped the band onto his wrist, "Careful! Take it off at once if . . ."

The band dangled loose and harmless from Tib's wrist, so he slipped it up to the thicker muscle above the elbow, where it seemed to fit snugly. The dangling legs spread themselves, and the feet, without actually gripping, seemed to adhere lightly to the skin, like those of a wall-climbing gecko. A faint shimmer ran through the mesh and, without any movement he could sense, it seemed to lose substance and fade until for a moment he could see his skin through it. Then it was gone, melted into the flesh of his upper arm.

Aunt Ellila put out a trembling hand and lightly touched the place, but instantly snatched it back with a cry of pain and sucked at the first three fingers. When she withdrew them from her mouth Tib saw that the fingertips were scorched white, as if she had laid them on a hot roasting pan. But when, gingerly, he held his palm over the place and then himself touched it, he could feel nothing but his own natural warmth.

At that point the magician returned with a clerk wearing the badge of the Slavemaster's Guild on the shoulder of his long coat and carrying a writing-case and a small parchment roll. Aunt Ellila cleared a space on the counter and the clerk unrolled the parchment, weighting the corners with knick-knacks from the stall. He told Tib to take off his smock and compared the tattoo on his shoulder with the copy on the parchment. By now Aunt Ellila was weeping openly.

"It's not that uncommon for owners to become over-involved with a slave," the clerk said chattily, as if neither Aunt Ellila nor Tib was present. "Women with younger men, especially. It's less offensive the other way round, of course—we'd have broken this relationship if we'd known of it. Come now, madam. . . ."

The magician turned and gazed coldly at him. The clerk doubled in pain, clutching his side. The magician nodded. The clerk straightened, pale and sweating.

"You should see a leech for that problem, my friend," said the magician, still unsmiling. His glance flicked for a moment to Tib, as if to check that he had seen the episode and understood.

From then on the clerk went efficiently about his business, clearly anxious to get it over. He wrote three lines on a fresh sheet of parchment, which Aunt Ellila and the magician signed. He took Tib's left hand, pressed the thumb onto an ink-pad and then onto the parchment below the signatures and compared the imprint to the much smaller one on the original deed of sale. As he did so, Tib was able to look briefly at this. His eye was caught by the one almost blank line on the crowded sheet—"Parentage:" and then, simply, a dash.

Lastly the clerk watched as the magician counted out the payment to Aunt Ellila, made a note of it on the new document and sealed that with the Guild seal and attached it to the original. He accepted his fee and left. Tib hadn't been surprised to see that his own price was nothing out of the ordinary—the Guild had strict rules—but as soon as the clerk had gone the magician gestured towards the items he'd originally chosen from the stall and counted out more coins from his purse—six of them, gold, and larger than Tib's thumbnail. Tib knew all Aunt Ellila's asking prices, as well as what she'd happily settle for. If the coins had been only silver, they'd have bought half her wares. She picked them up as if in a dream, shaking her head and still barely mastering her tears. The magician seemed not to notice.

"You'll need a man to help you home with your goods," he said.

"I . . . I'll find somebody," muttered Aunt Ellila.

The magician crooked a finger as if beckoning somebody from among the passers-by. A wizened little man squirmed his way through. His smile was so wide it seemed to split his face in half. His ears were upside down.

"Help the lady home," said the magician. "Stay with her as long as she needs you, and then go back to the place from which you came. No earth-wandering. Now, boy, say your farewell and come with me."

As Tib was stammering his thanks and good-byes, Aunt Ellila glanced sidelong at the magician.

"Tib," she whispered, "that thing you're wearing—it's more than a protection, much more. And the man who sold it to me—it's not the same man, but there was something about him. . . . And this man—those things he bought, he doesn't need them. And they're dangerous—in the wrong hands, I mean. But he's a good man, all the same. I'm sure of it. You'd better go now. . . . You've been a good boy. . . . Think of me sometimes."

Choking, Tib forced himself to turn away. The magician had been waiting for him without apparent impatience, but as soon as he saw Tib moving he turned and strode rapidly off. Anxiously Tib hurried to catch up with him before they were separated by the scrum, but found that he need not have worried because the magical influence now seemed to extend to him, so that no matter how quickly he moved or what path he chose, there was always a pace or two of clear ground immediately ahead of him, though nobody seemed deliberately to move aside to make way for him. All did so for their own reasons.

As they passed the roast-crab stall the magician tossed the little parcel of what he'd bought from Aunt Ellila onto the brazier, which immediately erupted into an amazing flare of coloured lights. Again, nobody seemed to notice. All heads other than Tib's happened to be turned away.

Yes, Tib thought. Aunt Ellila had been right. The magician had had no need of his purchases, except to be able to make up the slave-price, so he'd deliberately bought stuff that would be danger-ous in the wrong hands and then destroyed it. A good magician was said to be rarer than the Phoenix, and there was never more than one of those at a time. But this was a good man.

They reached wider and less crowded streets, through which the magician strode on, not once looking round. Tib was starting to pant with the effort of keeping up by the time they turned from a main thoroughfare into a narrow, windowless alley. The magician strode, unpausing, at a closed door that opened to let him pass and closed as soon as Tib had followed. They crossed a bare courtyard, unswept for a year. Dead leaves and scraps cluttered the paving. They descended a musty-smelling stairway into darkness, but the magician moved in a mist of pale light that Tib could follow down, and then along a stone corridor. A heavy door swung open, and again shut as soon as Tib too was through.

The magician faced him, smiling for the first time.

"Hard quarters, I'm afraid," he said. "There is a reason, you will find. I cannot explain. My time is up. Good—"

With an explosive snap as the air rushed to fill the space where he had been, he was gone, and Tib was left in darkness.

It took him a little while to realise that he was naked. He knelt and felt around for his clothes, but found nothing but close-fitted paving stones. It was the same when he explored the walls. They were bare masonry, apart from the door through which he had come and a window-opening in the adjacent wall, with a hefty iron grill, its bars as thick as his two thumbs laid together back to back.

A minor strangeness struck him. Why didn't he feel chilly without his clothes, down in this sunless cell, after hustling through the hot and crowded streets? He didn't, in fact, feel any sensation of temperature at all, apart, perhaps, from a faint inner glow emanating from his upper right arm and now beginning to spread quietly along his veins and nerves. This, he guessed, must come from the arm-band, and was the now-germinating seed of whatever was coming next.

He felt perfectly calm about it, as if he were merely a spectator, fully aware of what was happening to the young man in the cellar, but at the same time completely inside it. He, Tib, the young slave who had said farewell to his owner with such heartfelt grief less than an hour ago, was now two separate entities: a new, emotionless Tib occupying the body in the cellar, and the old Tib, the real Tib, a disembodied watcher.

He settled down with his back against the wall to wait. Something, obviously, had to happen. Everything so far today, since the arrival of the magician at Aunt Ellila's stall—no, since long before that, if she was right about the man who had sold her the arm-band the day she went to the slave school to look for him—perhaps further back still—had been part of some purpose. It couldn't end here.

Perhaps he slept. If so he didn't dream, but after a while became aware of a smell of burning. He opened his eyes, not having realised that they were shut, and found that he could see. An orange light filled the cellar, coming, he first thought, from nowhere. But when he raised a hand to test his vision, he saw that the whole arm, and the hand too, were glowing like hot coals. The light came from him. Stretched out on the floor in front of him, his legs and feet glowed with fiery currents. The smell of burning came from scorching dust particles on the pavement where he sat and in the crevices of the wall against which he was leaning. The surface of the masonry was turning powdery from the heat. His clothes, if he'd been wearing them, would have been ashes long ago.

But Tib himself felt only his own comfortable warmth. The cell, he realised, was now a furnace. No living thing could have survived more than an instant in it, but he breathed the roasting air as though in the cool of a pleasant evening.

This, no doubt, was why the magician had brought him here. It was a place where he could undergo this transformation without burning the building down, perhaps setting fire to a whole quarter of the city. But still there had to be some purpose beyond this change, and even the magician had been no more than part of that purpose. Despite his obvious powers, he could not have stayed a moment longer than he'd done, but had been whisked away as soon as his task ended.

Without impatience, Tib waited as the heat grew slowly more intense. When the light from his body steadied to a pure, even gold, so pale that it was almost white, he knew that the time had come. His purpose slid into his mind.

He rose to his feet and found that the cell had shrunk. He could now reach up and touch the vault. He strode to the window opening and laid a hand on each end of one of the bars of the grill. The metal melted at his touch, running in rivulets down his forearms but bubbling away in vapour before they reached his elbow. He melted out the remaining bars, lifted the grill clear and climbed through the opening. By his own light he made his way along the passage and up the stairs that he and the magician had descended. He needed to bow his head to pass through the doorway into the courtyard. The leaf-litter around him rippled into flame. The oak of the outer door charred at his approach and burst alight. He crashed through its roaring timbers and strode into the streets of Haballun, a burning giant.

It was past midnight, but the city never slept and the streets were still bright and busy. Screams rose as the giant flared like sunrise into their centre. A section of the night watch was stationed there to deal with riotous drunks. They formed a line, raised their crossbows and loosed a volley of bolts whose shafts and fins were already aflame in mid-flight, and the heavy iron heads melted before they reached their target, spattering the giant with molten drops that he felt no more than flesh feels a sprinkle of warm rain.

Tib, filled with purposes not his, but for which he had been brought to the slave school and bought and raised by Aunt Ellila, equally unknowing, moved through the maze of the city, his giant stride carrying him faster than any news of his coming. He stopped in front of a building. With his remaining human awareness he recognised it as the house of Dr. Cacada, the minor but still powerful magician with whom Aunt Ellila had maintained an uneasy relationship, giving him first choice of her latest purchases, and in exchange asking his advice on items that she felt might be tricky to handle. Sometimes she had sent Tib here on errands, and then he had seen it as a shabby little house squeezed in between two much grander ones. Now the blaze of his eyesight melted the illusion and he saw it as it was, fully as handsome as its neighbours but shielded with symbols of power that created between them a network of magical protection, glittering and pulsing.

The giant strode forward and grasped the network with both hands. Instantly it reacted, reaching out and flowing round his body like a many-tentacled sea-thing engulfing its prey. He ignored the pressure and ripped the whole net from the building. It shrivelled into squirming tatters round his feet. He kicked in the main door, grasped the door-posts, tore out the whole front wall and walked through. At once the building burst into flame, and in a few moments more was a furnace.

He stood at its heart and rested, drinking in the heat, much as an old woman, sitting in her porch on a summer morning, drinks in the sunlight, remembering under its caress what it was to have been young and strong. Invisible in the glare, a small lizard, white-golden like the giant with its own inward heat, came scuttling through the embers, up over the giant's foot to his calf. It hung there for a moment, moulding itself to the shape of his fiery flesh, then sank through the skin and disappeared. The giant emerged from the ruins of Dr. Cacada's house, taller by the height of a man than when he had come.

By now the remaining twenty-six magicians of the city knew of the giant's existence, and if they had been capable of cooperation, they might have combined to stop him. But all the magicians were, effectively, enemies of each other. Hatred, fear and distrust were the only relationships they knew. At first each simply assumed that one of the more powerful of them must have conjured the giant into existence in order to destroy a lesser one and used time he could not spare trying to elucidate how the thing was done and how the event might be turned to his advantage. By the time they realised that the giant was something new, a manifestation of a previously unknown force, he had destroyed the houses of three more magicians. He had grown in stature each time one of the little lizards crept into his body and added its powers to those already there, and was now as tall as the houses between which he strode and filled with the energies that fuel the stars.

The magicians were masters of their art, but its prisoners too, because it was the only art they knew. It made little difference what defences they built around themselves, what weapons they deployed against the giant, walls of brass, ramparts of ice, downpours that turned the streets to raging torrents, thunderbolts and shafts of lightning, monstrous beasts and demons, spells of utter destruction, spells of stillness and of binding, mailed legions of dead men— nothing delayed his march. A canyon opened at his feet. He spanned it with a bridge of fire and strode across. As he reached each magical household, the spells of its owner lost their power and the unhappy creatures that for centuries had been bound there to serve his will were freed and fled away.

Such was the giant's power that he could control the fires he set. Though the buildings nearest them might char, they did not catch, nor the flames spread, so individual column after column of smoke rose above the moonlit roofs to mark his progress. By the time twenty-seven such columns were in being, he was taller than the tallest tower of the Great East Gate.

Those fires were still raging when dawn whitened beyond it, but by then the giant was gone. Sentries on the wall had watched him dwindle to a distant spark, and by daylight they could see his track spearing northwestwards, a ruler-straight line of burnt crops, grassland and scrub that vanished as it crossed the ridge of hills that rimmed the northern desert.

They turned and looked back over the city. The smoke of twenty-seven fires still floated up and drifted away on the wind, but that was not what struck them most strongly. Seeing it even from here, they could tell at once that Haballun had become changed overnight. Both for good and ill, it had overnight been stripped of all its high magic.

Meanwhile the giant who had been Tib was striding down into the desert. His huge paces carried him through the roasting heat of its day and the bitter chill of its night. Soon after the next daybreak, a mile-wide canyon barred his path. He climbed down the nearer cliff and walked along the canyon's floor until he came to a place where the canyon narrowed to a deep slit that he could span with his arms, resting one hand on either cliff.

He gathered his giant strength and pushed. The whole wide desert groaned, and distant cities trembled as he ruptured the rind of the world and gazed down into its roiling central fires.

He settled down, dangling his legs over the edge of the crack, and waited. One by one, twenty-seven golden lizards rose through the skin of his thighs, cast their purple gaze on him for a moment, crawled as far as his knee-cap and cast themselves over the edge. As each one left him, some of his heat went from him and his stature dwindled. By the time the last emerged, he was Tib again, a naked young man with ordinary human flesh, sitting on bare rock, and forced now to draw back from the furnace heat that rose from the crack.

He felt a tingling in his upper right arm. The final lizard rose through his skin, formed no longer of metallic mesh but of living gold. Instead of leaving him, as the others had done, it crawled up his arm and over his shoulder, coming to rest out of sight on his shoulder-blade. He felt a patch of intense, pure heat that did not hurt or burn him. It lasted only a few seconds and then the lizard crept back up, stopping this time on the point of his shoulder. Squinting sidelong down, he saw it reach up with a long, dark tongue, forked at the tip. The lizard crept closer, out of sight now, and clung to his neck. Something smooth and warm slid into his ear, further and further. A whispering began inside his head.

"We are the salamanders. Our normal mode of being is outside time, where we have no material form. To exist in time we take this form. Our gateway between our two modes of being is the central fire of the earth, where the material elements are made and un-made. Long ago in time we watched fragments of the material world shape themselves into stars and planets and then, on this planet, into living things and, finally, people. Until these came into exis-tence, we were unable to act in the material world, but now, through them, we could. At first we did so very seldom, but continued to watch from a distance.

"Then the people began to develop the powers that you call cottage magic, through which, we saw, humankind might evolve into its next stage. Some of us were eager to study the process, so took material form and came to live secretly in the households of those who possessed these powers, in order to watch more closely. I was one.

"I lived secretly in the house of a man called Vered, in the city of Haballun. He possessed unusual abilities and great intelligence—too great, for he discovered my existence without my being aware of it. What is more, he devised a means to trap me into this mode of existence and keep me caged. Worse yet, he prevented me from warning my fellow salamanders what had happened to me, and told certain of his friends what he had done, so that they could do the same. Before we could move to prevent it, twenty-seven of us had been likewise trapped. Whether we liked it or not, these men—they were all men—could use our mere presence enormously to increase their power. They discovered high magic.

"Despite all this, Vered was a good man, just in his dealings. His aim had not been power or wealth but to understand the deepest causes of things, and he believed I would be a doorway to such knowledge. But as soon as he learnt more of my nature he realised the wrongfulness of what he had done and set me free, and further-more tried to persuade the rest to do the same, but the corruption of power had already done its work on them and they refused. Vered, with my help, then set about mastering them one by one, but they combined against us and destroyed him.

"I fled into my other mode of being, and conferred with the rest of the salamanders. I was determined to rescue my friends. The others were willing to help me, but seeing what had happened to me and my friends, they were not prepared to risk entering the material world while there were magicians there of such power. We ourselves have considerable powers in our other mode of being. I can move easily enough across material time and enter where I will, but once within it, I am bound by it until I choose to leave it, and it would take all my strength to move even a small material object with me into another time and to keep it there for a little while before it was snatched back.

"I needed to act through someone of great natural powers but uncorrupted by them. I knew of only one, Vered himself. But even with my help, working in his own time, he had been impotent against the combined powers of the other twenty-seven magicians of Haballun. So I persuaded the salamanders to transfer him out of his time to the present age, when the magicians had become so corrupted by their powers that they could no longer trust each other enough to cooperate. They agreed to do it, and said it was possible if we all worked together, but even then we would be unable to hold him here for more than a morning.

"I re-entered Vered's time on the day before he would be destroyed, when he could already foresee his failure, and told him what I planned. Though it would all happen long after he was dead, he was eager to undo the harm that he had done.

"I then searched a little back from this time and found a newborn child who had no ties to any other person. This was you. Your mother was a girl of the hill people. She became pregnant without her brothers' permission. They killed her lover, but not her, since she was their sister and their customs forbade it. But they would not send for help when she gave birth, and she died. You lived, so they carried you into the desert and left you for the wild animals. Instead I caused a hunter to find you and carry you to Haballun to be raised as a slave.

"When the time came, I took the form of an artificial salamander and caused a woman who dealt in magical objects to buy me from a street vendor, and then to choose you. This was to keep you safely hidden, and ready for our purpose. The rest you have seen for yourself. Now you are Tib again, with your human life to live. The blessing of the salamanders is on you."

The salamander withdrew its tongue and crawled swiftly down Tib's body and across the rocks. It paused on the rim of the crevasse and turned its head. For the last time he looked into the depths of those purple eyes, and then it crawled on down out of sight. With another desert-shuddering groan the crevasse closed.

Now that he had his natural body back, Tib could feel the heat of the rising sun. As he looked around for shade, a glint caught his eye. He went to look and found a golden nugget, still too hot to touch after having been squeezed up, molten, from the central fires between the lips of the crevasse as it closed. As he waited for it to cool, he saw another a little further on, and another beyond it. He walked along the line of the closed crack, picking the nuggets up as he went, until the trail ran out. Near that point stood a huge leaning rock, forming a kind of open-sided cave and casting the shade he needed. There were strange painted patterns on its under-surface, and a rough stone hearth to one side.

Tib settled down and waited. His position was apparently desperate, a naked man with nothing to his name but a double handful of useless gold, and nothing to give him hope but an abandoned hearth and some old painted patterns. But he was filled with the same confident calm that he had felt after the magician had left him in the dark of the cellar, waiting for whatever had been going to happen next. There was something still to come. The gold was a sign to him, a reward from the salamanders for allowing himself to be used as he had, and that meant he would live to spend it; while the hearth and the paintings meant that people came to this place, and would come again.

Sure enough, they arrived well before the sun was overhead, a dozen adults, very dark skinned, wearing nothing but little leather aprons patterned with blue and red beads, and a few naked children. The men carried flint-headed spears and short bows, and the women yellow gourds slung in nets. Silent as ghosts, they stole along the floor of the canyon in single file. The line halted in front of the rock. They turned towards him, stared for a moment and then with a low, sighing moan, knelt and touched their foreheads to the ground.

One grey-haired man came crawling forward while the others remained kneeling. Tib rose and went to meet him. The man looked up, imploring, from his crouch, but Tib took him by the wrists and pulled him upright. The man raised a shaking hand palm forward. Smiling, Tib placed his own palm against it. The man gave a great shout, stepped back, flung up his arms in a gesture of exultation and shouted again, and the rest came crowding round, whooping and laughing.

Tib stood smiling in the middle of the melee until they had shouted themselves hoarse and drew apart. A woman offered him a gourd of water, pleasantly flavoured with some kind of aromatic bark. He thanked her and stood aside, watching them prepare a meal, gathering fuel, kindling a spark from a fire-bow, opening gourds and satchels, cutting the meat of two small animals into strips with a flint knife, chattering and laughing, even the smallest children knowing their tasks.

He understood what was happening. He had heard of these desert people, older, far older, than Haballun itself. The hunter who had first found him must have been of their kind. This was one of their sacred places—the paintings showed that. They had heard the double groan of the crevasse as it opened and closed, so had come to ask the desert spirits what it meant, and had found him waiting for them. That was enough. He was sacred. They had seen his little pile of gold and left it alone—it was sacred too. They would feed him and clothe him and guide him to the edge of the desert.

And then what? Slaves do not own anything, let alone nuggets of gold. A thought struck him. He reached behind his shoulder to the place where the salamander had rested just before it had talked to him. His fingers touched not the ridged scars of the slave symbol that he had felt so often before, but smooth skin. The slave-brand had gone. He was free. He was also rich. He could go anywhere and do anything he chose. He realised that he had already chosen.

He would go back to Haballun and find Aunt Ellila and help her run her stall. Objects connected to high magic might have lost their powers, but they had been only a minor part of Aunt Ellila's trade, and there'd still be a good living to be had from the rest for the two of them. Or rather, for the three.

He was wondering what Zorya would turn out to be like when the grey-haired old hunter came and bowed before him and took him by the hand and led him to be the guest of honour at their feast.

FIRST FLIGHT

ROBIN McKINLEY

My parents had it planned that I'd be a wizard. Eldest son drag-onrider, second son spiritspeaker, third son wizard, you know? My dad was a carpenter, but he was a fourth son. I think that was part of the problem, he felt he had something to prove, even though his next-older brother wasn't a wizard but a merchant. A wealthy merchant, so everyone thought, oh, how clever of him, since most wizards are poor. And my mum made candles, but then she was a daughter, and daughters get to choose what they want to do. (There aren't very many women dragonriders, spiritspeakers, or wizards. There are some, but not many.)

Obviously not every first son is a dragonrider but it's every fam-ily's dream, and the problem is, my mum's family had done it right, and now my dad's local brother's family had started doing it right (the other two brothers lived on the other side of the country and were easier to ignore). Their eldest had just graduated from the same academy his dad had gone to, and had already been assigned to his first working dragon. Although it was only a little civilian one that ran up and down our coast and his rating was only Fourth Wing, he was still riding his own dragon. And their second son had just been apprenticed to a popular spiritspeaker.

I'd've hated being a dragonrider because I don't like heights, and I would've hated being a spiritspeaker because they're all so stuck on themselves. (Both my mother and my father admit that their spiritspeaker brothers are a trifle self-important.) I think I would have liked being a wizard, but it wasn't going to happen. I was all thumbs and I couldn't do the maths. You're always having to measure stuff when you're a wizard. If Mum sent me out for a dozen apples I'd come home with eleven, and even I can count to twelve. It's just something that happens with me.

And then Dag got into the dragon academy, and not just any academy but *the* Academy, the first, oldest one. When the Academy started we weren't even a country yet. Fhig, our cousin, had gone to Whimbrel Academy, which is only about three hundred years old, so we were one up there. Dag wouldn't admit it but he was dead chuffed, and when our parents assumed that he'd go, he let their pride and enthusiasm sweep him along. But he told Kel and me when he was home for his first half-year break that it was nothing but rules and history and getting the form right when you addressed anybody and the air smelled of eight-hundred-year-old dust and he hadn't even seen a dragon yet.

He'd sat for the entrance exams assuming he wouldn't get in, but he's too honest not to have given it his best shot, and he's the big bold capable type so he passed the physical just by showing up. I'd always privately thought he was a shoo-in but I may be a little prejudiced. He was the big brother who'd saved not only me but the bagful of kittens I was trying to rescue from drowning—I'd just got hold of the bag when the bank gave way, and the river was running hard in the spring rains. Dag dove in after me and we all got swept downstream but it was Dag who kept his head and pulled us out. He didn't even yell at me afterward. (One of the kittens has been keeping Dad's workshop a rodent-free zone for the last five years.)

But it was really bothering Dag that he knew Mum and Dad were staying up all night to earn money for the fees and there was still

Kel and me to come, and he didn't even want to be a dragonrider, especially not if it was tangled up in all this pointless rigmarole. "And of course it would be," he said gloomily. "Nobody ever crowns sheep." In any war pretty much as many dragons as human soldiers are awarded the crown medal for courage, and most of the Academy tutors and dragonmasters were ex-army. Dag had wanted to be a farmer.

Mum and Dad didn't seem to mind working all night. They were also busy trying to get Kel signed up to apprentice to this speaker named Jwell who was even more stuck on himself than usual and Kel was pretty dismal about it.

It was kind of depressing because of the three of us I'm the only one who wouldn't have minded the training I was due for. Although it wasn't exactly a wizard I wanted to be. I had this fat-headed idea that I wanted to be a *healer*. It takes a lot of work to learn and then nobody wants to know you after they find out what you do for a living. Nobody's supposed to get sick. And if you do it's probably your fault. And then it's a huge loss of face to admit you don't seem to be getting better on your own and need help. But everybody gets sick, and almost everybody at some point has to go to a wizard who admits doing healing (not all of them will; it's rough being a social exile), so pretty much nobody will risk saying any more than "good day" to a known healer for fear someone will see and draw the wrong conclusions.

Injuries are even worse than getting sick. Injuries, unless you got them in battle, mean you're a careless slob. Before the king made duels illegal about a hundred years ago, there were a lot more duels than were fought, if you follow me, so people had an excuse for having hurt themselves ("And you should see the other guy!"). But real duels also killed a lot of people, so it was a good thing the king forbade them.

The only healers that make any money are the smoothers—the ones that make the evidence go away, the scars and so on. But they're not respectable. You don't invite them to dinner or encourage them to marry into the family. Even soldiers don't go to smoothers, although they wear their medals and duty badges outside their clothes so everyone knows they're soldiers. My dad is a seriously good carpenter, and a smoother once tried to interest him in making artificial limbs. A really good smoother can give a wooden arm or leg some movement like a real one, but the fake one has to be nearly perfect. Working with a clever smoother would have meant more money, but my dad wasn't interested. My parents are nothing if not respectable.

Since I was always bumping into things, maybe that's why I had some sympathy for the careless slobs of the world. Every mother (and most fathers) knows about gimpweed for bruises. Nobody's going to advertise that they might need it by growing it in their own garden but you can find it near the edges of any deciduous forest. I used to pick it when I saw it as a kind of charm against bruising and I think it must work because I don't have nearly as many bruises as I should for all the running into things I do. It also means that I can kind of slip a stem or two to anyone I can see needs it and because I'm only a clumsy kid and no threat to their dignity they mostly let me. One or two of the mothers in the village have even told me that it seemed to work better when it came from me but I knew that was just them feeling sorry for me. Or too busy to go find some themselves. I did tell them that they didn't have to say that, I was happy to let them have some any time.

Our village did have a wizard, an all-sorts wizard, which is to say she did a little bit of everything. Most all-sorts aren't very good at anything but she was good at almost everything, good enough that if she told you she didn't feel like doing something you believed that she didn't feel like it and it wasn't that she couldn't. Nobody could understand why she stayed here in Birchhome. She'd come when I was three or four and she was still here. She could get you or your parcel somewhere faster or easier than a horse or a messenger could, if dragons made you nervous. Her love philtres were so good that she had an almost equally good business in antidoting her own philtres, and if you needed a few words to say over your new house or your pregnant wife or sister or your winter solstice party when you really needed a better year next year, she'd give you some weird little verse that didn't look like much but that you could feel *thunk* into place when you said it out loud.

She'd made Dad one of her verses the year his workshop burnt down (he and the cat got out but nothing else did). He was standing in the framed-out door for the new shop, which didn't even have walls yet, and he was afraid we were going to run out of money before the walls got built, and Mum was mad at him for spending money on the verse. So it wasn't a great atmosphere for any charm with Mum standing there throbbing with annoyance, and Dad was so tired and discouraged he couldn't even straighten up properly and he read the words in such a low mutter you could barely hear them.

And then there was this really strange pause that didn't seem to have anything to do with time, and you could feel something like a big wet fog of discouragement roll itself up and go away, and then Dad straightened up and Mum sort of got shorter as the anger drained out of her, and they looked round and smiled at each other, so then Dag and Kel and I did too.

But what I really liked about our wizard is that she also did healing, and she did it like it was no big deal. Wizards, even all-sorts, are really conscious of their dignity, aside from worrying about whether anyone will ever talk to them again if it gets out that they do healing or that they don't make you beg for it first. Maybe they make a big fuss about dignity because they're only third on the list after dragonriders and spiritspeakers.

Ralas lived a little outside of the village, which made it easier to sneak off there and ask about your chilblains or your old dad's cough or whatever. I should know because I did—sneak off to ask her things I mean—some of the mums that asked me for gimpweed asked me about other stuff too, and if I didn't know, I asked Ralas. She never seemed to mind, and she always told me anything I could use, that I could pass on. She always seemed pleased to do it too. She liked helping people. Wizard training is supposed to make you want to help people if you aren't that way to begin with but I bet she didn't have to be taught to want to. And she never made me feel like a dumb clumsy kid when she said she'd have to see someone herself, that what was wrong sounded sort of complicated. And she never said "Tell the old so-and-so to come here and pay my fee and stop trying to get it for free out of a kid."

Also although I'm really healthy, I have a sort of negative gift for finding sick hedgehogs and birds with broken wings and stuff, and I always brought them to her. A lot of them stayed on after they got better. So when I say "sneak off" you can sneak as much as you like but you won't surprise her, because she's got all these three-legged or bald or blind or somehow crooked-up creatures going squawk and squeal and chirp and yelp and so on, every time anyone comes near. And a lot of people did come to see her, people that weren't from our village too, so it was pretty noisy out there a lot of the time.

Mum and Dad and I were at a craft fair once and a foogit pup got trod on by a horse. Nobody knew who the pup belonged to and it was lying there crying with its leg at a funny angle and all sort of mashed looking. Everybody stared the other way. Once the animal was damaged no one was going to claim it, not when everyone else could see, and it was near noon and the craft fair wouldn't be over till sunset. It was weird somebody had brought it at all—it was way too young to be useful—and while foogits aren't the brightest lamp at the festival, you don't get wild foogit pups in the middles of craft fairs, so it must've belonged to somebody.

I asked someone where the town wizard lived, and I picked the pup up as carefully as I could—although it was amazingly good about this and sort of relaxed into me as if company was better than nothing—and went there. It was a grand house in the middle of town with stars painted all over it and a long fringe of charms hanging over the front door. It gave me the creeps—Ralas didn't use any of that show-offy stuff—but it didn't matter so long as he knew how to set broken bones. But whoever it was who answered the door wouldn't let me in to trouble "the master." I'd just managed to say, "He has a broken—" when Stoneface said, "The master doesn't deal with vermin," and shut the door. I'm not sure if he meant me or the pup. It's true I hadn't thought about how I was going to pay, but I don't believe the door thug had got that far in his thinking either.

So I went back to our waggon and stole a bit of lath from my dad, because I knew he'd say no if I asked but I also knew he wouldn't ask any questions if he recognised what I'd stolen, and then I had to use my belt and some of my sleeve because Mum would ask if some of the stuff she wrapped her candles in disappeared, and I splinted the pup's leg as best I could from having watched Ralas do it a lot better, although it was harder than that because, as I say, it wasn't just broken, it was kind of crunched up. There were a couple of places where the bone poked through the skin and I didn't have a clue what to do about that, I just made a big green smelly poultice of pretty much any plant I could find that hadn't been stomped flat by everybody at the fair and slapped it on. Mum was really annoyed, but mostly about my shirt (she said something about vermin too but I think she meant fleas) but she let me keep him till we got home. Nobody came around asking about him either.

But we didn't get home till ten days later and the bones had already started to knit (Ralas said) and, as I say, I didn't know what I was doing so the bones healed a bit funny and Sippy has been lame ever since, which is why he stayed with Ralas, but I don't think Mum would have let me keep him anyway. Ralas tried to make me feel better and kept saying that I was only eleven and Sippy's leg would have been tricky even for her, but the point is I'm a screw-up and Sippy is lame for life. Sippy's always really glad to see me when I go to Ralas' and that makes me feel both better and worse.

There was a joke in the family that the reason I didn't grow is because I kept wearing the growth off the bottoms of my feet with all the running I did for Mum. In finding all the best shortcuts through woods and fields, I found the best places for gimpweed, so I started looking for other stuff too, especially the common stuff that Ralas got through pretty fast. Ralas started letting me keep watch on her supplies so I could collect what she needed at the right time of year. That felt *really* good.

I started looking for new things when people would ask me, after I'd checked with Ralas what it was and where it grew and if it was good for what whoever wanted it for. Since you're not supposed to be sick in the first place, a lot of people are really dumb about what they think will make them better. Often I got the latest gossip as a kind of payment. It's less embarrassing than saying thank you. I was the first one to bring it to Birchhome that our councillor's daughter had run off with a smoother and her parents were going to disown her. I was also the first to hear when Fhig did something clever and got bumped up to Third Wing. Drat him.

But during the second year at a dragonrider academy you finally meet the dragons. And dragons and Dag were . . . *wham*. Suddenly all the stupid rules and the boring history and the human hierarchy just disappeared, because it was all about dragons.

And then Kel didn't go to Jwell after all but some young guy named Chooko who'd never had an apprentice before but who told good stories and furthermore amazingly would smile and look at you (even when you're the youngest and short for your age) when he came to your village and dropped in on the family of the second son who's going to be his first-ever apprentice in a few months. And he and Kel really hit it off.

So two sons down—and both of them happy—and one to go. Mum being Mum, I'd've thought she'd get going on me right away but maybe I was too much even for her tactical skills. Unless I started growing unexpectedly I could go on pretending to be fourteen forever, and never be apprenticed at all. Maybe I'd deliver candles for the rest of my life.

Dag came home on his half-year leave from the Academy right before Kel was going off with Chooko and they were both full of excitement and the future. Their future. Dag's *wham* with dragons was so spectacular he'd been jumped a class—Fhig hadn't done that either—so he was going to be eligible for his First Flight only next year. Which, just by the way, was the year I'd be fifteen and so far as I knew Mum and Dad hadn't even started looking for some desperate wizard they could bribe heavily (except they couldn't afford to, although Chooko was a lot cheaper than the Academy) to take me on as apprentice.

Dag and Kel's way of dealing with this awkwardness was to talk over my head about their own stuff (since they're so much taller than I am, this was very easy). They didn't mean to make me feel lower than a foogit pup. But what could they do, anyway?

Maybe my parents thought hanging out with Ralas would make me marginally more desirable as an apprentice. I would have flown like a starling and swum like a fish to be Ralas' apprentice but I knew that wasn't going to happen. When I was still only a little kid I'd overheard Mik, who had a third son to find a place for, asking Ralas about apprenticeship. Ralas had been very polite but said that she didn't take apprentices. I reminded myself of this a lot. At least it meant I didn't have to go through being turned down by her personally—and I didn't have to die of jealousy when she took somebody else. Although I'd still have to go away and be apprenticed to someone somewhere about something some day and stop hanging around her. I didn't really think Mum would keep me delivering candles forever. Maybe I wished she would.

Sippy believing I was wonderful was nice, even if he was only a foogit and it was only because he didn't realise it was my fault he was lame. He'd grown up a lot handsomer than I was expecting. Bigger too. Foogits are good watchdogs—nobody sleeps through a foogit howling—and tend to be less trouble than real dogs so you see them around pretty often, but only at the backs and edges of things—no one invites a foogit to lie by the hearth during its off-duty hours. Also foogits can move so fast, in that sort of goofy dance they do, they can make you dizzy if you watch them. And if you're a burglar, you probably will be watching them, because a good guard foogit will bite too, and their teeth sink in a ways. Not that Ralas needed that kind of protection. Some of the strangers who came to visit her were scarier than any burglar but I never saw her worried or bothered.

I've often wondered why it's okay to despise foogits. So that a foogit pup with a broken leg can lie crying in the middle of a hot fairground and no one will even bring it a bowl of water. I suppose it's because we hero-worship dragons and foogits play the fool in dragon stories. Usually there is no fool in a dragon story, because stories about dragons are always big and grand and solemn and exciting. But if you want something funny or ridiculous to happen somewhere in a dragon story you'll probably put in a foogit. I don't know why a foogit. But there's a connection between them and dragons somehow. Foogits are a bit dragon-shaped, although they're hairy and a dragon is scaly. And even the biggest foogit would look pretty silly next to the smallest dragon. Also dragons don't have topknots of hair that look like huka nests. No one can look dignified with a huka nest on their head.

I've seen dragons a few times, and around here the only dragons you're going to see are the smallest and the oldest and the slowest. But even they have that air about them: that they rule the world and they know it. I don't know why they let us little thin-skinned squeaky wingless humans order them around. I suppose that makes us feel kind of conceited too. Or maybe awed or even just confused. So then you look at a foogit and I guess it's sort of a joke, but the joke's in bad taste. Hard on the foogit, who didn't ask to look like a small hairy dragon with a silly dance. But if Sippy knew he was a buffoon he never let on. Or maybe he liked it. He was always cheerful and he always cheered me up.

You don't hear from your apprenticed relatives all that often. They're too busy being apprentices. We got a letter from Dag about twice a year, depending on there being someone to bring it, and because of the unpredictableness of this, it never seemed strange if we didn't get any letters. And there hadn't been any gossip, and now that our village had someone at the Academy every tinker passing through had an Academy story for us. There was just Dag, one day, turning up a week before we were expecting him for his half-year break, looking grey and hollow-eyed. We started out being delighted to see him but it was immediately obvious "delighted" was the wrong response. It had been raining for weeks and the first thing I thought was that he'd caught a chill, and started patting my pockets for gislarane; I'd been carrying extra in case anyone I was delivering candles to was feeling shivery and sneezy. I gave him the gislarane but it wasn't a chill.

The story came out in jerks over the rest of the evening. I'm putting it together in more or less the right order now but he didn't tell it like this.

At first we thought he must be feverish after all because what he said didn't seem to make a lot of sense. Then for a while we thought it was about having been jumped a year. But bullying or social exile wasn't the kind of thing that would get Dag down. I even wondered if he might be in love. I had probably a strange view of love from Ralas' clientele.

That was closer. But it wasn't a girl. It was a dragon.

"I couldn't believe it, when the First Flight list went up. I don't know . . . I don't understand . . . *Hereyta,* for all the gods' sake," Dag said. "I know they say it's all handed down in the signs and so on. But they could just not do it—or they could tell me they'd changed their minds and I'd take my First Flight next year with my old class."

Typical of Dag that it didn't occur to him that this might be awkward or embarrassing.

"I can't believe they'd *do* this to Hereyta. But they're not going to change it. Some of the other cadets are pretty upset about it too. Fistagh says I should refuse to Fly." A grimace that had very little relationship to a smile passed briefly over Dag's face. "I've thought of that—it's about the only thing I have thought of—but not for Fistagh's reasons." Fistagh was one of the fourth-years who thought a third-year jumper was a bad idea. "But I've decided—I *think* I've decided—that refusing to Fly—to try to Fly—would be even worse for Hereyta."

Some of why I didn't get it at first is that I'd been around Sippy too much, and I'd unconsciously begun thinking of dragons as being a kind of very large foogit with less sense of humour and better posture. I'd maybe forgotten about the awe part. And the honour part.

Hereyta was pretty old, although not all that old for a dragon, and mostly retired. She'd flown for the king in the last border wars and been pretty special. They used her at the Academy now for the practical stuff, when the cadets get out of the classrooms their second year and start working with the dragons, and she was a big success there. If Hereyta liked you it really meant something. He'd mentioned her before so I kind of half recognised her name. They'd also been breeding her but while she'd been bred this year she hadn't settled. "I knew she was barren this year," said Dag, "and I've been worried about her because I'm afraid if she doesn't settle next year too. . . ."

There are no romantics on a dragonrider academy staff. They can't afford it. All the dragons used for training in all the academies are rotated back into the income-earning world every few years to make some money, usually including the breeding stock. Nobody could run an academy if they had to feed all their dragons all the time, and nobody but maybe the king could afford to send their kids to an academy if they had to pay total dragon upkeep as part of the tuition. And a young dragon doesn't start earning its living till it's twelve or fifteen years old—some of them don't reach their full strength till they're twenty. Hereyta was very special indeed to have been granted the luxury of even semi-retirement, although coping with a lot of cadets can't be too restful.

"But why humiliate one of their best?" Dag was so wrapped up in Hereyta he kept on leaving the crucial bit of the story out.

"Humiliate," said Dad. "I don't understand humiliate. You mean she's too—too injured or arthritic to fly? That sounds . . . cruel."

"It *is* cruel," said Dag. "She can still get off the ground, yes. She can fly under the blue sky, yes. She's got one stiff wing—that's another old war wound—but it still works. But no, she can't Fly. She only has two eyes."

Even so it took a moment for this to sink in. Most people don't get close enough to any dragons to have to think about how they do what they do, and it's pretty eerie besides. You don't really want to think about how your expensive parcel or your more expensive visitor got here—what it or they might be trailing in from the journey. Dragons are too big and heavy to fly like birds fly for long; they do it to get going, and they do some pretty fancy blue-sky flying during courtship (and afterward they've burnt up so much energy they do nothing but eat and sleep for days) but mostly, as soon as they get a few spans up, poof, they aim their three eyes however it is that they do it and zap, they're into the Firespace, or the red sky, or the secret way, or the Endless Fire, or the haven, or the centre of the world, or whatever you choose to call it. And anything they're carrying—back on the ground in its net at the end of its special rope—disappears too. (With a jerk. Careful packing is crucial. Dag says you loop up any parcels while you're in the Firespace, so they come out *with* you and the dragon. Otherwise they'd be liable to brain you coming down.)

Most of the academies, and the companies that use dragons, don't call that other place anything; it's just how dragons get around—*officially* they don't call it anything. But that's because they don't want us ordinary people getting too spooked. A lot of your taxes go to the dragon regiments in the army. I've wondered sometimes how the tradition got started that you want your first son to go to a drag-onrider academy. It seems to me a really convenient counterbalance to the uncanniness of Flying. But some of the old magicians could have cast a spell that huge, so maybe one of them did.

Anyway, when your dragon zaps back out of the Firespace again you're a lot closer to where you wanted to be than when you went in—or that's the idea. Depending on how good you are at commu-nicating with your dragon you may be very close to where you want to be or you may not, and if you're not you may have to go back into the Firespace and try again. Every now and again a dragonrider gets really awful vertigo in the Firespace and has to stop being a dragonrider. (Passengers are securely tied in on the dragon with its rider, and a lot of people only do it once, even the ones who can afford it.) Everybody gets some vertigo so aside from needing to be as fast and efficient as possible because that's your job—and because dragons are staggeringly expensive to keep—you want to zap in and out of the Firespace as few times and for as short a stretch each as possible. Except for really short hops, when it's about the same, it's a lot quicker, going from point A to point B through the Firespace. Which is why it's worth it, although time as we know it goes a bit funny in there too, which they think is part of the vertigo.

I had been looking forward to Dag telling us what you could see when the dragon does whatever it does. There are stories that you can see three thin shiny lines like threads or ribbons or tiny light-ning beaming out of the dragon's three eyes, and where the lines cross is the way in, somehow—although I wasn't expecting anything too exact since dragons have been Flying through the Firespace for as long as there have been humans to see them disappear and reap-pear, and still no one knows anything really about how they do it. Except that they need all three eyes. A two-eyed dragon is grounded under the blue sky.

I'd heard him say his dragon—Hereyta—had only two eyes, but I hadn't taken it in. I'd maybe half assumed that First Flight was mostly a ceremonial thing or something. Once I understood what he was telling us I was really upset. No wonder Dag looked haunted. And I didn't even know this (or any) dragon. My mind started flicking through all the stuff Ralas had taught me, because that was what my mind automatically did now whenever there was any hurt or distress around. But nothing I knew could come anywhere near this. I couldn't help wondering if Ralas could do anything, but she was still only an all-sorts wizard, even if she was a good one, and all-sorts wizards don't mess with dragons.

Foogits have three eyes too, by the way, or they did, although it's getting rare. The third one is usually covered up by the topknot, but it's ornamental or vestigial or whatever, and a foogit can't see out of it even if it has a haircut. As I sat there thinking miserably about Dag's dragon it occurred to me to wonder if maybe that's another part of the reason everybody treats foogits like an ugly whining poor relation, because they have the gall to pretend to have three eyes like dragons, like the only creature there is who can get in and out of the Firespace—but the third eye's a fake on foogits. Their habit of silly dancing doesn't do them any favours either. But why do they have something that looks like a third eye? Nothing else does. Maybe they use it really secretly? Maybe the third eye has an extra eyelid that zooms back when nobody else is around and . . . nah. If Sippy was at all typical—and Ralas seemed to think he was—I couldn't see an entire species of Sippys hiding something like being able to get into the Firespace.

At the same time a third eye on a foogit—even though it's not a real eye and the foogit can't see out of it—is considered lucky. Sippy had a third eye.

Mum had been wittering away about how Dag must be mistaken, the Academy staff wouldn't do what he said they were doing, and Dad was making rumbling support-of-Mum noises, and I wasn't listening. I started listening when Dag broke in on this well-meaning clatter. "Have I told you how she lost the eye? She was in the war with the Srandems fifteen years ago. She took a spear meant for her partner. They were up in the wild lands, up beyond Ogan, and were ambushed. She still got them home, although Carn says he doesn't know how she did it, since they could only go under the blue sky, and the wound wouldn't stop bleeding, for weeks, he said, the spear was probably poisoned, so that it kept bleeding is probably what saved her life but even a dragon can only lose so much blood, and he was already pretty out of it himself because the spear-thrower had already had a go at him. . . . Carn's a tutor at the Academy now. He introduced me to Hereyta himself. Carn's still pretty lame, and every now and then he turns really grey and has to sit down. You'd think he'd've stopped it, assigning her to First Flight. You'd think he wouldn't care if every Seer ever born stood in a row and told him she had to be assigned to First Flight, after what she did for him, that he'd *find* a way to stop it."

◆ ◆ ◆

I woke up really early the next morning, thinking about Dag's dragon and how much she was going to mind what happened, just like Dag said, and eventually thinking about it bothered me so much that I went downstairs to boil some water. I'd decide if I wanted blastweed to wake up or snorewort to put me back to sleep after I had the hot water to do it with.

I found Dag still sitting by the fire where he'd been when the rest of us went to bed. He looked even worse than he had when he arrived. Coming home hadn't helped. Usually when you tell somebody else something that hurts, it hurts less after. "Want some blastweed?" I said, making up my mind.

Dag stirred. "Sure," he said absently. "Thanks, Tinhead." Mum would stop my brothers calling me that if she was around, but since they'd always used it when she wasn't it came out automatically. I was supposed to call him Geezer back but I didn't have the heart. I put the mug by his elbow and sat down opposite him with my own.

The blastweed started exploding through my veins and the silence got too loud to bear. "Want to come out to Ralas' with me?"

It took Dag about two minutes to come back from wherever he was and answer me. Was it his life he was looking at being wrecked before it got started—even I knew that if you failed First Flight you were pretty well doomed—or was it the dragon? That took about two seconds to decide. Dag and I don't have much in common but we're both nutty about animals.

"Okay," he said. "Thanks."

Sippy always knew when I was coming. Don't ask me how; he usually met me halfway between the village and Ralas' which means he has to have got started almost as soon as I did. Ralas said she always knew when I was coming because Sippy disappeared. He rushed up to us and cavorted like a puppy the way he always did, except unlike puppies foogits are green(ish) and don't wag their tails. If you didn't know about his leg you probably wouldn't guess; he'd adapted really well, although his run was a little strange. But foogits all run a little strangely. Dag actually smiled.

I knew Ralas would take one look at Dag and know something was badly wrong but being Ralas wouldn't ask. She just took him on a tour. There was someone coughing in the back of her house but we all ignored it. I knew it was Moga, the cooper's son, who was

allergic to wood dust. Ralas was trying to talk his dad into appren-
ticing him early to get him away from home, but Gakan was a
stubborn old so-and-so, and since Ralas couldn't actually say what
she meant outright—including that she'd be happy to do the tricky
negotiating for an underage apprentice that didn't include any mention of the crime of illness—poor Moga was still coming out to
Ralas' to cough pretty regularly. Ralas would load him up with gil-
berry tincture and he'd go home and be okay for a few weeks. And
then he'd start to wheeze, and then he'd start to cough, and then
he'd be back to Ralas' again.

I let the tour get ahead of me. Sippy wanted to play his charging
game, which involved running at me full tilt and at the last minute
swerving aside and leaping straight into the air. I guess it was some
kind of variation on the foogit dance, maybe because Sippy didn't
have any other foogits to do it with. Fortunately he'd begun teaching
me this game when he was still small and unsteady so I was willing
to stand still while he charged me because he didn't go that fast and
wasn't big enough to do either of us much damage if the purpose of
the game was to slam into me after all, like maybe when I wasn't
expecting it. Except it wasn't. So I held my ground as he got older
and bigger and cut the last-minute swerve till I almost had to shut
my eyes, and the breeze of his turn would hit me instead, and maybe
the tickle of the end of a flying ear.

I'd asked Ralas if he ever charged her, or anyone else, or maybe a
tree or something, or if he ever just leaped in the air and did his
trick out of nowhere, and she said she didn't think he ever did.

So I stood there so Sippy could play his game, and moved around
a little to go on facing him when he charged, which seemed to be
what he wanted, and thought some more about Dag and his dragon.
When Sippy got tired—which didn't take long; this was a very high-
energy game—we went off to find Ralas and Dag.

I could tell he was telling her about his dragon. People do tell Ralas things. I suppose we were both secretly hoping that she'd say, "Oh, your dragon is missing an eye? Why, I had a case like that last month. Apply this night and morning for a week." But she didn't of course. She just looked really sympathetic. I wondered if maybe she could give a two-eyed dragon a home but she didn't say anything about that either. And a dragon does take up an awful lot of space (and food) and the woodland where Ralas lived isn't that big and Birchhome is on one side and Twobridge is on the other side.

Dag was just finishing when Sippy and I arrived. We sat around (in Sippy's case lay around) in silence for a few minutes drinking Ralas' tisane (Sippy had most of a bowl of water) and then Ralas said to Dag, "Why don't you take Ern and Sippy with you when you go back to the Academy?"

She said it in this really reasonable voice like you might say, "Be sure to pack enough sandwiches, and don't forget your oilskin because it's going to rain some more." Dag opened his mouth and closed it again. He may call me Tinhead but he's not a bad guy. So since he wouldn't say it, I did.

"Why?"

Ralas laughed. "I don't know," she said, in that maddening wizardy way of hers. "It feels like a good idea."

It's true that when your wizard suggests you do something—especially a local wizard who usually gives pretty good advice and who furthermore has done your family a good turn or two already—you tend to do it. However useless or insane it sounds. Even so, when Dag looked into the bottom of the mug he was holding and sighed and said, "All right," I wondered what she'd put in his tisane.

I could think of about six *buts* immediately and, give me a minute, I'd think of six more. But I looked at Dag with his big shoulders all slumped staring into the bottom of his mug with his hands cupped over the brim like the answer was in there and he was trying to prevent it from jumping out and running away, and didn't say anything after all. No, that's not true. After a little while I said, "When do you want to leave?"

"Tomorrow," he said.

Mum blinked once or twice when Dag told our parents what Ralas had said, but Dad didn't even do that much. He was polishing a fancy carved chair leg he'd just mended and neither sons nor wizards were going to interrupt his train of thought. Mum tried to get him to pay attention by repeating the news but all he said was, "Ah? When're they leaving then? Maybe you can get Jardy to do some of your deliveries." But when he came in from his workshop he gave me a very clear, sharp, paying-attention look, and then nodded. I knew that nod. It was the nod he used when he'd been going around a craft fair or something looking at all the other carpenters' work and found something he really liked. It rattled me, that nod, but it also made me feel good, although I wasn't going to risk it by saying anything like "What do you mean?"

But it was even stranger, later on, when I was doing the washing up, and Mum came up behind me and said, "Ern." Dag had already gone to bed; he'd had no sleep last night. I braced myself. Mum tended to know everything and to be generous about spreading her superior intelligence around. Or maybe I just wasn't cleaning the dishes well enough. But she didn't say anything for so long after she'd said my name eventually I turned around (dripping water and soap-suds) and she was standing there with her face all screwed up with worry.

"Mum—?"

"Take care of him, won't you?" she said. "You'll take care of Dag."

This was more worried than I'd ever seen her. I tried to look taller and older. She didn't even say anything about the dripping when I put my arms around her. "Of course I will."

In more of her usual manner she said, "Don't patronise me, young man," although she didn't shake me off. She added, "But you've got a good head on your shoulders, and Dag has . . . temporarily mislaid his. I don't suppose Ralas can do anything about the dragon?"

I shook my head.

"Be careful," she said. She hesitated and then said, "Maybe I should—" and stopped. "You're dripping on the floor."

I turned back to the dishes, trying not to let her see me grin. She put her hand on my shoulder. "We'll talk about your future when you get back."

And then I bent lower over the dishes so she couldn't see my face.

"Yes, I know, we should have done it before." She added, "We haven't forgotten you, Ern."

I didn't say anything, and she patted my shoulder and left me.

It was sunny and clear when we set off the next morning (but we had our oilskins because it would rain later, and lots and lots of sandwiches because Mum always believed her sons were about to starve to death). If it had just been Dag he could have stayed a week because he'd be able to find a dragon to hitch a ride on; there were always dragons going to Clare, which is a big town in its own right as well as being the Academy town. Even the smallest, slowest dragon doing hop-stops (which is all you find around here) is still days faster than human feet. But cadets aren't allowed to bring their little brothers let alone their little brothers' foogits when they hitch. So we were going to walk.

I tried not to sound like I was looking for a way out when I asked Ralas if Sippy could walk that far on his leg. But she said immediately, "He'll be fine." And she gave me this enormous pot of liniment in case he seemed stiff. "Good for everybody," she said smiling. I hadn't thought about that; I spent nearly all day every day walking somewhere. And Dag—Dag was my oldest brother and a dragon academy cadet. They don't get stiff, do they? It's probably forbidden in the rulebook. It wasn't till a lot later that I thought about what she'd meant by "everybody."

Sippy was obviously a bit puzzled when Ralas made a slightly more than usual fuss over him when she sent him off with me that morning. Since we were going to Twobridge it seemed easier to pick Sippy up on the way than get into a flap with Mum. She preferred to know about Sippy from a distance. (Although occasionally after a long day delivering candles I brought Sippy with me, and smuggled him upstairs to my bed which is conveniently tucked way in under the eaves. But I didn't do it very often. And as long as I didn't do it very often Mum gallantly pretended not to notice.)

Sippy was even more puzzled when we got to Twobridge and went over the river to Waysmeet and then kept on going. Waysmeet was my candle-delivery limit. But he followed me like he always did even if his eyes and ears seemed to be whirling in five different directions at once, taking in all the new sights and sounds. Not that the village after Waysmeet looked much different. But the next day, after sleeping not-as-uncomfortably-as-it-sounds under a hedgerow, you could start to see the landscape getting flatter and more open, and for days after the towns were still small and there were plenty of fields and hedgerows and streams. Once we camped by the edge of a little forest and collected enough dead wood to have a (slightly damp and sullen) fire. When it spat and fizzed at us Sippy hid behind me.

When we got to Montuthra we turned right instead of left and then I was on new territory; the big craft fair my parents went to every year was in the other direction. And after Montuthra was West Cross and then East Cross, and after that Leton.

Dag and I didn't talk much so I stumped along beside or behind him like nothing was a big deal. I don't know if he knew I'd never been this way before. He was getting more and more shut in on himself as the road disappeared under our feet and out behind us in the wrong direction, and the towns got bigger. As he got closer to the Academy, to Hereyta, and to First Flight. With a runty little brother and a lame foogit at his heels.

It was like he was waking out of a trance the last day at sundown. We were getting to what looked like the end of the town we'd been walking through (Sippy so pressed up against me I kept tripping over him; the only other town this size he'd seen was the one I'd found him in with a smashed leg) and I was wondering if I should say something before we walked past what might be the last inn we'd see before midnight. I didn't think much of the local hedge-rows, and I didn't feel like walking till midnight, and in spite of picking up some food at markets on the way we'd eaten all of Mum's sandwiches by then (she didn't realise, because I'd been careful not to let her realise, how much Sippy eats). And we were short of sleep.

Last night's hedgerow had been a little too well populated and the family nearest us had a crying baby. Eventually I put on my best harmless-and-reassuring manner, although it works better in daylight, and went over there. I could see the mum in question was trying not to snap at me—if I was going to complain, I was also going to force her to admit that her child wasn't perfect. She said, "I'm sorry, but he's teething. He can't help it. *I* can't help it."

"I know," I said. "But this will help. Just rub a little on his gums."

I wasn't sure she'd try it—I'm good at looking harmless, but not so good at looking like I know what I'm doing—but she was desperate. The baby was asleep before I got back to Dag. He said, "You should have gone over earlier."

"Yeah," I said. But I knew he was saying "well done."

I prepared to take advantage when he stopped and looked at the inn sign hanging under the lantern—looked at it like he was paying attention to something outside his thoughts for the first time that day. A girl in an apron was coming out of the inn with a long spill to light the lantern.

"Sippy and I'll sleep in the stables, if you'll bring us some supper," I said quickly. I had my hand in my pocket for the coins Dad had given me; most inns would give a cadet in uniform free room and board, but Dag wasn't wearing his uniform. And sleeping in the stables was cheaper, but I also knew that no respectable inn would have a foogit indoors, and I didn't want to imagine what Sippy might do locked up all by himself in a little dark box in a strange town.

Dag wouldn't take Dad's coins and when he found us in the stables later on he was carrying a big tray with enough for three, and threw his pack down beside mine. He seemed almost cheerful. I'd already piled up straw so high that it was going to be a much more comfortable bed than we'd had the last several nights, and was feeling relatively cheerful myself. "Hope you don't mind if I join you," Dag said. "If I sleep in one of their rooms I'll just lie awake and . . . think. I find Sippy's snoring soothing."

The tray included a big jug of beer, which Sippy promptly knocked over, or maybe I did. Dag had put the tray on the ground because there wasn't anywhere else, but Sippy assumed it was for his benefit, and made a lunge for the plate of meat, which was still warm, and even my mere human nose registered that it smelled really good. I lunged for Sippy and the beer went over. Dag looked at the spreading pool for a moment and then laughed. "I'll take that as a sign," he said, "that I'm to be stone cold sober tomorrow; but it was only small beer."

We'd get to Clare tomorrow.

Maybe it was the beer he didn't have but Dag was awake before dawn the next day. Well, so was I. So we got up and left. I hope the horse that had the stall after us didn't get drunk on the straw. The sleepy kitchen maid—the same one we'd seen lighting the lantern the night before—wearily found us a couple of chunks of last night's bread, and we trudged off down the road. I loitered momentarily after Dag so I could give the kitchen maid a little coldleaf for the angry new burn on her wrist, which I was pretty sure was why she hadn't slept very well, and told her how to use it. She looked at me, surprised, but she took the leaves, and I was pretty sure she'd do what I said. Especially when she gave me a handful of apples to go with the bread.

The overnight dew had laid the dust, and the road before us was cool and white in the dawn fog. It looked, I don't know, magical somehow, like it was going to lead us to some great adventure. Not to a First Flight where one of the dragons would be left behind. The one my brother was with.

I've already said that Dag and I didn't talk much but that last day it was like his silence had a wall around it, that even if I had said anything my words would have bounced off like arrows against a shield. I wouldn't even have known that we'd get to Clare today except that I'd heard one of the ostlers the night before telling someone's groom that Clare was less than a league away and they'd get there in a morning even if the roads were crowded. That and Dag's barricaded silence told me we were close. I wanted to ask him what he wanted Sippy and me to do when we got there. I didn't think he'd want to bring us into the Academy grounds—his dim little brother and his dim little brother's defective pet foogit. He had enough to deal with. I started worrying all over again about why we were there at all. It was stupid to think that Sippy and I could do anything but make Dag's humiliation more complete. But Ralas wasn't stupid. And even Dad—even Mum—had seemed to think it wasn't a bad idea. Take care of Dag? How?

But here I was. Why hadn't Ralas told me what I was supposed to do?

The road was busy, but not so busy it slowed us down. Also I'm sure Dag speeded up. It was like, we're here, might as well get on with it. I would have preferred a little loitering myself. I don't know where Clare really began; it all pretty much ran on from the last town. It just got noisier, and there were little roads that branched off from the big road and if you looked down them they were lined with buildings too; and there were a lot of inns, and all their yards were busy. We wouldn't have been walking till midnight last night after all.

I was getting ready to hang off Dag's sleeve and bellow in his ear, something about if he'd recommend an inn that wasn't too expensive but didn't have too many bedbugs either, Sippy and I would go there and we could meet up later after Dag had checked in or whatever returning cadets did. I'd already put my hand out when I felt Dag stiffen and turned my head to look where he was looking, and saw the big ugly guy in a cadet's uniform.

But I was too slow, and as I was about to drop back into the crowd so Dag could pretend we had nothing to do with him, Dag grabbed the wrist of the hand I hadn't pulled away fast enough. The big ugly cadet walked straight up to us and to my surprise his face broke into an enormous smile. This wasn't necessarily an improvement—too many teeth—but he thumped Dag on both shoulders like they were best friends and I saw Dag was smiling too, if more restrainedly, but that might have just been from being thumped.

Big and Ugly now turned to me and if he was thinking "Who is this gnome and what is this vermin with him?" (Sippy was attached to my leg again; this town was even bigger and busier than yesterday's), it didn't show. "This is my brother, Ern," Dag said, and then Big and Ugly thumped my shoulders too and this sure made my smile feel strained. "And this is Eled," Dag continued. "He—he's on for First Flight too."

"That's right," Eled said. "You know your brother showed us all up, don't you? He's taking First Flight a year early."

I glanced at Dag but the smile was still fixed in place.

Sippy from behind me was craning his long neck toward Eled, or anyway Eled's trousers. Foogits' nostrils are like gathered or pleated, and foogits make the most revolting noise when they blow out through them to clear the way for new smells, and he was doing it a lot lately, because of the extra town smells, I suppose. But he sounded like he had at least forty nostrils when he did it now. Eled glanced down. It was a long way down for him so maybe he really hadn't noticed Sippy before. "Clear skies and great dragons," he said. "It's a little dragon. He yours?"

Nobody calls foogits little dragons except in folk tales. Eled had to have been being sarcastic, but I couldn't hear him doing it, so I muttered, "His name's Sippy."

"Hey, Sippy," he said, and offered his hand to be snuffled, which was gallant of him. Sippy came out from behind my legs and tried to frolic, which is what he usually does when he's decided he's made a new friend, but there wasn't room, so he banged into all our knees in turn a couple of times and subsided with a wounded look at the hurrying passers-by who were cramping his style. Eled laughed. It was a nice laugh.

"I've never heard anyone call a foogit a little dragon," Dag said, who knew the same folk tales that I did.

"Didn't your dad ever—" Eled broke off, looking embarrassed. I'd already noticed that Eled didn't have the manner of a carpenter's son.

"Eled's dad is a dragonrider," Dag said calmly to me.

"And my mum's oldest brother and four of my cousins," Eled said, grinning again. "And both granddads and all four of their granddads. My dad has two brothers and two sisters. And all of their first sons went to the Academy. And three of their daughters. And one second and one third son. I'm the youngest first son in this generation—and I have four older sisters, and one of them is a dragonrider too. I had the worst childhood you can imagine."

I didn't mean to laugh, but I did, and for the first time since Dag had come home and told us about Hereyta, some part of me I couldn't name stopped feeling quite so gloomy.

Eled looked pleased, and even Dag's smile softened a little.

"Is everyone else here?" said Dag.

"Pretty much," said Eled. "A few of you with a long way to come are still on the road."

A long way to come trailing extra cargo, I thought. And can't afford coach fare. Not that any coach would take a foogit.

Dag nodded.

After an uncomfortable little pause Eled said to me, "Most of us First Flighters get back early from this break. We can't stay away. Everybody else turns up at the last minute like normal. First Flight itself happens first day of term. We're supposed to get back one day before to check our gear over one last time, not like we didn't leave it in blisteringly perfect order, and to look our dragons over too, but the dragonmasters have been doing that while we're on leave a lot better than us dumb cadets can. A lot of the dragonmasters say that we shouldn't be allowed to come back early, because we fret the dragons. Most Academy dragons take First Flight every year."

Dag's silence was getting louder and louder.

Abruptly Eled added, "I'm hungry. Let's go back to halls and get something to eat."

They set off but I just stood there. Sippy started to follow them and then stopped when I didn't move, looking at me and them and back at me again.

"Come on then," said Eled, "no reason to block traffic," as a great rumbling cart went by and Sippy shied into me so violently he nearly knocked me down.

"I—er—Sippy and I will go to an inn if you'll tell us which one," I said. "I mean, cheap."

"Not necessary," said Eled. "Nobody does it much lately but in my dad's day First Flighters always brought someone from home to see them off. It's good luck."

"Not foogits," I said, stubbornly standing where I was. I held on to a handful of Sippy's ear to make him stand still. This would work for approximately two minutes but was good for emergencies.

"Nonsense," Eled replied. "Exactly what they are is lucky."

Maybe fool's luck, I thought. Maybe sometimes that's good luck.

"My aunt keeps foogits," said Eled. "I've always liked 'em. I miss having 'em around at the Academy."

Dag was smiling again, but he looked genuincly amused. "If Eled says you and Sippy should come, you'd better. It's easier than arguing with him."

Eled grinned a slightly different kind of grin and I thought, I just bet people don't argue with him much, and I wondered when Eled had befriended Dag and what Fistagh thought about it.

"And besides, Tinhead," my brother went on graciously, "do you really think I'd drag you all this way and then pitch you in an inn? Ralas would be ashamed of both of us."

"Ralas?" said Eled.

"Our wizard," said Dag. "And she's a good one. I don't know how our little boring village keeps her. She told me to bring Ern and Sippy."

"Did she then?" said Eled, looking at me thoughtfully in a way I didn't like at all. I let go of Sippy's ear and started off in the direction they'd been walking before Eled said anything else. In a minute I was struggling to keep up—Eled's legs must have been twice as long as mine. He said casually, "My granddad on my mum's side, he had a foogit. She flew with him and his dragon. It was rare in his day but he told me that in his granddad's day all the dragonriders had foogits. They were mascots—they were good luck."

Dag, equally casual, said from Eled's other side: "I don't suppose your granddad had any good stories about two-eyed dragons, did he?"

There was a pause full of stall-holders shouting, "Three a penny! Your best deal *here*!"

"I don't get it," Eled said finally. "It's making me crazier than a blind cawgilly in spring, trying to find a way to think about it. And okay, the grown-ups have to huff and blow and tell you you're a bad boy and so on and so on—"

I was startled enough to look up here, but Eled was waiting to catch my eye. "No, he didn't tell you that part, did he? He's a bit of a brawler, your brother, when the virtue of one of his dragons is impugned. And they're all his dragons. But that's why he got jumped, you know? He has what Dorgin—he's the chief dragonmaster—calls the *grace* of dragonriding."

"Eled, shut up," said Dag.

"I knew he wasn't telling you the whole story," said Eled, imperturbably. "If Hereyta still had three eyes we'd've probably all expected her to get him, even if she's old. She's that good. She was the best before she lost an eye, and she's been the best drill dragon the Academy ever had. And she doesn't lose her edge even though she never gets to cycle out like the rest of 'em. That's just it. She's just as proud—and as merciless—as she was when she still Flew. A lot of the drill dragons numb out, they've been through too many beginners and all they think about when they're here is food and sleep and when they cycle out again.

"I don't know if any mere rubbishy little human is up to Hereyta's standard but your brother is pretty close. I bet she brawled in her youth too—I bet her dragonmaster, when she was a youngling, had nightmares about her, when he wasn't dreaming of what she'd accomplish when she was grown, if she didn't kill off too many dragonmasters in the process. Did Dag tell you she has *three* crowns? She got the third one for the spear she took for Carn—that, and getting him home anyway."

"Maybe," I said, thinking about Ralas, "maybe their wizard told them to do it."

They both looked at me. "The Academy doesn't like wizards much," Eled said at last. "We're supposed to do without what wizards do—charms and spells and so on—it's all about dragons here. We do have a bonesetter and stitcher, but he's only for the cadets—the dragonmasters do for the dragons—and he's expected to keep out of sight. I can't imagine anyone going to him for advice, or listening to him if he was rash enough to give it."

"We have Seers," said Dag grimly.

"Yes, we do," said Eled, the way you might say "we have rats."

Ralas had once said of one of her scariest-looking visitors, "Oh, he's a Seer. They get like that. He started as a wizard—most of them do—but he didn't stay there." She'd made a quick, ironical face, as if perhaps he should have.

Dag glanced at me. "They're supposed to read the signs and so on. The Academy won't take you if the Seers find against you. And the Seers read for First Flight."

"Maybe we should try wizards," said Eled.

We were getting near what even I could guess had to be the Academy gates. We had crossed what must have been the oldest part of the town, where there were lumpy, bulgy, much-mended walls which ran in all directions and sometimes they made sense and sometimes they didn't. But the way we were going now was getting more open and less crowded. I hadn't realised I'd been breathing shallowly till I started breathing normally again. All those buildings and people really lean on you. The problem was that as soon as I took a few deep breaths I was zinging all over with a different kind of tension. I didn't remember when the wall had changed from an ordinary town wall to something else, but as we neared the huge gates—big enough, I guessed, for two dragons to go through together, although it seemed kind of unlikely they'd want to—it was obvious that the wall that led up to it was anything but ordinary. There were pillars built into it at intervals, and the mended places were a lot neater, and it was twice as high, which presumably meant it was twice as thick.

My mind went blank and I started walking jerkily, like my legs were trying to turn me around and run me away, which they probably were, but I was too scared even to think about that. There was a guard at the gate although the gates were open. The wall there was twice as wide as I was tall. "Clear skies," Eled said to the guard affably.

"And to you," replied the guard. His gaze lingered on me and Sippy, but he didn't say anything. I was still on the other side of Eled from Dag. Eled put his hand on my shoulder and pointed with the other, saying, "That way." I'm sure the guard thought my presence was his fault. I didn't know whether to be flattered or embarrassed.

Sippy and I got some funny looks and both Dag and Eled said "clear skies" or "hey" to what seemed to me to be a lot of people but probably wasn't. The food halls were nearly big enough for dragons, and nearly empty, or maybe they just seemed that way because of their size. Eled evidently was hungry and Dag and I should have been but weren't, and Sippy got most of ours. When we left the halls Sippy staggered after us, obviously wishing he could lie down somewhere and sleep it off.

We stopped just outside. "You're going to go see Ansilika," said Dag. "She's always anxious before a First."

"Trust you to know that," said Eled. "Yes. I would've come back early anyway but maybe I came back a little earlier still because I knew she'd be worrying. Probably about me. 'Can that great oaf stay in the saddle on the day or will he dishonour his family's proud name?' But I'll see you there later."

"Yes," said Dag. "And Ansilika won't let you fall off. You'd have to jump. I'll see where to stow all of us and then I'll be along too." He turned away and I glanced at Eled before I followed. I knew I should say something but "my open-handed thanks, excellent sir," which would probably have been the correct form, or anything else along those lines, felt like it would sound the opposite.

"See you," said Eled.

"Yeah," I said courteously.

He hesitated. "If you want to know something about anything around here, you can always ask me. Dag's maybe a little obsessed with dragons."

I glanced at my brother. Tell me about the brawls, and about grace, I thought, but I didn't say it. "Yeah," I said again. "Thanks."

"If your brother calls you Tinhead, what do you call him?"

"Geezer," I said.

Eled laughed.

"His sisters call *him* Ogre," said Dag. "Dyla told me. She's the one graduated from here."

"And I keep forgetting to grind her bones for my bread," said Eled. "Families—who needs 'em?"

As I followed Dag it seemed to me his shoulders were squarer than usual. We went into a slightly less huge building and climbed a lot of stairs, all of our feet making funny noises on the tiles. We had wood floors at home, and Dad's workshop was packed earth. "This is mine," Dag said on about the ninety-fifth landing, and pushed open a door. I fell in after him, gasping. "You can have the bottom bunk in case Sippy wants to join you." Dag didn't even sit down, and he wasn't breathing hard. He dumped his pack on the upper bunk and looked at me. "I'm going to go see Hereyta. D'you want to come?"

I was sure I should let him greet her in private, but I rolled up instantly off the bed where I had flopped and said yes. It wasn't even anything to do with not wanting to be left behind in a really strange place and wondering what I would say if anyone knocked on the door looking for Dag. I wanted to meet Hereyta.

The dragon *hsa* were on the far side of the training fields which meant a long hike, although the training fields went on and on and on out to either side of us a lot farther yet than what we were walking across. I wondered if a piece of this ground was used for First Flight or if it happened somewhere else entirely. Dragons have tremendously powerful wings to get themselves off the ground at all, and they really lash 'em. And gods help any mere paltry human caught in the backdraft. So maybe the First Flight field, where there would be a whole lot of dragons stirring up storm winds, was some special separate place. In which case I wouldn't see it. Whatever it was like in Eled's granddad's day.

Nobody knows if dragons really can spout fire any more, or whether that's all a complete myth (like whether or not foogits ever had a working third eye), or if over several thousand years of selective breeding humans have managed to get rid of the fire-spouting (in which case we'll be in a lot of trouble if we have a nasty-tempered throwback some day. The myths include whole countries burning if they get a big enough dragon mad at them). Dragons spit a little fire at you no more often than a horse tries to kick you. Which is to say if you treat your dragon nicely you're fine. Or that's the standard line. It's different though because horses are twitchier animals generally; they're prey. Dragons aren't. They can afford to have a look and a think before they do anything about it; nobody's going to bite them on the back of the neck and then tear out their entrails. And domestic dragons have been bred for good temper for a long time. People do get burned, but it's rare, and when it happens it's a huge story and it's told all over the country and everyone's horrified and there's always an investigation because the presumption is the human did something wrong.

But dragons still smell of fire. It's a hot, charred smell, and when you smell it for the first time it's pretty scary, even if it's only one of the little ones carrying freight, and even when it's the other side of the jammed-with-smells fairground from where you are and behind the long series of warehouses there. It's scarier yet when you're walking toward a whole *hsa* full of them. I can't begin to imagine who the first human was who decided to try and tame one. It's like who thought of trying to eat a cawgilly for the first time? They sure don't look like they'd be good to eat and they smell bad too, raw, even after you've got rid of the scent glands. But at least a cawgilly isn't as big as a mountain. Also they run away if they see you coming after them, like a wild horse does. And there's no fire involved.

I kept reminding myself that not only were these tame dragons I was walking toward but this was the Academy, and furthermore I was with my brother who was a First Flighter at the Academy. What was really interesting though is that Sippy, who'd spent most of the last ten days skulking and cowering, wasn't. When we first set off he had made an attempt to run a few circles around us, since he had the space to do it in for the first time in several days, but he was still too full of food and had to give it up. He trotted along behind, panting rather, but then he picked up and trotted past us, with his head and ears up and his tail straight out behind with the guard hairs on it raised, which in foogit language means, "Hmm, what's this?" If he'd been frightened or worried the guard hairs would run backwards the full length up his spine, eventually up to his topknot, which would have bushed out (or tried to) like a sort of extreme mane. Among other things this exposes the third eye, if there is one, and I'd never seen Sippy in that much of a strop, although I'm told a big male foogit ready for battle isn't funny any more.

And then I smelled the dragons too, but it made me want to slow down, not speed up.

They're properly called *hsa* but they're often slangily just called barns, Dag told me, and they're huge enough to look at, but huger still from inside, because they're dug into the ground and the hillsides as well. The Academy was where it was because there was this huge flat plain with these sudden hills leaping up at its edge, and the hills are mazes of underground caverns. A mountain over your head keeps the temperature down, and a lot of dragons all rubbing up against each other generate a lot of heat. Supposedly wild dragons lived there once, before the beginning of time. It's been the Academy *hsa* since there was an Academy, and there are pretty much only folk tales about the time before the Academy existed. But even so people had been riding and breeding dragons for riding a long, long time before anyone thought of establishing an Academy about it.

I'd never been there before of course. None of our family had except Dag. I don't know if he remembered what it had been like for him the very first time—but it was the dragons themselves that had made him change his mind about staying at the Academy, and maybe the *wham* had happened while he was walking across this field just like I was. Maybe, if he thought about me at all, and I wouldn't've blamed him if he didn't, he only thought that I was potty about animals too and that I'd have the same reaction to the dragons that he did so he didn't have to worry or think about me, except maybe how lucky I was that I was going to meet, really meet, a dragon, which almost nobody outside the academy system ever does. There are handlers at all the regular commercial stations, but they only handle whatever the dragon is carrying. The only person the dragon pays attention to is the rider—the partner. And that's true several times over in the army.

I felt myself starting to walk stiffly, like I had approaching the Academy gates. But this was worse. I fixed my eyes on Sippy's happy, interested tail a few paces in front of me, and told myself that if my foogit could do it, so could I.

There was a beyond-enormous door in front of us. The funny thing was it was built like an ordinary double stable door, and the top halves were open. Any of the four quarters was big enough to be the roof of our house with some left over. When you got close enough you saw there was an ordinary human-sized door cut into the right-hand bottom half. I didn't mean to giggle but I did, although it sounded more like I was being stabbed than laughing. Dag said at once, "I know. But dragons don't like draughts. It makes them restless. So we keep the bottoms closed all year, and the tops closed in the winter."

Sippy squeezed through the little people door with me and I took hold of his topknot on the far side to keep him near me. Holding an ear isn't fair for long; it's just for when you really need him to pay attention. His topknot was nice and long and I could get a good grip and he could still turn his head.

There was the rustle of vastness all around us. It took an effort of will to look up from the top of Sippy's head. I looked up. There was a sharp slope down from the doors and then a *big* empty sandy space just beyond that. It was pretty scuffed up but at the same time you knew it got raked all the time, and there were the rakes, leaning on either side of the doors. The piece at the bottom with teeth was about as wide as I am tall, and the length of the handles was twice that. Beyond the sandy space it was too far away and dark to see clearly, but that's where the rustling came from.

Dag set off at once down a corridor. We were still mostly above ground and there were windows here although they were over our heads, and the corridor slanted downwards. Pretty soon it was more shadows than light, and then the lanterns began, sitting in niches in the walls (the first ones low enough for mere humans to fill and trim and light them; then when the second overhead rank began there also started to be the occasional ladder hung against the wall). Every so often there was a wide gap in the walls—a gigantic doorway—with its own shadows and its own flickering light. And its own hot charred smell.

We met the occasional other human. I recognised the cadet uniform, but there was another uniform too. One of the men in the other uniform stopped as we came toward him. "*Singla* Dag, honoured sir," he began. "You sand-for-brains chucklehead, Dag, don't you know enough to climb back into your uniform before you come to the *hsa*? I won't report you, but there are plenty who will."

"I forgot," said Dag, humbly for Dag.

"I believe you, or I'd send you back. I still should send you back. If you hear anyone coming, hide behind a dragon, will you?"

"Yes, *Hlorgla* Dorgin," said Dag, still humble.

"Mmph," said Dorgin, and looked at me. "You must be one of his brothers," he said.

"I—er—yes, sir," I said.

"You look like him," said Dorgin.

"No, sir," I said.

Dorgin smiled suddenly. "You'll grow into those feet," he said. "I've seen dragons like you. Keep your brother in order, will you? I wonder what else I should be telling you, besides don't let him go to the *hsa* out of uniform?" He gave Dag another glare and walked on.

"That was Dorgin," said Dag unnecessarily.

"Have we met anyone who's going to report you?" I said.

"I don't think so," said Dag, whose mind was obviously leaving this uninteresting topic.

"You wouldn't want to tell me what Fistagh looks like?" I said innocently.

Dag gave me a sharp look and then laughed, although the laugh was almost as sharp as the look. "I'll hide behind a dragon like Dorgin said, okay?"

After a lot more corridors and a lot farther going down, we came to another big sandy space. There was a fire burning in a stone-ringed fire pit in the centre of it. The smoke rose cleanly and straight up, and I looked up to see where it was going, but the ceiling, assuming there was a ceiling, was again lost in darkness, along with the chimney-hole. Dag made a curious humming, crooning noise. It wasn't very loud and I don't think it was just the creepiness of the surroundings that would have made me take special notice of almost anything, but it was a very attention-catching sound.

And an immense heap of darkness at the edge of the firelight uncurled itself, and made a crooning noise in return. This sound was no louder than Dag's had been, but it could no more have been made by a human chest than a human could fly. It was like the echo of an earthquake. I was surprised the earth didn't tremble underfoot. Sippy, however, was trembling like seven earthquakes, and he made no attempt to get away from my now-convulsive grip on his crest, but I thought the trembling was more excitement than fear. I was trembling too, but I wouldn't want to say it was mostly excitement.

We stood still as Dag went toward the humming blackness. Against the firelight I could see what I guessed was a head and neck untwist itself from the top of the mound, and arch down toward Dag. Dag reached a hand up toward it; it was like a leaf trying to pat a forest.

But the forest liked it. The hum dropped down a few more earth-shaking notes and the gigantic spade-shaped head—which I could now just make out in the twilight—came to a halt within human arm's length of Dag's hand. I thought dizzily of the sensation of a gnat landing on your skin; you could just about feel it if you were paying attention. And dragons must have thick skin. Maybe not on their noses. I hoped dragons didn't blow through their nostrils the way foogits did.

Dag left his hand on the dragon's nose and turned his head toward me. "Come say hello. She knows you're here and that you came with me. But it's polite to greet her yourself."

I walked toward them, feeling as if I was in a dream. The weird light and the weird echoy rustling noises that came from everywhere—and the sense of being so far underground—was part of it but it was mostly the dragon. This dragon. Her humming was almost inaudible now but she didn't seem to want to dislodge Dag's tiny hand, so as Sippy and I came closer, rather than turning toward us, there was a sort of half-imaginary tremor through the blackness that was perhaps her acknowledgement or her acceptance of our approach. When I was standing right beside Dag there was a ripple at the top of the head that I thought might be ears.

Dag said sheepishly, "I don't know how to do this. I've never introduced anyone to their first dragon. When we do it as cadets, we kneel."

This seemed perfectly reasonable to me. I knelt. Sippy prostrated himself without any prompting from me. I let go of his topknot and bowed my head so I didn't see her move her head at last, but I heard it—do I mean heard? Underground in the dark next to a dragon your senses do funny things—and felt the surprisingly gentle whisper of her breath through my hair. I don't know if she quite touched me or not, but I felt the heat of her on the top of my head.

Everything was fine. Then Sippy leaped up from his imitation of a hearth-rug, and licked her nose.

The head disappeared instantly, whipping back up and away from us into the darkness, and the rest of the darkness blurred at the edges as it shifted backward. "Oh, *Sippy*," I wailed. I didn't suppose an unwanted lick on the nose would be one of the things that made a dragon spit fire, but I didn't want her even a little bit mad at Dag five days before First Flight either.

It took me half a minute to realise that the noise I was hearing was Dag laughing—a normal, easy, proper laugh, like it wasn't costing him anything. And there was another noise too that later on I learnt was the sound of him scratching one of her forelegs. Dragons' claws are very flat, so you can just about reach their ankles when they're standing up. "I was going to take her outside anyway. Let's go now before Sippy gangs up on her." He set off at a brisk trot and I heaved myself along in his wake. I wanted to protest the pace, but when you think about it, you running flat out is still a slow amble to a dragon. And furthermore it was *uphill*. Sippy dashed ahead of us and then dashed back, but he had to make do with jumping straight up in the air since Hereyta was keeping her head well out of reach. It looked a little like his swerving-and-leaping game.

Outside in daylight . . . dragons are *beautiful*. Their skin shines rainbow colours, although a green dragon is green under the rainbows, and a red dragon is red, and so on. As I say, I'd seen a few little ones that did hop-stops to the bigger towns near us, and I thought they were beautiful and proud and just a little bit arrogant— which they were. That's what dragons are like. But Hereyta just about knocked me over, just looking at her. She was a kind of red-gold; when she stretched her wings the iridescence made them look like they were on fire, and when she gave them a flap you would swear you could see the fire running down their edges. I mean, yes, all dragons are beautiful—all the ones I've seen, anyway—but Hereyta was special. Hereyta was amazing. I knew this, even if I had never seen a dragon up close before, and even if she was Dag's dragon so I was going to like her even if she was foogit-sized, dung-coloured, and warty. And even if she had only two eyes.

Dragon eyes vary in colour the way dragon skins do, but all dragon eyes glitter. I know that you talk about eyes glittering— the evil enchanter in a fairy tale always has glittering eyes; so do the things in dark corners when you're little and trying to go to sleep— but dragon-eye glitter is the real thing. I suppose almost everything about a dragon is scary, because they're so huge, and also, of course, because they're the only creature (that we know of) that can fly through the Firespace. But the glitter of their eyes isn't like anything else.

I think that it's the glitter of dragon eyes that's the origin of all those stories about the beds of jewels that wild dragons are supposed to have made for themselves back in the days when dragons were wild, and used to eat children when they couldn't find any sheep. Where all those jewels are supposed to have come from was always beyond me; even if you put all the kings and emperors and enchanters (good and evil) together and stripped them of everything they had, I still don't think you'd get more than about one jewel-bed for one medium-large dragon out of it. But you see the glitter of the eyes and you do think of jewels. Nothing else comes close—not fire, not stars, not anything. Of course I, and most of the other listeners to fairy tales, have never seen more than the mayor's beryl or topaz or whatever the local badge of office is, but we can all dream. When you see a dragon's eyes up close—if you're lucky enough to see a dragon's eyes up close—you don't have to dream.

It was Hereyta's left eye that was gone. Dragons have that great knobbly ridge over their eyes, and some of the breeding lines still throw out horns sometimes, but no really top-class dragon has horns any more. Hereyta didn't. And she had two eyes—which shone so vividly I felt I'd be embarrassed ever staring into a mere bonfire again—and one black crater. It wasn't ugly, any more than a dark hollow in a mountainside is ugly, but it looked all wrong.

She didn't seem to favour that side. As soon as we got outdoors—and this was true every time we came outdoors together for the few days left before First Flight—Sippy went into his full rushing-and-leaping-into-the-air routine. Dag just about killed himself laughing, that first time. In other circumstances I'd've probably got pretty mad at him laughing at Sippy like that, but it didn't actually feel like he was laughing at Sippy. It was like Sippy was doing him this enormous favour by letting all the laughter he hadn't been able to laugh out, where it ought to be, instead of all pent up inside and squashed by worry and misery. Like Sippy licking Hereyta's nose had knocked the bung out of the barrel, and now the laughter came flooding out. And because I wasn't getting mad, I noticed what it really was: love. Dag really loved Hereyta. I understood that. It's so much easier, loving animals. They love you right back, and it doesn't get complicated. Unless it's a two-eyed dragon who you've been partnered with for First Flight at your dragonrider academy.

I don't know if Hereyta just had really nice manners (yes) or if she was amused by Sippy too, but rather than ignoring the tiny lunatic doing his nut around her feet, by the end of that first game she'd developed her own side of it. When Sippy did it to me, the only rule I played by was that I had to move between rushes, so he had to keep adjusting and re-aiming. It was like, if you're going to be this insane, I'm at least not going to make it easy for you. Hereyta used her head. She'd arch her endless neck (I swear the top of the arch had clouds hanging over it) so that her nose was just above ground level—say the top of my head, which is just above ground level to a dragon—and as Sippy rushed at her, she'd twitch it aside. I don't think he started to develop his mid-air twist till he was playing with Hereyta; I was too easy a target. Then she'd move her head along sideways—keeping it amazingly the same distance above the ground—as if she was daring Sippy to try again, which of course he did.

I wasn't laughing like Dag, like that giddy relief when the painbane finally kicks in, but I'd almost forgotten all our problems, watching Hereyta and Sippy having such a good time. And then Dag suddenly shut off like he was a door that had been closed. There was a little breeze, and between the sound of that, and Sippy's panting (and thudding back to the ground), and Dag's laughter, I hadn't noticed anything else. But there was another dragon in the field with us. Fancy not having noticed a dragon. But I was fully occupied watching our dragon.

This one was a kind of midnight blue, and it was only about two-thirds the size of Hereyta, which was still plenty big enough. There was a tiny person tearing along beside it with his hand on its ankle, the way Dag had had his hand on Hereyta's. They'd come out of the *hsa* after us. It was half rousing its wings as I turned my head, although I don't know if this was a greeting or an "I can take you with one wing tied behind my back" show for Hereyta's sake. Hereyta went on playing Sippy's game as if it was all that mattered. I can't believe she didn't know the blue dragon was there, but I still don't know nearly enough about dragon behaviour and I didn't know anything then.

So I made do with the fact that Dag wasn't happy to see whoever it was. He didn't say anything to Hereyta, but I don't know if you call off a dragon like you call off a dog (or grab your foogit by the topknot). I know I keep saying how they've been bred for thousands of years to be amenable to human commands, but I defy you to get anywhere near a dragon and not utterly and profoundly believe that a dragon obeys any human only because it is a *bizarrely* good-natured creature. Or maybe because it has a bizarre sense of humour, in which case maybe dragons have something in common with foogits after all. Anyway, Hereyta went on with her game as Dag stiffened himself to greet the other dragonrider.

"May you fly over a clear horizon," said the other, with that funny lilt that goes with a formal ritual greeting. I thought I saw his eyebrows go up as he registered that Dag was out of uniform but if they did they came right back down again.

Dag without preamble said to me, "This is Setyep." I was horribly embarrassed. I was sure there was a proper response to the greeting before you even got to the introductions, and then there is no way that a younger brother should have been introduced first to a dragonrider, even a pre-First-Flight cadet dragonrider. But that was Dag. He'd sit the dragonrider exams to please his parents (and maybe a little to show his cousin we weren't the useless branch of the family) but once he found himself in the Academy, he was going to do it his way. "Setyep," he went on, "this is my brother, Ern."

If Setyep was offended, he didn't show it. Maybe he was used to Dag. His eyebrows didn't even twitch. "That's a foogit, isn't it?" he said, sounding interested. "How did you train it to do that? I could use a foogit myself, if I'd known."

I may have made a gargling noise.

"Arac"—this was presumably the dragon, who was now staring off over the trees as if it hadn't seen Hereyta either, and hadn't roused its wings in an attempt that failed to get a response out of her—"can be remarkably lazy about paying attention to which direction I'm trying to send him in, and I live in dread that he'll go some other way entirely, from not paying attention."

I felt Dag relax a little. I wondered what Setyep had done to annoy him. He'd stiffened for Eled too when we'd first met him but this was a stiffer stiffening. "I'm not sure Ern would call it training, would you, Ern?"

I tried to swallow the large boulder in my throat and with a heroic effort made a semi-intelligible answer. "He's always done that. When I—er—when I found him he had a broken leg, and at first when he could use it again, this seemed like a good way to exercise it. But it was his idea. I just didn't, you know, try to stop him."

Setyep seemed to find this amusing. "I'm only a cadet, of course," he said, "but I guess that's pretty much how dragons get trained too. We don't stop them doing things and then pretend it was our idea. The big question has always been why they happen to do things we might want them to do—and why they let us get away with pretending it had anything to do with us."

This was so much what I had been thinking I was temporarily distracted. I hadn't seen either dragon move; it wasn't that they were standing like statues, but I hadn't seen them move purpose-fully. But somehow or other they had squared themselves off so that Sippy was suddenly like the third point of the triangle. I don't know why it looked like that to me. If you have three things plonked down somewhere you can always make a triangle out of them, can't you? And Sippy—it's not like he ever stayed plonked.

But as he ran around making hexagons and dodecagons and things—like a street fair juggler moving his hands fast enough to fool you about where he's hidden the pebble or the ball—it was like when he ran over the correct triangle point something happened. Or something almost happened. I know how dumb this sounds, but for like half a breath where we were was somewhere else. It was hotter there, wherever it was, and the trees had a funny pink halo. If they were trees.

Then Hereyta turned her head, and whatever it was—whatever dragon magic it was—was broken. Arac turned his head too, and looked at Hereyta. Then they both looked at Sippy. Sippy nodded his head and shook himself all over . . . and then flung himself on the ground and rolled around wildly as if it was all too much for him. Whatever it was. Having two dragons to run at, maybe, as-suming what I'd just seen was his adaptation of his game, for two dragons. I wondered if either of the other humans present had no-ticed anything. Anything like hot wind and pink trees.

Dag was in fact looking at the sky. "There aren't any clouds," he said. "And the trees are motionless. Am I losing my mind or is there a weird breath of hot air that keeps gusting over us?"

"You're probably losing your mind," said Setyep. "It's a well-known phenomenon, First Flight nerves. But I've got it too, if it's any comfort—it's more like opening an oven door, rather than a breeze."

"Yes," said Dag. "That's what I thought."

There was a little silence. "Even Dorgin says he lives in a state of perpetual surprise, living around dragons," said Sctycp. "It'll be suppertime by the time we get the dragons back to the *hsa*. You hungry?"

Sippy, who has a limited vocabulary, understood "hungry." The way he tore around he was always hungry, and playing with dragons had evidently worn off lunch. He shot over and pranced around Setyep who had said the magic word. Setyep bent to pat him when he came to a halt for long enough, and ruffled the forelock that fell into his eyes. "He's got the vestigial third eye, doesn't he?" he said. "I've always heard that's lucky in a foogit."

I shrugged. "It's supposed to be rare. People always make rare stuff lucky, don't they?"

"Getting killed by a roc is rare," said Setyep. "And I've never heard that it's lucky."

Dag laughed and Setyep looked pleased. "Come on then, supper for you too," he said, and stretched up to put his hand on Arac's nearer ankle spur. Arac turned—obediently, carefully, setting each enormous foot down as gently as a feather, as if testing for the presence of small crunchable creatures before he put his weight on it. Also when you're that big even stepping along really slowly eats up the landscape, and gives the small crunchable creatures you're being careful not to stand on a chance to keep up with you—and started back toward the hill.

"That was interesting," said Dag as soon as Setyep was out of earshot. "Setyep said a long time ago that he thinks jumping lower-class cadets is all wrong and it's no wonder trouble comes of it. At least he admits it. Fistagh doesn't think he has to admit anything. But it's not that much easier to live with your enemy even when you know who he is. Not that he's exactly my enemy."

I said, "He's nothing like your enemy. He admires you. He wants you to think well of him."

Dag looked at me like I'd grown a second head. Or a third eye. "You're raving. But he may be making an effort because Arac has a crush on Hereyta."

"People change," I said. "They grow up. They learn things. They change their minds."

"Gods, Tinhead, you sound like Dad," said Dag. "Or a wizard." He looked up and Hereyta, with that weird consciousness good dragons have of their partners, looked down. For some reason the sun was glaring right across her brow crest, and shining into her missing eye. The blind black hollow showed suddenly, shockingly, red, and full of light.

The last few days before First Flight went way too quickly. Some of it was just trying to get along in this very strange new place Sippy and I found ourselves in, but that should have made the time crawl by, wondering every time you put a foot down if it's the wrong foot on the wrong piece of ground. And trying to make yourself invisible is very tiring. (Also impossible, if you have a foogit with you.) But time with Hereyta—and most of our time was with Hereyta—flew by.

It wasn't till dinner the day after we arrived that Eled said to Dag, "Haven't you got Ern a visitor's ribbon yet, you chucklehead? What happened, getting yourself back into uniform absorbed your total non-dragon powers of concentration? And there's old *Zek* Darab

with his eagle eye at the tutors' table now." Dag got me the ribbon
the next morning. After that I felt a little better, especially after I
saw someone else wearing one.

But mostly I was too busy identifying with Dag to think about
how I was feeling. Every minute that went by was another minute
closer to First Flight. And there weren't enough minutes in all of
history to spend with Hereyta, even if First Flight hadn't existed.

At first I helped polish Hereyta's harness, not that it needed it or
Dag needed any help; but that meant he could spend a few more
hours polishing Hereyta herself, which they both enjoyed. Not that
she needed it either. From a little distance she glowed in the dark,
like she was all over eyes—those magical, shining dragon eyes—like
every single faintly-hollow-curve scale was an eye: thousands and
thousands of eyes. It can't all have been Dag; there'd have to be twenty
Dags to keep one Hereyta polished, if she really needed polishing.

I admit I found harness boring when there was a whole mountain range of dragon available, and it was almost like Hereyta left
bits of herself near me as a lure or an invitation, so I polished the
odd toe and fraction of cheek and a few human-hands'-breadth of
tail myself which I knew was just a special treat for a new worshipper. Up close you could lose yourself in the reflections, running a
soft cloth over her scales. The reflections went on forever, down and
down and down, into, who knows, the Grey Place, maybe. Maybe
the Grey Place is grey and cold because the dragons stole all the
colour and all the fire. If they did, I'm sure they didn't mean to. Or
maybe the Grey Place had been the first worshipper, and gave the
dragons everything.

I woke up with a crick in my neck the second night at the Academy, which I discovered was the pot of ache ointment that Ralas
had given me. None of us had needed it and I'd forgotten about it
(although how it got under my pillow I have no idea) and that morn-

ing before breakfast while I was waiting for Dag to sew a last-minute escapist button on his jacket (cadets, even or perhaps especially rogue cadets, had better not ever be seen outside their own rooms in a uniform missing a button: Dag was muttering and scowling, but he was also sewing) I sat on my bed tossing the pot from hand to hand. Sippy, having made sure it wasn't edible, let me do this without getting in the way. I could feel my face frowning.

Dag stopped scowling when he bit off his thread and looked up. "What's wrong? You look kind of like the morning after the night before, except we didn't have one."

I stopped tossing the pot. "This is the stuff Ralas gave me, in case we got road sore. And then we didn't. I was just thinking . . . about Hereyta's stiff wing . . . I mean, it can't hurt. If she'd let me. If you'd let me. It's only a little pot." Hereyta had a long scar across her belly from her first crown, which didn't seem to bother her at all, and a stiff wing-joint from her second. And a missing eye from her third.

Dag looked surprised, then thoughtful. "We'll ask Hereyta."

I was dragon-besotted enough by then that asking her seemed perfectly reasonable, but I had enough brain left over to wonder how we were going to do it. Dag and she had long conversations—even I could see that—but I didn't think they were about anything much, most of the time, or if they were, I couldn't translate. This was going to be one I could actually watch, and maybe I'd learn something.

Except that it wasn't like that. We brought Hereyta outside and found a little space (which is to say a vast space) away from all the other cadets with their dragons, behind a grove of trees that must have been almost as old as the Academy. There weren't many of them but they were big gnarly old things and they weren't totally dwarfed by our dragon. Then Dag told me matter-of-factly to take the lid off my pot and hold it up toward Hereyta.

"She's not going to pay any attention to me," I muttered.

"Yes she is," said Dag. "Do try a little less hard to keep yourself crammed into that dim-little-brother mould of yours."

I looked up at him, startled, and forgot to keep my shoulders hunched up.

"Better," he said. "You keep coming with me, and she pays attention to me, doesn't she? She's not stupid."

"But—I—"

"Yes. Exactly," said Dag. "You're going to have to choose. You're going to have to give it up that you're a worm, because Hereyta notices you, and Hereyta wouldn't notice a worm, would she? Or you can think she's stupid. Your choice."

I stared at him with my mouth open.

"Open the pot and hold it up," Dag said inexorably. "You can leave your mouth open too if you want."

I took the lid off and held it up. Hereyta's enormous nose descended toward it and then paused, waiting politely.

"Dab a little on your fingers, and then gesture at her wing, like this," said Dag, and showed me a kind of sweep-and-point motion, which I half recognised from watching him groom her, and then clumsily followed. Her wing immediately unbent down, toward me, the bottom edge splaying against the ground, and the red lights bucking up out of the creases like live things themselves. Then her head came all the way down till it was resting flat on the ground, the nose pointed straight at me. Her breath poured around me, gentle as a caress, endless as the sea.

Dag nodded. "I knew she liked you. Climb up. She'll take you to where you want to go. Pat her with one hand and then point with the other, and she'll take you in that direction."

"Oh, but—"

"Don't worry. She's taught dozens of terrified and adoring cadets how to talk to a dragon. She'll teach you too."

"Oh, but—"

"We only use the tapping sticks on formal occasions or when we're flying," Dag said nonchalantly as if he thought that would be what I would be asking him about. "Your hand'll be fine." Dag has a lot of force of personality. I can see why dragons liked him, but it's hard on little brothers. I swallowed hard. I don't *like* heights, and Hereyta was big even for a dragon. I looked at her. Even her *nose* was taller than I was. But I spent the rest of the day climbing and patting and pointing . . . and rubbing, since there were several leagues of shoulder once I got there, and even through a dragon's thick skin I could feel some of where the tension and stiffness ran. I almost forgot about how high up I was, at the crest of her spine, where the wing-joints were.

"You could help," I said, panting, to Dag.

"I could," he agreed, from somewhere out of sight around her rib cage. His voice echoed slightly. "But I'm not going to. This is your show, I think." The way he said it I didn't even feel like my older brother was telling me he wasn't going to do something I wanted him to do. What I thought of was the way he agreed when Ralas told him to take Sippy and me with him. Just like that. No fuss. Although that was about Ralas, of course. And it was me she gave the ointment to.

Dragon skin isn't, I guess, quite as thick as you think—or anyway as I thought—it's just that they're so big, dragons, everything is all about how big they are. Also the bumps and knobs and ridges are thick and hard, but they're supposed to be protective. The scales in between feel surprisingly like skin—warm and unexpectedly elastic. Although you still have to get down on your hands and knees and lean as hard as you can when you're trying to rub liniment into a dragon. And the occasional scale-edge bites into your palms. But you know you've finally started to get where you want to go when the dragon begins to hum.

◆ ◆ ◆

By that third day the other cadets were coming back. A few of the fourth-years came around when everyone was eating to gloat at the First Flighters, but it was a nice sort of gloating, a "see you on the other side" kind. Most of the different years did kind of stick together, the first-years together and so on, but you could sure tell that the third-years were a tense bunch. They were huddled together like a regiment in enemy territory. Dag being Dag, he joined the First Flighters but always managed to stay at the edge. I could guess that he'd been like this before the First Flight assignments went up, but it made it easier for the third-years to overlook him now. Except it seemed to me that they didn't. If anything they were trying to welcome him but he wasn't making it easy. Dag is a stubborn old geezer and I guessed that whether it was conscious or not he was damned if he was going to be accepted at last because everyone was (nearly) as upset that Hereyta was on the First Flight list as he was. I swear he got taller every time we approached a third-year group.

But there was more to it than that. I didn't notice, the first two days. One or two people wandered as if idly past where we were sitting and said something to Dag about a dragon, and Dag answered, and they went away again. Then once I did notice that someone seemed to have passed by our table an awful lot for one meal unless he was very hungry or very absent-minded, and finally Eled said to Gham, who were both sitting with us, "Let's go pester the cooks for a few minutes and let poor Chort ask Dag whatever he's dying to ask him. Ern, you come with us."

"No, Ern, you stay here," said Dag. "Chort has to grow up some day, and Ern's not even a cadet."

So Eled and Gham strolled away and Chort, after a moment, sidled up, looking at me in a sidly kind of way, and then asked Dag what seemed to me a completely harmless question about the grooming mixture he used on Hereyta. Dag answered calmly and Chort sidled away again. Eled and Gham came back with a plate of sweet buns the kitchen had given them to make them go away, and we all went on eating. I would have started noticing more after that anyway, but by the next day when the Academy started to fill up again for the next term it got so obvious that a lot of people turned to Dag for answers about dragons that I didn't have to.

But I was totally not expecting it when one of the tutors came to our table at breakfast on the fourth day. The cadets all shot to their feet so I stood up too. Facing us was a tall, white-haired, straight-backed, commanding old fellow in the red and blue of the seriously senior higher-ups. He let everyone scramble to his or her feet and come to some kind of dazed, early-in-the-morning, not-expecting-any-ordeals order, but he had the sort of presence that makes you feel after the fact that whatever you've actually done, it's the right thing. So the line of half-stupefied third-year cadets was transformed under this man's eyes into a crack troop, alert and ready for anything. Ralas has a quieter version of it. It makes you like her even more at the same time as it makes her even more intimidating.

Then he said, as politely as if he were the cadet and we were the tutors, "*Singla* Dag, please introduce me to your brother, as I have not yet had that privilege."

Dag was less flustered than the others, maybe because big impressive in-charge types were all, to him, both inclusively and individually responsible for Hereyta's presence on the First Flight list. The higher you were in the hierarchy the more responsible, and this guy looked pretty high. He answered promptly enough though, and maybe only I could hear the edge in his voice: "*Zedak* Storkhal, this is my brother, Ern. Ern, I wish to present you to *Zedak hri do lun* Storkhal."

I made sure I had my visitor's ribbon on straight, but the *zedak* didn't look like someone who'd be ironic before he laid you out. I didn't know how to address a tutor, let alone a *zedak*, which were the really important ones, and I had no idea what the *hri do lun* meant, but the way everyone was behaving, it probably meant "god." Oh, well, I thought. "*Zedak* Storkhal, my honour is already in your hands; anything else I can give you is yours."

"Your honour is gift enough," this scary old man said, which is the correct response, of course, but he said it as if he meant it. I tried to stand straighter. "But I would ask you for something else. I have heard that you have an ointment that heals old aches, and I, like Hereyta, have a sore shoulder, and I would beg a little of your ointment if I could."

If he had said "the Academy is being dissolved tomorrow and all the dragons set loose to go feral" it couldn't have been more astonishing. Around me I felt everyone turning to stone, and tables all over the hall were falling silent. The *zedak* was standing a few feet away from us and he had a carrying voice.

Back home I was used to giving people stuff for things like aching shoulders. But I was used to having them ask me quietly, and offhand, as if they weren't really asking. I was not used to being addressed like an audience was watching, which there was. And I wasn't at home either. But Ralas had drummed it into me that you were responsible for the stuff you gave people, and you did not automatically give them what they asked for. You asked questions first. I should have been saying "yes, sir, no, sir, how high do I jump, sir?" and I was going to interrogate him instead.

At least I remembered to call him sir. "Honoured sir, I must ask you about the pain in your shoulder, because the liniment may not be the best choice. Sir."

He looked positively amused—and still perfectly at his ease. That made one of him, in the length and breadth of the food halls. "Ask away, respected brother of *Singla* Dag."

So I did, and at the end I took a deep breath and said, "It's not the liniment you want, sir, but"—here patting my pockets; I'd brought all the stuff I knew how to use with me to the Academy because I couldn't help it, it would be like leaving your trousers behind, but most of it was upstairs in Dag's room under the bed—"but delor leaf. Ah." At the same time, I wouldn't feel like myself if my pockets weren't lumpy, and one of the lumps had just proved to be a little cloth wallet I knew contained, among other things, delor leaf. I was fascinated to observe that my hands weren't shaking as I unfolded it. I don't suppose the *zedak* was really ten feet tall but I felt mouse-sized as I went round the table to give him his leaves. "Sir. That's, uh, about three days' worth. Steep it in boiling water. Sir."

"I rejoice in your assistance," said the *zedak* gravely, and turned and left the hall. There was a sigh as big and gusty as a dragon's when everyone started breathing again. I went back to my place and fell into my chair. Dag took one look around and said, "Ern, we're late. Come on." I didn't say, "What do you mean, late? Late for what?" I scrambled gratefully to my feet, grabbed what was easily grabbable from my plate for Sippy, who had missed the excitement by scrounging for crumbs under the table, and both of us followed Dag.

We were heading straight for the *hsa*. After a few minutes I risked glancing at Dag. He was smiling faintly. He noticed me looking and looked back. "I don't know what's in Firstarrow's mind, but whatever it was he was pleased with you. I know you're not a cadet or anything but people gibber and fall over when he appears from no-where like that, which is what he does. You can see where he got his nickname. Although there's a story that when he was a zero level soldier waiting in reserve on his first battle he let off an arrow before the command, except that he killed the assassin that was trying to sneak up on their troop's colonel with it, so he got promoted for disobedience."

"But he stood there in front of everybody and asked for help. Healer's help. From a kid."

"Yeah. Interesting, isn't it? And you're Hereyta's First Flight part-ner's little brother."

"I can't heal *Hereyta*," I said in alarm.

"I know, Tinhead," said Dag, but he reached out one arm and gave me an absent-minded big-brother hug. "If I knew of a wizard who could, I'd've stolen Dad and Mum's life savings and be gone over the Fabulous Mountains by now." All the best fairy-tale wizards live on the other side of the Fabulous Mountains from wherever you are.

"I wonder if his shoulder really does hurt," I said.

Dag snorted. "He spent thirty years fighting the Borogon. He's taken so many spears and arrows and swordstrokes he probably did eenie-meenie-miney-moe about what to use when he decided he wanted to talk to you. And now he has talked to you and . . ." Dag didn't finish. Two days till First Flight.

We saw Eled with his dragon, Ansilika, every day—Ansilika looked pretty serene to me—and Setyep and Arac too, till Dag stopped stiffening up when he saw them. I had been introduced to pretty much all the third-years, quite a few of the other cadets and a few tutors. And about twenty more dragons—I remembered the dragons best. They were all beautiful. One of the best—after Hereyta of course—was Munyinzia, who was purple and blue, and his partner was one of the few women at the Academy: Doara. "She'll be a city captain in five years," said Eled. "The girls are always like that. They're out there aiming and aspiring while a lot of the boys try to come back to the Academy as soon as they can and teach, so they can have regular meals and their baths indoors in hot water. Unless there's another big war on, which please the gods there won't be. My cousin was a city captain in *four* years and my sister's already a deputy."

"You said three daughters in your family went to dragonrider academies."

"Yes. The other one was in the last war. She went from city upper guard to colonel in one fell swoop, and lasted fourteen months on the Haksap border before they killed her. It's nearly a record. Her parents have a crown for it."

I finally found out who Fistagh was. I hadn't realised I was expecting him to have horns and fangs till I met him and he was normal. Short, even. Well, not as short as me but shorter than Dag. I found out I was relieved he didn't have horns and fangs because I'd've worried about his dragon.

Sippy went on playing his game. He never tried to play it when Hereyta was doing something for us, or we were doing something on the front bits of her. He didn't pester like a little kid, he just waited. Hereyta had so much neck she could perfectly well play the game so long as Dag and I were busy doing whatever we were doing somewhere else—the rest of her stayed as steady as a, well, a small mountain. Unless of course you were asking her to flex the top of her wing in and out so you could find the sore places to rub better.

When Arac (with Setyep in tow) came round Sippy played it

with the two of them. He never tried it with any other dragon, even Ansilika. I generally watched this show, waiting for that flash of dragon-magic when Sippy hit the right triangle point. I'd begun to recognise the flash—it wasn't a flash, I just don't know what else to call it; it was like a crumple or a crack more than a flash, but a crumpled what? Or a crack into what? Let's call it a flash. Whatever it was, it didn't bring a hot wind or pink haloes for the trees any more, and Dag and Setyep didn't mention it again. But in a funny way it seemed to get sharper, somehow, like it was being pulled together from being all spread out.

The weirdest thing of all was once when I was standing thinking about it right after Arac had left. I was almost as if glued in place, or like a little glamour had got itself laid on me from watching the dragon magic. This does happen, by the way, or something like it, it's one of the reasons you have to train to do magic with someone who knows what they're doing rather than try and pick it up yourself; you might go off in one of these trances and not be able to get out again. Dragons aren't supposed to be magical, not like rocs, say, but this felt like magic. So I was standing there, not noticing that I was kind of tranced, and thinking about the crumple-crack-flash. And I sort of noticed that Hereyta had kind of realigned herself since Arac left, but as if the game was still going on with three, as if Arac had merely changed location and become invisible. I had only just figured out that the invisible Arac was standing where I was standing. They were using me as the second point of the triangle. . . .

And Sippy found the third point.

Ever been caught in a crumple-crack-flash? I don't recommend it. It literally knocked me down. It was a little like what being stepped on by a dragon might be like—knocked over and very slightly stepped on and then the dragon snatches its foot back just in time. It was also hot and . . . I want to say loud, but the loud part was only sort of part of the being-stood-on part, I think. It was just too much in all the ways you have to feel that something is too much. And my ears were ringing although I couldn't remember hearing anything.

I sat up from where I'd fallen as Dag came trotting over to me. "Hey, are you all right? What happened? Do you need food? It's almost lunchtime and I know how tiring working on a dragon is if you're not used to it." He was pulling stuff out of his pockets as he spoke. Various bits and pieces of dragon equipment emerged first, and then he produced an only slightly beat-up sandwich. Usually we had a midmorning break and ate something then, but Setyep had interrupted it. "You just stay sitting down. I'll sit too," and he did. "What happened?"

Sippy was standing perfectly still—Sippy never stands perfectly still—looking at me. Hereyta was perfectly still too but she usually is unless she's deliberately doing something. But her two eyes were clearly focussed on me.

"I have no idea," I said firmly, broke the sandwich in half and gave half to Dag. Sippy drooped, and then came over to me and fell down, only in standard Sippy falling-down style, nothing serious, and laid his head lengthwise along my legs so he could stare into my eyes, and stared. As if he was asking me to forgive him. Or to understand something. I gave him half my remaining half sandwich.

"Hey," said Dag, still bothered, and gave me half of *his* half sandwich. "Look, even Hereyta's worried about you." Hereyta was still staring at me.

"I'm okay, I'm fine, I'm anything you like, I'm eating my sandwich," I said, and leaned over to pull my fingers through Sippy's topknot. It's one of those comfort things, like rubbing your lucky pebble, but in this case it dragged the hair away from his third eye, which seemed bigger and shinier and more eye-like than usual. I looked up at Hereyta. *What is going on?* I thought at her. She didn't answer, but she threw her head back suddenly to look at a dragon flying over us, the tiny bump of its rider just visible only because you knew where to look.

◆ ◆ ◆

Most of the other First Flighters flew their dragons—real-time flew, I mean, not Flew. Dag didn't. I didn't say anything, but he saw me watching the other ones. The world turns the colour of the dragon's wings when a dragon shadow passes over you. It's like magic. It *is* magic, even if it isn't the kind you have to measure and count. I was sure that if I knew the right incantation I could do anything, standing in the shadow of a dragon's wing. I believed it so hard that I found myself holding my breath when it happened, as if waiting for the words to come.

"First Flighters fly our dragons for us, not for the dragons," Dag said, half dreamily, and I knew he wanted to fly too, and wasn't going to, for Hereyta's sake. She'd taught Dag everything he needed to know, and it was up to him to remember it, not to play schoolboy games with her because he could. She'd get him off the ground again on the day, but real-time flying, especially flying toward the Firespace, is gruelling at best, and it might hurt her. Just not as much as what followed would hurt her. "It's only we still don't believe we can. That they'll do what we say, you know?"

I nodded.

"They will, or they wouldn't be at the Academy being fumbled by cadets in the first place. Young or stroppy dragons don't get cycled through the academies, not till they get middle aged and cooperative. And flying's not the thing, not really. Taking your dragon into the Firespace is. Being able to. Anybody with the nerve could get an old mellow dragon off the ground after fifteen minutes' training. You could fly Hereyta. She'd go sweet as a lark. The Firespace—in there you can only so much as keep breathing because you're with your dragon. Here's something they don't generally talk about—it's not just the first time into the Firespace tied in behind a tutor or a dragonmaster that most cadets pass out. Or even the second or third. A lot of the three years most of us spend working with dragons before we're ready for First Flight is just learning to keep your head on straight after you make that transition. And the most important thing about working with dragons is the connection to the dragon. *Nobody*—no human—is any good in the Firespace, and it's obvious pretty soon if you're going to be one of the ones who can cope at all, or not. In there, there's no place to stand—at least no place any human has ever found—so you have to keep flying—and there's something funny about up and down too. It's too hot to breathe and you can't see anything except cloud. Red cloud. And you still have to be able to remember how to get where you're going. Out here comparatively speaking we're almost equal." He looked up at our scintillating red-gold mountain, and then looked at me and smiled.

Equal. Right. At least I could be glad I wasn't going into the Firespace. I couldn't be very glad, though, when Dag and Hereyta weren't going there either.

I thought Dag deliberately didn't stop or look up when the other dragons flew over us. For Hereyta's sake. So I stopped stopping or looking up too. Besides, now I knew what might make her hum, nothing was more absorbing than trying to please her enough that she did it again. When you bring your dragon outdoors, she usually preens. This includes stretching her wings out as far as they'll go and then vibrating them like plucked strings. The morning after my interesting conversation with the *zedak*, when we brought Hereyta outdoors, she stretched her stiff right wing out as steadily and straight as her left one, and when she shook them she hummed, and I about thought I'd died and gone to heaven (one of the better heavens, one with dragons).

But that was a very odd day all around, because for the rest of it it was like being back home, except the people who kept sidling up to me and trying to pretend they weren't were all wearing Academy uniform. And they were mostly First Flighters who certainly weren't going to go to the Academy healer and admit there might be anything wrong for fear they'd be pulled out of First Flight. After the first few I kind of wanted to sidle myself into the kitchens and drop a lot of quietleaf in the kettles they kept hot over the fire, to lower the general tension level, but I'm way too cowardly. But I had to tell the last two who wanted something to help them sleep to come by our room after dinner because I'd run out of the quietleaf in my little wallet by then. I hoped I still had some in my pack.

◆ ◆ ◆

The day before First Flight I don't think Dag said a word to me. It was worse than the last day of the journey to get here had been. His silence the day before First Flight had not only a wall but a moat and a lot of jumpy sentries with bad attitudes around it. But I don't think any of the other First Flighters said a word to anyone either. It was like you could tell a First Flighter by the fact they weren't saying anything. I don't think anybody even said "pass the salt" at meals. If they wanted salt, they grabbed it. If they couldn't reach it, they went without. And all their dragons had three eyes.

We went down to the *hsa* last thing, after dinner, after dark— after curfew, except most if not all the other First Flighters were doing exactly the same thing and there are always tutors and dragonmasters around, and nobody said anything. Sippy had the good sense to be subdued, at least by his standards and almost by mine. I could feel it—don't ask me how—that Hereyta was waiting for us, that she knew we'd be there, last thing at night, after curfew, after any time a cadet is allowed to be visiting his (or her) dragon, the night before First Flight. Did that mean she knew that she was in it? Did that mean she knew . . .

She didn't move into the firelight this time, but I was beginning to learn to feel my way around the darkness that is dragon as opposed to the darkness that is just darkness. She was belly-flat to the ground although her head was up, the long neck carrying it some unguessable length above the reach of the firelight. Her eyes were closed when we stepped into the firelit circle, but then she opened them and we had shining dragon eyes beaming down on us like stars. Two stars.

I leaned against the bottom of her shoulder. She'd moved the foreleg out a little from her body on the side with the stiff wing, which I'm sure was about the wing and not about expecting me or knowing where I'd want to lean, but it meant I could get in between it and her body. I never thought about how this might be dangerous, me being bug-sized and all, and maybe her not paying attention. She was paying attention. I don't know where Dag went. Sippy came and leaned with me. We just stood there and leaned and nobody said anything or hummed anything either. But I felt better after and I was pretty sure Dag did too.

But she still only had two eyes.

I know Dag didn't get any sleep to speak of that night because I didn't either. I did offer him some quietleaf—I did have some left in my pack—but he refused so I didn't have any either in some kind of stupid loyalty. I lay there trying to be quiet while he tossed and turned and muttered to himself and periodically sat up and stared out the window like he was thinking about running away. Maybe he was. But I bet he was thinking about running away with Hereyta. He wouldn't have left her behind to face the shame of a First Flight without her partner, even if it maybe looked like the way to spare her shame, because if Dag wasn't there she wouldn't have to fly. She was only a dragon, what did she know? But why had she been waiting for us that evening? She knew. Whatever was going to happen he wouldn't do that to her. But smuggling a dragon out of anywhere, even a place already full of dragons and built to have dragons moving through it, would be a little difficult. So that's probably why he kept lying back down again with a long sigh.

Mum and Dad had told us lots of stories when we were all little, and a lot of those stories had dragons in them. There was always lots of flying and lots of heroics in those stories. Dragons lost eyes in these stories occasionally but you never heard about what happened to them after. You always knew it was tragic though—worse than the old human veteran limping home leaning on his cane.

Except there was one story I'd been half remembering, but more to the point half forgetting, ever since Dag had come home looking like a condemned man, and told us about Hereyta and First Flight. It was a story Ralas had told me, a long time ago, when I'd first brought Sippy home, and it was mostly about a foogit, which was why Ralas thought I'd like it. But I was sure there was a dragon in it. And I could *almost* remember that this particular dragon had only two eyes. And as I say, dragons don't stay in stories when they lose an eye. But I couldn't remember anything else about the story—the two-eyed dragon should have stuck better, but I was foogit-obsessed at that point. I kept trying to remember anybody's name—the dragon's, the foogit's, even the human's or humans', since there had to be humans in it too—because if I could remember a name I'd ask Eled, casually, if he knew a story with someone named whatever in it. I just wasn't going to say to him, hey, you don't happen to remember some weird old story about a foogit and a two-eyed dragon, do you? With Sippy standing there. And Hereyta.

Sippy was still subdued at breakfast, although being subdued didn't stop him from eating everything that came his way. I've said that years tended to stay together but the third-years on First Flight morning had invisible "don't come near" signs all around them. I would have hung back myself except Dag broke his twenty-four hours of silence to say, "What? Come on. Watching Sippy eat may give me some appetite." It didn't seem to.

I probably knew all the First Flighters by name but my eye lingered on the ones I'd had conversations with or slipped some quietleaf or gimpweed or something to. Setyep was looking as green around the edges as Dag was. Doara actually smiled at me, but it was a smile that said "Yes, I know how bad I look, don't even try and guess how I feel." I smiled back. Maybe it was the colour of the cadets' formal uniforms, yellow and red, that makes fair people look grey and dark people look purple and anybody in between green. And the third-years seemed to walk ever so slightly funny because they had their tapping sticks in their boots. The sticks are really slender and your formal boots have a loop for one anyway, so it wasn't that a tapping stick in your boot was crippling you. It's just you knew what having it there meant.

Eled still just looked like Eled, but I thought it was costing him. And Fistagh was looking rather too well, as if he was under a small glamour, which I think he was. He had a funny half smell about him that I recognised from Ralas. I did wonder if it was legal, which I doubted, but even if I'd ratted him out it wouldn't have given Hereyta a third eye.

Fistagh had a girl with him. She was extremely pretty, and they both knew it. One other First Flighter, Vorl, had someone who had to be his brother with him, they looked so much alike, but Vorl's brother wasn't small and scrawny except for his ears and feet, nor was he accompanied by a demented foogit.

When Dag stood up with the others I grabbed Sippy's topknot and looked uncertainly at Dag.

"You don't have to come if you don't want to," Dag said in this awful flat voice that didn't sound anything like him. "It's okay."

I shook my head violently. "It's not that—you must know it's not that. It's okay with *me* if you want Sippy and me to stay out of the way and not, you know, not embarrass you. I can go back up to the room and sit—sit on Sippy—till—till—"

"Till it's all over?" said Dag. "Yes. Well, if it's really all the same to you, I'd actually rather you came." He turned away, not checking to see if we were following. Of course we were. I let go of Sippy's topknot but he stayed right beside me, nearly as glued to my leg as Fistagh's girl was to his side.

The First Flighters drew lots for the order they filed out of the *hsa*. We were near the last. It gave us plenty of extra time to adjust, readjust, de-adjust, and super-adjust every scrap of Hereyta's harness six times. Maybe sixteen. I say "us" but it was mostly Dag. He knew where the bits went and I still only sort of knew. The tip of Hereyta's nose followed Dag's every tiny motion, back and forth, up and down, round and round. She did this a lot anyway but this morning the nose-tip was about a hand's-breadth away from the back of his neck.

I was watching Dag and didn't really think about what I was doing so I started petting one of Hereyta's ankles. I was reassuring me, not her, but when I stopped Hereyta's nose left the nape of Dag's neck just long enough to point at me. I started petting again. The nose went back to Dag. Sippy, like we were a pair of bad comedians, was licking the side of her other foot. He couldn't reach her ankle.

It was our turn—Hereyta and Dag's turn—finally. I wondered how many times Hereyta had made a First Flight. Maybe never, because I think she hadn't been an Academy training dragon till after she lost her eye. Why had she been waiting for us last night after curfew? I trotted behind Dag and Sippy trotted behind me.

I'd never counted the First Flighters. There were probably about twenty; Academy classes are small. But twenty dragons look like they go on forever. I couldn't even recognise the dragons at the far end of the queue. Unfortunately Fistagh was about halfway along and I could recognise him and his yellow-gold dragon. She was beautiful too; I might as well get used to it that all dragons are beautiful. I couldn't see Eled or Doara. Setyep and Arac were two behind Fistagh, so like only the distance between one end of my village and the other from us. There were only three more dragons and riders after us.

I was just noticing that Fistagh's girl was in the saddle with him when Dag said, "Up you go." He'd unrolled the double belt that the dragonrider uses to tie himself in place in case of unexpected acrobatics or vertigo (also the Firespace is just so strange, Eled had told me, that you can get numb or breathless as well as dizzy: lots of ways to lose it and fall off), which doubles as a mounting ladder, since it has rungs between the two long bands. It's an awkward climb because the rungs are made of the same soft tough cloth that the belts are and you worry about grinding your toes into your dragon's side, but on formal occasions you use the ladder.

I gaped at Dag.

"Tuck Sippy under your arm; I'll be right behind you and I'll give him or you a shove if he looks like he's slipping." I'd only been up and down the mounting ladder once—and unhindered by a foogit passenger—most of the time you either climb the dragon as you can, or ask for the head to come down and lift you up somewhere. Dimly I was thinking, Dag let me climb the ladder that once just because he knew I was interested in anything to do with dragons.

"Come on," Dag said impatiently. "Stad is halfway up already." Stad was next behind us in the queue. I climbed.

Sippy, who was really not himself this morning, hung like a package over my arm, and while my shoulder was coming out of its socket—and my other arm and side were fiery from strain—by the time I got to Hereyta's saddle, we did both get there. "Push up forward," Dag said, "I'm coming in behind you." Hereyta's saddle was bigger than usual because she was bigger than usual, so there was plenty of space, and I now noticed that Dag must have been doing some secret alterations because the bumps and bulges for both padding and helping keep the rider in place had been rearranged for two. Or three. I had thought Dag had been spending a lot of time ripping out bits of the saddle and sewing them back together, but I'd thought it was general reflex obsessiveness. But Dag had been planning for us to come with him. Why? When had he decided? *Why?* Ralas had only said take us back to the Academy with him.

I settled Sippy in front of me so he could look out over the pommel. Dag dropped a loop of the ladder-belt over me. I stuck my arms through a couple of the rungs and snugged Sippy down with another.

"Comfy?" said Dag.

I would have liked to say no but I wasn't sure if truth disguised as humour was a good idea right now so I said thanks instead. I was feeling so stunned and flabbergasted and appalled I wasn't feeling anything really. Dag grunted. Maybe he thought that truth disguised as humour wouldn't be a good idea either.

The three dragons after us were all mounted and their riders tied in too. I couldn't see Vorl so I couldn't see if his brother was riding with him. Fistagh's girl was behind him.

My heart was beating so hard I thought I was going to throw up. The Academy officers were making a long queue in front of the dragon queue. Dag had told me they read out a lot of historical stuff that probably nobody ever heard except maybe some of the onlookers. Onlookers. I'd forgotten. Some First Flighters' families, the ones who either lived nearby or were wealthy enough to make journeys that weren't about buying or selling anything, came to watch. I looked around. There was a rope fence that wasn't usually there at the edge of the field. There were probably a hundred people behind it, but they were scattered in little clumps behind the dragon they were interested in. The officers were now bellowing something at us. There was one almost right in front of us and one more near the end of the queue and then five or six stretched out along in the other direction, and they were reading just not in unison enough that it made it impossible to hear what they were saying. I could hear words like *honour* and *heroic* and *stalwart* flying over my head.

I couldn't think of anywhere I belonged less. Sippy was actually shivering. I put my arms around him. We'd heat up in the Firespace, I thought.

Except we weren't going to the Firespace. How could I have forgotten? Hereyta had only two eyes. I still didn't know why Dag wanted us to come with him, but he must have thought it would make it easier somehow, in spite of our extra weight for Hereyta's weak wing. I had a really ignoble moment when I thought that Dag might have brought us because we were foolish and ridiculous and maybe that would make it our fault somehow when Hereyta couldn't Fly with the other dragons. But I realised immediately what a really rotten thing that was to think, and I knew it wasn't true. Maybe it was because Hereyta liked us. She played with Sippy and when I'd stopped petting her ankle she'd noticed. Maybe Dag thought it would be better for her to have three friends with her rather than only one. I wasn't sure he was right. Dragons are very proud.

The officer-heralds had stopped shouting and were leaving the field. It was a blue clear day, cold for the time of year; Sippy's and my excuse for shivering. We seemed to be in the sky already, sitting so high up, in the saddle at the base of Hereyta's neck, with her standing at full attention. And I don't like heights. The heat of her beat through the heavy leather of the saddle and flowed off her neck in front of us like a mane, but it barely touched me; it was like it broke and swept past, like water around a rock. I wished I felt more rocklike, steady and solid and untroubled. I wished I'd never come. I wished Ralas hadn't sent us.

Poor Hereyta.

The neck in front of us quivered. I don't know how I knew that. It wasn't anything I saw. But Hereyta knew what was coming. I leant forward, squashing Sippy into the pommel, but after years of illicit lying between my feet and the wooden foot of my bed he knew how to squash. I let go of him and put both hands on Hereyta's neck.

I was so busy feeling Hereyta through the palms in my hands I didn't notice when the first dragon launched itself into the air.

The backdraft, even from the far front of the queue, was amazing. Not that it disturbed the other dragons one whisker, except that the tension level arced up like a firework on a solstice, but it nearly pulled all my hair out. Sippy rearranged his squashedness a little but he stopped shivering. I was feeling something else, not just heat, beaming up from Hereyta, through my hands, into the rest of me, into Sippy.

Another dragon hurled itself into the air. The ground shook and the trees bent back, their leaves streaming in the wind like a girl's long hair. And another. And another. It was like being in a series of small, violent, curiously self-contained storms, each one closer than the last. . . .

I wasn't anything like ready, and I can't begin to describe it. I wished that it wasn't just my body tied to the saddle but that I had a neck brace as well. I thought my head might just about part from my shoulders. I couldn't breathe. My stomach seemed to have been left behind, which was just as well, because if it had come too I might have been sick. My arms felt like they were being dragged out of my shoulders, my legs from my pelvis, my eyebrows and nose just shoved off my face from the pressure, my eyelids peeled down with them. My eyes were trying to weep from the blast, but the wind snatched the tears away and my eyes felt dry and sore. I couldn't see anything. And it seemed to go on and on and on.

Hereyta went on spiralling up and up and up with great thunderous heaves of her wings. I finally managed to drag my head from crushed backward against my spine to crushed forward against my chest. This way I could kind of see some of what was going on around me, when the vast, country-wide wings on either side of me allowed it. The other dragons were disappearing, and I realised that some of the noise that I thought was Hereyta's wings was actually the rumbly, echoey, huge *whomp*ing noises the disappearing dragons created as they slid into the Firespace.

Whomp and *whomp* again. There weren't many dragons left. And Hereyta carried on, climbing and climbing and climbing. The last dragon I saw was Arac, Setyep an unrecognisable speck. And then they disappeared too.

There was only us left.

And then the worst thing happened. The thing that was even worse than Hereyta not being able to make the jump. And I don't know how it happened. I'd tied him in myself, and I knew how to tie him, because I knew what a wriggler he was.

Sippy snaked out from between me and the pommel. Out of the harness that kept him safe.

And jumped off Hereyta's back. Into the air. Into nothing.

He might have landed on a wing—he should have landed on a wing; Hereyta's wings are big enough to hug the world—but he didn't. I swear he aimed. He aimed for the little triangular gap where the wing met the shoulder. And fell through it. I could see him, a little hairy lump—the wind fanned his hair out till he looked like a greeny-brown dandelion clock—getting smaller and smaller and smaller and farther and farther and farther away. . . .

I heard Dag cry out behind me. I only know because of how sore my throat was later that I must have been screaming. I was busy trying to get out of my own harness—like that was going to do any good—and Dag was busy trying to stop me.

And Hereyta turned in the air like a swallow, neatly, gracefully, impossibly, and plunged after Sippy.

My memory gets pretty confused after that. We'd climbed much higher than where a dragon usually finds its navigation points and goes into the Firespace, I think, so I guess we had some room to manoeuvre. Maybe it makes some kind of sense that Sippy, Hereyta and I—because despite Dag's efforts I had got out of my harness— arrived at the same little piece of air at the same time. I don't actually remember falling. I remember seeing Sippy rolling in the air as if he was perfectly at ease, like he rolled on the ground sometimes when he was so excited he couldn't think what to do with himself.

And I seem to remember Hereyta turning her head toward us, keeping her deadly wings at almost the full distance of her long neck—although even so, with every stroke, Sippy and I bobbed up and down on the air-waves like little boats pitch in the wake of a ship—but we were falling, falling, *falling*. . . .

And then I do remember the roaring and the squashing, which could just be the air, but then the *heat,* and the sharpness of it, almost like being cut with a hot knife. And I have a vague, crazy flash of memory of being still in the middle of the roaring and the squashing but having got my arms around Sippy somehow; and then an even crazier flash of glancing off the rough tip of Hereyta's outthrust nose which was suddenly right there under us to be fallen on, and into the concavity farther back, behind the nostrils, just in front of the steep higher-than-a-man-is-tall crag where the dragon's array of eyes is. We hit and rolled and juddered . . . and thumped against the bottom of the empty left eye socket.

Hereta threw her head up and I managed to think, "Oh, *no*, we're just going to fall *off* again," when . . .

. . . the heat really hit me. It wasn't like a knife any more. More like being rolled up too tightly in a blanket that had been lying by the fire too long, and it's high summer. And the *redness*. It was like looking at the sun through your eyelids, except your eyes were open, and there was nothing to see except the redness. And the weightlessness. Or almost weightlessness. That was what made me think we were falling off again, I think, when we weren't. But you didn't feel what you were on properly. Sippy and I weren't quite floating off Hereyta's face but even if we did we wouldn't fall very fast. Not here.

It's pretty weird to think of a dragon floating like a feather in a breeze, but it was pretty much like that, except there was no breeze. Hereyta's wings still went on and on and on and on, stretching away on both sides of us, but they lay almost still now, like landscape. With an occasional un-landscape-like tremor, like a hawk on an updraft.

The Firespace. We'd done it. Somehow. Thanks to Sippy. Thanks to Sippy being totally deranged and stupid and a troublemaker and thinking he could play his game *in mid-air* and if we got out of this alive I'd tie him up *for the rest of his life*.

Noise seemed muffled. Or maybe it was just shock. But there was a funny dull quality to what my ears were trying to tell me. I could hear something going on—I thought—pretty close but at the same time I couldn't hear it. And then Arac's head rose over the leading edge of Hereyta's left wing and several leagues of neck passed Sippy and me still lying on Hereyta's nose and then Setyep was hovering right in front of us. You can get quite close to another dragon in the Firespace. Everything moved so slowly, and if two of the floating mountains actually collided, it would happen gently, and they'd just drift away from each other again. But Arac didn't touch us, and there was no backdraft from the soft riffle of his wings.

"I think your brother wants to kill you," Setyep said in close to his usual laconic manner, although he was having trouble with it. He looked alarmed, amazed, delighted and completely bewildered all together, which made laconic hard to hang on to. It was probably the effect of the Firespace again but even his words seemed rubbed and soft somehow. "But you're probably safe enough for now." He shook his head—slowly; it's hard to do anything quickly when you don't weigh anything, it seems to turn your muscles to jelly, that and the heat, which makes you not want to try to move anyway. Arac managed to give me quite a sharp look, however, full of all the questions Setyep wasn't asking, including "what are you doing on Hereyta's nose anyway?"

But I thought about his "for now." We've got here. Hurrah and all that.

But how do we get out again? Presumably a dragon needs three eyes to get out too. And I wasn't looking forward to trying to duplicate what we'd just done. Especially the coming out into the ordinary world again and falling off Hereyta's face. And falling and falling. Although I supposed staying where we were and frying or starving to death wasn't a great choice either.

Sippy was puffing away like a bellows; I was panting too, my mouth open, gasping. The hot air tasted funny and felt funny in your throat and lungs; it didn't feel like air, and you weren't sure you could breathe it, whatever it was. You felt it pressing against your eyes too. In the murky reddish light Sippy looked sort of maroon, and the usual bright glint of his eyes was dull. When I turned my head I could see that Hereyta had her third eyelids closed; Dag had told me the third eyelids seemed to be some kind of Firespace protection or focus since they were never closed in our world and always closed in the Firespace. Hereyta's eyes were also half closed. I couldn't see Arac's so I don't know if she was squinting because of the Firespace—how well could she see in the Firespace with only two eyes?—or because of the little things on her nose. She was obviously aware of us though; I could tell by how carefully she was moving her head, keeping it perfectly level as she twisted it around and down, and then down some more. Dragons can scratch the napes of their own necks with their teeth. Or, in this case, they can lower their heads to within reach of someone sitting in a saddle there.

I saw Dag looking grimly determined, standing on the saddle. He still had his harness on, but he'd untied it from the saddle and it hung in loops around his shoulders; his tapping stick was still in his boot. He made one of his peculiar chirruping dragon-calls and Hereyta stopped her nose where it was and angled it very slightly downwards, not enough to tip Sippy and me out of our convenient hollow, and Dag pulled himself gingerly up over her chin and lips, walked gently up the length of her nose and sat down beside us with a heavy sigh.

I waited for the lecture. For the shouting and raving.

It didn't come.

For something to do while I waited I looked around. Arac had taken a long slow circle off to one side and now, wings slightly tilted, came sweeping back. His upper wing sailed over me and then some-impossible-how he and Hereyta were floating right next to each other again with their enormous wings as if in layers, and I don't know, pleated. So Setyep was actually comparatively near us. Hereyta had her neck sort of folded up too, like a scarf, so Arac was only a little bit (in dragon terms) below us. I could see Setyep's face—a congested-looking bricky red, like Dag's and I'm sure like mine—and see the expression on it although I wouldn't have wanted to say what that expression was. The alarm and amazement and so on had kind of all blurred together and become something else.

I looked at Sippy then. There weren't even any dark green glints in the maroon; it was like green just didn't exist here. He was flat out on his side—or as flat as you can get on the wavy scales of dragon skin—and in spite of how hard he was panting the fine fur on his belly was matted with sweat (foogits only sweat on their underparts). He looked exhausted, but maybe it was just the heat. I'd never seen him exhausted before, even in the heat of high summer when everyone else is.

But maybe he was exhausted from getting us here. And we still had to get out.

Then I stared at Arac, wondering what the Firespace was doing to my sight aside from eliminating green. Arac looked like a god in the Firespace: noble, incredible, glorious. It was probably just as well I couldn't see Hereyta properly; it would probably kill me, like it killed the king who actually made it to the Mountains of the Sun and looked into the pool at the top of the tallest one and saw into the heart of the world. There are some things you're better off not knowing. Although the story says that king died happy.

Why wasn't Dag yelling at me for being a dangerous, suicidal, brainless fool?

"That was interesting," Setyep offered after a few silent minutes of drifting.

Dag made a short muffled barking noise like a foogit having a bad dream. It wasn't a laugh.

Sippy, as if answering, yipped.

"I suppose," said Dag, after another reflective spell of drifting, "we could at least go where we're supposed to."

Setyep's silence this time had a different quality to it. I looked over at him and he was frowning. "You . . . er . . ."

Dag made the barking noise again. "Yes. I did learn my route. It seemed only, you know, polite. Since they'd given us one and everything." Both Setyep and I knew it wasn't the Academy he cared about being polite to.

"We won't be going the same way," said Setyep.

"I know," said Dag. He pulled his tapping stick out of his boot and looked at it.

More worried silence. Nobody knew if a two-eyed dragon could navigate *in* the Firespace either, but since two-eyed dragons couldn't get into the Firespace in the first place, there hadn't been anything to find out. Like a question that begins "if humans could fly, then what if. . . ."

"If I don't see you, I'll come back," said Setyep. "I can get the coordinates out of Thispec. And Arac is happy to find Hereyta."

"Thanks," said Dag. And again, "Thanks."

"Um," said Setyep, and then he tapped Arac on the shoulder and made a talking-to-dragons noise, and Arac slid away from beside us, unpleating his wing from Hereyta's; and then he banked and did one of those impossible bird-like turns and was gone away from us. I turned my head to watch them, but they disappeared into the murk almost at once.

Dag looked at his tapping stick. "We're trained to use these on their shoulders. They're trained for us to use them on their shoulders. The idea is supposed to be that our arms aren't long enough and when you're flying you want your directions to be as easy and clear as possible. But speaking of easy and clear, nothing ever is here, and the view feels like it's better from up here, or would be if there were a view. There's no way to tie yourself in up here for the transitions of course but that didn't work so well last time, did it?"

I braced myself again. Now Dag was finally going to yell at me.

But all he said was, "I think all rules are suspended." He reached over and tapped the tip of his stick as far as he could toward the right-hand edge of Hereyta's face. "*Hrroar*," he said, or something like that. And Hereyta, still keeping her face perfectly level, did a swing right and set off . . . somewhere or other.

"Coordinates?" I said. "It's like flying in soup."

"Yes, it is, isn't it?" Dag said calmly. "Most of your second year at the Academy is about learning to work with dragons. Then your third year is about getting around in the Firespace. Ever noticed the little tattoos on the palms of our hands? You get those at the end of your first year, with your first cadet star for your uniform. That's to give the magic somewhere to stick, and you have to use a little magic. Sometimes they sizzle faintly so you know they're working—although they don't make you go in the right direction, they just let you go somewhere rather than around in circles. If Hereyta has trouble . . . *Hekhuk*," he added to Hereyta, and she sank a little, through the soup. I was half expecting a squishing noise as she beat her wings, but they were more silent here than in the ordinary world. In our world. After a moment he added, "It's not like there's another special mark for if your dragon has only two eyes."

Great puffs of redness gusted out under Hereyta's wings, like clouds, only with iridescent threads through them. Not like soup. I was still glad the navigating wasn't up to me. I felt faintly sickish, and trying to look around made me dizzy.

I'm not sure how long we flew through the gloom. Dag murmured and tapped a few times. Once I saw him scratching the palm of his left hand with his fingers—the hand that didn't have the stick in it. But he and Hereyta seemed so calm. Well, I'd never seen Hereyta anything but calm, and maybe Dag was just in shock. Like me. Sippy's breathing had slowed down but he was still collapsed. If I hadn't had a lot of other things to worry about—and having him collapsed was extremely convenient at the moment—I'd've been worrying about him too.

After a while, a short or maybe a long while, I have no idea why, but I started to feel that we were getting near . . . something. Whatever. Wherever. And I guess I was right, because Hereyta . . . stopped. Mid-air and all. Mid-murk. I hadn't thought about it before, but when we first came through, we'd still been gliding. Slowly, but moving. If there were an up or a down here you might almost say soaring. And it was as if her wings unfolded a whole extra length that they never had in our world, or maybe they'd picked up some of the murk, maybe the murk weaves itself onto the edges of dragon wings . . . maybe my eyes had gone funny. But when she stopped, it was like her wings shuddered out another span, like shaking out a wadded-up bedspread, except Hereyta's wings already went on forever.

Dag leaned forward and patted her, her nose, I guess, the part of her nose right in front of where he was sitting. And then he stayed that way, leaning forward. He put his tapping stick down, and pressed both palms against her. Kind of like I had, just before she jumped into the air and started flying. And he bowed his head. I don't know if he was thinking or . . .

I didn't think he saw me. I stood up. Carefully. Even with leagues of wing stretching out on both sides standing on a dragon feels pretty insecure. (How did she manage to stay so still?) When I stood up, I was right in front of the great black hollow that was her missing eye.

Sippy stood up with me, pressing himself against me. I gently dug his face out of my thigh and turned him to look the direction I was looking—the direction Hereyta was looking, with her other two eyes. I rubbed the place between Sippy's two ordinary eyes, where the little ridge and hollow in the skull had produced the myth that foogits had once had a third eye. The place that's supposed to make a foogit lucky.

And I thought about something Ralas had told me about healing. "A lot of the time you haven't got a clue. It's not made any easier by the fact that no one will tell you even as much as they know themselves what's wrong because they're ashamed that it is wrong. So you just wade in and do it. It's all you can do."

This had been about a year ago. She often told me things like I was another grown-up, or like I was her apprentice, and I never knew whether to shut up and be grateful, like she'd forgotten who she was talking to and if I said anything she'd remember and not say any more, or whether to risk asking her a question—letting her see that it was me paying attention. This time I couldn't help myself. "Do *what*?" I said.

She laughed. "It. *It*."

I looked into the murk. I rubbed Sippy's head. I leaned back against the spiked rampart that was the bottom front edge of Hereyta's empty eye socket. I chose a direction. I braced myself. I tried to remember Arac and Hereyta and Sippy in the field behind the *hsa*. I looked at Sippy. He was already looking up at me. And there was a waitingness under my feet too. Hereyta was waiting.

I chose a direction, and shifted slightly to face it. Sippy shifted slightly too, to face me. Hereyta's face slowly, slowly turned, and Sippy and I shifted slightly in response. Sippy was watching me intently. I could almost believe he was watching me with three eyes. I stared out over the end of Hereyta's nose. You know how when you stare at something, anything, too long, it starts to sort of break up and turn into something else? It doesn't have to be anything specific, like a foogit or a candle flame or the back of your brother's head. It can be darkness or redness or a pool of water. The nothingness I was staring at was breaking up and turning into something else. I raised my hand and pointed—not so much to point, I think, but to give us, me anyway, something stable to stare at in all the disintegrating nothing. I think all three of us, even Hereyta, although for her it must have been like trying to focus on a gnat standing on her eyelashes, looked at the end of my finger.

And the heat had got even hotter. We would definitely fry before we starved.

I nearly fell off when Hereyta dived. Not quite. I grabbed a lesser spike and held on. I lunged at Sippy and got him round the neck. He scrabbled a little, but he didn't slip either. The redness whipped and churned around us—it was probably just dizziness, but I almost *felt* it streaming by, like very fine fabric, like the stuff my mum's best shawl is made of. It wasn't a steep dive—and it didn't last very long—although there was a very nasty upside-down-inside-out moment of what I suppose is the crossover and briefly the redness felt like cables, trying to hold us there—

—and the moment we were back out into the ordinary world, our human world, Hereyta levelled off again, long enough for Sippy and me to sit back down, and Dag threw a couple of loops around us, reflexively I think, but if we fell off we'd all fall off together. And then we swirled and whirled and circled down and down and down—

And landed in a field almost as enormous as the one we'd set off from, except that it looked like a field of trolls when the sun has just come up. There were a couple dozen dragons and at least a hundred people, but they were all frozen, like trolls in sunlight, staring up—

At us, twirling down.

Hereyta landed as gently as a butterfly.

And Arac *roiled* forward—trained working dragons mostly move slowly on land, careful of all the little squishy humans that are likely to be nearby—and thudded against Hereyta's side in what I think was a friendly tap, like you might thump someone on the back and say, "Well done!"—but it just about shattered our bones, I think, Dag's and mine and Sippy's, or at least it made me feel even more fragile and crumbly than I'd already been feeling, since the fragile crumbly feeling had started when I'd seen the nothingness breaking up, back in the hot red murk. I felt like a piece of overdone toast. The thump also knocked us an alarming several arms'-length to one side, but Hereyta just twitched her head like keeping people on her nose was something she'd been doing forever, and we jolted back again.

Hereyta made a kind of low purring grunt, which was either "it was nothing" or possibly "I have no idea," which would have made at least two of us, or maybe it was something else entirely, like, "be careful, you clumsy oaf." Setyep, still gallantly hanging on to Arac's saddle, suddenly shouted something I didn't catch—it sounded like one of those old ritual phrases Academy cadets have to learn—but it must have meant something like "cheer now" because everybody, and I mean everybody, started cheering like they'd gone mad. Even Fistagh and his girl. I saw them. And maybe they had all gone mad. After all, everyone knows a dragon needs all three eyes to get in and out of the Firespace, and it probably needs them to navigate around inside it too.

◆ ◆ ◆

I think they put me to bed right after that. It was kind of embarrassing. I'm more or less used to being small, ugly and stupid, but I've kind of imagined I'm fairly tough. But I slept all the way through the rest of that day and halfway into the next.

I didn't know where I was when I woke up. I'd never seen it before. But there was a familiar weight on my feet which, when I looked at it, was indeed Sippy and not an impostor, and then I looked a little farther and discovered Setyep sitting tipped back in a chair, reading something. He looked up when I moved and put the book down. He didn't waste words. "Hungry?" he said.

The water rushed into my mouth so fast I could barely say yes. He had a basket of rolls and a ewer of water next to him, which he shifted to the table at the head of my bed, and then he stuck his head out the door of the strange room I was in and shouted, "He's awake! Bring supplies!"

I don't remember much of the next hour or so either. I was too busy eating. (Then someone had to tell me where the loo was, and then I came back and ate some more.) When I could finally think of something besides food again there were only a few people left in the room, although I had some memory of a lot more people coming in and being forced back out again, protesting, and the door being not only closed but bolted behind them.

By that time I'd noticed that the room was a kind of small dormitory although mine was the only occupied bed, so there was room for everyone who was still there, plus Sippy weaving through the chairs scrounging for crumbs and attention (in that order). Dag was there (who'd been the first through the door when Setyep shouted and almost broke some already-sore-from-bouncing-around-on-a-dragon bones when he hugged me) and Setyep and Eled. The one I didn't know was the old guy from breakfast in the food halls two (three?) days ago—the one who'd wanted something for his aching shoulder. *Zedak*-something Something. I couldn't remember his name either. Lormon? Ormlo? I hadn't noticed him coming in or sitting down. (I was *really* hungry.)

I was seeing him up close for the first time—or anyway I was looking for the first time. I'd been kind of preoccupied with other things that time in the food halls. His white hair had the occasional black thread running through it, and the wrinkles on his face were so deep, some of them, you could've planted corn in them. The person-in-authority aura was worse close up, like sitting too close to the fire, and having him staring at you from only a few handspans away was a little like being pricked with the end of a very sharp dagger. I had to restrain myself from jumping to attention. Or running away. But I wasn't going to do either one. All I could think of, now, after what had just happened, and still feeling as wobbly as a convalescent, was, he was one of the people responsible for letting Hereyta's name go on the First Flight list. I was just as bad as Dag. Once I'd met Hereyta I'd probably always been as bad as Dag but it had *solidified* after what we'd been through. I knew I didn't have the courage to tell him what I thought about him for that, but I could at least try, I don't know, to stare back.

He was sitting down but he sat just as straight as he stood, as if he had a broomstick up the back of his coat; and those big square shoulders hadn't sagged at all over the years he'd been carrying the world on them. Or maybe that was just the most comfortable position for him. I wondered if the delor leaf had helped.

In almost any other situation he'd have scared me witless before he said anything but . . . we'd done something, you know? Dag and me and Sippy and Hereyta. The Academy—who at the moment was this guy—had tried to do something horrible to Hereyta, and we hadn't let them. Rot them. Rot them all. See if I cared. I even had the cheek to ignore him long enough to ask Dag, "How's Hereyta?"

"She's great," he said, and I thought I saw something of my feelings in his face too. "She's not even stiff." I risked a quick look at the old guy, and he was looking just a little amused. A little ironic maybe. Even a little guilty? No, I was imagining that. Authority stays in charge by never feeling guilty. Although when I say things like that at home my dad says wait till I have kids of my own.

There was a general air of barely suppressed frenzied impatience which began to make itself felt even in my still-half-zonked state. I was still in my clothes from First Flight—yuck—I had Sippy drool down my front and dragon dust and oil over most of the rest of me—next thing was a bath—but at least it meant I could sit in a chair too and pretend I was a part of the group. As long as no one asked me anything and I had to try to answer sanely. Like, "What the *hells* did you think you were doing???" The kind of authority that had kept Dag in a classroom for a year and made him think about six hundred forms of correct address doesn't like you doing stuff you shouldn't, even when it works. Maybe particularly when it works.

Although I didn't like this old guy looking amused.

"There will be a council meeting about First Flight later," he said. "But I thought a few of you—especially Dag and Ern as the most closely involved—might like the, er, simple version first. There will probably be a bit of an uproar at the meeting." He paused and looked thoughtful. And not at all amused.

"The story goes back a long way. Most of it will be familiar to you from your studies—Ern, you can get Dag to tell you anything you want to know, or Eled, who knows more of the history of this place than I do." He flicked a glance over Dag and Eled and I was startled—no, shaken—by the affectionate look on his face. He almost looked like my dad, trying to explain about authority and guilt. But he was talking again: "The Academy was founded on certain principles; the invisible structure of our Academy is based on these principles and they may not be broken."

He paused. Into the silence Eled said, "Intinuyun." Dag shifted in his chair and Setyep sighed.

The old guy nodded and waited, looking at Eled expectantly. You could imagine this guy standing in classrooms in front of generations of cadets, squeezing stuff they didn't think they knew out of them. Ralas did the same thing to me. Some days I felt like an old dishrag.

Eled said reluctantly, "Intinuyun broke one of its founding principles. Their Commander wanted his own choice to succeed him as Commander, not the Seers' choice. The Commander won out. But his successor died in a freak accident less than two years after he took over, and when the Seers tried to read for the next Commander, the signs only gave them nonsense. Intinuyun was disbanded about a year after that."

The old guy nodded. "One of every academy's principles is that dragons and cadets are matched for First Flight by augury and token, although exactly how this is done varies a little from academy to academy. Ours are called up and laid out very carefully, exactly and secretly every year by our Seers. Although most of our dragonmasters are almost half Seer themselves; those in charge of training cadets have to have a gift for deciding which cadets will learn most from which dragons, before we even begin trying to teach the cadets how to watch and listen and respond to their dragons.

"Even those of us not directly involved in the practical lessons follow this progress very closely, and when the First Flight lots are drawn and our Seers read the signs, we usually know what they will tell us. Sometimes there are surprises. But in the history of the Academy—possibly in the history of all the academies—so far as we know, no one has ever had quite such a surprise as this year when we were told—nay, ordered—that Hereyta was to Fly, and that Dag was to partner her.

"I know you, Dag, have held me personally responsible."

Dag scowled but didn't deny it. Dag held *him* personally responsible? Then who was he?

"And if it's any comfort to you—which it probably isn't—I haven't had a good night's sleep since the drawing. I've looked for ways out—gods know I've looked for any possible way out—and there was none. I know Carn, who flew with Hereyta on the journey when she lost her eye; I had partnered her a few times myself, and thought she was the best dragon I ever worked with. I wished I was as lucky as Carn, who Flew with her so much oftener."

He sounded almost human when he said "I wished I was as lucky as Carn." That's the sort of thing an ordinary person might say.

"Carn stopped Flying when Hereyta did; the official reason was the severity of his wounds, but as I say, I know Carn. That wouldn't have stopped him. They might have invalided him out, but he wouldn't have quit. But he told me he didn't have the heart for it any more: not when the best dragon he'd ever known had crippled herself saving his life.

"She's produced some brilliant babies in the years since she stopped Flying and I swear that the cadets who've worked with her leave here with a better understanding of dragon-nature than any of the others. I've wanted to feel that this was a good use of her talents—but dragons were made to Fly. Other than Hereyta, all the other Academy dragons alternate a few years here and a few years outside, Flying with experienced riders, doing what they do. Hereyta's been here almost twenty years, either raising babies—or raising cadets. And she's not so old that if she had three eyes she couldn't still Fly—there's no strain on her wing in the Firespace.

"I admit that for all those sleepless nights since the First Flight auguries were read out I've been harbouring a small terrible absurd hope that maybe there was an answer in—in what you've called cruelty, haven't you, Dag. In the apparent cruelty of sending Hereyta on a Flight she cannot make. That maybe a two-eyed dragon can find the way into the Firespace. I got a lot of reading done all those nights I didn't sleep, and in one—just one—old tale there was a reference to a dragon who'd lost an eye, who still Flew. But it was only one, and it wasn't even a history, but a ballad. Poets will say anything if it makes a good story."

"Which one?" said Dag, as if the words were torn out of him. I was sure he should have said "sir." The old guy was definitely a "sir" kind of guy. What was the title he'd used in the food hall?

"*Erzaglia and Sorabulyar,*" the old guy said. "It's in the Old Library; I'll give you a pass if you want to read it."

I didn't mean to move, I was just so startled. Then I was even more startled when everyone turned and looked at me. And I'd been relieved when the old guy had stopped staring at me.

"Ern?" said the old guy. I didn't like the way he said it. It wasn't unfriendly, but it had that interested, open-ended sound, like *Ern?* was only the beginning.

"It's just I know that story. A little," I said. "If it's the same one." The one I'd been trying to remember enough of to ask Eled about. I was thinking: *Erzaglia and Sorabulyar,* gods have mercy. No wonder I couldn't remember the title.

"Indeed," said the old guy, sounding even more interested. "And how do you happen to know it?"

"R-r-ralas tells it," I said, wondering if I was betraying her somehow. "It's got a foogit in it, you know. After I'd—uh—found Sippy, she used to tell me all the foogit stories she knew." I went on, knowing I was blithering, but the old guy's interest was unnerving, "F-f-foogits aren't very popular, at least not where I—Dag and I—are from. S-she was trying to make me feel it wasn't s-s-silly or dumb to have—uh—adopted one, sort of. I mean, he stayed with Ralas most of the time."

"Not silly at all," said the old guy. "Foogits have a long and honourable history."

"Rescued," said Dag. "He rescued Sippy. Sippy'd've died."

I could feel the blood beating against my skin as if the Firespace had got inside me. I knew Dag was trying to say that I'd done a good thing, but it was way too near my secret, that I wanted to be a healer. Besides, I hadn't done such a great job healing Sippy.

"And who is Ralas?" the old guy went on smoothly.

I didn't say anything. I could feel the stutter waiting to happen some more. I stared at the floor. Then Sippy inserted himself between my knees and I had to look at him instead. He put his head on my leg and stared up at me with his two big fringy eyes—foogits have amazing eyelashes: they're good at everything to do with hair—as if he was trying to tell me something. He needed a good brushing. He was covered in dust and dragon oil too. The third eye was hidden again, under his topknot.

After the pause got long enough to be uncomfortable, Dag said, "Ralas is our village all-sorts wizard. But she's a good one. She can do all kinds of stuff and never makes a fuss about it. None of us knows why she stays in our little nowhere village."

"And how did you come to adopt—rescue—your foogit?" the old guy went on implacably.

This time when I still didn't answer Dag leaned over and banged my foogit-free leg with his hand. "Hey. Wake up. This is your story."

I raised my eyes to the old guy's face and sighed. "We—my parents and I—were at a craft fair a few towns away from home. Sippy was just a pup, and he was lost, and he had a broken leg. He was crying, and everyone was ignoring him because he was a foogit and he had a broken leg. So I picked him up. The town wizard's doorkeeper wouldn't even let me in, so there was only me, and I made a mess of setting his leg and by the time we got back to Ralas, who will help anyone, it was too late and he'll always be lame, but at least he's alive. And he doesn't seem to mind. And he eats pretty well. Sir," I finally remembered to add.

The old guy took his way-too-penetrating eyes off me for a minute and looked at Sippy. As if Sippy could feel that gaze burning into his butt he lifted his head off my leg and pranced around the room a time or two.

"I don't see any lameness," said the old guy.

Dag made a little grunt I knew well. It was a big-brother-about-little-brother grunt. "Sippy hasn't been lame in years. Ern seems to need to go on believing he did it wrong."

Stop, I thought at my brother. Just stop.

"Are you Ralas' apprentice then?" said the old guy.

"No, sir," I said, trying not to look miserable, which is how I felt every time I thought about not being Ralas' apprentice. And before he asked me the next obvious question, I said, "I'm not anybody's apprentice." I could feel the old guy's eyes boring into the top of my head again but I refused to look up.

"Hmm," said the old guy. "Well. I had better warn you you'll be expected to come to the council meeting."

I jerked my eyes up then, really fast, to see if he was talking to me, and he was.

"You and Sippy are rather the heroes of the hour, you know," the old guy went on, "and the fact is that most of the Academy is very eager to know more about how you did it."

"Did *what*?" I said. I was too terrified to stammer, but my voice went up about three octaves.

"Brought Hereyta into the Firespace, and brought her back out again, of course, you idiot," said Dag, before the old guy could say anything. "It wasn't me!"

"I didn't do anything!" I squeaked.

"You jumped off Hereyta's back when she was about a league up in the sky!" said Dag.

"That was just stupid!" I said.

The old guy laughed. "It worked," he said.

"It was still stupid," I said, truthfully. "And I didn't jump. I went after Sippy. Which is even stupider."

The old guy looked at me thoughtfully for a minute or two. I glanced at him sideways. I was longing to know about the delor leaf. I couldn't see any self-protective rigidity when he moved but he'd be the kind of guy who wouldn't let pain show until it killed him. "You said your Ralas told you a lot of stories about foogits. What sort of stories were they?"

I stopped looking at him sideways and stared. What sort of stories?

As if I'd said it aloud, he said, "When there's a foogit in a story, what usually happens?"

"Oh," I said slowly. "The foogit usually does something really stupid." I added reluctantly, "And then something good happens that wouldn't've if it hadn't've."

"Yes," said the old guy. "And since I think getting the rest of what I want out of you would be rather harder than wringing blood from a stone, I'll say it myself: and usually the person who then makes the something good happen after the foogit does something ridiculous—I'm not going to call it stupid—is a rather special person, and often the hero of the story."

"Or if he isn't the hero he steals the story away from the hero," said Dag dreamily. I hadn't realised he'd ever listened to any of Ralas' foogit stories. But Dag likes all animals, like me.

The old guy laughed again. He had a rather nice laugh. If only he'd slouch a little. "We all saw what happened when you disappeared—I don't think anyone on the field was looking at any dragon but Hereyta from the moment the first one lifted off the ground—did you dive after Sippy to get back out again as well?"

"No," said Dag. "Ern just stood up and looked around a minute and then pointed."

I hadn't known Dag had seen any of it. Last thing I knew he was leaning on his hands with his eyes shut. "No," I said in my turn. "It's something about making a triangle with three of us looking in the same direction, Hereyta, Sippy and—someone. I think the two of them and Arac had been doing something like it as part of Sippy's running-around game, on the ground. I don't know why it seems to take three of us when Hereyta's only missing one eye. I don't know *anything*. I don't know why it worked and I don't know how to do it again. Maybe you can train Arac to do—whatever."

"Maybe we can. And if important discoveries were easy more people would make them," said the old guy.

"Maybe it's not an important discovery!" I said. I wanted to lie down again and put the pillow over my head.

"Oh, I think it is," said the old guy. "If this were a battlefield situation you might be right—at the end of everything anything is possible, and the gods sometimes send a miracle that will not be repeated. But this—pardon me, Dag, Eled and Setyep—this was only one year's First Flight at this Academy. What you did, Ern, is something that can be done. We need only learn the mechanism for it."

Only. I wanted worse to lie down and put the pillow over my head. And for everyone to go away.

"You're tired," said the old guy. "And not surprising. What you did . . . well. You've proved it was possible but it was not easy. The council meeting is tomorrow. You and Dag will be called for mid-morning. You can rest till then."

"He doesn't need any more sleep," said Dag in the brutal way of brothers. "He's had plenty of sleep. He gets tired as a way of making himself invisible. It doesn't work as well as it used to, before Sippy. And before he was always looking around for people who looked hurt or worried and then groping in his pocket for some stinky leaf or dirty root that was going to make them feel better. I know," he said to me, "that sidling around and looking tired and harmless is the reason why so many people let you give them your stinky leaves and dirty roots, but it's not going to work here, okay?"

"Yes, I'd noticed the sidling and harmless," said Eled.

"It's the little ones you have to watch out for," said Setyep. "You don't want to underestimate a little one."

"With those feet you'll always hear him coming," said my brother blandly.

The old guy actually reached out and put his hand on my arm. "Take it easy, you lot," he said. "He's four or five years younger than you and has important work to grow into." He stood up. I stumbled to my feet—maybe not only because he still had his hand around my wrist—while the three First Flighters shot up like arrows released from bowstrings. They were all in fresh uniforms and—I only now noticed—all had a shiny new bit of purple ribbon over their cadet badges. "Don't let them bully you," he said to me. "Maybe you have a—er—stinky leaf for that too."

"Sir," I said, and stopped.

"Ask," said the old guy. "I haven't eaten you yet, although I'm aware you're waiting for me to try."

"Why did you," I said confusedly, "in the food hall that morning—ask me. Ask me at all. But in front of everyone."

Some of his wrinkles seemed to smooth out when he smiled. "I told you I've been cherishing a small terrible hope that there might be a good reason why the signs demanded Hereyta Fly for First Flight this year. When Hereyta's First Flight partner came back to school a fortnight ago with a brother and a foogit—a foogit with a lucky third eye and a brother who had a secret calling as a healer—"

When he said "healer" the Firespace started beating against the inside of my skin again.

"—I wanted anything you could do for us, for Hereyta," he said, and for a moment he looked a lot like Dag, that fierce, intent, passionate look Dag had when he talked about his dragons. "So I wanted to flush you into the open. I wanted you to feel your healing gift was welcome here."

Welcome, I thought. Healing welcome. "Did you use it, sir? The delor leaf. Did you use it? Did it work?"

For the first time his authority wavered, and he looked almost embarrassed. "Yes. I used it, and it worked. And when the council meeting is over, I would like more delor leaf, if you would be so kind. I haven't decided if I'm going to make the half-dozen other of us old smashed-up veterans who'd like to try it too ask you themselves or not. I probably will. You'll tell me you need to speak to them individually anyway, won't you?"

I stood up straight. Straighter, anyway. "Yes, sir. I will."

"Good."

There was a brief, strained silence after Eled, who had jumped first as the old guy turned toward the door, closed it gently behind him. Then Dag said, "I'm going to make Ern have a bath now—"

"You don't have to make me," I said with the dignity of the truly filthy. "I *want* a bath."

"And then we'll come to supper. In the hall," he added, just in case I wasn't listening.

"But—" I said feebly. I was trying to think but what. Dag had already said that saying I was tired wasn't going to work.

"And you," Dag said over me, "you two can come sit with us and keep off his admirers."

Midmorning the next day came way too soon. I'd still been pretty much starving at supper, so it wasn't too bad. The only people who gave me a hard time were the three I was sitting with. Doara and Chort came round to say "well done" and I got a few "hey"s and "blue skies and clear horizons" of my own and I tried not to show how much this pleased me. And a lot of people wanted to push Sippy's topknot back and check out the third eye. Which was fine with him. All attention is good attention. Even Fistagh nodded to both Dag and me: two nods, one each—and his girl actually smiled.

We spent the night back in Dag's old room. Dag slept. I didn't. By breakfast I was too scared—and tired: no joke—to be hungry. Dag made me drink some blastweed, saying it would make me alert, but I didn't drink very much, because I was sure being this scared was going to make me need to pee all the time.

We went back upstairs for Dag to climb warily into a spotless new cadet uniform like it was a booby trap. It had been waiting on a peg outside the door when we got back to Dag's room after supper the night before, and he'd wordlessly pointed to the new stripe on the shoulder and chest. I'd seen it on the fourth-years' uniforms, so I said, "First Flight?" and he nodded. This morning it seemed to glitter in the light but that was probably my eyes. I thought Dag's hands shook a little when he pinned his old badge and new bit of ribbon to it.

They'd found some clothes for me too. They were too large but they were a little more dignified than anything I'd brought with me. I didn't have dignified clothes. What would I ever need them for? At least they were dull, invisible-making colours. It didn't occur to me when I put them on that this would have the opposite effect, making me stand out among all the Academy uniforms.

The meeting was held in the big hall at the back of the main building—the building that had been the whole human end of the Academy when it first opened eight hundred years ago. The hall was still big enough to hold everybody who went there—but I swear everyone who had anything at all to do with the Academy was there, not just the students and the tutors and the dragonmasters. There were people standing at the back and sitting in the aisles. Fire hazard, I thought. But no one made them leave.

You know how on winter solstice nights after it gets dark and you've done all the rites—or maybe it's the night after the solstice, depending on, you know, how well the rites get done, especially the ones with lots of libations—and you sit around the fire with your friends and tell stories about the really scary things that happened to your ancestors? Because telling those stories around the solstice is supposed to stop them from happening again, like to us. Our ancestors had a really rough time is all I can say. So maybe it works.

Sooner or later someone asks what everybody's worst nightmare is. Telling it out loud at the solstice is supposed to stop it from happening too.

I'm here to tell you that this doesn't work. Because my worst nightmare is being in front of a lot of other people who are staring at me. And here I was. And they really were staring at me. Nobody else. Me. It was much worse than the food halls. The halls are open all the time, and people sort of stream through, and there's never that many of them at the same time, and the tutors and dragon-masters mostly eat somewhere else, and it's all groups around tables, not rows and rows of chairs all pointed in the same direction with a stage at the front, organised for staring. Everyone would've known that Hereyta was in First Flight this year with Dag, and word would have got round that they'd actually made Flight. And I knew from yesterday that they'd decided to pin that on me. So everybody was staring at the one person up on that horrible great stage that wasn't wearing an Academy uniform. Who also, just in case they missed that bit, had a foogit with him. Maybe telling your worst nightmare hadn't worked for me because I could only bring myself to tell it out loud if it was only my own family listening.

So I took one look at that sea of faces and closed down and went off in my head somewhere. Well, not quite. Sippy wanted me there so I had to leave a little of me behind in the hall to keep him com-pany—and get ready to grab if he got reassured enough to want to go cruising for new friends. I don't know what his worst nightmare was. Maybe taking a dive off a flying dragon, and he'd lived through that.

But I was enough not-there that it took me a minute to recognise the person coming down the centre aisle toward the stage platform where Dag and I and Sippy and half a dozen more blue and red and yellow coats from the Academy were sitting. Setyep was the only other red and yellow cadet besides Dag; the rest were all the blue and red higher-ups. The old guy from yesterday was the only other person I recognised, although how much you can say you recognise someone when you don't know his name I don't know, but what he'd said yesterday was kind of etched into me. (Even if I'd forgotten to ask Dag later what his name was and *who* he was. I was kind of concentrating on what he'd said.) I was actually staring at him (which meant I was facing away from the audience, which was the crucial part) and vaguely thinking about it that all the other blue and red coats seemed to be deferring to him, like he wasn't just another blue and red coat, he was *the* blue and red coat.

So I didn't notice her till she was walking up the steps to the platform. I'd seen her out of the corner of my eye but, so? There were a million people out there, what was one more? Even if she was walking down the aisle and coming up on the stage. But the walk was familiar. I wasn't looking at the person but the way she moved was familiar.

It was familiar. She was. It was Ralas.

She seemed perfectly calm. Well, she was always perfectly calm. It occurred to me she was like a dragon that way, or anyway like Hereyta. Someone falls at Ralas' feet with bright red blood coming *wham wham wham* out of somewhere so you know they're not going to last long, she's still calm. I saw this once. I'm the one stood on the wound—because I was too small and feeble just to press on it—to stop the rest of the blood coming out while she dribbled a little green herbal goo under his tongue and stuck a *xan* leaf on his forehead with a little *dir* paste and then got out her needle and thread and went to work. He lived too.

What was she doing here? She looked up as if she felt my eyes on her—she looked up so quickly it was like she'd been waiting to feel my eyes on her—and gave me a friendly, level look back like she was going to be interested in what I had to say for myself and she was keeping an open mind. She'd given me that look when I'd brought Sippy to her the first time, after I'd bungled setting his leg. I don't know why I always expected her to yell at me. She never did. She was always kind and she always had an open mind.

What was she doing here? I couldn't think of any way it was going to be good news. Maybe she was going to tell them how I always meant well even if I usually messed it up. But that was hardly worth dragging her all this way for. They must have sent for her—they must have sent a *dragon* for her—before I woke up and told them I didn't have a *clue* how Hereyta got in and out of the Firespace and I couldn't tell them how to do it and no, I wasn't going to make a habit of waiting till she was a league in the air and then dropping Sippy over the edge and jumping after him. Not even for Hereyta. If I'd've done it for anyone, I'd've done it for Hereyta, but . . . no.

There was an empty chair on the other side of Dag and she sat down in it. She smiled at me. It was a "there are more people out there staring at us than there are in the world and this bothers you why?" sort of smile. I came a little more out of my daze for that smile. But I still kept my eyes away from the audience. Sippy had to say hello to Ralas of course but she even makes crazy foogits calmer so he said hello and then he came back to me and lay down, sort of wrapping himself around my ankles like he was making sure I didn't try to run away.

The old guy stood up and everybody fell silent like they'd all turned to stone. I would ask Dag again after this was over (if I lived that long) who he was. The problem was that both times I'd seen him before the experience was so extreme I forgot. And this time was going to be even more extreme so I'd probably forget again, and harder, if you can forget harder.

"We've called this general session to tell everyone what happened three days ago during First Flight and so, we hope, put an end to the rumours. What did happen is quite remarkable enough and the absurd stories that are already being told and listened to and passed on are doing no one any favours, least of all the Academy."

He said this in such a way that anyone who'd let one of those rumours go through them would now be feeling about ant-sized.

No one moved. Maybe the rumour-tellers really had turned to stone, and when everybody else got up to walk out, they'd just stay there forever.

Then he started explaining what had happened, starting with what he'd told us yesterday about choosing the First Flight list, but the moment I heard my name—"Cadet Dag also took his younger brother Ern with him on Hereyta, and Ern's foogit, Sippy"—I went back into my daze again and stopped listening. So I don't know how long that part of the story lasted or how he told it, but I don't think it was very long and I don't think he'd have made it any more gruesome than he had to.

Then there was a staccato bit when different voices spoke, and I think that was people from the audience asking questions and the old guy answering them. After a few minutes it started getting sort of uproary like the old guy had said it would. I kept hearing my name. Early on the old guy turned and looked at me, and I probably had "no one home" on my face, even though I was staring at him again. I was staring at him because staring at Ralas would only make it harder to stay in my daze because I kept wondering what she was doing here, and I still didn't want to look at the audience. He got that amused look again, and then turned away and answered the question. I think he had been thinking about asking me to answer the question. It's a good thing he changed his mind.

I heard Dag say something twice, I think, and Setyep once.

And then the next thing I knew was that everybody in the audience was getting up and filing out. I was so surprised I looked at them. There was a heavy sense of disappointment and frustrated curiosity in the air and a few audience members looked back over their shoulders as they left like they knew they were missing something and didn't want to—I was reminded of the way your parents send you to bed when you're dying to know what's going on and they think you're still too little—but that was as rebellious as anyone got. Most of the ones looking over their shoulders were looking at *me* so I didn't look back at them very long. But I doubted anyone was going to lurk around and then press their ears to the door either.

The old guy must have turned the rumour-spreaders back to human again because everyone left.

And then the eight of us on the stage were coming to our feet (I got up because everyone else did) and following the old guy out behind the stage, another way than the way we'd come in. And we were in this hallway, and there was a door with someone in *hsa* livery standing by it and we all went in and were waved toward a long oval table with chairs around it and pots and ewers and stuff to drink and plates of other stuff to eat in the middle of it. Like we were all going to sit down and relax and have a nice cozy chat. Because you always notice the stuff you don't want to notice when you're trying not to notice, I noticed that there were more chairs and plates than there had been people on the stage. So there were going to be more of us now.

I found myself sitting between Dag and Ralas, with most of Sippy wedged under my chair. I kept scraping my knuckles on the bottom of the chair when I leaned over to pet him. Ralas poured out some blastweed and put it in front of me. When I made no move to touch it Dag pushed it a little closer to me. Oh, well. I took a big gulp and it half scalded me going down. Which brought me out of my daze . . . just long enough for the old guy to nail me.

"Ern," he said, "I realise this will not be popular with you, but the fact is that this meeting is mostly about you. We want to know—we badly want to know—how you got Hereyta into the Fire-space and how you got her out." He was almost half laughing as he said it at the same time as he was absolutely deadly serious. The other old guys—they were all old—around him mostly weren't bothering with the half laughing part. Their stares really were like being stabbed. All but one of them, and he was just sitting there smiling like somebody'd given him the biggest present in the world and he hadn't got over it yet. Some of the wrinkles on his face were scars and there were two sticks leaning on the wall behind him and I wondered if, just maybe, he was Carn. I didn't think he'd been on the stage. But he was smiling and he was the only one, so without thinking I smiled back and his face just lit up. When he spoke I figured some of the wrinkles on his neck must be scars too. "Ern. Anything you can tell us. Please."

"I don't know," I said, desperately, knowing that I had to say something, and knowing they weren't going to leave it at that. I looked back at the original old guy and I knew, suddenly, that the on-stage part had been a lot shorter than planned, because the old guy knew I couldn't stand it. I told myself that he only cared because of Hereyta and the Firespace—and I thought, well, why not?—but then I also knew it wasn't true. He wasn't just some old guy that everybody has to obey, trying to make me obey too. I remembered the affectionate look I'd seen on his face yesterday, looking at his cadets. Maybe he was used to the weight of the world on his shoulders, but that didn't mean he didn't feel it, that he didn't have to remember, sometimes, to stand like he had a broomstick up his coat. He understood what he was asking me to carry, and he'd help me if he could.

Except he couldn't. "I don't know," I said again, knowing that it wasn't just they weren't going to leave it at that, they couldn't. If I were in their place I couldn't leave it either. But there still wasn't anything I could tell them. I'd taken my header off Hereyta because I was following Sippy. That just happened. I thought about when I'd taken Arac's place in Sippy's three-way game, and the way the other two had *looked* at me afterward. And then I thought about standing up, when we had to get back out of the Firespace again, and pointing, and how it had been that way, it had been how we could get out. But that wasn't anything anyone could use—it wasn't like "mash up some delor leaf and pour boiling water over it and drink it."

You just do it, Ralas had told me, long ago, and when I said, Do *what*? she'd laughed and said, It. *It*.

The head old guy—I don't know how to explain this—he was staring at me just as intently as the rest of the old guys, but he was doing it *softer* somehow. Him and Carn, if it was Carn. I thought, I'd tell you if I could, and the old guy's expression changed briefly, as if he'd heard.

He said, "Ern. Believe me. It doesn't just happen. The Academy has been here for eight hundred years and no dragon who has lost an eye has ever crossed into the Firespace again. Or if they have there's no record, and there would be a record. Or rather, the only hint of a record is from the tale of Erzaglia and Sorabulyar, which I told you about yesterday, and which you, interestingly, had heard of, although it's an old obscure tale that no one tells any more. We don't teach it at the Academy." He added gently, "Ern. I can see how much you hate this. But think about how important this is to us, to our dragons—to all dragons, maybe—to Hereyta."

I could feel my face getting hot. That was unfair.

"No, it's not unfair," said the old guy as if I'd said it aloud. "I love Hereyta myself. She was the leader of the king's guard for twenty years, did Dag tell you that? The king loved her too. I've hated seeing her crippled. Seeing her carry her authority—as she does still carry her authority—among the other dragons, when she can no longer Fly."

I could see Carn shift in his chair, and heard him sigh, a scratchy sigh from his damaged throat.

"I'm willing to believe," the old guy went on, "that perhaps it's something about her specialness, her uniqueness, that made it possible, what happened; that it also has to do with her being partnered with a cadet whose empathy with dragons is so extraordinary that he was jumped a year. We only have about one jumper a decade at the Academy. But I also know, as sure as dragons Fly, that it wouldn't have happened without you and Sippy. I can't believe it's all just a peculiar accident that the only two-eyed dragon who's entered the Firespace in any history we know went there while carrying a young man and his foogit. Ern. Think. Try."

And I did try. I closed my eyes and—Sippy having emerged from under the chair and put his head in my lap—buried both hands in his topknot and thought as hard as I could about those few moments after Hereyta leaped up from the ordinary earth and her wings beat us up and up and up in a spiral into the sky. And Sippy struggling out of his harness and out of my arms—and I still didn't understand how that happened; I know I'm clumsy so I'm really careful—and over the edge of Hereyta's wing. And how I went after him . . . and the heavy *floosh* of the air as I dove and the sort of counter-*floosh* as Hereyta plunged after us, veering up under us again in a way wholly incredible . . .

. . . wholly incredible . . .

. . . like the sudden wash of heat and the pink haloes around the trees on a clear cool autumn afternoon. . . .

I was suddenly staggering against Hereyta's side, her wing, I had my arms around Sippy, we were supposed to be dead (or about to be dead) and we weren't, but then how had any of this happened, starting with Ralas telling Dag to take Sippy and me with him. . . .

I could remember the pink trees, hearing Setyep and Dag comment on the bizarre breath of summer wind, knowing I wasn't imagining it, knowing that it was something the two dragons and Sippy had done among them—but it was remembering like you might remember watching your wizard stop someone from bleeding to death. They could do it, you couldn't. When it happened to you you were just standing there saying, Huh? What?

But thinking about wizards made me remember Ralas. Ralas who was here. What was Ralas doing here? It seemed as unlikely as Sippy and me flying on a dragon. Or a two-eyed dragon getting into the Firespace.

As if this was my answer I said to Ralas, "What are you doing here?"

Ralas smiled her funny, wry smile and I realised how glad I was to see her, whatever she was doing here, and however much it was her fault that *I* was here. "May I speak?" she said to the old guy.

"I invite you to do so," he said courteously.

"Ern has been my apprentice these three years," she began and I burst out, suddenly completely unaware of anything else, where I was or what was going on, anything but the words she'd just said: "Your *apprentice*? I'd *die* to be your apprentice! I'm *not* your apprentice!"

There was a tiny pause. Dag shifted in his chair. Ralas turned to look at me. I had never seen her disconcerted, but she was disconcerted now. "Ern? Of course you are. I settled with your parents right after your twelfth birthday. . . ." Her voice tailed off. She must have seen it in my face that this was completely news to me. She blinked once or twice and I could see her mind going back to what had happened. "Your mother was worried about tying you so young, that's true, even though as the third son you might be expected to be apprenticed to a wizard. But I pointed out that you were already interested in the work and that I wasn't merely willing to have you but wanted you as well. And that since you were already trying to learn as much as you could, why not let you? Why not accept that you'd chosen your path and begin to help you along it?"

I shook my head again, but the shaking just seemed to make my head hurt. Sippy moved his head on my knee as if to say, What's wrong? Can I help?

"Your mother," Ralas went on slowly, "as a stipulation to their agreement, said that the apprenticeship was to remain secret, and part-time only, till you turned sixteen. I agreed to this. It meant I could begin teaching you, which was all that mattered to me; and I did not see that anyone needed to know beyond those of us involved. It never occurred to me that when your mother said the apprenticeship should remain secret that she meant it should remain secret from you too."

I thought bitterly, she just wanted someone to deliver candles a few more years. And then I thought, no. I thought about all the food she kept trying to stuff in me and how she worried that I stayed a runt. And I thought about . . . about Dag saying that I needed to believe that I'd done Sippy's leg wrong. Mum was like that too. Nothing she did was ever really right; everything she did she thought she should have done better. She'd've seen me doing the same thing.

She was trying to let me grow up a little more. Apprenticeship was serious. You didn't apprentice twelve-year-olds because it was too difficult for twelve-year-olds. Even a twelve-year-old who already knew what he wanted to do. Especially a twelve-year-old who passionately knew what he wanted to do and equally passionately believed he'd be hopeless at it.

If I'd been being fair I'd've admitted three years ago that someone like me probably wouldn't be apprenticed till they were sixteen—it wasn't really true that everyone went at fourteen. It depended on the kid. But even if I'd been taller than Dag and brighter than Kel and didn't worry about everything all the time (just like her) my mother probably still wouldn't have let me be apprenticed early. My dad might've. He didn't think about things like maturity. He would've just thought, the boy wants to be a wizard, here's a wizard wants to apprentice him, great. I remembered now that Mum'd had a funny spell of going around the house muttering, "Twelve is *much* too young to be apprenticed," when I was twelve, which I'd thought pretty strange. I wasn't worrying about being apprenticed then—and at twelve I looked about eight—but I was already worrying about it for when I was fourteen.

But my parents knew that I spent every spare minute with Ralas and by letting Ralas apprentice me they were also doing their best for my future. And—this was even harder to admit—my mum was right about making me wait. If she'd let me go even at fourteen I'd've believed that I had to learn everything in the first six months—I had too much to prove because I was the youngest and the least of the three of us brothers. And I realised with something like amazement that it was the last three years of giving people stuff that would help them feel better—of learning more stuff and learning to read people better—that was teaching me patience.

Even my parents didn't know that I didn't just want to be a wizard, I wanted to be . . .

Ralas had turned back to the others. I missed what she'd begun saying but I heard: . . . "the strongest gift for healing of anyone I've ever met. It's one of the things that's kept me there, in Birchhome, because as we all know healing is not a popular form of wizardry and while I'm not the best teacher he could have I'll do to start with—and there are not many who will teach it at all."

"Birchhome," said one of the old guys who hadn't spoken before. "We did wonder."

"Why shouldn't I want a bit of peace and quiet for a change?" Ralas said briskly and I stopped thinking about myself long enough to want to know what she was talking about. Nearly everybody who had ever met her wondered what she was doing in Birchhome. Now that I was her apprentice maybe I could ask her what she'd done before. "I suspect one of the reasons his parents wanted a secret apprenticeship is because they know healing is the area of wizardry Ern is drawn to, and a three-year head start would help ground him in the difficult field he's chosen—or that has chosen him. Fortunately Ern's healing gift is nearly matched by his stubbornness." She turned her head and smiled at me, and there was no wryness in it at all.

Apprentice. I'd been Ralas' real honest-to-wizardry apprentice for three years. The rest of what she'd said still pretty much went past me. Gift? Me? Keeping her in Birchhome? But if I was going to have a gift, it would be for the wrong thing. Except that I *wanted* to be a healer. Badly wanted it. And she was right about this much: I was stubborn.

I could feel a huge stupid smile breaking over my face. I turned to look at Dag and a great grin spread over his face too, and suddenly he looked about twenty years younger. I hadn't realised how old he'd been looking, from the day he'd showed up at our parents' house and told us about Hereyta and his First Flight—the smile looked like what had happened on that First Flight was finally sinking in. And maybe a little bit that he could stop worrying about me. He was our mum's son too, after all.

"I don't have any idea how Ern did what he did for your dragon," Ralas went on. "And I doubt that Ern does either. I don't think it's only his well-known aversion to being the centre of attention that's making him uncooperative today. But I will tell you also that when he turned up at my house with Sippy as a broken-legged pup and I'd seen what he'd done I realised that my suspicion that he was a healer was truer than I'd guessed . . . and I was also very interested in why he'd been given a foogit as his familiar. Foogits used to be quite popular as familiars hundreds of years ago, but I know of no wizard who uses one now. And a wizard who specialises in healing and furthermore uses a foogit . . . Ern will need all the grounding he can achieve, and all the stubbornness he is capable of.

"Most of us do without familiars altogether, which I think is rather a pity. And I thought of the tale of Erzaglia and Sorabulyar the moment I heard about Hereyta. I had no sign to send Ern and Sippy back with Dag to the Academy but it seemed the obvious thing to do. It seemed too obvious to need or ask for a sign."

I muttered to myself, or to Sippy, as you might mutter an old familiar charm when recent events were too wild and strange for you, "I didn't do much of a job for you, really. I messed up your leg."

Ralas said out loud, so everyone could hear, "You did *not* mess up Sippy's leg. Sippy's leg wasn't just broken, it was shattered. He should have been dead of fever before you got him back to me. He should at least have lost the leg. He's not even lame on it any more. It's a little scarred . . . but I'm a little scarred, and I don't feel the healers who saved my life messed me up. And you were *eleven*. It was after that I went and asked your parents to apprentice you to me—and of course I had to explain why I was so interested, although I tried not to emphasize healing too much. I won't have you long—I'm still only an all-sorts wizard—"

A muffled grunt from the old guy who'd commented on Birch-home. "'All-sorts' in your case covers a bit more than usual."

"As you like," said Ralas, unperturbed. "Whatever my skills are, they will serve to get Ern started. Which they have done."

The original old guy said carefully, "We—the Academy—are quite interested in Ern's future ourselves."

"Let me have him three more years," said Ralas, as if what the old guy had said was only what she was expecting him to say. "Till he's eighteen. I can cram quite a lot in in the next three years," and she smiled a conspiratorial smile at me before turning back to the old guys. "We might—I would hope to—begin to find out why or how Ern's gift could shape itself to Hereyta's need. It was not an ordinary sort of healing—which makes me wonder—hope—if perhaps it might be the beginning of a new discipline of healing—one which might even make that crucial branch of wizardry respectable at last.

"When your messenger came of course his parents heard something of what had happened during First Flight, but it was clear to all of us that as his master I should come to the Academy and contribute what I could to the discussion. I can, if you wish it, begin to prepare them for the future. But they will hardly turn down a place at the Academy for him once he turns eighteen."

They'll think there was some huge mistake, I thought. A new discipline of healing! And a healer with a foogit! I'd better stay short and goofy-looking. That'll be the easy bit.

The old guy who'd mentioned Birchhome said, "I'm sure you have recognised me, Ralas, as I have recognised you."

Ralas nodded, and her smile, at its wryest, appeared and disappeared. "Yes. Even among those who stood at variance with me, you were—er—conspicuous, Cladharg."

Cladharg turned to me then. I managed to meet his eyes for about three seconds and then I looked at the table. "Ralas was apprentice to my master for a year. She's only an all-sorts wizard, as she describes herself, because that was her choice. My master begged her to stay and let him train her to be a Seer."

"The ordinary world needs good wizards too," she said. "Not only the kings and queens, the councils . . . and Seers for the academies."

There was a little silence that bristled with unspoken words. Then Cladharg said, "We will not agree now any more than we did thirty years ago."

"No," Ralas said pleasantly.

"But you are willing to see your own apprentice come here?"

"That is up to Ern. But I think what has already happened indicates that he has work to do here."

"And you also think he might shake us up," said Cladharg.

"I am looking forward to it," she said demurely, and he laughed, a proper loud crack of laughter, and something in the room cracked too, and after that we were all more comfortable with each other.

I started to open my mouth and then closed it again, but the first old guy said, "Ern. It is time you said something. This is your life we are prescribing for you. What did you want to ask?"

"Not about my life," I said. "I—" I stopped. Not yet, I thought. I can't think about that yet. "But I'd like to know who you are." I glanced quickly around the table and then back at the first old guy. "I don't even know your name. I mean, I should know, that morning in the food halls, but . . ."

The first old guy said gravely, "But you have had many things on your mind and you have been introduced to nearly an entire Academy of new people. It is very discourteous of us not to have identified ourselves in the beginning—that I have not ere now is the worst of all. I'm afraid we have been too interested in what you could do for us—what you have done for us already."

One of the other old guys who hadn't said anything yet said, "We believe we are looking at our future, and that we are already the past." He didn't sound unhappy about it though.

"It was the story of Erzaglia and Sorabulyar that told me to send Ern and Sippy to you," said Ralas. "The past remains vital."

"The past holds the present and hands it to the future," said the first old guy. "I am Storkhal, First Commander of the Academy—"

I blinked.

"This"—the old guy who had just spoken for the first time—"is Sfector, First Dragonrider. This is Mjorak, First Professor of Practise; Nonoran, First Professor of Theory; and Cladharg, who is First Seer."

I started missing the names; everything had been way too much for way too long. Even Sippy seemed content to sit quietly with his head in my lap as if he was feeling it too. First Commander of the Academy! But I was listening again in time to hear Storkhal say, "And Carn, Five-Crown Sukaj Colonel of the Inban Regiment—"

Carn interrupted in his harsh voice: "Storkhal, stop it. I'm a minor tutor here, that's all. But I'm guessing Ern has heard my name, and can himself then guess why it is I begged a place here today—and why I was granted one."

I said the only thing I could think of to say: "Hereyta is lovely."

"Yes, she is, isn't she?" said Carn, and smiled his wonderful, contagious smile again.

But Carn was the last. I'd missed some names, but I checked back in my mind for the sound of Storkhal's voice rising and falling through the introductions, and I didn't think I'd missed what I'd been—what I should have been—listening for. I remembered the day Dag and I had arrived at the Academy and met Eled, and Dag and Eled had looked at each other and said, We're supposed to do without wizards. I swallowed. "No First Wizard," I said. And then, ridiculously, I added, "No First Healer."

"No," said Cladharg. "There was once a First Wizard; perhaps there should be again. There has never been a First Healer. Perhaps that is an error. I look forward to beginning that discussion in three years."

"Oh, but—" Dag burst out, and then turned to the First Commander and said, "*Zedak*, my apologies."

Storkhal was wearing his amused look again. "No, please go on, *Singla* Dag." He sounded as if he knew what Dag was going to say. I know I did.

"You're not going to send him away for three years? What about Hereyta?"

"That is up to Ern, and his—your—parents, and Ralas," said Storkhal. Now he was using his smooth voice. I only knew what Dag was going to say, I hadn't thought about what it meant. I looked at Ralas and then at Cladharg. Ralas was looking disconcerted again—the second time I'd seen her off balance in all the years I'd known her—and I'd known her all my life—only half an hour after the first time. Cladharg, on the other hand, had the look of a man undergoing a revelation he wasn't sure he approved of. "Ern and Ralas are welcome here as soon and for as long as they wish to stay," added Storkhal.

"Oh, dear," said Ralas.

"There is certainly no one here who can teach him what you can teach him," said Storkhal, still smooth.

"No," she agreed. Cladharg twitched but didn't say anything. "Ern, what do you think?"

What did I think? I had no idea what I thought. I had no more idea now how Sippy and I had got Hereyta in and out of the Firespace than I had when we'd first come in here and sat down at this table and the old guy whose name I had forgotten had asked me how I'd done it. But I did know I was Ralas' apprentice, which I hadn't known then. And she said I was going to be a healer. And Hereyta . . . and the other dragons . . .

"Ralas," I said wistfully, "would you really hate it here?"

Ralas looked around the table and back at me. She was smiling again, and if it was a wry smile, it was also amused. "Fate finds you out," she said. "I knew I wouldn't stay at Birchhome forever—but I did think I'd have three more years. And the Academy is the last place . . . I'll have to tell Fran I need her at Birchhome three years early."

"We'll have to go back to Birchhome for me to talk to Mum and Dad too, but I'm pretty sure I can talk them round," I said, and I was surprised at how strong and clear my voice was. "I still want to be your apprentice more than anything else—but I want to find out what happened during First Flight. And I need Hereyta to do that. And I don't think there's room for Hereyta in Birchhome."

Ralas laughed. "No. But we might ask if she'd come for a visit some day."

And don't forget

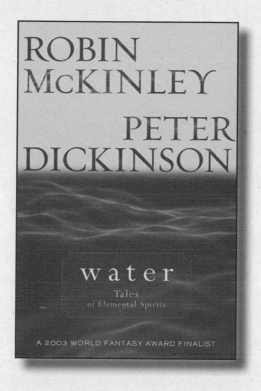

ROBIN
McKINLEY

PETER
DICKINSON

water
Tales
of Elemental Spirits

A 2003 WORLD FANTASY AWARD FINALIST

Turn the page for the beginning of
Robin McKinley's

"A POOL IN THE DESERT"

A POOL
IN THE DESERT

There were no deserts in the Homeland. Perhaps that was why she dreamed of deserts.

She had had her first desert dreams when she was quite young, and still had time to read storybooks and imagine herself in them; but deserts were only one of the things she dreamed about in those days. She dreamed about knights in armour and glorious quests, and sometimes in these dreams she was a knight and sometimes she was a lovely lady who watched a particular knight and hoped that, when he won the tournament, it would be she to whom he came, and stooped on bended knee, and … and sometimes she dreamed that she was a lady who tied her hair up and pulled a helmet down over it and over her face, and won the tournament herself, and everyone watching said, Who is that strange knight? For I have never seen his like. After her mother fell ill and she no longer had time to read, she still dreamed, but the knights and quests and tournaments dropped out of her dreams, and only the deserts remained.

For years in these desert dreams she rode a slender, graceful horse with an arched neck, and it flew over the sand as if it had wings; but when she drew up on the crest of a dune and looked behind her, there would be the shallow half-circles of hoofprints following them, hummocking the wind-ridges and bending the coarse blades of the sand-grass. Her horse would dance under her, splashing sand, and blow through red nostrils, asking to gallop on, but she would wait for the rest of her party, less wonderfully mounted, toiling behind her. Then she would turn again in the direction they were all going, and shade her eyes with one hand, talking soothingly to her restless horse through the reins held lightly in the other; and there would be the dark shadow of mountains before her, mountains she knew to call the Hills.

As the years passed, however, the dreams changed again. She left school at sixteen because her parents said they could spare her no longer, with her mother ill and Ruth and Jeff still so little and her father and Dane (who had left school two years before) working extra hours in the shop because the specialists her mother needed were expensive. When Mrs Halford and Mr Jonah came to visit them at home (repeated efforts to persuade her parents to come into the school for a meeting having failed), and begged them to reconsider, and said that she was sure of a scholarship, that her education would be no burden to them, her mother only wept and said in her trembling invalid voice that she was a good girl and they needed her at home, and her father only stared, until at last they went away, the tea and biscuits she had made in honour of so rare an event as visitors in the parlour untouched. Her father finally told her: "See them out to their car, Hetta, and then come direct back. Supper's to be on time, mind."

The three of them were quiet as they went down the stairs

and through the hall that ran alongside the shop. The partition was made of cheap ply, for customers never saw it, which made the hall ugly and unfriendly, in spite of the old family photos Hetta had hung on the walls. The shop-door opened nearly on the kerb, for the shop had eaten up all of what had been the front garden. At the last minute Mrs Halford took Hetta's hand and said, "If there's anything I can do—this year, next year, any time. Ring me."

Hetta nodded, said good-bye politely, and then turned round to go back to the house and get supper and see what Ruth and Jeff were doing. Her father had already rejoined Dane in the shop; her mother had gone to bed, taking the plate of biscuits with her.

Ruth had been told by their father to stay out of the way, it was none of her concern, but she was waiting for Hetta in the kitchen. "What happened?" she said.

"Nothing," said Hetta. "Have you done your homework?"

"Yes," said Ruth. "All but the reading. D'you want to listen while you cook?"

"Yes," said Hetta. "That would be nice."

That night Hetta dreamed of a sandstorm. She was alone in darkness, the wind roaring all round her, the sand up to her ankles, her knees, her waist, filling her eyes, her nose, her mouth. Friendly sand. She snuggled down into it as if it were a blanket; as it filled her ears she could no longer hear the wind, nor anything else. When the alarm went off at dawn, she felt as stiff as if she had been buried in sand all night, and her eyes were so sticky, she had to wash her face before she could open them properly.

✦   ✦   ✦

It had been a relief to quit school, because she was tired all the time. There was more than she could get done even after there was no schoolwork to distract her; but without the school-work she found that her mind went to sleep while her body went on with her chores, and for a while that seemed easier. Sometimes months passed without her ever thinking about what she was doing, or not doing, or about Mrs Halford, or about how she might have used that scholarship if she had got it, if her parents had let her accept it, which they wouldn't have. Months passed while her days were bound round with cooking and housekeeping and keeping the shop accounts, looking through cookery books for recipes when her mother thought that this or that might tempt her appetite, sweeping the passage from the shop twice a day because of the sawdust, teaching Ruth and Jeff to play checkers and fold paper air-planes. When she had first started keeping the accounts, she had done it in the evening, after supper was cleared away and there were no other demands till morning, and the kitchen was peaceful while everyone watched TV in the parlour. But she found she was often too bone weary to pay the necessary attention, so she had taught herself to do it in the edgy time between breakfast and lunch, when the phone was liable to ring, and her mother to be contemplating having one of her bad days, and her father to call her down to the shop to wait on a customer. One afternoon a week she took the car to the mall and shopped for everything they had to have. After the narrow confines of the house, the car park seemed liberating, the neon-edged sky vast.

The months mounted up, and turned into years.

One year the autumn gales were so severe that ruining the

harvest and breaking fences for the stock to get through out in the countryside wasn't enough, and they swept into the towns to trouble folk there. Trees and TV aerials came down, and some chimney-pots; there was so much rain that everyone's cellars flooded. The wood stored in their cellar had to come up into the parlour, whereupon there was nowhere to sit except the kitchen. Everyone's tempers grew short with crowding, and when the TV was brought in too, there was nowhere to put it except on counter space Hetta couldn't spare. The only time there was armistice was during programmes interviewing farmers about how bad everything was. Her father watched these with relish and barked "Ha!" often.

That season in spite of the weather she spent more time than ever in the garden. The garden had still been tended by her great-grandfather when she was very small, but after he died, only her grandmother paid any attention to it. As her mother's illness took hold and her father's business took off, it grew derelict, for her grandmother had done the work Hetta did now, with a bad hip and hands nearly frozen with arthritis. Hetta began to clear and plant it about a year after she stopped school; gardening, she found, was interesting, and it got her out of the house. Her father grumbled about having to contain his heaps of wood chips and discarded bits too broken to be mended, but permitted it because she grew vegetables and fruit, which lowered the grocery bills, and she canned and froze what they didn't eat in season. No one else even seemed to notice that the view from the rear of the house looked any different than the front—although Ruth liked bugs, and would sometimes come out to look at the undersides of leaves and scrape things into jars—and so long as Hetta wasn't missing when someone wanted her, nothing was said about the hours she spent in the garden. Their house was the oldest on the street and had the largest garden. It had been a pretty house once, before the shop destroyed its front, but the shop at least made it look more in keeping with the rest of the row. There were proper walls around their garden, eight foot tall on three sides, and the house the fourth. It was her own little realm.

That autumn there was a heaviness to the air, and it smelled of rain and earth and wildness even on days when the sun shone. Hetta usually left as much as she could standing over the winter, to give shelter to Ruth's bugs and the birds and hedgehogs that ate them, but this year she brought the last tomatoes and squashes indoors early (where, denied the wet cellar, she balanced them on piles of timber in the parlour), and she cut back and tied in and staked everything that was left. Even with the walls protecting it, the wind curled in here, flinging other people's tiles at her runner-bean teepees and stripping and shredding the fleece that protected the brassicas. Sometimes she stopped and listened, as if the whistle of the wind was about to tell her something. Sometimes at sunset, when there was another storm coming, the sky reminded her of her desert. But she didn't dare stop long or often, even in the garden; her mother's bedroom window overlooked it, and the sight of Hetta standing still invariably made her hungry. She would open her window and call down to Hetta that she just felt she might eat a little something if Hetta would make it up nice the way she always did and bring it to her.

When the meteorologists began predicting the big storm on its way, the family gathered round the TV set as if the weather report had become a daily installment of a favourite soap opera. Her father snorted; he hated experts in clean business suits telling him things he didn't know. But he didn't protest when the TV was turned on early and he didn't declare the forecast rubbish, and he told Hetta to do her weekly shop early, "just in case."

Two days later the sky went green-yellow, grey-purple; *soon*, sighed the prickle of wind against her skin, and for a moment, leaning on her hoe, the sky was some other sky, and the smooth wooden handle in her hands felt gritty, as if sticky with sand. Her fingers, puzzled, rolled it against her palm, and she blinked, and the world seemed to blink with her, and she was again standing in the back garden of the house where three generations of her father's kin had lived, and there was a storm coming.

When the storm came in the deep night, Hetta was asleep. She knew she was asleep, and yet she knew when the storm wind picked her up . . . no, it did not pick her up, it plunged her down, forced her down, down into darkness and roaring and a great weight against her chest, like a huge hand pressing her into. . . .

She was drowning in sand. It wasn't at all as she'd imagined it, a peaceful ending, a giving up: she did not want to die, and what was happening *hurt*. She gasped and choked, nearly fainting, and the sand bit into her skin, sharp as teeth. She could feel the tiny innumerable grains hissing over her, offering no apparent resistance as she beat at them, pouring through her fingers, down her body, into her eyes and mouth, the unimaginable multitudes of them covering her till they weighed as heavy as boulders, a river, an avalanche....

Where were the others? Had they set out knowing a storm was on the way? Even in this area a storm this severe gave some warning....

In this area? Where was she? There was nothing to tell her—nothing but sand and wind roar and darkness. And ... who were *they*? She could not remember—she would not have set out alone—even a guided party had to take care—in the last few years the storms had grown more violent and less predictable—parties rarely went mounted any more— she—remembered—

Perhaps she slept; perhaps she fainted. But there were hands upon her—hands? Had her party found her again? She tried to struggle, or to cooperate. The hands helped her up, held her up, from her wind-battered, sand-imprisoned crouch. The wind still shouted, and she could see nothing; but the hands arranged the veil over her face and she could breathe a little more easily, and this gave her strength. When the hands lifted her so that one of her arms could be pulled around a set of invisible shoulders, and one of the hands gripped her round her waist, she could walk, staggering, led by her rescuer.

For some time she concentrated on breathing, on breathing and keeping her feet under her, tasks requiring her full attention. But her arm, held round the shoulders, began to ache; and the ache began to penetrate her brain, and her brain began to remember that it didn't usually have to occupy itself with negotiating breathing and walking....

It was still dark, and the wind still howled, and there was still sand in the heaving air, but it pattered against her now, it no longer dragged at and cut her. She thought, The storm is still going on all round us, but it is not reaching us somehow. She had an absurd image that they—her unknown rescuer and herself—were walking in a tiny rolling cup of sand that was always shallow to their feet just a footstep's distance before and behind them, with a close-fitting lid of almost quiet, almost sandless air tucked over them.

When the hand clutching her wrist let go, she grabbed the shoulder and missed, for her hand had gone numb; but the hand round her waist held her. She steadied herself, and the second hand let go, but only long enough to find her hand, and hold it firmly—As if I might run off into the sandstorm again, she thought, distantly amused. She looked toward the hand, the shoulders—and now she could see a human outline, but the face was turned away from her, the free hand groping for something in front of it.

She blinked, trying to understand where the light to see came from. She slowly worked out that the hand was more visible than the rest of the body it was attached to; and she had just realised that they seemed to be standing in front of a huge, rough, slightly glowing—wall? Cliff? For it seemed to loom over them; she guessed at something like a ledge or half-roof high above them—when the fingers stiffened and the hand shook itself up in what seemed like a gesture of command—and the wall before them became a door, and folded back into itself. Light fell out, and pooled in the sand at their feet, outlining tiny pits and hummocks in shadows.

"Quickly," said a voice. "I am almost as tired as you, and Geljdreth does not like to be cheated of his victims."

She just managed to comprehend that the words were for

her, and she stepped through the door unaided. The hand that was holding hers loosed her, the figure followed her, and this time she heard another word, half-shouted, and she turned in time to see the same stiff-fingered jerk of the hand that had appeared to open the door: it slammed shut on a gust of sand like a sword-stroke. The furious sand slashed into her legs and she stumbled and cried out: the hands saved her again, catching her above the elbows. She put her hands out unthinkingly, and felt collarbones under her hands, and warm breath on her wrists.

"Forgive me," she said, and the absurdity of it caught at her, but she was afraid to laugh, as if once she started, she might not be able to stop.

"Forgive?" said the figure. "It is I who must ask you to forgive me. I should have seen you before; I am a Watcher, and this is my place, and Kalarsham is evil tempered lately and lets Geljdreth do as he likes. But it was as if you were suddenly there, from nowhere. Rather like this storm. A storm like this usually gives warning, even here."

She remembered her first thought when she woke up—if indeed any of this was waking—*Even in this area a storm this severe gave some warning.* "Where—where am I?" she said.

The figure had pulled the veiling down from its face, and pushed the hood back from its head. He was clean-shaven, dark-skinned, almost mahogany in the yellow light of the stony room where they stood, black-haired; she could not see if his eyes were brown or black. "Where did you come from?" he said, not as if he were ignoring her question but as if it had been rhetorical and required no answer. "You must have set out from Chinilar, what, three or four weeks ago? And then come on from Thaar? What I don't understand is what you were doing alone. You had lost whatever kit and company you came with before I found you—I am sorry—but there wasn't even a pack animal with you. I may have been careless"—his voice sounded strained, as if he were not used to finding himself careless—"but I would have noticed, even if it had been too late."

She shook her head. "Chinilar?" she said.

He looked at her as if playing over in his mind what she had last said. He spoke gently. "This is the station of the fourth Watcher, the Citadel of the Meeting of the Sands, and I am he."

"The fourth—Watcher?" she said.

"There are eleven of us," he said, still gently. "We watch over the eleven Sandpales where the blood of the head of Maur sank into the earth after Aerin and Tor threw the evil thing out of the City and it burnt the forests and rivers of the Old Damar to the Great Desert in the rage of its thwarting. Much of the desert is quiet—as much as any desert is quiet—but Tor, the Just and Powerful, set up our eleven stations where the desert is not quiet. The first is named the Citadel of the Raising of the Sands, and the second is the Citadel of the Parting of the Sands, and the third is the Citadel of the Breathing of the Sands.... The third, fourth, fifth, and sixth Watchers are often called upon, for our Pales lie near the fastest way through the Great Desert, from Rawalthifan in the West to the plain that lies before the Queen's City itself. But I—I have never Watched so badly before. Where did you come from?" he said again, and now she heard the frustration and distress in his voice. "Where do you come from, as if the storm itself had brought you?"

Faintly she replied: "I come from Roanshire, one of the

south counties of the Homeland; I live in a town called Farbellow about fifteen miles southwest of Mauncester. We live above my father's furniture shop. And I still do not know where I am."

He answered: "I have never heard of Roanshire, or the Homeland, or Mauncester. The storm brought you far indeed. This is the land called Damar, and you stand at the fourth Sandpale at the edge of the Great Desert we call Kalarsham."